DUNNI OLATUNDE

WestBow Press books may be ordered through booksellers or by contacting:

WestBow Press
A Division of Thomas Nelson & Zondervan
1663 Liberty Drive
Bloomington, IN 47403
www.westbowpress.com
1 (866) 928-1240

ISBN: 978-1-9736-6997-5 (sc)
ISBN: 978-1-9736-6996-8 (e)

Print information available on the last page.

WestBow Press rev. date: 03/16/2020

Chapter ONE

THE ONLY PLACE SHE ever wanted to be was her grandmother's house where she was born and had lived all her life. She loved the beautiful blue house with white shutters and tidy rooms. She would never forget the huge tree by the gate that always had so many leaves but never any fruits. She remembered her grandmother saying it was only good for shade on sunny days. She loved the small garden best of all. It was the only garden she ever saw that had roses and bachelor's buttons, though her favorite flower was the queen of the night. Sometimes she wished she smelt like it. There were also tomatoes, okra, peppers and spinach. Her grandmother had had a little bench made so she could sit when she tended the garden. It was also where she liked to sit and talk to Lily. Mama talked about a lot of things, some of which Lily thought she understood, and others, well, she had had no idea what the old woman was talking about; but had listened anyway. Lily loved listening to her. She always spoke with such passion, especially when she talked about God. Lily was certain her grandmother was the person that God loved the most, and she wanted God to love her too. Mama told her that He did, more than she could ever know, and that nothing in the world could ever change that.

Lily's grandmother, Belema Parker, took care of her from the day she was born to Amanda. Amanda returned to school soon after Lily was born because Belema wouldn't have it any other way. She promised to take care of Lily for as long as she needed to because she didn't want anything to stand in the way of Amanda's future. Belema had lost her own opportunity to study to become a doctor, her life-long dream, because of an unplanned pregnancy. Horace, the British accountant at the company her father worked for married her and returned with her to the UK soon after she had their first child, Melissa. After their son Henry was born, she studied Nursing. Amanda came a few years later. Those were the happiest days of Belema's life, a wonderful and loving husband, beautiful children and a good job.

Then Horace suddenly became ill. At first it was just a fever and Belema thought she could handle it. Then he passed out one night and was taken to the hospital. The doctors said his illness was caused by an infection. He died a few days later. His family blamed Belema. They said she had kept him at home for too long. The doctors insisted that an earlier arrival at the hospital couldn't have saved his life. The course of the virus was so remote that it wasn't discovered until the extensive autopsy.

The truth was that Horace's family never really accepted Belema. They were not happy when he returned from abroad with an African wife and a child. But he loved her. And he stood by her and defended her over the years. And when they saw that he was truly happy, they tried to tolerate her and keep their feelings to themselves. It was only Nigel, Horace's younger brother that really liked her, and he was the only one that stood by her after Horace's death. The rest of the family wanted nothing to do with her again.

With Horace gone she had no reason to stay in England. Horace was her life and it was difficult to live there without him. Four months after the funeral she returned to Nigeria with her children. Her family tried to be supportive but she couldn't stop grieving. She thought she would never be happy again, and that when she died it would be of grief.

That was before she met Matron Onengiya Briggs. She had just got a job at the Heroes of Faith hospital, and was particularly glad because it was the highest paying and best-equipped hospital in Rivers State. She had waited six months for the response to her application, and had spent the period working at a smaller hospital. The matron was on leave when she started working there and she wasn't able to meet her until three weeks after. The other nurses had said so much about her that Belema couldn't wait to meet such an extra-ordinary person. Before they met she had learnt about the matron's loss of her husband and son in a tube accident in London and how her only daughter had died during childbirth. Belema was shocked at how so much tragedy could befall one person, but what amazed her really was how the matron was said to have overcome her pain and grief and become the shoulder everyone cried on.

When they finally met, Belema understood. The woman had an inner strength that defied any challenge she faced. She met every problem head on and seemed to know that she would always win. It was a joy working with Matron Briggs and spending time with her made Belema realize that she had been depressed for long enough. It was really hard to believe that though this woman had lost her entire family, she could still be so full of life and joy. Yet Belema still had her own children. They meant everything to her now and she couldn't imagine her life without them. She knew that if anyone was going to help her, it was this woman. They became close friends and Belema soon discovered the source of the matron's inner strength.

"He is a Person, Belema," the matron said to her one day. "Not just an object of worship or religion or part of history. And He wants a personal relationship with us as individuals."

Belema knew that this was what she had been looking for all her life, a relationship with Jesus like the matron had. Soon after, her life took a new turn. She began to face her challenges with a new energy as she always felt His presence with her. Even when things didn't turn out the way she expected she still held on to her faith that He would come through for her somehow.

Her children were her greatest challenge. Melissa and Henry left home as soon as they could. They both chose universities far from home and stayed away most of the time. Even Amanda started showing traits of independence at an early age. Belema wanted more than anything to give them the best education they could get and she was greatly disappointed when Melissa dropped out of school to get married. Shortly after, she ran off to the United States of America with her husband.

Henry on the contrary finished school, got his degree in Civil Engineering, but refused to stay in the country. When he told her he was going to England with or without her help she quickly contacted her late husband's brother Nigel, who willingly sent for him and gave him all the assistance he needed.

Belema had wanted her three children close to her but she was soon left with only Amanda. And she knew that Amanda too would leave. That was the other reason she offered to take care of Lily. And that was why she never discouraged Amanda when she announced after her graduation from the university that she was going to live in another state and was going without Lily. And so Lily had stayed with Belema.

Lily drew her knees up to her chest and wrapped her arms around them as she sat on the small bed next to the one her brother and sister slept on. She didn't know what she would do without her grandmother. They had played together, prayed together and even cried together when either of them was overwhelmed. And they had comforted each other. Mama was the most important person in her life and Lily had thought she would always be there. But she died two weeks ago and everything changed. Agnes, her grandmother's niece took care of her till her mother could come for her. Actually Agnes was more than just Mama's niece. She was their closest friend.

Lily had hoped that her mother would let her stay with Agnes after the funeral. She knew she would be happy with her because Agnes loved her. They had shared so much together. Besides, Mama had loved Agnes dearly and she had been a part of the small family, but Amanda had decided that Lily was returning with her to Benin. Saying goodbye to Agnes was almost as painful as losing her grandmother. Fresh tears rolled down her cheeks and dropped on her thigh as she remembered how she had clung to Agnes that morning and wept bitterly until her mother had literally dragged her to the waiting taxi and refused Agnes's offer to accompany them to the taxi park. She had wept as she watched Agnes through the rear window of the departing taxi try to wave with both hands and wipe the tears from her face at the same time. She would miss her. She'd hoped then her mother would let her visit soon.

Throughout the journey from Port Harcourt to Benin, Lily had tried to convince herself that living with her mother would not be so bad even though they hadn't spent that much time together. Her mother had two other children that were younger than she was, a boy and a girl, and she felt it would be good to live with her own brother and sister. She hadn't been lonely at her grandmother's house, but she had sometimes wondered what it would be like to live with her own siblings. She'd hoped her mother's husband would like her. She had never met him and she knew he wasn't her father. She knew her mother and grandmother argued about him a lot. She had heard Mama describe him as domineering. She'd said that he controlled her mother's life. She remembered one evening her mother had visited and was to stay till the next day. After Lily had gone to bed, she had overheard an argument between the two women about something Sheyi wanted her mother to do but Mama had thought was wrong, and had told her mother so. Her mother, as usual, had defended him.

"This is really none of your business, Mum, and you always carry things too far," Amanda had complained.

"It is my business, Mandy. I am your mother and I am concerned about you. Getting involved in such practices is not of God…" Lily remembered her grandmother trying to make her mother understand.

"Oh, spare me please!" Amanda had interrupted her.

"I am just telling you it is not Christian to visit herbalists and make sacrifices to idols," Mama had explained.

"Well, I am not a Christian!" Amanda had snapped. "Look, it is their family thing and they've been doing it forever. You just hate him for no reason, that's all."

"You know that is not true! I am just saying you don't have to do something that's not right just because he said so!"

"He is my husband! If he left me would you find me another one?" Amanda was screaming. Lily hated it when she screamed at Mama.

"Listen Amanda," Mama had maintained her soft tone. "I just don't want you getting involved in what you will later regret. Remember what happened when he asked you to…"

"I know. I know," Amanda had cut her short. "You were right then and so you think you are right all the time."

Mama had sighed. Even as young as Lily was she knew her grandmother was right whenever she warned her mother about the decisions she made because of Sheyi. Some of the results were nearly disastrous. Once Amanda had almost lost her life because of an abortion he had insisted on as a condition for them to stay together. He had also made her and their baby girl stay with his mother in the village for eight months because he had said he couldn't cope with a family at the time and would send for them when he thought he had enough money. During that period the baby ingested contaminated water and almost died. Mama was upset, because she had begged to have them with her in Port Harcourt and he had refused.

"I just don't want you to get into any trouble…" Lily's grandmother had pleaded that night.

"Stop interfering…. stop trying to…! You don't… you can't know everything. OK?" And then Amanda had stomped into the room where Lily was, picked up her unopened bag and marched out the front door before Mama could say a word! That night Lily had crawled into her grandmother's bed and wept until she fell asleep. She had always wondered what kind of man Sheyi was. Well, now she didn't have to anymore.

When they finally arrived at the house in Benin that afternoon Lily was tired and also hungry. A man opened the door when her mother knocked and she knew immediately that it was Sheyi.

The first thing that struck her as she entered was how chaotic the sitting room was. The seats were strewn with clothes. There were used cups and plates on the coffee table, little odd shoes under the dining table, food crumbs on the rug, and toys just about everywhere. The dining table was covered from one end to the other with books; more used cups and plates and other bits and pieces. *Mama would have a fit if she walked into this place,* she thought to herself. The second thing was the way the man Sheyi looked at her. His eyes never left her from the moment he saw her at the door until she was seated on one of the chairs by the dining table at the other end of the room where her mother took her. He reminded her of a lion she had read about in a story in school. It had invited a different animal to its cave every day until the tortoise refused to enter the cave when it noticed that at the entrance there were only hoof prints going in and none coming out. There was something about him that made her feel unsafe.

"So, how was the journey?" Sheyi asked, still looking at Lily.

"It was fine," Amanda replied as she dropped the bags on the floor. "But why is this place in such a mess? How can I come back from a four-hour journey to face this?"

"Why don't you relax?" He lazily took his eyes off Lily. "We can tidy up later. How did it go?"

Amanda sat heavily on the chair closest to her. She looked so weary. "Agnes and some of Mum's cousins handled most of it. Everything went well, I guess."

Sheyi sat down too and looked at Lily again. Then he turned to Amanda. "So how long will she be here for?"

Amanda looked surprised. "I beg your pardon?"

"Of course you know she can't stay here. I'm not in a position…."

"Excuse me," Amanda said lifting up one hand. Then she spoke to Lily. "Lily, take your bags and go to the room on your left as you walk through that door." She indicated a door that led to the rest of the house.

Lily got up and did as her mother said. The room she found herself in was almost as untidy as the one she had just left. She put her bags in a corner and began to tidy it up. After picking up the pile of dirty clothes she had gathered round the room she held them to her chest, wondering what to do with them. Then she remembered that she had seen what she thought must be the laundry basket in the tiny corridor that led to the room. She left the room to put the clothes in it, and overheard her mother and Sheyi arguing.

"Be that as it may," Sheyi was saying, "you still need to find a place for her soon. I simply cannot afford to take care of another person."

"Everything is always about money to you, Sheyi," her mother said. "What you can afford and what you can't. Well, there's more than money to be considered here. Lily is my child and she has never lived with anyone apart from my mum."

"If you so badly want her around you, as you say, we can ask around and find a family here in Benin that would take her."

"What?" Amanda sounded shocked. "As what?"

"Whatever you want to call it. I don't care," was Sheyi's reply.

"We are talking about my child, Sheyi. I don't want her with strangers; I want her to be with me now."

"Well, she can't. I don't even understand what your stress is all about. You've never wanted her with you."

"It's not like that…"

"She can't stay. And I don't want to talk about this anymore. Sort yourself out as soon as possible."

"Please, Sheyi." Lily heard her mother beg.

"No!"

Lily was still standing with the clothes in her arms when Sheyi walked through the door into the corridor. He slowed down when he saw her, and then he just brushed past her into another room and shut the door.

She couldn't stop thinking about all that she had heard for the rest of the day. She could barely eat the lunch her mother prepared for her. Even seeing her brother and sister when they returned from school did very little for the way she felt. Though she loved them the moment she set her eyes on them, knowing that she would be leaving them made her feel even worse.

Not long after Lily went to bed her mother walked into the room and told her she couldn't stay. She said it was Sheyi that wanted it that way. It was his house and he alone could decide whom he wanted there. And he didn't want her.

"But I'll always be good," Lily begged. "I'll take care of the children and clean the house every day. Please tell Uncle I'll........"

"Stop it! You can't stay and I can't do anything about it. And that's it." Her mother headed straight for the door.

"Am I going back to Aunt Agnes then?" She asked hopefully.

"No," her mother replied, confirming her worst fear before leaving the room. She was going to live with strangers.

Why was God letting this happen to her? Aunt Agnes said He was the one that took Mama. Why would He do that? God was supposed to love her too. Mama said he did. Now Lily wasn't so sure. She tightened her arms around her knees and wept as if her heart would break.

A week later her bags were packed again. Her mother said she was going to live with Sheyi's aunt in Lagos. She said she lived in a beautiful mansion and had lots of money. Lily didn't care about any of that. She didn't want to live with a stranger even if they owned the whole world. Why wouldn't her mother take her back to Port Harcourt? She wished Sheyi wasn't such a cruel man. She had grown to dislike him in the short period she had spent at his house. Mama really knew the kind of person he was for her to have spoken about him the way she did. Lily couldn't remember her grandmother ever speaking unkindly of anyone, not even those men everyone in Port Harcourt seemed to hate, that went about quarrelling with shop owners when they couldn't get any money from them. Lily thought they were greedy because they kept coming back for more money, but Mama said they worked for the Local Government Council and were only doing what they were told.

Well, Sheyi didn't like her either. She knew because he never smiled at her or spoke to her, only stared in that strange way that made her very uncomfortable. And so she had stayed out of his way as much as she could.

Though she was sad when she left Port Harcourt, she was hopeful. Now as she traveled to Lagos despair tore at her insides. Tears stung her eyes as she thought of her Aunt Agnes. Will she ever see her again? Will she ever feel loved again? The closer the taxi moved towards Lagos the farther she felt from all that made her secure.

At the taxi park in Lagos they went in search of another taxi that would take them straight to Sheyi's aunt's place. Lily had never seen so many people in one place and so much filth on the road. Every time she stepped on something soft she fought hard not to imagine what it could be. Her mother held her hand tightly as they both trailed behind people because there was no way around them and by the time they got to the main road she had bumped into three women already. She saw children, some of whom were younger than she was, hawking different things to motorists and passers-by. She was fascinated by the way they got on the road and darted between moving cars so dangerously. She watched as a motorcycle nearly knocked down a man and how the argument that ensued almost turned into a fight.

Finally her mother was able to get them a taxi and as she talked with the driver Lily noticed some young children pointing at her and her mother and chanting, "Fine *Oyibo,* sweet *Oyibo.*"

She was still staring at them when her mother took her arm and guided her into the taxi. As the taxi pulled away the children began to wave and shout, "*Oyibo* bye-bye, *Oyibo* bye-bye."

"Here we are," Amanda announced as the taxi stopped in front of a storey building. She paid the driver, picked up Lily's bags and helped her out. "This is Aunt Melody's restaurant. See the sign?"

Melody's Restaurant was boldly written on a signboard by the gate. As they walked in, Lily noticed that it was also written on a larger signboard on the building. There were lots of little colored light bulbs around the sign, which made her believe that the restaurant was also open at night. Her mother took her round the back of the building and into a long corridor. She stopped at a door marked 'Manager' and knocked. Without waiting for a reply she opened the door and peeped in.

"Good afternoon. Is she in?" Amanda asked a lady sitting behind a table with a computer.

"Yes. Madam is in. You are?"

Amanda walked in with Lily. "Amanda and Lily. She is expecting us."

"You'll have to wait. She's with someone. Please sit down."

"Thank you." They sat on a four-seat sofa behind a large round coffee table with a stack of magazines.

A few minutes later a door opened and a fat lady dressed in purple lace and more gold than Lily had ever seen, emerged with a man. She looked from Amanda to Lily and back to Amanda. And then she beamed and held out her ample arms. Amanda got up and walked into them smiling.

"Amanda, Amanda. How are you? I hope you have not been waiting long." And then she turned to her secretary, "Why didn't you let me know my niece was here?" Not waiting for an answer she turned back to Amanda. "It's been quite a while. I heard about your mother. Accept my sympathy."

"Thank you," Amanda said.

Then she looked at Lily. "Is this Lily? What a beautiful girl," she expressed with obvious wonder. "You look just like your mother. How are you?"

"I'm fine, thank you," Lily replied and thought the woman's accent was rather strange.

The man beside Melody coughed and she looked at him as if just realizing he was still standing there.

"Oh, Chief. I have completely forgotten about you. Forgive me." Then she addressed Amanda. "Please excuse me, my dear; I'll only be a few minutes." She smiled at Lily again with a mild shake of her head before leaving the office with the man.

A little while later, the secretary turned and looked directly at Amanda and shifted in her seat. She looked like she was going to say something but she turned back to her computer and continued punching the keys. After a few seconds she stopped and squirmed in her seat. Again she looked at Amanda and Lily was convinced she would talk this time, but she turned away again and pretended to look busy. Lily felt like giggling. Finally the lady cleared her throat and turned her swivel chair to face Amanda. *Well, here goes,* thought Lily.

"Excuse me," she said to Amanda. "Please don't get angry. Madam said a girl would be coming to live with her. Is your daughter...she is your daughter, right?" She continued when Amanda nodded. "Is she the one coming to live with Madam?"

"Yes. I brought Lily to live with Aunt Melody," Amanda replied with a frown.

Something was troubling the lady and Lily couldn't imagine what it could be.

"Forgive me. I don't mean to 'poke nose'. Don't you have any other person she can stay with? Please, forgive me," she added quickly. "I know it is none of my business, but a restaurant is no place for an innocent young girl, especially one as beautiful as your daughter." She looked at Lily from her long plaits down to her small sandaled feet.

"She won't live in the restaurant." Amanda sounded slightly irritated.

"I know." The lady looked down. She seemed to know more than she was letting on. "But there is no way she would live with Madam without being at the restaurant. And she is so beautiful."

Lily wondered why she kept saying that, but she never got the chance to find out, at least not that afternoon, because Melody suddenly bustled in with three other women. Lily's eyes were still on the secretary who had with incredible speed turned back to her computer.

"Ladies," Melody said loudly. "I want you to meet my niece, Amanda. She has brought her daughter to live with me here in Lagos."

Lily thought she saw the women exchange looks but couldn't be sure. Her mother greeted them. She hoped her mother would talk to the secretary some more and find out what was eating her when Aunty Melody went into her office, but the secretary was called in immediately. Several minutes later Amanda looked at her watch. She still had to return to Benin.

Melody soon came out and Amanda told her she had to leave.

"Don't worry, my dear. Your daughter is in good hands. I would take care of her as if she were my own. You don't need to be shuttling between Lagos and Benin. Just remember to always give me a call first whenever you want to visit."

"Thank you," was all Amanda could say as Melody hugged her again.

"Give my regards to Sheyi."

"I will. Goodbye." Amanda held Lily's hand and took her out of the office.

Tears were already building up in Lily's eyes as her mother held her by the shoulders outside the building, looking like she didn't want to leave her there after all. Lily wished she would go back into the building and tell Aunt Melody it was all a big mistake, pick up her bags and return with her to Benin. Her mother just hugged her and promised to visit soon.

When would this nightmare end? First her beloved grandmother dies, and then she is separated from her aunt Agnes who was a major part of her growing up. Now instead of being with her mother she is left alone in this faraway place.

Her mother stood before her looking so sorrowful. "How long?" Lily heard her ask in a barely audible voice. "How long would I have to…?" Her voice trailed off.

Lily walked back into the office downcast after the taxi her mother took was out of sight. Melody was standing by her secretary's table, looking through some papers.

"Is your mother gone?" She asked Lily without looking up.

"Yes, Aunt Melody," Lily replied with a small voice.

"Patricia, have these ready for me in ten minutes," Melody said as she handed the papers to her secretary and walked towards her office. At the door she looked back at Lily. "And you, you call me Madam."

Chapter TWO

I AM LYING ON a soft blanket in a grassy field. The trees are full of birds singing sweet songs just for me. I am surrounded with flowers of different kinds, roses, daffodils, daises, lilies…especially lilies. A soft breeze carries their mingled fragrances to my nostrils. I am so happy. The sun is high in the sky. I can feel the warmth on my skin. I hear the sound of the…

"Lillian! Lillian, you lazy girl. Where are you hiding?"

Lillian groaned as her mother's voice broke into her reverie. She didn't like being disturbed when she lay under the old wooden door leaning against the fence behind the little house she lived in with her parents and younger brother and sisters. That was why she always finished her work first.

Ever since she got a calendar from one of the fresh graduates that worked in the school she attended, she had fantasized about the pictures on each page. She would imagine herself in one of them and dream endlessly. It was her way of escaping the dreariness of her life in her small hometown.

She peeked first to make sure her mother wasn't near enough to see her come out from her secret place, and then she got out and walked round the side of the house in the direction her mother's voice was coming from. She wondered what her mother wanted her for now. What else could it be if not chores, chores and more chores?

"There you are," her mother said angrily as she saw her coming. "Where have you been hiding and wasting your time? Don't you know that an idle mind is the devil's workshop?"

"But Mama, I am never idle," replied Lillian defensively. "I have been working since I got back from school and I have finished."

"Which work?" Her mother asked looking her up and down. "Tell me which work."

Even though Lillian knew she didn't really want an answer she decided to fill her in anyway. "I…I washed all the uniforms and socks, I washed the plates and charcoal pot, and filled the two drums. I even went to empty the rubbish even though I.K. was supposed to do that."

"Shut up!" Her mother cried. "Don't you know that a woman's work is never done? Do you ever see me idling away like you?"

"This is your own choice, Mama…." Lillian began to mutter.

"Close that mouth of yours, you ignorant girl!" And then her mother sighed. "I don't blame you. I don't blame you at all. It is because times have changed. At your age I was already married to your father, and having real responsibilities."

Lillian groaned inwardly. She knew it was time for another lecture on her mother's unhappy past. She was 'given' to Lillian's father at the age of thirteen and the only reason she didn't start having children immediately was because her period didn't start until she was almost sixteen. And so she was made to stay with, and take care of her new husband's parents and aged grandmother until she was able to bear children.

Lillian was grateful she hadn't been born in that era because she knew she would never have consented to such a thing. She always felt that her mother was too timid before her father. In fact she was convinced that he terrified her. She could never marry a man that terrified her; neither could she marry a man twenty years older than she was, like her mother did. No, she was going to meet and marry a man she loved and who loved her more than anything in the world. A man like one of those characters she read about in her romance novels.

"That is how to be a woman," Lillian heard her mother conclude. "Not by hiding from work or expecting a man to do it for you."

"I don't hide from work, Mama, and I.K. is not a man," Lillian grumbled.

"Take these clothes!" Her mother scowled as she thrust the bundle of clothes she was holding into Lillian's arms. "As you can see, they are white. Your father needs them washed, starched and ironed for an important meeting tomorrow evening. If you know what is good for you, you'd better start on them immediately. I am going out." She let out a long hiss and marched into the house, leaving Lillian glowering at her back.

"I'm no better than a maid in this house." Lillian was fuming as she walked towards the well. "Everyone has their own duties but I am expected to do mine as well as everyone else's. Is it a sin to be the eldest? And that stupid boy I.K. only plays all day and no one seems to notice. Shouldn't he be the one washing Papa's clothes?"

She found a clean bowl to put the clothes in. Then she dropped the little rubber bucket into the well and let the rope attached to it run freely between her palms. As she drew up the full bucket, she wondered when she would live in a house that had running water like the flats the graduates lived in. She envied them. They were out of the university. They only worked in dead end places like her town because the government made it compulsory for all graduates below the age of thirty to do so in service to the nation. But it was only for eleven months. And then they returned to whatever exciting place they came from while she remained stuck here, in this house, with these parents and that horrible brother of hers.

She had made friends with one of the graduates, Shade, who had returned to Lagos. Lillian had got her precious calendar and romance novels from her. It was also from Shade that she had learnt about Lagos. And she had known from that time that whenever she managed escaped from this place, her destination was Lagos.

She put the clean, starched clothes on the line to dry and went in search of her sister, Mary, who was the only person in the family she could relate to. The fact that Mary always listened to her, always had time for her, made Lillian look beyond loads of bible passages and sermons and seek her out each time she had something on her mind.

Mary had changed a lot in the three years she had been part of the Youth Christian Fellowship in the town. She had become more mature in the way she handled everything. Also there was this thing about her that made her appear respectable that even I.K. listened to her. And she prayed and sang a whole lot more. The best part of it though for Lillian was that Mary had defied her parents, especially her father, and had survived it. Not only had she survived, she had won. No one ever disobeyed Papa, not even her mother. His word was law.

Her father had stated that no child of his was to attend any other church apart from the Catholic Church. He was a knight in the church and well respected and he wasn't going to let his own child bring any disgrace upon him by leaving the church to join a bible thumping, halleluiah shouting group. Mary stood her ground and insisted that she had found the Lord, and wasn't letting go. She tried fruitlessly to explain to him that it wasn't about any denomination or religion but a personal relationship with the Lord. Mama begged and threatened. She asked their aunties and uncles to try to reason with her daughter. She even invited the local priest, but Mary only preached to him about the salvation of his own soul. Her father's next action took everyone by surprise. He gave Mary an ultimatum, to give up her newfound faith or leave his house. And one night Lillian watched her father push her sister out of the house and tell her not to return until she had agreed to do as he said. No one was able to do anything as they watched Mary disappear into the night and Papa slam the door shut. But something happened the next day that had never happened before or ever since. Mama stood up to Papa. She told him that she would not fold her arms and lose another child and that if anything happened to Mary, he would never have peace again in his lifetime. Papa left the house for hours and when he returned she continued raving. This went on for days until finally Papa told her to go and bring Mary home. Mary had become Lillian's hero ever since.

She found Mary peeling cassava outside the small kitchen in a corner of the yard. She was singing as usual.

Mary stopped singing and looked up as she saw Lillian approaching. "I heard Mama calling you earlier on," she said. "Where were you hiding?"

"That is exactly what she asked me," Lillian said with her palms raised. "Why does everyone think I was hiding?" She drew up a small stool and sat on it.

"It's because you can see just about the whole of your father's yard from one spot. Come on, Lillie, were you under that door again?" Mary asked.

Lillian put a finger to her lips as her head darted from side to side like that of a cat burglar that had just heard an alarm go off. "And I should have stayed there," she whispered mischievously.

"Why?" Mary couldn't help giggling. "What did Mama want?"

"You mean apart from wanting to give me a lecture on the woes of being a woman? She wanted me to open my eyes wide," she said as she put a forefinger beneath each eye and drew down her lower eyelids, "and see that Papa's clothes were white before I ventured to wash and starch them." She shook her head. "One day I will leave this house, this town, and go to a place where I will be appreciated and treated with respect."

Mary dropped the cassava she was peeling and laid the knife down carefully. She folded her hands on her lap and looked directly at her sister. "Lillie, there is something I have been praying about for some time now."

"What?" Any time Mary talked about her prayers, Lillian knew they were always about something serious.

"I don't know any easy way of telling you," she continued, "but I pray God will help me."

"What is it?" Now Mary had her full attention. She couldn't imagine what her sister would need God's help for to tell her. There was no way she could have been prepared for what she heard next.

"Papa is planning to marry you off to one of his friends."

The stool Lillian had been sitting on fell back as she jumped up suddenly, covering her mouth with both hands. She took a few steps back and tripped over the upturned stool. Her sister got up quickly and reached out to support her as she fell.

"No! It can't be!" She ranted as Mary helped her up. "It can't happen to me! He can never do that to me! I will never agree! Never!"

"Calm down, Lillie. It doesn't mean it's going to happen."

"Over my dead body!" Lillian cried as she waved her hand around her head and snapped her fingers, as she had learnt to do over the years when something she was expected to do was totally unacceptable.

"Don't say things like that," Mary said. "Calm down."

Lillian tried to be calm, but she was trembling too much. She let Mary guide her to the bench by the front door of the house and they both sat down. Their parents were out and the younger ones were inside the house, so they had some privacy.

"I want you to be calm." Mary tried to soothe her. "At least let us be sure that he really means to do it."

"How...how did you find out?" Lillian wanted to know.

"I'd had this burden for some time but I didn't know what about. So I kept praying and waiting for the Lord to reveal it to me. Then I overheard Papa talking to Uncle Festus about it being the only solution to..." She shook her head and shrugged, "...whatever. It won't happen, Lillie, if it is his plan. I want you to rest assured that it won't happen." And she punctuated each of the last three words with her fist on her lap.

"Papa must be a very wicked man, but he will be surprised that I will never do it. The worst he can do is to throw me out of his house, and I will gladly leave."

"Don't talk like that," Mary said, looking really concerned. "Where will you go?"

"I will leave, Mary. I will find a place." Lillian was determined and Mary looked troubled. Lillian knew she was troubled because she knew that if their father really meant to carry out his ludicrous plan then it would only mean one thing. She would have to leave their home.

The two girls sat silently for a long while, each occupied with her thoughts. Finally Lillian broke the silence with a chuckle.

"I wonder which one of them Papa has in mind."

"What?" Mary asked as her sister's voice broke into her thoughts.

"I said, I wonder which one of Papa's friends he has packaged for me."

Mary was surprised that she has moved so quickly to such a light mood in spite of the devastating news she has just heard.

"Don't make fun, Lillie."

"No. Seriously. It's possible that Papa has money problems. And in that case Chief Ernest would be the likely one. You know he has a lot of money, though he doesn't have any classmates."

Mary smiled. "Not even in Kindergarten."

Lillian continued. "So when the priest asks if he will take this woman to be his lawful wedded wife he might say 'I don't' instead of 'I do'." They both laughed. "And imagine the problem we will have when he is asked to sign the marriage register."

"Thumb print?" They laughed again.

Mary was so glad that Lillian had lightened up that she decided to play along. And so she raised a forefinger as if an idea had suddenly come to her. "Chief Chike?"

"Who?" Lillian laughed out loud. "Chief Two-feet-nothing? I would have to be careful for the rest of my life not to tread on him."

"Or that man that bought the land opposite the Post Office. You know the one that gave Papa that contract for steel."

Lillian turned and looked at her sister as if she didn't know her. "Man? You call that...thing a man?" Disgust was written all over her face. "He is more like..." she cleared her throat rather loudly and then pretended to spit on the ground. Then she pointed to the ground and said, "...that thing."

"Oh, Lillie!" Mary shook her head at her.

"Have you forgotten what he did to Mama Nduka's daughter?"

"No," Mary replied.

Lillian shook her head and narrowed her eyes. "If it was left to me..."

"It wasn't. And I don't want to talk about it," Mary added quickly. Then she remembered something. "Chief Daniel has been coming here more frequently than before. Haven't you noticed?"

"Come to think of it, yes," Lillian replied and then she shook her head and grimaced as if in pain. "That man smells so badly I can't even stand next to him. He stinks! Like something between...ammonia and...and...and that dead animal I.K. found in the..."

"All right!" Mary quickly interrupted her.

"You know, there's one of Papa's friends I could really consider," Lillian said pretending to look thoughtful. She looked at Mary and smiled mischievously. "Elder Chinedu."

"He's older than your grandfather!"

"Exactly! And so all I have to do is jump out from behind a door and shout 'boo!' Then I would become a widow on my wedding night and be back here in no time!"

"Stop that!" Mary said. And then she sighed. "Well, whether they are old, uneducated, smelly, or whatever, you are not going to be married off to any of them. God will never permit it."

"Amen!" Lillian said firmly and held Mary's arm. "Just keep praying for me Mary. I believe so much in your prayers."

Mary put her arm around her sister's shoulders. "Lillie, Jesus wants a relationship with you. He loves you and wants to be close to you, closer than anyone. He wants to give you peace and real joy." She smiled and her face seemed to light up. "He wants to make your life beautiful. If only you will yield and give your life to Jesus, Lillie."

Lillian folded her hands on her lap and looked down at them. She knew nothing would make Mary happier than for her to do as she said. And she felt it was probably the right thing to do. But she wasn't sure she was ready. She wasn't sure she was ready to give up on all her dreams and she wasn't sure God approved of them. She didn't think she could be like Mary. Sweet Mary. She was just thirteen months younger at sixteen but she was so mature and could easily be taken for the eldest daughter. Though she was slightly plump and not so tall she had a pretty face with dimples on both cheeks that deepened pleasantly every time she smiled. Lillian, on the other hand, was tall, slim and very beautiful.

Sometimes she wished Mary were the eldest. Lillian would have been quite happy as the second child. Her mother wouldn't have been saying all those things to her. Actually then she would have been the third child. Some time ago they found out that they had an elder brother who had died when Lillian was a toddler.

She looked up at Mary. The sincerity and love she saw in her sister's eyes almost moved her to tears and all she could manage was, "I will one day. I promise. You just keep praying for me."

"You know I will. Always. Just remember that God has a special plan for your life and no matter what happens, that plan will come to pass." They hugged each other and held on for a while.

"I wonder when Papa will break the news to me," Lillian said when she finally let go of Mary. "When Mama finds out, that is if she is not the initiator, she will be overjoyed."

"Why do you say that?" Mary queried with a puzzled look on her face.

"You don't know the things she says to me." Lillian shook her head. "She pretends to be contented with her life but really she is bitter; bitter that her own childhood was taken from her. She couldn't go to school or learn any trade; except if you want to call going to the farm and selling her produce in the market a trade."

"You shouldn't be angry with her. No one can go through all she did and be happy."

"But why take it out on me?" Lillian spread her hands. "She acts as if it is my fault and not hers."

"No, she doesn't. Lillie, come on. And it wasn't her fault either."

"What was she looking at?" Lillian sat up straight and put her hands on her hips. "Didn't she go with her parents to Papa's house with her own two feet? I bet she was smiling and curtsying and saying 'yes sir, yes sir, three bags full sir.'"

"What could she have done?" Mary asked. "You know those times were different. Things were different with Mama. She…"

"She didn't have a sister like you." Lillian's smile was warm. "I feel so lucky. I know you will never let that happen to me. Besides I would rather run away than end up like…"

"Lillian!" The sound of their mother's voice startled both girls and they jumped up from the bench they had been sitting on. For a moment neither girl could say anything. Then Lillian let her shoulders slump.

"Uh oh. Enter the…"

"Don't say it!"

Lillian gave Mary a knowing look before dashing towards the gate while Mary quickly returned to the cassava she was peeling.

When she got to the gate Lillian didn't see her mother anywhere. A bundle of yams, two new brooms and a bag were by the fence, but no Mama.

"Mama!" She called out. "Mama, where are you?" She began to walk towards the path that led to the road.

"Keep quiet there!" She heard her mother whisper fiercely from the bushes somewhere behind her. "I am easing myself."

Lillian had to stifle her laughter. She should have known. It wasn't the first time her mother had decided she couldn't make it to the toilet on time after returning from an outing.

"Ok, Mama, I'll just take the things inside."

Three weeks later their mother announced that they would be having some important visitors and so the whole yard had to be cleaned inside out. Lillian and Mary exchanged looks but said nothing. They both knew that life as they knew it was about to change.

A few days before the visit, Lillian was in the sitting room putting up newly washed curtains when Elizabeth, her nine year old sister walked in and told her their father wanted to see her. At first she pretended not to hear and continued with what she was doing. This was the moment she had been dreading for weeks and she wasn't sure she would be able to go through with it. Why did this have to happen? Why did her father have to…?

"*Sister*, I said Papa is calling you." Elizabeth interrupted her thoughts.

"Ok, I'm coming!" She snapped. And then as if realizing that none of this was the little girl's fault added in a gentler tone, "Where is he?"

"He's sitting under the tree at the backyard."

"Ok, thank you."

Still wondering how it would go she got down from the stool she had been standing on and went to the back of the house. She saw her father sitting on the shabby green and orange easy chair the older children had nicknamed 'the throne'. This was because no one else dared sit on it. They often joked that sitting on it would invite a death sentence. She walked up to him and curtsied.

"Papa, Eliza said you wanted to see me."

"Yes. Sit down." And he pointed to the wooden chair facing him.

Sit down? Her father was asking her to sit before him? It had never happened before. For as long as she could remember she had always stood to speak to him. Now he was inviting her to sit down himself. This was definitely it. She sat down slowly on the edge of the chair.

"Ada," he began as soon as she was seated. "I have a very important matter to discuss with you."

Ada? When was the last time he called me that? She couldn't remember.

"It is a matter that will change your life forever. I have given it a lot of careful thought and concluded that it is best for you. All parties involved have given their consent."

How could he say that?

"As a matter of fact all that is required is just to tie up a few loose ends."

Oh, so that is all I am, a loose end.

"I am sure it is for the best." He picked up his cup from an old stool beside his chair, drank from it and set it down again. "I want you to know that your education will not be affected so you can still be anything you want to be in life. Besides, you won't have to worry anymore about what the future holds for you as a woman. Let me say the future has come to you."

He laughed heartily. "You know my friend Chief Daniel Onu, don't you?"

"Yes." Lillian's answer was barely above a whisper. She knew the only reason she could speak at all was because she had been preparing for this moment.

"Very good. Yes. I have known him for a very long time." The way he stressed 'very' made Lillian feel sick. He was really comfortable with this. "And he is a good man," her father continued. "He is not that old. In fact he is the youngest man with a chieftaincy title from our village. Also, he is from a very respectable family. And he has promised to take good care of you. What I am saying is that he wants to marry you and he is coming to make his desire known."

By now Lillian was seething. So Mary was right. Her father really planned to carry out this hideous thing. She had fixed her gaze on the patch of grass around her feet while he was speaking so he couldn't see her face. When she looked up she saw him flinch. Her face was contorted in anger. She rose slowly to her feet.

"So all parties have consented?" She shook her head vigorously. "I don't think so." She knew her boldness was fueled by her anger and she would probably regret acting on it but she couldn't help herself. "This one in front of you says never! I will not marry Chief Daniel or anyone of your friends. Never!"

"Are you crazy?" Her father asked in obvious disbelief. "Am I the one you are talking to like that? Is something wrong with your head?" He stood up, towering above her.

"I am sorry for being disrespectful, Papa," she said and curtsied even though she sounded nothing like it. "But I cannot marry a stranger to me. Besides, I am only..."

"Keep quiet!" He shouted. "Are you better than your mother? Did she know me before she agreed to marry me?"

"Isn't that why she's always so bitter?" The words had spilled out of her mouth before Lillian could stop them and if she hadn't ducked on time she would have felt the brunt of her father's palm across her face. He looked murderous and she backed away quickly. She knew she was likely to be thrown out but she didn't have to leave with a black eye.

"You will marry Chief Daniel! You hear me?" Her father was trembling with anger and she kept backing away. "You will say yes to him when he proposes, otherwise I will disown you! You hear me?"

When she thought she had put enough distance between herself and her father she said gently but firmly, "I will never marry a stranger to me, Papa."

"Get out of my sight!"

She turned and marched towards the front of the house. Her mother was sitting on the bench by the front door. She looked like she was going to say something but quickly changed her mind when Lillian glared at her.

Mary was already waiting by the time Lillian stormed into their bedroom and slammed the door behind her.

"Calm down, Lillie, just calm down."

"Do you know he has already settled everything with his friend Chief Daniel? Oh you should have heard him go on and on about how it was best for me." Lillian started pacing. "According to him all parties concerned have consented and they only needed to tie up a few loose ends." She stopped pacing and turned to Mary. "Mary, I am nothing but a loose end in the matter."

Mary sighed. She didn't know what to say to her sister. "All I can do is to trust in God that everything would work out."

Lillian sat on the bed and placed her head in her hands. One thing she was certain about was that there wasn't going to be a wedding. Another thing was that there would be grave consequences.

She started avoiding her father from that afternoon. Though she was fuming herself, she was still scared of what he could do in his temper. Her father was a violent man. And everyone knew to stay out of his way when he was angry. So she got up earlier than usual to fill the drums with water and quickly returned to her room to wait for him to leave the house. She was returning with the last bucket of water on her head some days later when his frame suddenly filled the doorway. Her heart almost leapt out of her chest when she saw him and she stopped suddenly, spilling some of the water. She wanted to greet him but no words came.

"No child of mine will bring this kind of disgrace on me," her father said in a tone she could only describe as the growl of a hungry beast whose prey was determined to get away. "I won't have it! I will give you another chance to come to your senses. And if you don't, I will show you that I am still your father and you must obey me! I promise you that you will regret ever defying me." He turned and went back into the house leaving her standing there with her heart beating wildly and still unable to find her voice.

Lillian got a final warning from her father the next night. She was not to disgrace him or let him down. Chief Daniel had been very generous. If she did anything other than what was expected of her, she would leave his house, but she would suffer before she did. She left his presence without uttering a single word. There was nothing left to say.

Since the day Mary broke the news to her Lillian had begun making her own plans. As she lay on the bed she went over them again. No one had noticed her secret trips to the business center and to the bank. She reached into the pocket of the khaki skirt that was lying on the chair next to the bed and pulled out the envelope inside. She brought out the money in it and counted it for the umpteenth time. Shade had exceeded her expectations. She had also given her directions to where they would meet. The directions were clear enough, Lillian believed. Anyway she had Shade's phone number. She had had it in her head for ages. She looked at Mary who had fallen asleep a short while earlier. She would miss her best friend and confidante. If only there was another way…

There was no sound as the over-stuffed duffel bag landed in the bushes outside the fence. Neither was there any as the owner landed beside it. She'd be long gone by the time they realized she was missing. She had left a note for Mary apologizing for not telling her about her plans. She was careful not to write anything about her destination. About an hour and a half later their mother would go to their room to wake them up. Then they would find out she was gone. She would be on the bus going to Lagos. She went over what Shade had told her. Her bus would arrive at the Interstate Park in Lagos by evening and she was to take a taxi to Herbert McCauley Street. The third turn to the right was Mainland Road. Shade would have closed from work but would be waiting for her at the restaurant on the ground floor of number 23. It was called Melody's Restaurant.

Chapter THREE

MELODY'S INSULT-RIDDEN SCREAMS ROSE and fell from somewhere in the building. Though no one seemed to pay any attention they all pitied whoever was at the receiving end this time. Anything could happen when she was in a rage, anything from a slap to a sack letter. The good thing was that the restaurant was on break and there were no customers. This was the period when the place was transformed from the regular restaurant to a nightclub. It was usually re-opened by half past 7 and from about 8pm people started trooping in. It stayed open till 4am in the morning, sometimes 5am when the last set of people left. And then another transformation took place before breakfast time.

Lily had been at Melody's for eight months now. During the first two months she worked with the staff on the day shift. Then she laid tables and helped in the kitchen; fetching things for the cooks, washing vegetables and doing whatever she was told to do. She learnt the routine and knew the regular staff very quickly. She also learnt the different terminologies used for those that came to the restaurant. She knew the 'biggies' and the 'smallies' were the workers from big and smaller companies that paid their bills monthly. She knew the difference between customers and clients. Customers were the people that ate at the restaurant, while clients were those that paid a lot of money but didn't eat. They only came at night and always left with one of the female workers.

She hardly had any encounter with Melody then even though she lived at her house. She usually left for the restaurant very early in the morning and returned home by six. She didn't know what time Melody got home or left the house. Sometimes she wondered if she ever came home. She also wondered when she would go to school because her mother had told her that she would. She had wanted to ask Melody but she was terrified of her. Everyone was.

It was Sarah, one of the workers at the restaurant that Melody had handed her over to, to take her home and bring her every morning. Lily liked Sarah even though she found her to be an unhappy person. She had found her downcast, even weeping sometimes but Sarah always denied it when Lily asked her about it.

Then one day Sarah told Lily that Melody wanted her back at the restaurant later that night.

"She wants me there tonight?" Lily asked, not wanting to believe what she had just heard. "But I thought…I thought they said…you said…but you told me that…"

"She said I should bring you with me. Or do you want to disobey her?" Sarah cocked her head.

"No," Lily answered quietly, but still looked confused. She had been curious about the nightclub and had been told by the cooks that at night the restaurant was strictly for adults. And she couldn't understand why her friend looked so angry. "I just don't know what I would be needed for at night."

"Look at you!" Sarah said spitefully. The look on her face was completely alien to Lily. "Oh, you think you're better than the rest of us eh?"

"What do you mean? I don't understand." Lily was even more confused now.

"You think because you have been left alone for two whole months...ah..." She nodded very slowly. "I see. You may be related to Madam but that doesn't mean anything to her. A beautiful girl is nothing but..." she held up her right hand and rubbed the thumb over the tips of the other fingers repeatedly, "...money." Then she added. "Tonight we sail together."

"But I don't want to go."

"When we get there, you tell Madam. I am only obeying orders. And part of my orders is to dress you up. So please follow me, your majesty." She dragged her to one of the rooms and closed the door. She sat on the huge bed and looked at Lily who was already weeping.

"Look. I am sorry for being so hard. Madam is sending her driver for us soon. It will be good if we are ready before he arrives. Madam can do anything to us if we waste time."

The driver drove into the front yard as Sarah put finishing touches on Lily's hair. He was leaning on the car when they came out. He whistled softly as he saw them approaching but quickly turned and got into the car when Sarah gave him a hard look.

Lily sat confused in the back seat with Sarah; but much more than that she was scared. She didn't know what really happened at the restaurant at night but she knew she was too young to be there. She thought of her grandmother as she always did when she was scared, confused or sad. And then she thought of her aunt Agnes. If only one of them were here. She thought of her mother. What kind of a person was she to have abandoned her with Melody for so long? She had thought her mother would visit her often. But she hadn't seen her since the day she brought her to Melody's.

At the restaurant, the driver honked for the security guard to open the gate as the night club was not yet open to clients. He parked the car in Melody's space and the girls got out. Lily walked behind Sarah like a zombie to the office. Everyone stared at her as she walked past but she didn't notice.

Melody was in her secretary's office when they walked in. A smile spread slowly across her face as she saw Lily.

"Come with me, Lily," she said immediately and held the door of her office open. "I love what you did with her hair." This she mouthed to Sarah before following Lily in and closing the door.

Lily had never been inside Melody's office before. It was beautiful and everything looked expensive. Her shoes sank into the soft beige carpet as she took a few more steps and stood in the middle of the room. The curtains were red and gold and they matched the sofa in the corner. The huge mahogany table by the window had been polished until it gleamed. Melody walked round it and sank into the massive chair behind it. There were two smaller chairs by the table facing her. She pointed to one of them and gestured for Lily to sit. Lily walked to the chair and sat.

"So how long have you been here for?" Melody asked as soon as Lily was seated.

Lily almost smiled. She had completely forgotten about the odd accent. She cleared her throat. "Two months, ma."

"And how many times have I called you into my office in those two months?"

"Never, ma."

Melody nodded slowly. "That should tell you that something very important has come up." Then she smiled broadly baring most of her teeth and reminding Lily of a comic cartoon character she had seen on TV. "Would you like something to drink? What do you like? I have Coke, orange and malt drinks.

Lily shook her head. "No, thank you, ma."

"Are you sure?" Melody asked. "You don't have to be shy with me."

"I don't want a drink, ma. Thank you."

"Ok then." Melody leaned forward. "I want to know something. Where did you learn to speak so well? If I didn't know better I would believe you have lived abroad. I have heard you in the restaurant and I must say your vocabulary is really impressive. Was it at your school in Port Harcourt?"

Lily was surprised at what Melody just said. She thought that she had forgotten all about her. "My grandmother taught me how to speak well."

"Really? Your grandmother?" Melody looked doubtful.

"Yes, ma. She lived and studied in England for several years."

"I see. And you are seventeen? Eighteen?"

"I'm fourteen years old, ma"

Melody sat back surprised. "You look older."

Lily had always been mistaken for an older girl. Her grandmother had told her never to talk to strange men or boys and was to report to her any man that came anywhere near her in the neighborhood. She said it was because her body had developed too quickly and she didn't want men to take advantage of her like they did her mother. And so Lily had kept her distance from all the boys around their home and limited her interactions with those at school.

"Lily, you have been with me for some time now. You have lived in my house and I have fed you and bought you clothes... everything you need. I have made you comfortable just like I promised your mother. Or is there anything you should have that I haven't provided for you?"

Lily thought of school but didn't have the courage to say anything about it. "No, nothing," she replied.

"Now, if I was to do that for everyone that works here, will I still have a business?" Not waiting for a reply she continued. "No." She clasped her hands and laid them on the table. "You will start working from tonight, my dear."

Lily frowned. "But I've been working. I have been doing the tables and working in the kitchen."

"I don't mean that." Melody dismissed her protest with a flamboyant wave of her hand. "In the past couple of months you have just been kept occupied. I mean real work now. Not only will you earn your keep, you also will be making some good money for yourself."

"But I am still in school." What was this woman talking about? "I mean I should be writing my Junior Secondary School examinations in June."

"What school is that?" Melody asked surprising Lily.

What did Melody mean by that question? "My mother said I would...go to school when I get to Lagos."

"And did she drop any school fees?" There was no trace of a smile on Melody's face now or any evidence that there had ever been one. "To go to school you need money. And since your mother didn't leave any, I am afraid you will have to make some yourself."

Lily didn't know what to say. It seemed like Melody was not ready to send her to school like her mother had said and her mother had abandoned her. Finally she sighed. "What kind of work do you mean, ma?"

"Escort." Melody replied evasively. "All you have to do is to go with someone wherever they want to go."

"Escort?" Lily wondered what kind of dumb work that was. Why would anyone want to pay her just for going anywhere with them? And where would that be anyway?

"Yes," Melody replied. "A very respectable friend of mine has noticed you and has expressed his desire to meet you." Melody said.

"Why…would he want to meet me?" Lily asked, puzzled.

"Because he has seen you as the decent and very well brought up girl that you are and would want to spend some time with you," Melody replied.

"Spend some time with me? Is that what escort is?"

"Yes."

"And he will pay me for that?"

"Yes."

"But I still don't understand," Lily said, as she was still not sure why anyone would pay for that. "What would I have to do?"

"Just spend time with him, that's all." This was obviously taking longer than Melody had expected and it seemed like her patience was wearing thin. Most of the girls were willing to do what they were asked to when they found out about the money involved. A couple of them needed a little more persuasion though, but none of them was this naïve. Melody needed to be very careful where Lily was concerned. The truth was that she thought Lily was probably the most beautiful girl she'd ever had the good fortune to have in her clutches. Her glowing skin was flawless and her hair was so long and silky it was almost hard to believe it was real. And she was so young. If she played her cards right Lily would bring in a lot of money and also help open some doors. Alhaji Usman the billionaire had specifically requested for her. Melody had known Alhaji for years. It was his penchant for very young girls that had brought them together in the first place. But he had stopped patronizing her business when he could no longer get what he wanted. Since he was worth more than any three clients put together, Melody had missed his patronage a lot. And now he was back, because of Lily. He had somehow found out about her and he wanted her. Melody wasn't ready to lose Alhaji Usman again. "You know what? I suggest you give it a try," she finally said. "You go with him tonight and see. It's simple really. But you will be very well paid. You will have enough money to do whatever you want."

"Would Sarah be going with me?" Lily asked innocently.

Melody's eyebrows shot up in surprise but she smiled quickly. "Oh no, just you."

"You mean I will be alone with him? But I don't even know him!" She cried. "And I don't know where he will want me to go with him. And it is late."

"Will you stop? He is not a monster, you know," Melody said with her accent more pronounced. "I told you he is a very respectable and decent man. He will not eat you up." Melody looked at her watch. "Listen, I don't expect you to understand everything right away. But as time goes on you will." She picked up the phone. "I'll call him and find out what time he will pick you up tonight. Ok?"

Lily didn't answer. She was scared of whatever it was she was being asked to do. She knew it was dangerous to be alone with a man. Mama had said so. She also knew that women who went out with strange men for money were called prostitutes. She had seen them along the streets in Port Harcourt. She remembered one night she was returning home from a concert she had attended with Agnes at the Presidential Hotel. They had had a difficult time getting any means of transportation, and so had walked a long distance before having to share a seat on a rickety bus all the way home. While they were waiting for the bus she had seen some scantily dressed women standing along the road. She remembered asking about them and Agnes telling her they were waiting to be picked up by men they didn't know. She said they were prostitutes. Is that what she was now? People said very horrible things about prostitutes. Mama and Aunt Agnes had said what they were doing was wrong. But where was Mama now? She died and left her all alone. And her Aunt Agnes was too far away to help her. And wasn't it her own mother that brought her to live with Melody? What else could she do? She would have to work.

"Ok?" Melody's voice broke into her thoughts.

She looked up. Then realizing that Melody was waiting for an answer, she nodded slowly.

"That's my girl!" Melody was elated. "Now let me just confirm..." She dialed and waited, smiling at Lily. "Yes. Hello Alhaji. Madam Melody...I'm fine, thank you. What time will you pick Lily up tonight?"

Sarah had curled Lily's hair and tied it in a ponytail but she had left some tendrils to frame her beautiful young face and hang down her neck. They were like a soft waterfall as she bent her head and looked down at her hands. Her fingernails had never been painted before, but today Sarah had painted them black. She said the colour suited her fair skin. She looked up as Melody dropped the phone and announced that Alhaji would be picking her up in less than an hour.

A tall slim man walked into the restaurant forty-five minutes later and went straight to where Lily was sitting alone. He drew out the chair opposite hers and sat on it smiling at her.

"I am Alhaji Usman," he said with a slight Hausa accent as he extended his hand. Lily took it, though hesitantly, not knowing what else to do. "And I already know that you are called Lily. Tell me, who gave you that name?"

He still held on to Lily's hand and she felt nervous. "My grandmother," she said quietly and tried to free her hand.

"I see. She named you correctly. You look like a very beautiful flower." Instead of letting go of her hand he put his other hand over it and held on more firmly. "Ever since I found out about you I have wanted to meet you. Tonight I am the happiest man in the world and I promise to make you happy." Without letting go of her hand he stood up pulling her up gently. "Shall we?" He guided her to where he was standing and slipped an arm around her waist. Lily stiffened and her heart began to race but he didn't seem to notice. She noticed the other girls looking at them as they walked out. She couldn't understand the expression on their faces but she knew they didn't look pleased.

The car Alhaji parked outside the restaurant was brand new and Lily had never seen anything like it. He opened the door for her and she got inside. It was even more beautiful inside. Alhaji got behind the wheel and started the engine. The sound was so soft that Lily if lights hadn't come on both inside and outside she would have wondered if the car had really started.

"I hope you are hungry," he said smiling at her. "Because I am and I am taking you to one of the best restaurants in Lagos. Fasten your seat belt."

Lily did as she was told as the car slid on to the road. She had never been out this late since she got to Lagos. The traffic was much less and all the hawkers had disappeared. Alhaji turned left at the end of the main road on to a bridge. She had never been on this kind of bridge before. There were streetlights everywhere. She gazed at the buildings afar off and the numerous lights as they reflected in the inky black water. It was a beautiful night.

The sights on the island were simply breathtaking. Lily had never been anywhere this beautiful. This must be where the richest people lived. The houses were magnificent and there were lots of very tall buildings. Also the few cars she saw on the road looked as new as Alhaji's.

Finally Alhaji turned off the road and drove into an open gate. He found a space in the parking lot and parked the car. Then he turned to Lily and smiled revealing perfect teeth."Let me introduce you to an unforgettable experience," he said as he got out of the car and walked round to her door. Lily sat still. She didn't move even when he opened her door. He asked her to unfasten her seat belt and then he bent down to take her hand and help her gently out of the car.

The doors of the restaurant opened as they walked up to them. Lily noticed immediately that this restaurant was nothing at all like Melody's. There were no waitresses, only waiters, and they were all identically dressed in black three-piece suits, white shirts and black bow ties. The ceiling was really high up making Lily feel very small. The tables were exquisitely set and she was particularly intrigued by the way the napkins were folded. She made a mental note to open hers slowly and carefully so that she could study the way it had been folded.

When they were seated a waiter brought a tray of little folded towels. Lily had no idea what they were for. Then she saw Alhaji begin to wipe his hands with the one given to him and so she did the same.

"I am going to order for both of us." Alhaji announced. "Believe me you will be pleased."

Lily was only glad because she knew she wouldn't know what to order. She couldn't even bring herself to pick up the menu, let alone open it to see what was inside.

While they waited for their meal Alhaji leaned forward and smiled at her. She looked down embarrassed. She had never been this close to a man before. She felt very strange in this strange place with this strange man.

"So are you going to tell me about yourself, Lily?" Alhaji asked.

Lily kept looking down. What should she do? She could not talk because of her growing uneasiness. Besides a part of her kept telling her she didn't belong here with him doing this type of work. She felt an overwhelming need to separate herself from all this somehow, yet she had to make sure that this man did not return to Melody to tell her she was not a good escort. Where then would she get money to go to school?

She cleared her throat and tried to speak but she saw that she needed to clear it again. And then the words came out.

"My name is Lily Parker. I…"

"Pardon me. Is your father American?" Alhaji asked her when he heard her name. "Already I know you are not a full Nigerian."

"No," she replied. "Parker is my grandmother's surname. She was married to a British."

"Isn't it your father's surname too? Why do you refer to your grandmother?"

"She's not…She's my mother's mother."

Alhaji nodded slowly. "How come you have her surname?"

"She raised me and so she gave me her name."

"And what about your parents?"

Lily hesitated not sure how much of herself she wanted this stranger to know. She thought of her father whom she had never met, and her mother who had abandoned her. "They didn't raise me," she said simply.

Alhaji nodded. "Where is your grandmother now?"

"She died."

"I'm sorry," Alhaji said softly. "You must really miss her."

Lily nodded. Suddenly she felt very sad. If her grandmother hadn't died she would be safe with her at their house in Woji, Port Harcourt and not here in Lagos working as an escort to get money to go to school.

Shortly afterwards two waiters arrived with a trolley and served their meal but Lily couldn't bring herself to eat.

"If you don't eat I won't too," Alhaji said as he leaned back in his chair and folded his arms across his chest. "And then I will starve to death because I haven't had anything to eat all day. And my death would be on your conscience. People would want to know how I died, and these kind men," he turned to the waiters who had finished serving but were still standing by the table, "will help me tell them that a certain young lady starved me to death." And then he closed his eyes and let his head hang back with his mouth wide open.

Lily smiled shyly. With his head still hung back Alhaji opened one eye and peeped at her from beneath his glasses. Then he closed it again and said, "I'm still dying."

Lily picked up her spoon. She was still smiling.

Alhaji opened his eyes and turned to the waiters. "It seems I am not dying today." And they both laughed.

The waiters left and Lily and Alhaji began to eat. Throughout the time they spent at the restaurant Alhaji tried to keep the conversation light and funny. He was really pleased that Lily had relaxed and seemed to be enjoying the evening. She smiled at him though shyly and occasionally she laughed at something he said. By the time they left the restaurant Lily was in a much lighter mood.

Alhaji drove around for a while and soon Lily began to wonder when he would take her back to Melody's.

"I want to show you some of Victoria Island. And so I am going to drive a little."

She had no idea how long that would take but she really was enjoying herself. Is this all there was to escorting? She certainly hoped so. Besides, Alhaji seemed nice.

After about thirty minutes he said he was taking her back. He said that if he didn't, there wouldn't be anything left to show her the next night.

For several nights he picked her up and took her to a different expensive restaurant. And then he drove around for a while before taking her back and slipping an envelope in her purse. They had been going out for three weeks when one night he drove up to a very large gate and honked. Almost immediately the gate was opened by a man and Alhaji drove in. Before them rose a magnificent white and green house. It didn't look like a restaurant at all. The beautiful garden on the left of the driveway reminded Lily of her grandmother's own though this one was larger and had a boundary of large smooth whitish stones. Alhaji parked the car and as usual came round to open her door.

"Where are we?" She asked without making any move.

"This is where I live, Lily," Alhaji answered.

Lily became a little agitated. "Why did you bring me to your house?" She queried. "I thought we were going to a restaurant and just then you would drive to different places and then you would take me back."

"I'm sorry. I just wanted you to see where I live." Then he spread his hands and shrugged. "I have taken you to different restaurants every night and I just thought…" He really looked sorry. "I thought maybe…ok maybe I was wrong to have brought you here. Maybe I should have asked you first. Please forgive me."

Lily stayed put. She didn't think she should be here. But what was she supposed to do? He really looked sorry.

"Besides you're here now, and I have a surprise for you. Please, my Lily, forgive me for my foolishness." And then he got down on one knee.

Lily was both surprised and amused by his act. He was right though. She was here now. Besides he was a decent man and very funny and she had found herself beginning to really like him.

"Ok Alhaji," she said. "You don't have to do that." She stepped out of the car and he got up. He locked up the car and led her to the house. As he unlocked the door and held it open for her she gasped. She sight she beheld was unbelievable.

"This is the most beautiful house I have ever been in," she said breathlessly. "And it is so big."

"And boring," he said as he led her through an archway into a large luxurious sitting room. "Please make yourself comfortable and I'll be right back." And he was gone in a flash.

Lily looked around her. She loved this place. The chairs were covered in cream leather and the rug was so soft and beautiful. There were three large paintings on the wall as well as some art works. The television was huge. She had never seen anything like it. Then there was that nagging thought again that she shouldn't be here, and with it a strong uneasy feeling. She took a deep breath and let it out, but the feeling persisted. She sank into one of the chairs and decided that immediately Alhaji got back she would tell him she wanted to leave. After all he wasn't supposed to have brought her to his house in the first place.

He returned five minutes later with a large shopping bag under each arm. He dropped them on a sofa and before she could say anything he raised a finger and disappeared again through the door. He returned shortly after with yet another shopping bag, and two purses hanging round his neck. He put the third shopping bag on the floor beside her and removed the purses from around his neck. Then he knelt down in front of her and put his two hands together as if he wanted to pray.

"Please," he said. "Please be a 38."

"What?" Lily asked wondering what he was on about. "38 what?"

"Your shoe size," he replied.

"Oh…oh ok," Lily said nodding.

"Well? Are you?" Alhaji asked when Lily didn't say anything more.

Then she looked at him enquiringly. "How did you know?"

He smiled and rubbed his palms together looking pleased. "Because I'm good. I took one look at your feet and knew."

Lily didn't believe him. "No, really. How did you know?"

Truthfully?"

"Truthfully."

Alhaji drew the shopping bag he had dropped beside Lily to himself and said, "I looked at your feet long enough and guessed you were a 38. Then I hoped very hard and went to buy your shoes." He was smiling.

Lily couldn't help smiling too. "You hoped very hard."

"Very, very hard," he said with his eyes squeezed tight and his fists clenched.

Lily laughed. "And that's how you knew?"

"That and the fact that I am good," he replied as he took one of Lily's feet and began to remove her shoe. When she tried to protest he quickly put a finger to his lips to silence her and refused to let go of her foot.

"But…" She didn't think it was right for him to be doing this. And there was something about the way his hands felt on her skin.

"I meant it when I said I am the happiest man in the world because I met you. Please let me show you how much I meant it." Alhaji gently removed both shoes from Lily's feet. Then he reached into the bag and brought out a pair of red leather mules set with little white beads. They were so dainty Lily thought they would never fit. But when Alhaji gently slipped them on one after the other they were a perfect fit.

"I have always imagined how your feet would look in red," he said as he gazed at them. "And there is a little purse to match." He reached into the bag again and brought out the matching purse. He slipped the mules off and brought out a pair of black suede high-heeled sandals with a matching clutch bag. He put the sandals on Lily's feet.

"I don't think I can wear these," she said. "I don't think I can take any of these." She felt the need to be on her guard again.

"Why not?" Alhaji looked up from admiring her feet.

"You don't have to buy me expensive gifts. You don't have to buy me any gift at all. And…and I would like to leave now." She bent over to remove the sandals from her feet and suddenly found her face too close to Alhaji's. For a moment she froze. And in that moment he quickly reached out and cupped her face with his hands.

"Oh Lily," he said.

Lily could feel his breath on her face as he inched closer and closer. She began to feel some strange stirrings she had never experienced before. What felt like electric currents coursed through her body. She wanted to stop this. She needed to stop this. But she found she couldn't move a muscle. Her mind did not seem to belong to her anymore. Why couldn't she break out of this spell? Why couldn't she stop this?

Why couldn't I have put an end to it? Lily asked herself again as she had a thousand times since that night. Melody's shrill voice rang out again from the corridor, interrupting her thoughts. Someone was really in trouble tonight.

If she had had any idea how that evening with Alhaji would turn out, she would never have agreed to get out of the car when they got to his house. But how was she to know he had such intentions? How was she to know he wasn't really as nice as she'd thought? And she had begun to trust him. Why had she been so foolish and naïve as to think going to restaurants was all that would be required of her? She had hated him since that night. He still showered her with expensive gifts and took her to fine restaurants and the occasional party but some of the time he took her to his house. He even made her spend a whole weekend.

She hated Melody, the one who tricked her into all this. She had deceived her by lying to her about what was involved. She shook her head as she remembered how she finally came to her senses and begged Alhaji to stop, but he ignored her pleas. She cringed as she always did whenever she remembered everything that happened at his house that night.

When Alhaji finally dropped her off, she had gone straight to Melody, crushed, and told her that she could no longer continue to be an escort and why. Instead of the empathy she expected, Melody threatened to throw her into the streets where she would be available to every man. She told her that she ought to be thankful that a man like Alhaji Usman was interested in her. Didn't she know that she was the envy of the other girls? Then she pulled her into her ample arms and told her in kinder tones that everything would be all right. She would soon get used to it and the good thing was that unlike the other girls she needed to be with only one man.

She hated her mother. She hated her for bringing her to this place and abandoning her. She hated her for not standing up to Sheyi and keeping her in Benin. She had chosen to do what he wanted rather than love her own daughter. Now she really understood why Mama felt the way she did about him. He was truly a bad man.

The nightclub was almost ready for opening. The band was already set and was performing a popular song. Very soon people, mostly men, would start coming in. Most of the girls on night duty sat around in groups as usual. Lily didn't have more than a casual relationship with just one or two of them. She was always conscious of the animosity around her. Hadn't Melody referred to her as the envy of the other girls? If only they knew how much she hated her life. She would gladly give them the Alhaji if she could. But that wasn't even the only problem. She had overheard one of them standing up for her once and telling the others not to blame her for being more beautiful than they were.

Even Sarah avoided her now. Lily didn't blame her really. She knew she was just being loyal to the others.

"Hey! Cletus!" Selena, one of the bar girls called out to a waiter who was standing on a stool by the entrance fixing a light bulb.

He took his time to fix the bulb before looking in her direction. "What?" He asked rudely.

"There's someone at the door." Selena pointed to the glass doors.

Cletus got down from the stool and saw a young girl standing outside. "Can't she see that the restaurant is closed?" He half-asked and half-complained.

"At least find out whether she's looking for someone," Selena suggested.

Cletus reluctantly opened the door and stepped outside. His face broke into a smile as he got a better look at the visitor.

Though she looked exhausted and a bit roughened up, she was one of the most beautiful girls he had ever laid his eyes on. She was dressed in a simple khaki skirt and a t-shirt but he thought she looked like a model with her shapely figure and up-turned nose. He chatted with her for a couple of minutes before returning into the restaurant and walking to a table occupied by only one girl who looked up as he approached.

"There is a fine babe outside who says she's looking for you. She said her name is Lillian Obimali."

Shade smiled. "Please Cletus, show her in." She stood up and waited for Cletus to fetch Lillian. She opened her arms as Lillian approached. "I was beginning to worry about you," she said as she hugged her friend. "I expected you over an hour ago."

"The bus broke down on the way and it took a while for them to fix it," an exhausted Lillian said.

"The most important thing is that you made it safely," Shade said as she drew out a chair for her and they both sat down. "It's really good to see you, girl."

"You can't believe how glad *I* am to see you. This Lagos is something else. I was so scared of ending up in the wrong place."

"You look really tired," Shade said. "And you must be starving," she added. She looked at her watch. "Listen, I have to go out soon and I need to get ready. We have a lot to talk…"

"Out? Where?" Lillian asked, looking round the restaurant.

"Look, I'll explain when I get back. We have a lot to talk about, you know." Shade bent to pick up Lillian's bag.

"You want to leave me alone?" Lillian looked round again. "Here? But…"

"I'm not leaving you alone Lillie. Relax. I'm going to introduce you to the safest person here and I am going to leave you in her care." Shade reassured an obviously anxious Lillian. "Come."

She carried Lillian's bag in one hand and held her hand in the other as she took her to the far end of the restaurant, to the table where Lily sat alone.

"Hey Lily," Shade called out.

"Hello." Lily looked up and smiled. Shade was probably the only girl that didn't seem to have anything against her at Melody's.

"I want you to meet my friend… You won't believe it. Her name's Lillie."

"You mean we have the same name?" Lillie asked as she took the hand extended to her by Lily. "Mine is short for Lillian."

"And mine is just Lily, as in the flower. I am pleased to meet you."

Shade looked pleased. "Well, Lillie is an old friend of mine and she just came into town today. She will be staying with me. Could you please take care of her for me while I am out?" She asked Lily.

"Don't worry," Lily replied.

"She's hungry and tired…"

"Don't worry," Lily reassured her. "She'll be fine."

"Well then," Shade said. "I'll see you guys later."

As she turned to leave, Lily quickly reached for her hand. The smile on her face had disappeared. "Take care of yourself," she said.

Shade smiled. "I will," she said quietly. "Thanks." And then she waved.

"So Lillie, what would you like to eat?"

Chapter FOUR

OLISA CRESCENT HAD BECOME busier in the evenings in the past two weeks. Usually by 8pm the only people that could be seen on the road were those returning from their places of work and a few security guards and gatemen. But since the general outage that had persisted for over two weeks people now sat outside their houses or took strolls along the road, sometimes till midnight. They preferred to brave the mosquitoes and get some fresh air than suffer the heat inside their houses because they could not use their fans or air-conditioners.

It was the second prolonged power failure in six months. The first one had lasted for four weeks but that had been during the rainy season when the weather was relatively cool. It was frustrating to return from a hard day's work and not be able to stay indoors. The heat was almost unbearable sometimes.

A few more generators had been bought since the last outage. Some were brand new while others were second-hand. Some of the second-hand generators were really noisy and emitted a lot of smoke. Some people laughed when they passed by the houses of those that owned them, but they soon stopped laughing and just moved on when they suddenly realized that the owners were comfortable in their houses while they were outside battling with mosquitoes. Those that didn't find anything funny and couldn't just move on were those who lived next to the owners of the old generators. They had to continuously suffer from the noise and the pungent fumes without enjoying the benefits.

Amanda was one of such people. She groaned as Patrick's generator began to cluck like an agitated mother hen as it usually did before he managed to get it going. She knew she would have to go inside her flat soon if she didn't want to choke on the fumes that were sure to fill the verandah of the building in the next few minutes. If only he would stay out later or not even come home at all. She smiled as Esther, her friend and neighbour jumped up from the mat she had been lying on. She knew it was time for another one of her series of lamentations about the 'wickedness of mankind to mankind'.

"I wish something would happen to that...contraption your neighbour calls a generator!" She said with hands on hips. "Doesn't he know how offensive it is to the people around? Is it until we all die of...of...pollution-related causes that...that..."

Amanda chuckled. Esther always had that effect on her. She had such a pleasant nature that she couldn't be taken seriously even when she was really angry. She and her husband Timothy were newly married when they moved into the flat next to Amanda and Sheyi's. Esther was like a breath of fresh air and Amanda liked spending time with her. Her friendship with her was one of the few good things that had happened to her in a very long time.

"Ama?" Esther looked at Amanda enquiringly. Amanda had found out early that Esther shortened everybody's name any way she saw fit. "Why...why are you laughing?" This only made Amanda laugh the more. "This is not a laughing matter," she went on. "It is not a laughing matter at all." Esther was now struggling to look serious herself. "This man has a mission. And it has to do with annihilating all his neighbours with carbon mono-oxide and..."

"Esther!" Amanda interrupted her. "He's not the only one with an old generator in the area."

"They are all together, the wicked of the world that have no consideration for their fellow man," Esther lamented. "Why can't they just look for more money and buy a brand new one even if it is the small type? Why must they try to kill us?"

"We should be thinking of getting our own so that we can be inside our houses too, you know?" Amanda said.

"Hmmm." Esther seemed to be lost in thought. Then suddenly she brightened up and exclaimed, "Wow! That is such a wonderful idea! Why haven't you suggested it before?"

"Oh, go away!"

"No, it's true. If we spend enough time thinking hard..."

Just then the two women heard a cry from inside Amanda's flat. Akin, Amanda's little son had woken up.

She got up quickly and dusted her skirt. "Duty calls."

"Poor darling." Esther said. "Must be the heat." She picked up her mat. "I guess I'll be going in too if the wife of Timo is to be alive by the time her husband gets back."

"Well, goodnight then." Amanda smiled at her cheerily.

"Good night."

Amanda picked up her three-year-old son from the mattress he'd been lying on with his sister, Ola, by the large screen-covered open window. She went to the sofa and sat down cradling him in her arms. She touched his forehead and found he wasn't sweating. Something else must have disturbed his sleep. He buried his head in her arm and tried to make himself more comfortable, and in a few seconds he was asleep again. He felt so soft and comforting. This was one of the few luxuries of her life, to hold her children in her arms smell them and feel their softness. She loved to watch them play and comfort them when they got hurt. Amanda had learnt how to love her children from her own mother. They were the most important part of her life.

But there was one she couldn't comfort, one she couldn't reach; one she felt she had hurt beyond forgiveness. The burden weighed so heavily on her she sometimes felt she couldn't bear it.

The room suddenly went dark as the candle she had put on the dining table burnt out. She wouldn't bother lighting another one. The darkness suited her mood.

For as long as she could remember there had been a gaping hole in her life. It had grown bigger with time and had threatened to swallow her up when her mother died. Her mother had been her mainstay all her life. She had been the one Amanda looked at and knew there was a reason for living. Her mother had loved without conditions and had been able to forgive anything. She had also loved God with all her heart and had shown Amanda who a true Christian was. Amanda knew that a Christian wasn't just a title for anyone who attended a church; it described a person who had a personal relationship with the Lord Jesus by truly giving their heart to Him and nurturing that relationship. She knew that being a Christian brought about changes in your life that otherwise could never have taken place. She also knew it was the only way you could go to heaven when you died. She remembered her mother saying that the Holy Spirit of God bore witness in your heart that you were a child of God. And so Amanda knew she hadn't been a Christian all those years even though she attended church regularly and was raised in a Christian environment.

There had been a time when she was, but she was very young. Though she had never known her father because he had died when she was only a baby, she had been conscious then of an abiding presence of a heavenly Father who gave her comfort and an assurance that she was not alone. Later she had walked away from Him and that was when the feeling of emptiness began.

She was young and impressionable when she met Robert. He was an older man and he gave her a feeling of well-being and security. She was so thrilled that such a sophisticated man could be interested in her that she threw caution to the winds and gave herself totally to him. It was already too late when she found out that he was married and she had just been a pastime for the three months he had spent in the town to relieve one of his colleagues who had been away on a course abroad. She was already pregnant with Lily. He had returned to Lagos where he came from, to his wife and family without knowing and she was left heartbroken and unsure of her future. It was her mother that had come to her rescue. If it hadn't been for her support she didn't know how she would have survived that period.

Amanda leaned back and closed her eyes. She knew she'd been selfish and had always wanted her own way. She never listened to her mother but preferred to argue with her all the time. Her mother was always right and it annoyed her. Now she regretted being so disagreeable. She regretted not taking corrections because no matter how angry she was and how much fuss she made her mother always told her the truth and tried to make her see the wisdom in accepting it. If only she had listened a few times. Her mother had died before she asked the Lord for forgiveness and had her relationship with Him restored and she wished she hadn't waited for so long. At least she could have been kinder to her during her last days.

She wondered what time it was. Sheyi had been coming home late every night for a long time now. These days he blamed it on the power failure. He said there was nothing to come home to. Amanda had said nothing in response to that because she didn't care. Besides they both knew his late nights had begun long before the electricity problem.

Sometimes she pondered on what had drawn her to Sheyi. He wasn't tall, maybe just an inch taller than she was, but he was good looking, and he used to be charming. He spoke so well and he seemed like the kind of person she could have a good relationship with. She knew now though that that was just a scam. That charm had died a natural death a long time ago.

Everything she was passing through now was her own fault. They were the results of the bad choices she had made in the past. If she could go back in time she would change a lot of things. She would be obedient and gentle towards her mother. She would let her know that she admired her and truly loved her more than anyone in the world. She hoped she knew...

Another thing Amanda would have loved to change was her decision not to take Lily with her after her youth service year. She had got a good job and would have been able to cope. She'd also had the option of returning to Port Harcourt to live. Or at least she could have visited home more often and become a part of her daughter's life. But she had done none of these. Rather she had convinced herself that the child was better off with her mother, that she would grow up with all the love and care she needed at home. A man like Sheyi would never have been interested in her if she had had a child with her when they met. That would have saved her so much heartache for sure. It also means she wouldn't have had Ola and Akin. *It's like you can't win either way, Amanda,* she thought to herself.

She also wished she hadn't listened to Sheyi when he suggested that Lily be sent to his aunt in Lagos. It had seemed like an alternative at the time since he had refused to have her in his house and she didn't want her to stay in Port Harcourt without the watchful eye of her grandmother. She was afraid of Lily falling into the same trap she had fallen into. Besides she had been assured that his aunt would be responsible for Lily's welfare and Amanda wouldn't have to worry about a thing.

The moon was full and cast a warm glow through the window. She looked at the sleeping boy in her arms and for a little while she watched the steady rising and falling of his chest. He looked so peaceful and gentle though when he was awake he was a bundle of energy. He reminded her so much of her brother Henry.

Amanda was unable to contact him or Melissa when their mother died. He had had a big fight with her when she became pregnant with Lily. He had expressed his disappointment and called her names. She had screamed at him and told him that none of it was his business anyway. And as a result, in spite of their mother's pleas they had both sworn to break all ties between them forever. They'd kept away from each other until he left the country, and for fourteen years there was no contact between them. Even when their mother told her that he called from England Amanda was too proud and stubborn to speak to him or ask any questions about him. She pretended she didn't care even though she missed him so much. And as if their mother knew, she furnished her with all the details about him anyway. Amanda knew he was successful. She also knew he had married a girl from Mauritius and that they had a daughter. Tears had flowed down her cheeks when she saw the pictures Henry sent to their mother of his family. She had waited for her mother and Lily to leave for church that morning before taking the pictures from the table where her mother had left them for her since the day before.

Amanda and Melissa were never close. Melissa had moved out of the house long before they could really relate. Amanda only remembered her coming home once in a while and she never stayed for long. Amanda was only about twelve when she left for the US and she had never come back.

Thinking of Henry now made Amanda smile. Things would have remained the same between them if it hadn't been for Agnes. Good old Agnes. She had searched for Henry and Melissa's phone numbers when she had sorted their mother's documents with the lawyer after the funeral and found them. Then she had called Amanda and given them to her. What Amanda didn't know was that Agnes had already spoken to Henry. Amanda was able to speak to Melissa but didn't get round to calling her brother before he called.

Amanda would never forget the conversation they had, the first in fourteen years, as long as she lived. It lasted forty-five minutes and she wept for half of the time. Henry wept too. They both felt responsible for the separation. They forgave each other and both regretted not doing so before their mother died.

Henry now called her regularly. He wanted to know all about her and had pressed her until she found it difficult to hide most things from him. He later confessed that some things their mother had said in the past about her relationship with Sheyi had disturbed him. And when she opened up to him about her life with Sheyi he had only one thing to say: Leave him.

He assured her he would take care of everything. All she needed to do was make up her mind. Amanda knew it wasn't as easy as that. Sheyi would never let her take the children away and she could never leave them. And there was Lily. There was no way she could do anything now without Lily being fully in the picture.

Since she had taken Lily to Lagos Sheyi had always stopped her from traveling to see her any time she proposed to. He had told her it wasn't a good idea, that it would only make Lily feel worse because she would miss her more. He said it was better to let her grow older. Amanda didn't really agree with him but as always she had listened. She later spoke to Esther about it and Esther told her it wasn't right. And so Amanda began to call Melody more frequently and request to speak to Lily. At first Melody was friendly and assured her that Lily was fine and was settling very well. Then she started sounding irritable especially when Amanda insisted on speaking to her daughter. Melody would tell her how Lily had just left, hadn't arrived, was running an errand or was just not at the restaurant. And the day Amanda asked Melody to arrange for her to be present the next time she called Melody exploded in anger.

"Is this how you repay me for taking your daughter in when she had nowhere to go? Did you give me money to feed her and clothe her? How dare you command me to arrange for her to be here the next time you call?"

Amanda fought hard to control her own anger. "I didn't expect that my wanting to speak to my daughter could get you so angry. I'm sorry, Aunt Melody. I don't mean to offend you. It's just that I haven't seen Lily in such a long time."

There was a pause and then Melody spoke in a softer tone. "It's all right, my dear. Don't mind my outburst. You see, I have had a very difficult week and I am under a lot of stress." She cleared her throat. "Lily is fine. You don't need to bother yourself about her at all as I have always told you. I understand how you feel. You are just doing what any good mother would do."

Amanda only became more worried. Sheyi too was going to such great lengths to stop her from seeing Lily. She knew it could only mean one thing, and that was what she feared most. It was what had bothered her from the day she left Lily with Melody. The things Melody's secretary said had left her riddled with guilt for leaving Lily. At first it came as an uneasy feeling all through the journey back to Benin that day. And then in the days that followed it grew gradually to a full realization of what she could have exposed her daughter to. She had hoped that she was wrong, that she was worried for nothing, but with Sheyi being so adamant about her not seeing Lily and his aunt refusing to let her speak to her she knew she had every reason to feel guilty.

She'd decided to give Sheyi time before mentioning seeing Lily again. She'd hoped that if she kept asking he would give in and let her go. She was so wrong.

"It's been months since I saw Lily," she told him one evening two months earlier. She remembered his cold silence. She'd refused to let it sway her and continued. "I would like to go to Lagos on Saturday to see her. I am going to make arrangements for Ola and Akin to stay with Esther in case you already have plans. If I leave first thing in the morning I should be back..."

"You can't go," he said without any emotion.

"Why not?" She blurted out even though she already knew he would only give her the same old reasons and then tell her she couldn't go. "Sheyi, why can't I visit Lily? I have listened to you for almost six months. I have always listened to you. I have not seen or spoken to my daughter in six months just so there can be peace..."

Sheyi had sprung up from his seat and moved menacingly towards her. She remembered that murderous look on his face and how it scared her. When he got to where she was standing with her back against the wall he pointed to her face and thundered, "and if you want that peace to continue you would forget about going to Lagos and..." he grabbed her upper arm, "...never make demands on my aunt to speak to your daughter again. You hear me?"

Amanda wanted to cower and beg as she had always done. She wanted to reason with him and plead, but a sudden boldness came upon her. Maybe it was the talks she'd been having with Henry lately or maybe it was the effect of the heavy burden she has been carrying alone for months. Or maybe she had simply had enough.

With his grip still on her arm she looked up at him and said in defiance, "I can see you really think you can stop me!"

Sheyi's face had been close enough for her to see his eyes flicker. She had taken him by surprise. Even his grip loosened so she could free her arm and bolt across the room. He just stood there facing the wall. Then he turned slowly and it was her turn to be surprised.

"Ok, I'm sorry," Sheyi said. "I'm truly sorry. I didn't mean it that way."

Amanda had blinked twice and wondered if her ears were deceiving her. Sheyi was apologizing? She couldn't remember him ever being sorry about anything. She was silent because she was shocked, but he must have misunderstood her silence because he continued begging for forgiveness.

Amanda had felt like she was in a trance and was at a loss as to how to react. Sheyi then tried to assure her that he was not against her seeing Lily for any bad reason. He asked her to postpone the visit and promised that when his workload eased off a little at the office, they would all travel together as a family.

Amanda knew even then that she couldn't fall for that but she was overwhelmed by the way he acted and decided to give him a little time. Besides, she hoped that there might be a possibility he'd meant what he said because after that day his attitude towards her changed. He became nice.

She confided in Esther who was convinced that Sheyi was only adopting another way of stopping her because his previous scheme didn't work anymore. This made Amanda spend considerable time thinking about the situation until she finally made up her mind what to do. She would go to Lagos without telling Sheyi. He was gone the whole day everyday anyway. She reckoned she would be home before he returned late in the night. Even Melody would never find out about it, she hoped. She would find a way of seeing Lily and spending time with her, even planning how to take her away from there.

Everything would be fine, she thought. She would make Lily understand that she never meant to abandon her or hurt her in any way and that she loved her very much and wanted more than anything for them to be together. Lily would forgive her and then maybe this horrible pain in her heart and the heavy burden she had carried for so long would go away.

Chapter FIVE

PROSTITUTION? LILLIAN COULDN'T BELIEVE what her friends were telling her. She had wondered why they spent so much time at the restaurant and about all those women, but she had never imagined... Shade? No, it couldn't be. Not Shade and definitely not Lily. She looked from one to the other. This had to be a joke. Lily was the most decent, well-spoken girl she had ever met. She had liked her from the moment they were introduced. And Shade was...well...Shade. These two couldn't possibly be...they just couldn't be.

"But why?" This was all she could manage as she tried to understand.

It was Shade that spoke first after a full minute. "Let's just say I woke up one day and found out...I was a prostitute." She shrugged. There was another full minute of silence.

"But how?" Lillian asked again spreading her hands and looking more confused with every passing minute. Then she added, "I mean...I'm sorry for being so confused but..."

"But you can't understand why a girl would *choose* such a way of life, right?" Shade asked punching Lily playfully.

Lily smiled back at her.

"Forgive me. You know I am not judging you. I'm just…I just didn't expect anything like this," Lillian said. "I…" She took a deep breath and let it out through pursed lips.

"You're in deep shock," Lily said.

Lillian said nothing. It was her first week in Lagos. She had been staying at Shade's flat and had been indoors most of the time. She had spent the night she arrived in a little storeroom at the restaurant and when they left early in the morning she had wanted to ask Shade where she had been but was too tired. And by the time she woke up later Shade had already left for work and didn't return till after mid-night, exhausted. Somehow she had been unable to talk about it until this Saturday morning. Shade had an errand to run for Melody and had asked Lillian to come along. She said it was an opportunity for her to get out of the house. Lillian had only been too glad since it meant seeing Lily again.

Since they were not expected at the restaurant until evening, Lily had requested that they spend a few hours with her at Melody's house. They had joked for an hour or so until Lillian asked why they went to the restaurant every night and what kept them till morning.

Even now as she sat on Lily's bed thinking over what she had heard she still wondered if it was a bad joke. She couldn't imagine why any girl would sell her body. As far as she was concerned it was the lowest life anyone could live. There were a thousand and one things a girl could do for money. Was it the desire for expensive things that would make her resort to prostitution or what? She would rather clean gutters…

"What are you thinking about, Lillie?" Shade asked.

Lillian took another deep breath. "I'm just wondering."

"Wondering why your friend Shade is not who you thought she was?" Shade asked her.

"Actually, you'll always be Shade, no matter what," Lillian said with a half-smile. "You were my way out of the miserable life I had back home and I can't imagine how things would have been if you hadn't come to my aid. You were there for me when I needed you." And her feelings for her friend were evident in her eyes.

There was some silence again.

"It's just this prostitution thing," Lily said suddenly, shaking her head vigorously and frowning very hard. The way her eyebrows came together made the others laugh.

"I was brought to Lagos when I was thirteen years old," Shade began after a moment. "My mother had just died and there was no one to take care of me. We had been dispossessed of all we had when my father died earlier. We had to live like beggars because they left us with nothing."

"Who were they?" Lillian asked.

A humorless laugh escaped Shade's throat. "My father's brothers and sisters. My so-called aunties and uncles. They took our house, our cars, my father's business, my mother's shop, everything. They even threatened my mother or scared her or something until she let them have all the money she had access to. Then they threw us out into the streets. I never saw my mother smile again, not really. She had to sell her clothes to feed us.

"She took me to the Community Health Centre one day and left me in the waiting room. If only I knew I would never see her again… I didn't know she was very sick. She died that day. A nurse took me to my uncles and aunties but none of them would have me. She made further enquiries and found out my mother had a cousin in Lagos." She paused. "Melody is my aunt. I was brought to Lagos by the nurse's nephew and

Melody took me in. She took care of me until..." she sighed deeply. "Well...until I was considered ripe enough for work. I was fifteen and had no idea what they were going to do to me."

Overwhelmed by what she had just heard Lillian felt sorry for her friend. She had had no idea. Suddenly she was ashamed of the thoughts she had nursed about her earlier. "You didn't choose to be..."

Shade shook her head. "I wanted to go to the university. I had dropped out of school when my father died, of course, but I had a good foundation. Remember the nurse's nephew? He visited me every now and then. He said his aunt the nurse always wanted to know how I was doing. One day I asked him to bring me books and begged him to be my teacher. He agreed and began to call me his pet project. And for four years he faithfully taught me. I passed my O levels and later my JME and was admitted into the University of Lagos."

"And Melody didn't object to any of these?" Lily asked. She too was hearing Shade's story for the first time.

"As long as she didn't have to pay for anything and it didn't interfere with her ability to satisfy her clients," Shade shook her head, "she didn't mind me studying. In fact she prefers educated and enlightened girls."

"But what about your youth service? How come she let you leave town?" Lily wanted to know.

"Frankly, I was surprised myself." Shade replied. "I just told her I had been posted to the East. She asked me where exactly I'd been posted and if I would come back. That's all."

"And she didn't say anything else?" Lily was surprised.

Shade shrugged with her lower lip stuck out.

"Well, it's surprising that she would let you go just like that. Wasn't she bothered that you might not return?" Lily asked. "I can't even take a step in this house without being monitored."

"What's surprising about God wanting our paths to cross?" Lillian tilted her head and had a playful look on her face. "I see providence." Then she said more seriously, "you said Melody asked if you would come back." When Shade nodded she continued. "That means she thought there was a possibility that you might not."

"So why did I come back? That's what you want to know, isn't it?" Shade asked.

"Well…yeah." Lillian folded her arms and looked like a young child bent on having her way.

"Where would I go? I spent almost every day of my life dreaming of the day I would leave. And when I finally did I had nowhere to go."

Lillian didn't understand. "But you got a job at the insurance firm when you returned. You could have taken care of yourself."

"You don't get it." Shade said, shaking her head and looking weary. "I had been in the business for so long. I could leave…the restaurant. But I couldn't really leave," she struggled to explain. "You see… it doesn't leave you just like that. This is who I am." Her face was a picture of sadness. "I didn't show up for two months after I returned to Lagos. I kept telling myself I wouldn't go back." She laughed. "Who was I fooling? This is what I do. I wouldn't know how else to be. And Melody and the girls are my family. They are the only people I know that will accept me however I am. I have no one else. So you see; I had to return."

Lillian didn't know what to say but strangely she felt she understood. Shade was trapped in the only life she knew and she couldn't see any way out. She would need some form of miracle, like a brainwash or something. It seemed like Shade had sold more than her body, she had sold her soul.

"I wish Mary were here," she said to herself.

"I beg your pardon?" Shade hadn't heard her.

"My sister, Mary. I said I wish she were here. She would know exactly what to say. She believes that no matter where you find yourself, God has a purpose for your life and if you allow Him He will make it happen."

"And you believe her?" Shade looked surprised.

"Sometimes," Lillian replied nodding her head first to the right and then to the left.

"God? A purpose for my life?" Shade laughed mockingly.

"Sounds just like what my grandmother would say," Lily said thoughtfully.

"She's born again?" Lillian asked.

"She was," Lily said. "She died less than a year ago. That's when I came here."

"Are you also related to the woman?" Lillian asked.

"No…yes…well, not directly. My mother's husband is."

"Your mother's husband? You have a mother?" Lillian looked shocked.

"And get this: She is the one that dumped me here with Melody," Lily announced. And for the next few minutes Lillian and Shade listened to her sad story.

"So one day I was Mama Parker's little girl and the next, a highly paid Lagos prostitute," she concluded.

"Wow!" Lillian wrapped her arms around herself as if she was cold. After a while she looked at Lily. "Maybe there's a good reason why she hasn't come," she said. "You said yourself that it was her husband that didn't want you to stay with them. Maybe he's also responsible for her not coming to see you."

"Not coming to see her daughter or even calling?" Lily asked. "In eight months? The truth is that she would rather do what he wants. He is more important to her than anyone else. Than her mother, her daughter…" She shrugged. "I can live with that."

Lillian wasn't so sure. Lily looked too sad. She looked like she had a myriad of unasked questions. If only Mary were here.

"So what if she turns up one day and really has a good reason." Shade persisted.

Lily shook her head.

"Means the reason had better be good with a capital 'g'," Lillian offered.

Lily smiled at her. Then the smile faded and she said, "I know why she hasn't come. She probably never will. She has her own family. She has two other children and I know she loves them very much. She's never wanted me. I was a mistake. Now she's totally free of me, I guess."

"I wouldn't be too quick to conclude, Lily," Lillian said quickly. "I mean, I agree with Shade. She probably has a good reason. My guess is, take away that man from her life and perhaps things would be different. What you told us about your grandmother shows she seemed to know him very well. And besides, you said his family is into 'juju'. Maybe he has cast a spell on your mother to do exactly what he wants."

"No spell," Lily said shaking her head. "She's just..." She spread her hands. "I don't know."

"I won't be convinced until I have met her, and him. But I'm almost certain that I'm right." Lillian nodded slowly. "I'm a village girl. I know these things."

Shade laughed. "When did you become an expert in black magic, Lillie?"

"Just trust me on this one. That man is doing something." Lillian replied.

"And you are determined to prove it, right?" Shade got up from the bed.

"Right!"

"Before you start, we have to go. We still have to get home and I have to get ready."

"So soon? But you've only just got here," Lily lamented.

Lillian put her hand on her shoulder as they walked towards the front door. "Don't worry. You'll survive the next few hours without us."

"Us?" Both Lily and Shade echoed.

"Yes," Lillian said looking from one face to the other.

"Meaning?" Lily asked.

"I'm coming to the restaurant tonight."

"You can't be serious!" Lily looked aghast.

"No, you're not coming!" Shade protested.

"I…we can't let you do that," Lily said.

Lillian looked puzzled. "And why not?"

"We'd both be out all night. It's not a good place for you…" Lily replied.

"I'm older than you, Lily," Lillian interrupted her. "If you were my sister you would call me *Sister.*"

Shade doubled up in laughter and it took a while for her to recover. "Yeah, well, still…"

"I won't get stained, don't worry." Lillian too was laughing.

"But what would you do while we are away?" Lily asked. She really didn't want Lillian at the restaurant alone.

"I would sleep in that little storeroom you showed me. Just don't forget me there." Lillian said. "But that would be after I have satisfied my eyes with all the drama around me."

"Well, since you have decided to be stubborn, whatever you do, don't let Melody see you." Shade said. "She'll take one look at you and know she can never let you go."

"What? With this my 'village' looks?" Lillian asked.

Lily opened her eyes wide. "You? Never."

"I've always told you how different you look from everyone back home," Shade said "And if it's your hair you are bothered about she'll whisk you off to a salon so fast your feet wouldn't touch the ground. And I mean it Lillie, don't let her see you, ok?"

"Not even a glimpse?" Lillian teased.

Shade glared at her and Lillian quickly raised her two hands in surrender.

They were by the gate.

"I'll see you both later."

"Bye."

"Bye."

A rather loud badly done remix of a popular reggae song flowed from the bandstand at a corner of the restaurant. The unpleasant tune coming from the sporadic strumming of the guitar and the loud beating by an over eager drummer mingled with the thick cigarette smoke and the strong smell of alcohol to create a riotous atmosphere. The dance floor was packed with dancers who writhed and swayed rhythmically like one huge disjointed monster with many heads.

At the other end was an unlit part of the restaurant where chairs and tables were stacked. This was where Lillian sat and watched all that was going on. Shade had gone out over an hour earlier and Lily had just left with the tall Alhaji. It was very difficult for Lillian to imagine herself living like this. Yet her friends seemed to have no other choice. Hearing their stories had broken her heart and made her sadder than she'd revealed to them. It had also changed her views about prostitutes forever.

As she sat watching the people dance, laugh and drink in the dimly lit, smoke filled room she wondered what she was going to do with her own life. She was in Lagos as she had always dreamed but it wasn't as appealing as she had thought.

Things are never really as you plan. There are always hitches. Mary said it was only God that could make things work out perfectly in the end. She said it was because He always saw the end from the beginning and so He could direct one's steps. Lillian definitely needed some directing from Him right now. She wondered if she was qualified to ask. She had learnt to recite quite a few memorized prayers over the years but tonight she felt she needed more than that.

"Lord, I hope that you're listening. I know I have not been close to you, but I have always believed that you love me and will be merciful to me. Please keep me safe in Lagos and don't let anything bad happen to me. Also, show me what to do now that I am here… and watch over my friends too. Let them be able to stop what they are doing and help them to stop. Amen."

As the night wore on Lillian began to feel sleepy. She thought of the little storeroom round the back. She would go there in a little while but she had to make sure that no one noticed her, especially the evil Melody. She smiled as she remembered her friends' warning. When the music changed and even more people got on the dance floor she got up quickly and moved amongst them towards the side exit. As she tried to walk as fast as possible while trying to avoid too much physical contact she wondered how these clubbers could stand it. Many of them were literally touching bodies. Just a few steps from the door, someone grabbed her wrist and pulled her back. She looked round to see who it was and immediately regretted it as the strong smell of something nasty hit her like a slap across the face.

"And where do you think you're going, young lady?" A man asked smiling at her. He had a glass in his other hand with a cigarette between the fingers.

"I beg your pardon… leave me alone," Lillian said as she struggled to free her hand. This only made him tighten his grip. She stopped struggling when she realized that the man could cause the trouble she had been warned about and had been trying to avoid. She needed to get rid of him without attracting any attention.

"What do you want?" She tried to sound nice. This wasn't going to be easy.

"Just a dance," he slurred. "And then you'll have a drink with me. And who knows where it could go from there?" The man was already drawing her towards the dance floor.

An alarm went off in Lillian's head. Now she was beginning to wish she had listened to her friends. She had to think of something fast.

"That would be nice, you know," she said as she yanked her hand free. The man spun round and she quickly smiled. "My name is Tina. What's yours?"

"Alex." He smiled back. "But my friends call me Lexus." He winked at her and began to sway to the music.

"Hmmm. Yeah, I prefer Lexus." Lillian nodded slowly, as if to the music. Then she signaled for him to move closer. When he did, she said into his ears, "Hey Lexus, I was actually on my way to the *Ladies*. Would you give me a few minutes?"

He looked reluctant but she smiled sweetly at him. Then he shrugged and had barely turned away when Lillian hurried towards the door not caring how many sweaty bodies she rubbed against. She got to the storeroom and entered quickly and it wasn't until she had secured the door from inside that she was able to breathe again.

"Stupid creature," she mumbled to herself as she slipped off her sandals. "You think I escaped marrying Chief Daniel so that I can come and dance and drink and 'who knows where else' with you." She lay on the mattress by the wall. "Foolish creature," she added. And within a few minutes she was asleep.

Chapter SIX

ALHAJI'S AQUARIUM WAS THE first Lily had ever seen. It was in a smaller living room at the end of the corridor. She always enjoyed lying back on the sofa and watching the fish swim around. She could stay there for ages without getting bored. As she lay there she let her thoughts wander. She'd cried herself to sleep almost every night for months when she first got to Lagos. Her life had changed so drastically that she felt like she was alone on a speed train she couldn't control going nowhere and was very likely to crash. Other people controlled her life and she was so lonely and depressed. Then something happened that changed everything; her meeting with a new friend, Lillian. Her lively nature was so contagious that Lily found herself gradually being lifted out of her depression. Lillian's constant references to her sister Mary's admonitions and her interesting interpretations of them gave Lily a lot of food for thought. It also brought back to her memory the things her grandmother had told her that she had forgotten.

She didn't have to continue this way. She knew she didn't want to live like this but she had never had anything or anyone push her into doing something about it until now.

And Lillian made her laugh. She always had a way of adding humor to just about every situation. She hadn't been to the restaurant since her encounter with a man called Lexus. They had had a good laugh but they also knew that it could have turned nasty. It wouldn't be the first time a drunken man had turned violent because a girl refused to go with him. There had been broken bottles and stab wounds in the past.

Lily was glad it hadn't happen that way. It would hurt her deeply if something happened to her friend. Even though they had only known each other a short while Lillian had become her best friend. She was witty, friendly, kind and genuine. And she was the only person around her that was not involved in all this madness.

As she lay with one arm under her head she wondered how she would go through another night with Alhaji. Salamotu, one of the other girls, whom Lillian had nicknamed 'surly Sal', had told her to her face one night that Alhaji would soon get tired of her. She had said it to spite her and had had no idea how glad Lily was to hear it. How she looked forward to being free of the man. But being free of him also brought about some trepidation. Would Melody give her to another man or would she begin to sleep with a different man every night like Shade, Salamotu, Sarah and the others? She shuddered just to think of it. So far she had been able to keep her sanity because she had only been with Alhaji and he was behaving well enough. If things changed…

She made up her mind to share her thoughts with Lillian the next time they were together. Shade had recently helped Lillian secure a job as an administrative clerk at a travel agency and so she had been unable to visit for some time. Since Lily couldn't get out because Melody always had her locked up when she was at the house, maybe she would ask Lillian if she could come over next Sunday. She really needed to talk to her about her fears. She was sure that she would have something to say that would help.

Lily couldn't think of anything scarier than going out with different men. There had been lots of horrible stories. Some girls had contacted HIV and other diseases Lily had never heard of, some had been hurt, sometimes very badly, and others had disappeared, and were never found. Even Shade had had an incident that put her in a hospital for a week.

She heard the sound of a door opening. Alhaji was back. He had picked her the night before and told her she would be staying with him till Thursday. Four days. He said he would be traveling out of the country for a month and needed to be with her as much as he could. A whole month without Alhaji was something to look forward to. Yet…

"How's my flower?" He asked as he walked in. He dropped the bags he was carrying on the coffee table and walked towards her. "Are you all right?"

"I'm fine, thank you," she replied in her usual cool manner. She had stopped being friendly towards him since the first night he brought her to his house. She had long stopped caring about him going back to Melody to complain. It wasn't as if she behaved badly or was disrespectful at any time, she just simply didn't give him any more than the physical pleasure he got. Sometimes he complained about how she just stared at him when he talked, as if she wasn't there, and how she didn't speak unless he spoke to her. Other times it was about how she never asked for anything. He said he had never met anyone like her.

All Lily was trying to do was to put some distance between her and what was happening to her. She had told herself it was just a job and that all she was doing was trying to get enough money for her education. And she had to do it because she had no parents or anyone in the world to support her. Whenever she left for the restaurant to meet Alhaji she always told herself that she had left her mind and all her feelings behind and all she was going with was her body.

She swung her feet down from the sofa and sat up straight. If only he was traveling tonight.

He looked at her for a while and seemed to decide he would have to be satisfied with her reply. He reached for one of the shopping bags he had brought in and sat beside her on the sofa. "Neapolitan for you," he said as he brought out a tub and handed it to her, "and chocolate for me." He brought out another one and removed the lid.

She sat staring at hers while he ate.

"A spoon is attached to the lid. If you just open it…don't you want any?" He asked.

No, she didn't want any. She didn't want anything other than to be away from this man…this way of life. "No thank you," she replied. "I don't really feel like having any."

"That's the thing with you," Alhaji said as he leaned forward to put his tub on the coffee table. "You never feel like anything."

He sat back again with his hands behind his head, studying her. She used to feel uneasy when he stared at her like that, as if he was trying to understand something, anything about her. But now she was used it. He could stare all he wanted without her being bothered.

"Ok, what would you like us to do tonight?" Alhaji sat up and put his arm around her shoulder. How she hated him doing this, or touching her in any way for that matter. She steeled herself as she always did, in order not to cringe.

"Why don't we go out?" *If possible every night until you get yourself out of the country and I can get out of this house.*

"Out?" He looked hesitant, as if he really didn't want to go out.

"Yes, out," she said a little bit more cheerfully than she intended.

"And where exactly do you have in mind?"

"Oh...*Onyx's* or...or...*Undersea*...or that dome place in Apapa..." she shrugged.

"Hmmm." He smiled and kissed her cheek. "You have good...no... great taste." He removed his arm from her shoulder and rubbed his hands together. "Now we're getting somewhere." He stood up and held out his hand to her. "If the lady wants to go out, then out we shall go."

This part of Lagos Island was a spectacular sight at night. The tree-lined streets were brightly lit with streetlights, neon signs and what seemed like a million lights shining from tall and magnificent buildings. As people drove along the Bar beach, which stretched from one end of the major highway to the other they usually switched off their air-conditioners and wound down their car windows to enjoy the cool breeze from the sea.

Kingsway Road was Lily's favorite place on the Island. Apart from the fact that the road seemed endless, she liked the way you descended a bridge on one end of it and climbed another at the other end. Besides she thought the most interesting places Alhaji took her were on this road and she was always a little excited whenever she was on it.

But tonight she barely noticed anything. Knowing that Alhaji would be away for a whole month had suddenly filled her mind with a lot of ideas and she just sat in the car desperately trying to work them out. It wasn't until Alhaji drove into the massive grounds of the exclusive *Undersea World* that she realized where she was.

"You were so lost in your thoughts I didn't want to disturb you," he said as he parked the car. "I hope you are fine."

"Oh, I'm fine, Alhaji," Lily reassured him. In fact she had not felt this fine in a long time. She was so excited about what she hoped would happen in the next few weeks that she smiled at him warmly.

Alhaji looked pleased. "Ok then. Let's make the best use of the rest of the night."

The restaurant was dimly lit as usual with most of the light coming from the aquariums that served as glass walls round the large fish-shaped room. Lily had never really liked this particular aspect of the restaurant and would have preferred anywhere else. The movement of the sea creatures in the water around her always made her uncomfortable. She usually wondered at the other people in the room who never seemed bothered by it. She couldn't imagine how they could be so relaxed with such creatures squirming and thrashing around and staring with those bulgy eyes. Since she didn't like to offer her opinion about anything to Alhaji he must have assumed she liked it because he had brought her here quite a few times. She had no complaints about the food though.

As soon as they were settled at their table Alhaji began to speak. "I have to tell you something now because I know there will never be a perfect time. You know I am going to be away for a while and so I would like us to settle this before I go."

Lily looked up at him. With the way she felt tonight she was sure she was ready for anything. She was wrong.

"This is it, Lily. I want to marry you. I want you to be my wife." He kept quiet and leaned back in his chair as if waiting for a reaction.

"Marry?" Lily cried sticking her chin out further than she would have thought was decent. She couldn't believe her ears. Alhaji could have said any other thing. *But marry*?

"Yes, marry," he said. In spite of her shocked state Lily couldn't help noticing how confident he sounded, as if he was certain she would accept. Well, he was in for a surprise.

"I can't marry... I can't get married," she stammered. "Get married?"

"But there is nothing stopping you. I know you don't need anyone's approval and I am willing to have you..." He shrugged. "All you have to do is accept."

Of all the...! What is wrong with all these men? Lily remembered why Lillian had run away from home. She felt very angry and knew she really needed to calm down. She picked up her drink and stared at the glass, thinking of how best she could express herself to Alhaji. Finally she laid the glass down gently and looked up at him with an expressionless face.

"You're wrong," she said. "You're wrong about me not needing anyone's approval, because I do."

He looked puzzled. "Whose?"

"Mine. I don't approve."

Alhaji laughed out loud. "You're funny," he said after a while. "I actually thought there was really someone somewhere I needed to impress. You!" He laughed again. Then when he realized she wasn't even smiling he stopped laughing and frowned at her. "Oh, you can't be serious. You don't want to marry me?"

"No! I don't want to marry you," Lily replied with all the seriousness she could muster.

"But how can you not want to marry me?" It was his turn to stare in disbelief. "You have seen what I can give you, what I can do for you. You can live anywhere you choose in the world. You will never be in want of anything money can buy. The life I can give you is far better than you can ever have any other way."

"I've never wanted anything from you, Alhaji. And I have always made it clear that I..."

"Look, Lily, this is not the time for..." He waved his hand in the air. "Whatever this impression is you always try to give. I am really serious about this." He reached for her hand. "I can make you happy. Look, any girl would give anything to have what I am offering you."

Lily snatched her hand from his. "I am not any girl!"

"Ha!" Alhaji threw up both arms, clearly exasperated. He placed both elbows on the table and opened up his palms. "What do you have? Nothing, Lily. No family that cares about you. And I am offering you everything. Can't you see? I am your savior."

"No, you are not!" Lily couldn't help raising her voice and attracting some attention from the next table. But how could he say that? Only Jesus can be one's savior. Isn't that what her grandmother always said?

Alhaji sighed. He obviously hadn't expected things to be this difficult. He folded his arms and stared at the ceiling for a full minute. Then he seemed to come to a decision. "You know what? Let's leave it for now. We came here because you wanted to enjoy yourself. Let's eat something."

But Lily had lost her appetite. Still, she forced herself to eat as much as her unwilling stomach could take because not eating meant getting back to the house sooner.

To her surprise Alhaji spent a great deal of time away from the house in the next three days. Though Lily wondered where he went, she was glad. Especially since there was no more talk about marriage. But on their last morning together he brought it up again. Lily was packing her bags when he walked into the room.

"My flight is at midnight so there's really no hurry," he said and sat on the stool by the dressing table. "Plenty of time to pack."

"I know. I just want to be ready." Lily was still curious about where he had been going everyday but she had made up her mind not to ask.

"What would you like me to buy for you?" Alhaji asked.

Lily looked at him and shook her head. He knew she wouldn't ask for anything, so why was he asking?

"Anything. Please, Lily," he begged. "Even if it is a scarf."

"I don't need a scarf, Alhaji," Lily said almost pleadingly. "I don't need anything. You have given me so much already. You've bought me clothes, shoes, jewelry, two phones, more things than I could ever need. Please don't buy anything for me."

"But that's not possible, my Lily. You see I'm just warming up. You are going to be my wife and that means we will be together for..."

"Stop, Alhaji!" Lily raised both hands in protest. "I am not going to be your wife. I am only fifteen and I don't want to be anybody's wife!" How was she going to get through to this man?

She watched Alhaji stand up, but contrary to what she was expecting he looked unruffled. He just smiled at her and spoke calmly. "You are going to be my wife Lily. You are going to be...my wife." And he walked out of the room.

Lily didn't see him until he was ready to take her to Melody's Restaurant that evening. He still remained calm and sure of himself as he talked to her all the way back about his trip. She pretended to listen but she was getting increasingly troubled by his attitude. It seemed he was certain she would be his wife. That couldn't happen unless she agreed. And she knew she never would. So what was giving him so much confidence? He couldn't force her, could he?

For the next two days Lily couldn't think about anything else. So far she had had no control over what happened to her. She hadn't been able to stop her grandmother from dying, or her mother from taking her away from Aunt Agnes and dumping her with Melody. And she hadn't been able to stop Melody from getting her to work as a prostitute. So what if she couldn't stop Alhaji? What if she found herself married to him one day? Then she would be trapped forever. So who was looking out for her?

Her grandmother had told her that God loved her no matter what and she could always count on Him to be there for her. She had hoped with all her heart that it was true and had wanted to believe then that He could love her like He loved Mama. Now she knew it couldn't be true. Mama was wrong. Or all these things wouldn't have happened to her.

Well, she wasn't waiting around for Him either. She knew she had to find a way out by herself. She had to put a stop to all the control other people had over her. Her head was full of ideas but she didn't know how to take the first step. She couldn't wait till the next day when Lillian would visit. They would talk about it and come up with something. Besides, Lillian was the only one she felt safe enough to reveal her plans to.

The sound of the bell at the gate rang throughout the house. Lily didn't bother looking out of her bedroom window since she wasn't expecting anyone. A few minutes later there was a knock on her door. She found Melody's older maid standing outside her door when she opened it.

"Aunty Ella."

"Gateman say person find you," the woman said.

"Did he mention the person's name?" Then she remembered the maid understood very little English. "Gateman say which person?" Lily asked her.

"Person," she replied, shaking her head.

"Ok, thank you, Aunty Ella." Lily always had problems communicating with her so she just let her go.

As Lily walked down the stairs she wondered who it could be since no one ever came to see her except Shade and Lillian and the gate man always let them in. When Lily got outside it was just the gateman sitting on his chair by the gatehouse. The visitor must have been left outside the gate.

"Good afternoon. Aunty Ella said someone is looking for me," Lily said.

"Yes," the man said but didn't move from his seat. He held a small piece of cloth in his hand which he kept flipping over his shoulder as if he was trying to get rid of an imaginary pest.

"Where is the person?" Lily asked.

"Outside." He didn't even look at Lily.

"Who is the person?"

"I don't know. One woman," he replied, still not moving.

"May…I see the person?" Lily asked and began to doubt that he would let her. She had found out earlier that Melody had left instructions with her staff that she was not to see anyone they didn't know and she was not allowed to leave the yard except when the driver came for her.

"Madam said I should not open for anybody I don't know," the man said.

"So…what are we going to do?" Lily asked smiling at him. She had no idea where this was going. "Can I at least see who it is? Or can you help me ask for her name?" When he still didn't budge Lily moved towards the small gate and reached for the unlocked padlock. She had had enough of the man's attitude. Maybe this would get him off his chair.

"No! No, please! I beg you." He jumped up and rushed to the gate. He stood between Lily and the gate and addressed her. "You see, Aunty, as I don't know the person I'm not supposed to open." He looked really reluctant. "But because it is you. If it is another person…" He shook his head. Then he opened the gate, stepped out and gestured for the person outside to come in.

Lily opened her mouth to thank him when he came back in but the words froze in her throat as she saw the woman that walked in after him. Her eyes widened and her hand flew to her mouth. Both Lily and the visitor stood and stared at each other.

It was her mother that broke the silence. "Hello, Lily."

Chapter SEVEN

"WHAT ARE YOU DOING here?" Lily asked after a few moments.

Amanda, with her two hands clutching her purse, took a deep breath. "I came to…see you."

Lily studied her as anger bubbled up inside her like a seething pot. "You have seen me," she said. "And if that's all…" She took a step back and turned.

"No, Lily! Wait!" Amanda put a hand on Lily's shoulder. "Please don't walk away." Lily looked at the hand on her shoulder and Amanda slowly removed it. "I have a few things to…tell you."

Lily shrugged and began to walk towards the house. Amanda followed her quickly and closed the door behind her when they were inside. Lily flopped unto one of the chairs in the small anteroom, while Amanda sat on the edge of another.

"How…how have you been?" Amanda asked.

Lily sat up, putting her two hands between her knees. "How have I been?"

"I know how you must be angry and...and you have every right to be," Amanda said. "But I never intended for things to be this way. I never planned to leave you alone like this."

"Why did you? What did you plan?" Lily asked.

Amanda looked surprised. "You've changed. I mean you sound... and act different...older. You even look older, like it's been more than just a year."

"What did you plan?" Lily repeated as if she hadn't heard her.

Amanda sighed and shook her head. "I've made a lot of wrong choices in my life, Lily, choices I will regret for the rest of my life. But to leave you here in Lagos is not one of them."

Lily had been angry with her mother for so long that she had thought she was past caring. She had been sure she would be able to handle seeing her again but now it seemed more difficult than she expected. She struggled to muster all the hatred and anger she could. "Then why did you?" She asked through clenched teeth.

"I..." Amanda shook her head. Words seemed to fail her. "I..." She tried again.

"You wanted to be free of me, isn't it?" Lily accused, her voice quivering with emotion. "Your husband didn't want me in his house and you didn't either.

"That's not true!" Amanda cried.

Lily continued. "I was a nuisance to you. I was always a nuisance. The product of an unwanted..."

"Stop it!" Amanda cried. "Stop it, please."

You never cared about me when Mama was alive. And when she died you still didn't want me." She eyed her mother. "And why should you? You have your precious little family. And I'm not a part of it." Tears stung her eyes. "What I want to know is why you didn't let me stay in Port Harcourt. You knew Aunt Agnes wanted me to stay with her." She shook her head and the angry tears flowed. "Or did you just want me to disappear? Like I never existed, so you can have things the way you and your husband want it?"

"The reason I took you away from Agnes is so that you can be with me, Lily. That's the truth. Mum was…no longer there. And I was afraid that…what happened to me would happen to you too. I wanted to keep you safe. I wanted you to be with me." Amanda looked at her with eyes pleading for understanding. "But…but Sheyi didn't. It was his idea to send you here. I didn't know…" She looked down at her hands.

"And you always do what he says, right?"

Amanda smiled sadly. "Not anymore."

"Really!" Lily didn't believe what her mother had said.

"He didn't want me to come and he has never wanted me to come," Amanda said. "But I'm here."

"Well, good for you," Lily said and looked away. "Only there was really no need."

Amanda looked at Lily as if she was seeing a different person. "Please don't say that. There's so much you don't know." Amanda moved to the chair next to Lily's. "I beg you, Lily. Please listen to me."

Lily wanted to put up a bold front, to hide her hurt from her mother, but the harder she tried the more difficult it proved to be. She fought to control her emotions but failed. She looked at her mother with tear filled eyes. "There's so much you don't know as well." She got up from her chair. "Don't you see? You abandoned me here. You…you dumped me into something far worse than what you say you were trying to save me from." The words tumbled out and she didn't have the power to stop them. This wasn't what she had planned to do when she saw her mother again. "Melody said I had to work. She asked me to go out with a man. I…I didn't even know what he planned to do. He…he forced me. And that was only the beginning. I am a…a…prostitute." Then she broke down and wept.

Amanda looked ill and she leaned back in her chair. Tears began to flow down her cheeks as she listened to her daughter's heart breaking story.

When she finished, Lily took a deep breath. "You were able to see me today because he has traveled. I probably would have been spending the weekend at his house."

"I'm so sorry." Amanda rocked back and forth with her hands clasped beneath her chin. "I am so sorry."

Lily wiped her face with her hands, sniffing. "That can't change anything." Then she walked to the window. "I don't really care if I never see you again."

"You…can't mean that. I never meant for any of this to happen. I care about you…"

"Then you shouldn't have left me here. You are my mother!"

"I know," Amanda said huskily. "I was a coward. I was afraid."

"Of what? Or of who…that you couldn't call me on the phone at least?" Lily challenged.

"Call you? I called so many times, but Melody wouldn't let me speak to you. She kept giving me excuses why I couldn't speak to you and also reported me to Sheyi who…" Her voice trailed off.

Of course Melody couldn't afford to let her mother know what kind of life she was living. And she had teamed up with her nephew to prevent any form of communication between her and her mother. Still it had been a whole year, a period of loneliness, pain and degradation. If only her mother had loved her enough, enough to defy her husband and come for her much earlier. Now Lily wanted to know.

"Are you taking me away from here?"

Amanda hesitated before answering. "I came to see you and let you know that I plan to get you away from here."

"You didn't come to take me away." Lily felt like a lost little girl who would never find her way home.

"I haven't seen you in a long time. I didn't know what to expect…I came for you, Lily…I'm definitely taking you away," Amanda explained.

"But I can't go with you now," Lily said with a finality that put a worried look on her mother's face.

"I just had to see you first, even if I can't take you today. I need to put some things in place. I was hoping that we would plan together and come up with how to get you away from here." Amanda sounded desperate. "I made up my mind to come because I couldn't continue staying away from you. I've stayed away from you for too long." She went to Lily and knelt before her. "I know I should have done this much earlier and nothing I can say can exonerate me. But I will not leave you here. I will never leave you again."

Lily looked away, confused. How could she trust her after all she had done? Why should she believe her just because of all the things she had said? A part of her warned her not to because she would only be disappointed while another part of her wanted her to understand and put an end to the pain she had suffered for so long. But as she turned to look at her mother kneeling in front of her she realized that this was what she had always wanted, what she had spent the past months hoping for without knowing it, for her mother to come and tell her she wanted her. She had been sure that her mother didn't love her or want her in her life, but now she saw differently. This woman kneeling in front of her, pleading with tears running down her cheeks couldn't possibly be the selfish, evil person she had imagined her to be. Maybe Lillie and Shade were right. Maybe Sheyi was the problem. A strange feeling came over her and she began to feel all the anger and animosity slowly drain from her. She took a decision not to fight it. She wanted to forgive her mother and let her know it. She reached out and Amanda took her hand and held it to her face, still weeping.

"Thank You, Lord," Amanda whispered. "I know I don't deserve it, but thank You." She got up and drew her daughter into her arms. She held on to her as if her very life depended on it.

Lily then put her arms round her mother and closed her eyes. At that moment she knew she had made the right decision. "I thought that God didn't love me, even though Mama always said He did. Even if he did before I started… Melody said she would put me on the streets for every man...I was afraid. Then she locked me in here. I…I thought Mama was wrong." She drew back and looked at her mother. "And now here you are." She smiled. "I guess He doesn't want me thinking like that anymore."

"Lily, He loves you anyhow. That's one thing I learnt from Mum. And if He can love a person like me," she nodded slowly, "believe me, He loves *you*." She held Lily's face. "Listen to me. None of this is your fault. Don't ever blame yourself for any of it. I should never have left you. Or at least I should have come for you earlier." She paused. "Oh, I'm so glad you don't hate me," she said with a gush of emotion. "I have lived with the thought of you hating me for so long. I still can't believe I'm standing with you here holding you in my arms. I feel like I'm dreaming, Lily. Thank you. Thank you for forgiving me."

"I'm glad you came."

"I should have a long time ago. All these… Melody would not have…I'm sorry Lily. I really am. I don't know how I could ever…"

Lily smiled. "Lillie doesn't think you're a bad person." When her mother looked at her enquiringly she added, "Lillie is my friend."

"And she doesn't think I am a bad person?" Amanda asked, looking interested.

"No. She is convinced your problem is your husband, full stop."

"She said that?" Amanda asked.

"Yes. She is sure he is into, well, some form of diabolical… you know? And if you were to be free of him I would see that you were really a good person and I wouldn't have had to come here."

"Well, Sheyi is a problem, truly, but he is not responsible for all my faults. I am I told you earlier that I made a lot of wrong choices. And I pray that God will help me to somehow make it up to those I have hurt. Especially you."

Lily hugged her mother again. "I am just glad you came. I am so glad you don't hate me like I have thought. And I want you to know that I don't hate you either."

"Thank you." Amanda began to weep again. And in the midst of her tears she managed to say, "I've got more than I could ever hope for."

And for a long period mother and daughter held onto each other as their hearts healed.

Before Amanda left she promised Lily she would be back for her before Alhaji returned.

Lily went to bed that night, happier than she had been in very long time. Though she knew they had a long way to go, she was confident that her mother loved her and God loved her too. He had not allowed her to give up on Him. Somehow everything was going to be all right.

Chapter EIGHT

BY THE END OF her first month at the *Correct Travel and Tours*, Lillian had concluded that what they needed was not an administrative assistant but a Girl Friday. She got to work earlier than everyone every morning to clean up the offices, storeroom, toilets, corridors and the front desk. She also ensured that the kettle was boiling by the time the others arrived and she was ready to run around to buy their breakfast. The actual administrative work turned out to be all the tedious paper work no one wanted to do which included the sorting of numerous receipts dating back to three years or more and their documentation under codes and dates. It seemed like someone had failed to do his or her job for a long period.

Most days she was also one of the last to leave the office. By the time she was through with her work for the day the only other person left was the manager. She usually got home too tired to do anything other than take a shower and go to bed; therefore she always looked forward to Sundays and 'off' days.

She didn't mind the volume of work she faced. She didn't even mind getting breakfast and lunch for the rest of the staff as well as running all kinds of errands for them, but to be cheated by her boss was a little bit too much for her to take. At the end of the first month she was paid her complete salary at the due date, and on the days she was off duty she didn't have to go to work. But during the second month she was asked to work on two 'off' days with the promise of an overtime payment to be added to her salary and her boss defaulted. Not only did he not pay the overtime, he also held back part of her salary. He gave the excuse that the agency was short of funds and that he would pay her before the middle of the next month. And when she asked him about it then he told her to wait till the end of the month for everything to be paid. The month ended and she went to his office to ask him for her money but he was absent from work. She got to the office a few days ago only to find out that he had traveled out of the country. Lillian was angry though there was nothing she could do now. Whenever he chose to return, she would be waiting for him.

As she approached Melody's house she tried to remember how long it had been since she saw Lily. It had been too long and it was all because of this job. Of course she had to work. She couldn't continue living off Shade who never complained though. Some of Shade's money came from her job at the insurance firm but Lillian knew where the rest came from. She had felt uncomfortable from the moment she found out about the prostitution and she had pressured Shade into getting her a job, any job.

The gateman recognized her and let her in immediately. Lily who had seen her from her bedroom window ran all the way down the stairs to meet her as she walked through the front door.

"Ok, this must be very good." Lillian said as she let her friend hug her rather tightly. "I couldn't wait to hear what was so urgent that you had to summon me to your court, your royal highness."

"There are now two things," Lily said excitedly as she grabbed Lillian's hand and led her up the stairs to her room.

When they were in Lily closed the door and told Lillian to sit down. She walked to the window and turned around to face her.

"My mother came here yesterday," she said simply, and watched Lillian's facial expression transform as what she had told her sank in.

"What?" Lillian's eyes couldn't be any wider.

The maid came to my room to tell me someone was looking for me. And when I got downstairs, there she was!"

"Wow! Then what happened? What did she say? Why has she been away for so long? What did you do?" Lillian's questions came in quick succession.

Lily shook her head. "At first I was angry and I showed it."

"At first? Meaning you didn't stay angry?" Lillian's face was animated.

"Nope." Lily replied enjoying the look on Lillian's face.

"I told you she wasn't a horrible person. I told you. But did you believe me? No! But what did she say has been happening all this while?" Lillian cried. "So start from the beginning."

Lillian clapped her hands and bounced up and down on the bed as she listened to Lily's account of the time she spent with her mother the previous day.

"I think God did it," Lillian concluded when Lily finished. "Or how else do you want to explain it?"

"I can't," Lily replied. "All I know is that something came over me and all I wanted more than anything was that everything should be all right between us. I just wasn't angry anymore. Something just…washed away all the…sadness and…and grudge. I just found that I didn't hate her anymore."

"That's God. Believe me," Lillian said.

Lily cocked her head. "Really?"

Lillian laughed self-consciously. "Ok, I may not be like Mary, but I'm sure of this."

"I'm sure of it too, actually. My mother doesn't hate me. It means God is still there for me. It means He still loves me," Lily said. "I was convinced that my grandmother was wrong about God loving me for always. I had given up on Him."

"And then your mother shows up and in a flash everything between you is all right," Lillian said. "He didn't want you to give up on Him. I can't imagine how you must feel."

"Yes, it's really unbelievable." Lily sighed and came to sit beside Lillian. "So I've been thinking since yesterday and I feel something is missing, like there's something *I* should do."

"Something *you* should do? Like what?" Lillian enquired.

"I don't know. Maybe start going to church again or something. God has done the one thing I wanted more than anything," Lily replied.

"Going to church? I don't understand. Why do you feel you need to? And how do you even plan to get out of your prison?"

"I don't know. Maybe..."

I think what you're trying to do is meet God halfway," Lillian said.

"Preacher woman," Lily said smiling.

"All right, I don't really know what that means but I have heard Mary say it many times," she said. "She always said it wasn't a 'totally God affair'. You have a part to play and it is personal and...voluntary."

A few moments passed.

Then why aren't you born-again like Mary?" Lily asked.

Lillian took a deep breath as she weighed her answer. "I guess I haven't gone my half," she said looking down at her skirt and smoothening it with her hands.

The room was silent again. Then Lillian rubbed her hands together and looked at Lily. "You said there were two things. What's the other one?"

"You mean the bad news." Lily replied.

"Oh?"

"Something unexpected happened and I just couldn't wait to tell you because of how much it is bothering me."

Lillian let her continue.

"Alhaji asked me to marry him."

"What?" Lillian looked angry. "Is he crazy? Was he bitten by a rabid skunk?" Then she thought for a while. "But why should that bother you so much? Or why should it bother you at all? People turn down proposals every day. What happened to 'no sir I cannot marry you, sir'?"

Lily sighed. "I told him. Told him I was too young. How could he even consider it?" She shook her head in disgust.

"So you told him. Then what?"

He wasn't bothered," she tried to explain. "At first he was really surprised I said no. He thought… he actually thought I would be overjoyed, you know, as if it was what I had been waiting for."

"So he found out he is not the centre of your universe. Then what?" Lillian was getting impatient.

"Then he just kind of…became calm."

"Calm. How?"

"As if he was certain I would be his wife." Lily said. "He actually assured me that we would be married. As if it was settled." She looked puzzled. "The more I told him it couldn't happen the surer he seemed."

"Still can't imagine why it should bother you. Is it by force?"

When she saw that Lillian still didn't understand she stood up and faced her. "Ok what made you run away from home? Why didn't you stay and just say no?" Then understanding dawned on Lillian and she nodded. "You knew it would take more than simply saying no. And so you had to leave." Then she sat down again. "It's as if he has...sealed it."

"Uh oh." Lillian made a face.

Lily frowned. "What?"

"You have me worried now." Lillian said. "Did you just say 'seal'?"

"What I mean is..."

"Wait first!" Lillian stood up now looking very serious. "Did he give you any special drink, special food to eat or anything strange to lick? Or did you notice any strange behaviour...did you watch him closely...of course you couldn't have. You couldn't have known." She paced back and forth.

"What are you...?" Then it hit her. "No. No way. You don't think..." She shook her head while Lillian nodded.

"What can you remember?" Lillian asked. "Anything at all. Of course he wouldn't have done anything obvious for you to notice."

"That's very comforting." Lily said giving her friend a quick glance. Then she remembered. "Come to think of it he disappeared for a long time."

"Disappeared?"

"Yes. He was away the whole day for three days and... well...he didn't come near me in the night; which was strange." She frowned. "He told me when he picked me that because he was traveling he wanted to spend as much time with me as possible, and then he disappeared the whole time."

"When you told him you were not marrying him." Lillian folded her arms. "I think he went to 'seal it'."

"You think he has gone to a herbalist and...done something spiritual?"

"I'm sure of it, Lily. That's why he's so sure of himself. There can't be any other explanation."

"I thought he was sure because he knew I didn't have anyone…you know, because I was alone. He felt I didn't have a choice." She made a face. "He actually called himself my savior. Can you imagine that?"

"Your savior indeed." Lillian was disgusted.

"If what you're thinking is true, if he has 'tied' me somehow, what do you think will happen?"

"I will tie my own around your waist and take you everywhere I go so that…" Lillian did not get a chance to finish her sentence because the loud creaking of the gate caught her attention. Both girls went to the window and saw Melody's car. They looked at each other. Lily had never seen her at home at this time before.

"Melody?" She looked at Lillian enquiringly.

Lillian only stared back at her.

The car door was flung open and Melody had barely struggled out of the back seat when she started screaming at the top of her voice.

"Buffoon! Dunce! Good for nothing!" She walked towards the gateman who was still bowing in greeting. "How dare you?"

"Good afternoon, Madam."

"Idiot!" She ignored his greeting. "Who pays your salary? Who has not allowed your wife and children to live under the bridge and feed from dustbins? Eh? Answer me!"

"But Madam…" The gateman looked confused.

"Shut up your dirty mouth! I say who pays you?"

"It's…it's you, Madam."

"When you came here," she continued, "you were destitute. Your family was starving to death. I rescued you. I gave you a job and even paid your rent. Is that not so?

"It is so."

"Then why is it a hard thing for you to obey my simple instructions?" She poked her own head several times. "Is your head empty? Are you retarded?"

"But Madam…"

"I hope you have another job waiting for you…all of you!" She screamed as she turned towards the house. "Ella! Bernard! Nkeobuna! All of you!"

Lillian's mouth hung open as she watched the maids, and the other household staffs rush out from different parts of the house while Melody continued to rail at them.

"Useless!" Melody shook her head. "Even if everyone is stupid, eh, Ella, even if that idiot of a gateman does not know his left hand from his right, I expect that you at least, will not let me down."

"Excuse me, ma," was all Ella could say as she curtsied and stared at Melody in confusion.

"Did I not put you here so you can take care of my house and…and not treat it as a…a…public place?" Melody asked, still as angry as ever.

"Public?" Ella blinked at Melody.

"You are asking me." Melody looked her up and down. "You will still be asking me when you find yourself back in your village." Then she interpreted what she had said in the language that Ella understood.

"Ah, Madam, I beg. Please." Ella got down on her knees and held up her two hands to Melody.

"Oh, you know how to beg, eh?" All the others got down on their knees as well. "But it doesn't take anything for you to disobey my orders."

"But Madam…" Nkeobuna the cook began.

"Why did you allow a strange woman into my house yesterday?"

Lillian and Lily turned to look at each other and quickly moved away from the window.

"Your mother!" Lillian gasped. "But how did she find out? Of course she would go crazy. Your mother came to see you."

"Did she think she could keep her away forever?" Lily asked angrily. She obviously hadn't taken the time to think of the consequences of her mother's visit. She looked outside the window. "I just hope this will not affect all those poor people she's threatening."

"She really is a crazy woman," Lillian said. "But you can face her."

"I can face her." Lily looked defiant.

"She's afraid she's losing control and might not be able to do anything to you anymore," Lillian said. "But how did she find out so fast?"

Lily thought for a while. "Maybe Sheyi, her nephew."

"Of course," Lillian said. "He found out."

Lily sat down heavily on the bed. "Now I'm worried about my mother. You know she came against his will. I have to know she is all right."

Just then there was a knock on the door. Lily looked at Lillian, who motioned for her to go see who it was.

"Who is it?" Lily asked loudly.

"Ella."

Lily opened the door and saw the maid wringing her hands and looking down. Lily felt sorry for her.

"Madam," she said and pointed to the living room at the end of the corridor.

Lily thanked her and closed the door.

"She wants to see you," Lillian stated.

"Yes."

"I am coming with you."

"Do I look like I'm going to face the executioner?"

"No. Actually it's because you look like the executioner."

Chapter NINE

WHY YESTERDAY OF ALL days? She could have made this trip on any other day in the past few months or so and he would never have found out. He'd been getting back home very late and when he did they hardly spoke. And then she had made the grave mistake of taking a marked park taxi all the way home, making it difficult for her to lie about where she was coming from. Though she had no regrets about going to see Lily, she'd never forget how her heart began to race when she saw him standing there as the taxi pulled up in front of the house.

She was unable to breathe as she walked past him to their flat, deciding to leave the children at Esther's.

"Where are you coming from?" He asked the moment he walked in after her and shut the door. "And don't you dare lie to me!" He added when she hesitated.

"Lagos," she said simply. What was the point in lying? "I went to see Lily."

"Is that so?" His eyes flashed. "Do you know that you are very stupid?"

"Why, Sheyi? Because I went to see my daughter?"

"Shut up!" He yelled. The veins bulged from his neck thicker than Amanda had ever seen them. "Didn't I warn you not to go? And didn't my aunty ask you to call first? What was difficult in that for you to understand?"

Amanda thought of submitting, apologizing, anything to end it before it got out of hand. But she couldn't bring herself to be quiet. How could she? If Sheyi didn't know how ridiculous he sounded she was going to show him.

She took a deep breath. "What I find difficult to understand is how I have allowed you and your aunt to keep me away from Lily for a whole year." She saw Sheyi's eyebrows rise. "Yes," she affirmed. "I should have gone to see her sooner."

"Really?"

"Yes. Then I would have been able to stop you both." She knew that she was treading on dangerous grounds but there was no going back. "Then I would have been able to stop your aunt from turning my daughter into a prostitute!"

It took Sheyi only two strides to cover the distance between them. He stood just a couple of inches away and stared at her menacingly. She was truly afraid for a moment but she recovered and continued.

"You don't like the truth do you?" She looked straight into his eyes, hers filling with tears; her voice was no longer calm. "The only reason you offered your 'help' was just to secure a prostitute for Melody!" Amanda shook her head. "I should have known. You have nothing to offer anyone but pain and heartache and I should never…" She paused, wondering whether it was wise to continue.

"You're just a fool," Sheyi said spitefully.

"I know. That's why this is happening to me."

He moved even closer and she was certain he was going to hit her. But he didn't. He just turned around and walked out of the house.

It had been a whole day since the unpleasant encounter with Sheyi and as Amanda sat at Esther's dining table feeding Akin she kept wondering why Sheyi had come home earlier than usual. Surely she had picked the wrong day to travel to see Lily. But she had made the trip and the result far outweighed whatever punishment she might still get for it.

"It's not that bad really." She smiled at Esther when she saw the pity in her eyes.

"Your eyes are swollen because you have been crying," Esther said. "And I am supposed to believe that?"

"Well, he's not Prince Charming." She shrugged. "And yes, I am sad. But he only yelled and threatened and promised to make me pay. Remember I committed the abominable."

"I hope they are empty threats," Esther said, looking concerned. "I would hate for you to be hurt, and for doing the right thing."

Amanda waved her hand. "He has threatened me before. He resorts to that when he doesn't get his way or can't get me to do what he wants. Let's just say his bark is worse than his bite."

"Well, I'm just glad you're OK," Esther said after a moment. "When you came for the kids yesterday, I was really scared. The way you looked." She shook her head at the memory. "I wanted to come after you but Timo said I should leave you for the moment. He was sure we would talk later when you were… you know, a bit over it."

Amanda smiled. "Timothy the sage."

"Yeah," Esther agreed. "He always seems to know the right thing to do."

"He does."

Akin had had enough. Amanda gave him some water and let him go. He went straight to the corner of the room where his action figure was lying with the other toys Amanda had brought. Ola too slid from her chair and went to join her brother.

"Can't wait to have mine," Esther said.

Amanda followed her eyes to see that she was referring to the children. "You will, soon," she said. "You and Timothy are too good for your children to stay away for too long."

"Is that right?" The two women looked up at the sound of Timothy's deep voice. Neither of them had seen him walk into the room. He went to sit on the floor with the children and started to play with them.

"Hi," Amanda said.

"Hello Amanda," he said. "How are you?"

"Still in one piece," Amanda replied.

"Seriously."

"I'll live."

"Your friend didn't sleep a wink last night," he said as he tickled the children. The sound of their laughter filled the room.

"I'm so grateful for your concern, both of you. I can't imagine these past months without you."

"Thank God," he said.

Amanda was glad to find the place empty when she got back with the children. She hadn't spoken to Sheyi since he stormed out the previous day after yelling at her. He had returned very late, long after she had gone to bed and she'd heard him moving around because she was still awake. She knew he must have slept on the couch in the living room. She was also awake when he got ready and left the house early in the morning but pretended to be asleep until she heard him shut the front door. Then she noticed that his bible was missing from his bedside table. A little terrorism couldn't stop a religious Sheyi from being amongst the earliest to get to his church.

She looked in the mirror again as she had when she got up in the morning and noticed that though her eyes were still red they didn't look so bad. By the next day there will be no physical sign of her misery and then she would be able to take the first step in her next major plan. She knew that this time she would have to be extremely careful. She couldn't afford to make the slightest mistake at any point. This time Sheyi must not have any idea what she was up to because if he did he would go to any length to stop her. She had even decided not to think about it when he was around her.

By now Melody would have found out about her visit from her nephew. Suddenly she sprang up in alarm as a thought occurred to her. Could Melody move Lily to another place? She had to call her right away. Lily's phone rang twice and went off. She tried again and this time it didn't ring at all. After a few minutes she tried again and it just kept ringing. She frowned. What could be going on? She decided to wait for some time before trying again. If she still didn't get to speak to Lily then she would start to worry.

Lily walked into the large nicely furnished room she had spent so many lonely hours in. It was the only other part of the house she stayed apart from her room. It was where she had her meals and gazed at the TV without really seeing anything, her thoughts being too far away. She saw Melody standing by the window at the far end, looking outside. For a whole minute she stood by the door watching her. This was the woman that lied to her mother and then tricked her into becoming a prostitute.

She was truly heartless if all the stories told by the girls were anything to go by. She had taken advantage of helpless young girls and made money out of them.

As Lily waited for Melody to notice she was in the room she saw that she was not afraid of her anymore. Lillian was right. She was no longer the girl that was terrified of what could happen to her. She had grown; she was no longer penniless, and best of all she had a mother who cared for her.

Finally Melody turned around and their eyes met. For a moment neither said a word. Lily decided to stay by the door. She leaned against the door post and folded her arms. A few months ago she would have been nervous and unsure of herself, but Lillian had helped her see that she was the offended party here. She was the one who had been exploited and she needed to let this woman know that she knew it. She felt unusually confident.

"I learnt your mother came here yesterday," Melody said with a slight toss of her head.

"She did." Lily nodded, looking poised.

A few seconds passed. Melody kept looking at her and Lily held her gaze. Then she walked slowly towards Lily.

"And what did she have to say?" She asked in her false accent. "What stories did she have to tell you?"

"She didn't tell me any stories," Lily replied rather quickly.

"Is that so?" Melody stopped and sat on the arm of a chair placing one hand on her knee and gingerly placing the other on top of it. She looked at Lily with raised eyebrows and smiled mockingly. "So tell me, what did she say?"

Lily didn't reply. She wasn't going to tell her anything that would put her mother in any more trouble than she might be already.

"Oh, I see." Melody got up. "You let her get to you. She dumps you and disappears for a whole year, and then shows up unannounced for whatever reason, maybe a guilt trip and you let her get to you?" When Lily didn't reply she balled her fists. "Oh come on, girl." She'd dropped the accent momentarily but quickly picked it up again. She sounded incensed. "Wake up. Life is all about survival. She has abandoned you all your life because she sees you as a bother; first with your grandmother, and then with me. Goodness knows why she showed up here. But I can assure you that it's to her advantage and not yours, one way or the other!" When Lily still didn't comment she continued, her words now almost like a singsong. "Yes, life is hard! The people we trust turn out to be our worst enemies. They keep disappointing us because they always put themselves first." She started marching towards Lily purposefully like an activist who must be heard. "But we can't let that stop us by sitting back and feeling sorry for ourselves, can we?" She stopped in front of her and stretched her arms forward suddenly, taking Lily by surprise. "Look at you! You have survived!" She looked somewhat triumphant, her eyes shining with something Lily could not decipher. "In spite of her you have survived!" She placed her hands on Lily's shoulder. "Don't let her come now and manipulate you with lies and... whatever she had to say. You have to show her that you don't need her..."

"Did she lie when she said she called many times but you refused to let me know?" Lily had heard enough.

Melody was taken aback and for a moment she was at a loss for words. Her hands dropped from Lily's shoulders and she held them together.

"Well...well..." Melody stammered.

It actually felt good to see Melody like this. And Lily wasn't through with her. "Why didn't you let me speak to her or let me know that she called?"

"Skipped my mind." Melody shrugged after a moment. "She only called a few times or so. What difference does it make? Can a few phone calls make up for a lifetime of abandonment?"

"I would have loved to know."

"It doesn't make any difference to anything."

"It does to me."

"Well, it shouldn't," Melody said blinking repeatedly. "Don't you see? She'll only abandon you again the next time she feels like it. You have done well for yourself. You're young, beautiful and intelligent. Your wonderful future lies ahead of you and you can have it all." If this weren't coming from Melody, Lily probably would have been swept off her feet. But she knew her for what she was, a schemer and a manipulator. "Besides the richest man I know is...crazy about you," Melody said rolling her eyes. "What could your mother possibly have to offer?" Lily knew then that this woman and not Alhaji was her worst enemy. Melody reached out and Lily let her draw her into her arms. She let her hug her for a long while and pat her back gently. Then Melody spoke softly. "Think about it, ok? I have to be at the club in half an hour. We'll talk some more soon." She put her hands on Lily's shoulders again and looked into her eyes. Then she went and picked up her hand bag. As she walked past Lily she slowed down. "Be wise." Then she walked towards the stairs.

Lily stood there listening to the clicking of her heels as she walked down the stairs. She heard her call Ella and give her some instructions. It wasn't until she heard the front door open and close that she returned to her room.

"Well?" Lillian asked eagerly.

Lily sat on the bed and didn't say a word.

"Well?" Lillian repeated.

Lily took in a deep breath. "It's amazing."

"What's amazing?"

Lily shook her head. "I just can't believe it."

"Are you going to leave me here wondering what hit you or are you going to tell me what is going on?" Lillian stared at her as she kept shaking her head.

Finally Lily turned to her. "I could have been won over by the things she said," she exclaimed. "She was so…I could have just have been won over." She fell back on the bed. "That woman is a bad person!"

"Don't tell me," Lillian said. "She tried to make your mother look bad."

Lily sat up immediately. "How did you know?"

"It's what I expected her to do," Lillian replied. "Your mother's visit could mean the end of your…what's that word… 'lucrative' presence." Then she started laughing. "Forgive me. I've not used that word since my last Business Studies class."

"So she thinks…"

"It's either of two ways. She could try to scare you by threatening you, which won't work anymore, or she could sweet-talk you to make herself look like a saint and your mother the one responsible for everything that has happened to you."

Lily nodded. "You should have heard her." She sighed heavily. "Now I'm not surprised at the number of girls at the restaurant."

"Yeah. And each and every one of them probably feeling she should be there," Lillian said. "It's a pity."

"And I would have felt the same way if it weren't for a certain bold, stubborn and determined girl that has infected me."

Lillian looked at her. "Are you serious?"

"Don't you dare look like you don't know that I am serious," Lily replied. "You think all those stories you told me about your escapades in your hometown and those wonderful things that Mary taught you haven't had any effect on me?

Even if you didn't tell me anything, hanging around you alone can make a timid person begin to stand up for herself."

"Wow!" Lillian clapped her hands "All that and you didn't even come up for air."

The sound of the gate made them go to the window again. They saw Melody's car leave the yard and the gateman close the gate.

"Poor man," Lily said. "I hope Melody doesn't carry out her threats."

If you ask me, that woman is crazy and needs to be locked away," Lillian said as she went and sat on the bed. "Completely insane."

"My mother is planning to get me out of here."

"Why should it involve any planning?" Lillian asked. "She's your mother and she brought you here. Why can't she just come and take you away?"

"To where?"

"To...Port Harcourt," Lillian answered her. "Back to Port Harcourt. After all, your Aunt Agnes is there and you said yourself that she would have you."

"I think my mother has something else in mind."

"What do you mean?"

"She's up to something," Lily said. "She didn't really tell me, but I know."

"How do you know?"

"She kept saying I would be with her and the children. And I know that can't be in Sheyi's house. I'm convinced she's up to something."

"Could be that she's leaving him."

"Yes," Lily said. "It's what I've been thinking."

"Well, that definitely needs some planning. I pray she succeeds."

"So do I, Lillie, more than anything. And she wants to do it before Alhaji returns. If she needs to get away from that man…" Something was on her mind. "It's not as if I don't believe in her but I just feel like I should have my own plans too, you know."

"There's nothing wrong with that," Lillian assured her.

"Actually before my mother came, I already made up my mind to discuss it with you," Lily said. "When Alhaji said he would be away for a whole month I decided that this was it. When he talked about his marriage plans I became even more determined that I would not be here when he got back."

"You wouldn't. But you need money," Lillian said.

Lily got up and went to her wardrobe. She got out a box like twice the size of a shoebox. She brought it to the bed and opened it. It was more than half full.

Lillian gasped.

"Every time I saw Alhaji he gave me an envelope. See." She brought out a couple from the box. "I haven't even opened these ones."

"So he paid you directly?" Lillian wanted to know. She had expected that all the payments passed through Melody.

"No. He paid Melody and she put mine in a savings account," Lily replied. "She encouraged me to open the account because she said it would help me save."

"And she actually puts your money there?"

"Oh yes," Lily said. "I got my statements."

"But Alhaji still gives you more."

"Every time."

"I bet this is more than what you have in the bank."

Lily pulled out another envelope and handed it to Lillian. "Look inside."

Lillian opened it and brought out the contents.

"Foreign money? Dollars. He gave you dollars?"

"Count it."

Lillian gasped after counting. She shook her head. "I hope your dear Madam doesn't know anything about this."

"I didn't tell her." Lily went back to the wardrobe. "Alhaji has given me so many things." She brought back a smaller box from the wardrobe and opened it revealing little boxes and pouches. She sat and brought out a little velvet box containing a set of earrings and necklace. "They call this one white gold."

"Looks like silver to me." Lillian looked at it closely.

"No, this is silver." She showed Lillian an inch thick bracelet.

Lillian looked at it and shrugged. After looking at a few more she put everything back. "So you have money," she said. "Let's plan."

"And a car and a flat," Lily said flippantly.

"Wait, wait, wait, wait, wait!" Lillian exclaimed. "Did you say a car and a flat? Please what does your Alhaji do for money?"

Lily handed the box to Lillian. She stood up, took a few steps and struck a pose. "I am a very successful international businessman and I can make all your dreams come true," she mimicked, making Lillian laugh heartily.

"So where is the car?" Lillian asked still holding her stomach.

"At his house. I told him I didn't want it and didn't go anywhere near it. He was shocked. But he was even more shocked when he took me to the fully furnished flat and I told him I didn't need it." Lily said. "He just dropped the keys in my bag and told me to do what I liked with it."

"I'm not surprised he was shocked. A flat is supposed to knock a girl out," Lillian said. "So where is it?" Lillian asked.

"At Victoria Island or whatever they call the place," Lily replied. "Can you imagine? He said he wanted me safely tucked away and besides he couldn't keep picking me up at the restaurant."

After a few moments Lillian nodded. "Let's plan."

For the next hour they put together a plan that they hoped would get Lily out of Melody and Alhaji's reach permanently.

As they walked towards the gate Lillian remembered that Lily's phone had rung from one of her purses hanging on her wardrobe door while she was speaking to Melody.

"It rang a few times and I didn't want to go through your bags."

"I hope it was my mother. I'll call her immediately I get back inside."

As Lillian walked alone towards the gate Lily called out to her. "What happens when a person is bitten by a rabid skunk?"

Without turning Lillian whistled as she raised her forefinger to her temple and twirled it. "Madness, mainly!"

Chapter TEN

SHADE HAD BEEN ACTING funny lately. Even though she kept very late nights she always came home to sleep. But for some time now she had been staying away for days without offering any explanation. Now it had been a whole week since Lillian had seen her and she was worried. She decided that the next time she came home she would ask what was going on. Besides she wanted Shade to speak to her boss at the travel agency who had just returned from his trip.

She was in the kitchen preparing her breakfast when she heard the front door open. She turned off the heat and went to the sitting room. Shade walked in and when she saw Lillian she beamed and held her arms open with bags dangling from each end. Lillian stood where she was with her arms folded across her chest.

"Oh, stop it, Lillie. You can't be angry with me," she said as she kicked the door shut and walked towards her with her arms outstretched. When Lillian turned as if to go back to the kitchen she ran and went and hug her and refused to let go.

"Ok. Don't suffocate me," Lillian said, craning her neck and trying to wriggle free as Shade tightened her hold.

"Tell me you forgive me."

"I do! I forgive you." Lillian sounded almost desperate.

"All right. I'm sorry." Shade let her go.

"I was so worried. You didn't tell me anything and I didn't see you. How was I to know if something had happened...?"

"I said I'm sorry. Sorry, sorry, sorry," Shade sang. "I promise I'll never do it again."

"So what is going on?" Lillian asked after a moment.

"Things." Shade dropped her bags on the floor and went into the kitchen. "What are you cooking? Smells wonderful." She looked back with a placating smile. "Has anyone ever told you that you make the best omelet in the world? Even the aroma alone is good enough for breakfast." She cut a piece of Lillian's omelet and put it in her mouth. Then she danced around the kitchen like she could not contain her joy.

"Thank you very much." Lillian came and stood beside her when she stopped. "And I'm still listening."

"I know you wouldn't get off my case until I've spilled everything," Shade said with her mouth full. "Isn't that so?"

"You appear very different." Lillian observed her closely. "Where have you been?"

"All right." She dropped the fork and smiled. "I've met someone."

"Yes?"

She looked at Lillian enquiringly but with the stirrings of a smile. "What do you mean by 'yes'?"

"What do you mean by 'I've met someone'?"

Shade laughed heartily. "You!" She poked Lillian playfully. "It's simple. I'm in love with a nice young man who loves me and wants to be with me." She sat on a stool and Lillian hopped on a cupboard.

"How do you mean?"

"We met at a party and became friends. Then it just got better." She closed her eyes and took a deep breath. When she opened them she was smiling broadly. "I've never felt this way before. He said I'm the girl of his dreams."

"Sounds wonderful," Lillian said. "And he must really be something."

"He is. And guess what? He'll be visiting his mother soon and he has asked me to come along." She waved her arms in the air. "Can you imagine that? He wants me to meet his mother."

"That means he is serious," Lillian said nodding. "If a man takes a woman to see his mother in my village it's as good as proposing to her. I'm really happy for you."

"What now?" Shade asked after a moment, surprising Lillian.

Lillian looked at Shade and blinked. She had been struck by a sudden thought and though she tried to suppress it she couldn't. Apparently her face had given away the unpleasantness of the thought and Shade had been watching her.

"I... It's...Does he know?" She shook her head obviously finding it difficult to express what was on her mind. "I was just wondering...if you have told him... if he knows," she stammered.

"Knows what?" Shade asked, and then stopped smiling as she realized what Lillian was talking about.

"Forgive me for bringing it up, but me, you know...I just..."

"He doesn't," Shade interrupted her shaking her head slowly, ruefully. "I haven't told him."

"But you plan to." When Shade didn't reply Lillian stared at her in disbelief. "Don't you think you should?" She waited and still Shade remained silent. She jumped down from the cupboard. "Look, I maybe years younger than you and may not know much, but I think it's better for you to tell him as soon as possible. What if…"

"What if he finds out from someone else?" Shade cried. "You think I haven't thought about that? I think about it every day!"

"Then…" Lillian started mildly.

"Oh! Just like that! Do you have any idea what it's like to be where I am now? It's the most difficult thing I have ever faced in my life, Lillie. He respects me, as a woman, a companion, a friend; and not just an object of physical pleasure. This is the first time and it feels great."

"He still has to know," Lillian said quietly.

"I know!" Shade snapped.

Lillian didn't blame Shade for being angry and she felt bad for making her feel this way especially after seeing how happy she seemed about her new relationship. Maybe she should have kept her thoughts to herself and not said anything. But what kind of friend would she be? Besides keeping her mouth shut was not one of her strong points. And she cared about Shade so much. Still she felt responsible and decided she needed to do something about it.

"Maybe you don't have to tell him everything at once," she suggested. "Maybe you can break it to him bit by bit."

Shade was lost in thought for a long moment. Then she looked up at Lillian. "Like a little at a time?"

"Yes! You tell him gradually so he wouldn't have to deal with everything at once."

"Maybe you're right." She looked hopeful.

Lillian cocked her head and smiled. "Maybe I am." She was glad to see that her remedy was acceptable.

"I could even start tonight." Shade got up from her stool. "You remember the course I told you about? The one I said we would be having at the Sheraton Hotel with some resource people from the U.S?"

"Can I forget? You defaced our best calendar because of it."

Shade laughed though she seemed a bit subdued. "It starts this morning."

"Finally."

"Yes, and Fred is picking me up afterwards."

"His name is Fred."

"Yes." She started walking out of the kitchen. "Eat your breakfast while I get ready. Have to be there in an hour. I'll be back tonight to tell you everything."

By the time Shade was ready to leave Lillian was almost ready for work herself.

"I'll see you tonight." Shade walked towards the door. "By the way how is the job?"

"Well, I was going to wait till tonight to tell you since we are both rushing out and I don't want to keep you. The job is fine but I have not been paid in two months. Could you please call 'Mr. Stingy' and ask him to pay me?"

Shade laughed and promised to give Lillian's boss a call later in the day.

The first thing Lillian noticed as she approached her office building was the manager's car. He didn't usually come this early. She hoped that Shade would call early and he would send for her before she had to go to him. Either way she had made up her mind she was getting paid today.

"Young lady," Lillian's boss called as she walked past his office door. She had hoped to pass without being noticed.

"Good morning, sir," she said as she walked in.

"Good morning," he replied. "Please shut the door." Then he pointed to a chair facing him. "Please sit down."

He pulled a folder from under a pile and opened it. The sheet of paper in it had a cheque attached to it. He turned the file round and pushed it to her.

"Please sign at the bottom of the voucher," he said. "This is a cheque for all you are owed. Sorry for the delay."

"No problem sir," Lillian said as she quickly confirmed the amount written on the cheque. She was so glad.

After Lillian had signed, her boss detached the cheque. Then he held it at both ends and leaned back in his seat with a half-smile while she sat there wondering why he wouldn't just hand it over.

"It's quite unlike me to behave this way," he began after a few moments. "I usually don't withhold what is due others; therefore I don't want you to think I'm a bad person. Do you see me as a bad person?"

"Of course not, sir," Lillian replied even though she would like to tell him otherwise.

"That's good because I'd hate for you to see me as a bad person. You see I have seen how hardworking you are and I have also seen that you have great potentials. Such potentials should not be wasted. I know you're better than this job and I can help you."

"I don't understand sir." And really she didn't.

He laughed. "She says she doesn't understand." He sat up. "I can take you places."

"Places?"

He laughed again. This time he got up from his chair and walked round to where Lillian was seated. "You should understand me," he drawled. "You're a very pretty girl and a brilliant one too." Then he perched on the edge of the seat and draped one arm across her shoulder.

Lillian shot out of the chair like a bullet and stood some distance away too shocked to say anything. He stood up and began to walk slowly towards her. Lillian took a step back.

It took her a little time to get her voice back. "I don't think you should come any closer, sir," she warned even though she knew there was little she could do if he did. "I only came for my cheque and...that's all."

He looked slightly irritated but still kept approaching her. "I'm offering you an opportunity to advance." He looked her up and down. "You and I..." He was interrupted by a knock on the door and he quickly returned to his seat just before Fidelis the accountant opened the door and stuck his head in.

"Good morning, sir."

"Yes, good morning Fidelis," the manager replied. Then he turned to Lillian and addressed her in a purely business-like tone. "Here's your cheque, young lady. You may cash it at any time."

"Thank you, sir," Lillian said as she collected the cheque from him, grabbed her purse and left the room.

After putting her purse in a drawer she stood for a moment not wanting to believe what had just taken place at the manager's office. Did the man just come on to her? What if Fidelis had not arrived at the time he did? She suddenly felt discouraged as she realized how this could cause a big problem for her. How would she relate to him now? Did this mean she would have to get a new job? Absolutely, because there was no way she was going places with her bald-headed manager. What was the man thinking? She couldn't get the matter off her mind as she went about her cleaning duties. She couldn't stop worrying even as she washed the toilets that were usually badly used and were even worse now that there had been a problem with the water supply for days. She had needed to make several trips to the next yard to fetch water in buckets to get her job done. This wasn't the kind of life she'd expected to live in Lagos.

Two hours later she sat at her table exhausted. At least she had been paid in full. She wondered if it was because Shade had called her boss already. Suddenly she realized she had forgotten all about Shade. She truly hoped that everything would go well with her and her new boyfriend. She hoped that his love for her would be strong enough for him to overlook her history and still want to be with her. The possibility seemed remote though. If it happened Lillian knew she would be the happiest person. Shade deserved to be happy. If only things had been different for her. If only her father had not died, or her mother, or if only she hadn't fallen into the hands of Melody. The man couldn't really be blamed if he rejected her. He would just be a regular person. It would take an extra-ordinary man to love her in spite of everything. Yet the way she had turned out was not her fault. She was just a victim of vile people who took advantage of her vulnerability.

"What planet are you on?"

Lillian looked up to see Fidelis standing by the door.

"Oh, good morning," she said smiling. "I didn't see you."

"Just as you didn't at *Oga*'s office earlier on."

"I'm sorry I was…"

"Never mind." He waved his hand. "I'm a forgiving person. Besides, you were too far away just now. I envy him." He walked to her table. "I really envy him."

"Who?" She asked, her eyebrow furrowing suddenly.

"Him," he replied. "The guy on your planet."

"What guy is on your planet?" Lillian was already getting impatient. She was tired and had a lot on her mind. The last thing she needed was to listen to this drivel from a person whose company she didn't particularly enjoy. "Please go to your office. You're needed there."

Since she started working at the agency, Fidelis had been trying to get close to her. She had always known it but had pretended to be ignorant and tried subtly to discourage him. If he ever said anything out loud she would tell him off and start avoiding him completely. She'd had enough of this.

"Are you telling me to go away?" He asked her.

"Yes," she replied. "I am."

"It's too early in the morning to do that, don't you think?

"Then don't let me," she said struggling to remain civil. "Go to your office."

After looking at her for a while, he nodded. "Ok. I'll go." He turned and walked towards the door. "For now," he added as he walked out the door.

Lillian let out a deep breath and returned to her thoughts. Life is so unfair and it's the women that seem to suffer the most. She felt her mother had had no chance at all. Forced into an early marriage, she had grown up without a vision other than to feed and take care of a husband and children. No wonder she acted the way she did. She hardly ever laughed out loud and always rebuked Lillian for doing so. She said it wasn't decent to exhibit her teeth to all and sundry. Lillian always laughed the more when she said that. Even now she smiled as she remembered. Lillian had always thought her mother was too hard on her and she'd felt bad about it. But now when she thought of it she didn't really blame her. If she had had to marry under such circumstances she wouldn't even have lasted this long. She would have crumpled and died long ago.

One thing she knew for sure was that her mother loved her and her siblings fiercely. She didn't have any formal education and lacked exposure but no one could take care of them like she did. She always gave them the best she could and they all knew that. She tried her best to protect them from being hurt by other people and always rose up to defend them even when they were guilty, especially I.K who got into trouble all the time. But none of them ever got away with it. She made sure their father got to know about it so that the adequate punishment was meted out.

When Lillian heard Lily's story she wondered how the girl could still smile. Lily had described her as a strong person, but she knew in her heart that it wasn't true. Maybe she had her strength in other areas but she knew she could not have survived what Lily had, not even at eighteen. But Lily was fourteen when it all started and was still only fifteen. No, Lily was strong, not her.

And now Shade has to pay the price for crimes other people committed. She suddenly realized that she wanted more than anything that this Fred reacts favorably. Then she would be relieved. Yet she couldn't shake this bad feeling. Does such a man exist?

Finally she thought of her own situation. She had no business being so far away from her family a day before her eighteenth birthday. What made it worse was that they had no idea where she was and she couldn't let them know. And it was her need to escape an early marriage that had led to this. If only her father wasn't such a primitive man. She still felt she did the right thing by running away. She didn't have a choice. But she missed her family, especially Mary. It had been four months now.

As she strolled to the bus stop after work she promised to give herself a special treat the next day. But what could one do alone on a Wednesday evening? Then she remembered the new fast food place on Glover Street, which was a five minute walk from the travel agency. Yes. That was where she would go. She knew it would be expensive, but it was her birthday. If she was going to celebrate it alone she might as well make it as interesting as possible. Maybe she would buy herself a new pair of shoes. The nice one she had was bought for her by Shade amidst her protests. She had also bought her some clothes and taken her to a hairdresser to have a perm. When she refused to have her hair done in any way other than in a bun Shade complained that it was a waste of long hair.

"Some people don't know what they have let alone flaunt it," she had said with a toss of her head.

By the time Lillian got home she was exhausted as usual. After dinner she switched on the television. She wanted to be awake when Shade returned but she soon fell asleep. The TV was still on when she opened her eyes later. She looked at her watch. It was a quarter to two. Didn't Shade say she would spend the night at the flat? Maybe it was too late for her to return and she decided to spend the night with Fred. She switched off the television and the light and went to lie on her bed. If only she could stay awake.

What was that sound? She dozed. There it was again, like a persistent thumping. The door? Was someone at the door? Who could it be at this time? She reached for her watch. It was too dark to see. She tried to put on the table lamp. Where was the switch? She found it and the orange glow enveloped her. She looked at the watch and was shocked to see that it was almost five. She dragged herself from the bed and tied the sheet she used for a cover over her nightgown.

"Who's there?" She asked at the door.

She couldn't make out what the person said but she was almost certain it was Shade.

"Shade?"

"Lillie, open the door."

Lillian opened it quickly. Shade was leaning over the balcony rail backing Lillian and didn't move even when the door was opened.

"Shade?" Lillian knew something was wrong. Shade only groaned when she heard her name. Lillian stepped outside. "Are you all right?" She asked. "What's wrong?"

When she didn't get any response she pulled her up and dragged her into the house. She helped her onto the sofa and went and shut the door. Then she sat beside her and put an arm around her shoulder.

"Are you hurt?" Lillian asked as she looked Shade over and then suddenly realized that she had nothing with her. "Where is your bag? Were you attacked by armed robbers?"

Shade shook her head slowly. The light from the corridor dimly lit the sitting room and Lillian could see that she had been crying.

"Then tell me what happened." Lillian was almost desperate. "Come on, Shade, say something!"

"I'm finished," Shade said at last.

Lillian drew back. "What are you talking about? What happened?"

"My life is meaningless."

Lillian sat silently waiting for her friend to make sense.

Shade hung her head and shook it. "I should have known it was too good to be true." She sniffed. "My life ended a long time ago, but I think I'm just realizing it. I'm worth nothing."

Lillian knew then what must have happened.

"But that's not true." She tried to encourage her friend. "I mean…how can you say that? You are worth more than any two people put together. You're the kindest person I know and I would boast of you anywhere. You're a very special person."

Shade laughed mirthlessly. "Fred doesn't think so. Rather he thinks I am the filthiest, most deceptive and useless dog he has ever met and still doesn't know how to scrub himself clean of me and my memory." Then she burst into tears.

Lillian didn't know what to say, but regretfully she wasn't surprised. After all, Shade had been sleeping with different men for money. But did he have to be so nasty?

"He actually said all that to you?" She asked Shade.

Shade nodded and continued amidst tears. "He said more, much more. And he pushed my head." Shade demonstrated by pushing her temple with three fingers. "He said he would have taught me a lesson for allowing him to be seen with my type. He said he just didn't want to stain his hands." She drew a shaky breath.

Lillian felt hatred for the man.

"But did you tell him how it all started?" Lillian asked Shade.

"I did." Shade wiped her nose with the back of her hand and sniffed. Lillian went to the table and brought her a box of tissues. Shade took it from her and blew her nose. "I told him." She turned to Lillian. "I remembered what you said and started with just my childhood. Then he started asking questions. And before I knew it he seemed to know everything." She leaned back. "At first he was quiet and…and calm. I'd begun to believe he would understand. Suddenly he just shook his head and began to scream 'no', that he wouldn't take it. And then he unleashed insults on me."

Lillian felt truly sorry for Shade. She never asked for it.

"There's really nothing special about him," she said finally.

"Ok." Shade sniffed and nodded.

"He's just an ordinary everyday man looking for a perfect woman when he himself is full of faults," Lillian said. "I'm sure there's still someone out there who wants just you. It's just that you've not met."

"A man out there, looking for a prostitute to marry," Shade said tearfully. "Yeah right."

"But that's not all you are." Then Lillian shook her head vigorously. "What am I saying? That's not who you are."

"Well, whoever I may be, Fred doesn't want me."

"Fred is not the only man in the world."

"He is for me."

"Oh, come on..."

"I can't live without him." Shade burst into fresh tears.

"Please don't say that," Lillian said, soothingly. "You can and you will. You will show him that he is the one that is not worthy of you."

"Why couldn't he just..." Shade shook her head and cried harder.

"Look, you obviously didn't sleep all night." Lillian stood up. "Let me get you some hot water. You shower and get some sleep. When I return from the office we'll talk. I'm sure you would be feeling better by then."

After Shade was in bed Lillian got ready for work. She would have to cancel her birthday plans so she could be home on time to be with Shade. She decided to get some snacks to take home instead. They could still have a nice time when she got back.

By the time she got back from work Shade was gone. Lillian sat heavily on the bed disappointed. Where could she have gone now? She had told her that she would call her office to tell them she wouldn't be in today. Or could she have gone to the restaurant? Lillian didn't think so. She couldn't possibly have gone to see that man Fred. Not after the way he had treated her. So where was she?

She dumped her purse and the bag full of pastries on her bed and went out again. She needed to call her and there was a business centre near the bus stop she could call from. She felt exhausted as she walked down the road. She knew Shade kept a cell phone in the house but she didn't know where. She had said Lillian could have it but Lillian had refused, saying she didn't need one. Now she wished she had collected it.

The place was busy and she had to wait for fifteen minutes. She was so glad when it was her turn because that was when she got a seat. She punched the numbers and waited. The phone made a sound and went dead. She tried again and her call still didn't go through. The sales girl explained that there was a problem with the network and she would need to try another line if she had one. She punched Shade's other number. Good thing she knew three of her numbers. This time it rang but Shade didn't pick it. She tried once more before calling the last number. The phone rang also but there was no answer. Finally she decided to call Lily.

"Hello Lily," she said when Lily answered. "It's me, Lillie. How's everything?"

"Security is tighter," Lily replied. "Otherwise everything's the same."

"How's your mother? Have you spoken to her?" Lillian asked.

"Yes. She's fine. It seems like Sheyi didn't react as much as she expected. And she's up to something." Lily chuckled.

"Can't wait to find out what it is," Lillian said hurriedly. "Lily, I'm worried about Shade."

"What do you mean?" Lily asked.

Lillian turned away from the sales girl and lowered her voice. "She has a problem with a man. We need to talk about this."

"What kind of problem?" Lily wanted to know.

"They were having a serious relationship until she told him about herself.

"A serious relationship." Lily paused. "And what did he do?"

"He threw her out after verbally abusing her."

Lily became silent and Lillian was about to ask if she was still there when she spoke again. "How is she?"

"Not fine. In fact right now I don't know where she is."

"Have you tried calling her?"

"No answer."

Lily sighed. "Will you come tomorrow?"

"Yes."

"Ok then. You know I'm not going anywhere. Yet," she added.

"Tomorrow evening then."

"Ok."

"Bye."

"Bye."

Lillian paid and left.

Back at the flat she took a shower and settled down to eat alone. What a way to celebrate her eighteenth birthday. She had been planning this day for a couple of years. If she had been home she would have called a few friends and had a party if her father would allow it. Her mother would have taken her to the market and bought her some nice second-hand clothes and shoes. And Mary would have decorated their bedroom with her tinsel garlands and the few birthday cards Lillian would get. The picture on the TV screen blurred as her eyes became moist. She shook her head and wiped her eyes. She couldn't give in to this now, just as she didn't two months ago at Christmas. All her life she had traveled with her family from the town to their village towards the end of the year. They always celebrated Christmas and the beginning of the year there and spent no less than two weeks. It was the only family event Lillian really enjoyed taking part in. There were relatives from all over the country, and sometimes from abroad, and there were always lots of exciting activities and exchange of gifts. What Lillian enjoyed most was that she and her sisters were allowed to stay with their cousins for most of the period. She always longed for that time away from housework and her parents.

But the last Christmas had been lonely. Shade had seen it as any other holiday and had left the house as usual every day and returned very late. And Lillian had missed her family very much. Now she fought the same feeling of loneliness. She had to fight it, more so now that her friends needed her. Shade was going through a period of crisis and she had to be strong for her. And the plan to get Lily out was very close to being executed. Since she was seeing Lily tomorrow night it seemed like they could be starting earlier.

She reached into the bag from the fast food place and brought out a sausage roll. She knew she wasn't sleeping early tonight. She had too much on her mind.

Chapter ELEVEN

THE RING TONE WAS distant but distinct, and Lillian had heard it before. In fact she had heard it quite a few times. It was coming from the cell phone that Shade usually left in the flat. Maybe it was Shade. She hoped it would keep ringing as she got up quickly and went to look for it. She moved around Shade's room trying to locate the exact spot the sound was coming from. It seemed to be coming from the bed. She ran her hands over the sheets and quickly lifted up the pillows. Then she looked on the bedside table and in the drawers. She even got on her knees and bent to look underneath the bed. But it was nowhere to be found. Just as she was about to pick up the pillows again it stopped ringing.

"Oh why?" She flopped on to the bed and lay back. "Why do things like this happen?" She asked no one in particular.

She pulled a pillow on her knees as she got up, dug her elbow in it and rested her cheek on her palm frustrated. Suddenly the phone began to ring again. This time it was much louder and definitely closer. She sat up. It seemed to be coming from the pillow on her knees. She patted it all round until she felt something hard. She dug her hand in the pillowcase and found the phone. Quickly she brought it out and pressed the answer button.

"Hello."

"Lillie…" It was Shade and her voice was barely above a whisper.

Lillian breathed a sigh of relief. "Shade! Shade where are you? I told you not to leave the flat," she burst out.

"Lillie…" Shade seemed unable to go on.

"Shade, are you all right?" Lillian became more worried.

Shade began to speak but Lillian couldn't make any sense of her barely audible, incoherent answer.

"All right, all right, where are you?" Lillian asked and what she heard jolted her. "Hospital?" She threw off the pillow and jumped up. "Did you say hospital?"

"Yes." The reply was weak.

"What are you doing there?"

"Lillie…"

"Ok. Which hospital?"

"General…on the...Island."

"Look. Stay there." Lillian started walking to her own room. "Do you hear me? Don't go anywhere. Please listen to me this time. All right? Just…stay put."

"Hello. Hello." Lillian heard someone else's voice.

"Yes, hello. Who is this?"

"I'm a nurse at the Island General Hospital. Are you a relative of Shade's?"

"I'm her friend. What happened?"

"It's all right. I just need you to come down as soon as you can."

"I'm on my way."

Not knowing who else to call Lillian dialed Lily's number. It took some time before Lily answered and when she finally did the words tumbled out of Lillian's mouth as if they had been held back against their will. "Shade just called. Something is terribly wrong. I spoke to a nurse. She's in the hospital." She took a deep breath. "And I'm going there."

"What?" Lily sounded like she had been sleeping. "What are you saying?"

"Shade. She went after that man and now she is in the hospital," Lillian replied. "And I'm getting ready to go there."

"I'm going with you."

Lillian couldn't help chuckling and she paused for a moment before slipping her shoe on with her free hand. "You're still sleepy."

"No. I'm serious. I'm going to meet you in front of the bank close to our road junction."

"And how do you plan to get out?" Lillian asked.

"Just trust me," Lily replied. "I'm determined enough."

"Look, I don't think..." Lillian was doubtful.

"I can do it. You can't even stop me."

"Whatever you want to do, please be careful. I wouldn't know how to…"

"Listen, you're not going looking for Shade alone at this time of the night. I will call you later. And don't call me." Lily hung up.

The house was quiet as Lily tiptoed down the stairs. It was a quarter past midnight. She adjusted the strap of her heavy barrel bag across her chest. She had stuffed only as much as she could into it even though she had meant to take more when she finally left the house. Lillian had come up with a plan to move her things without raising any suspicion. She had planned to visit Lily twice the next week with a big bag full of old newspapers which she would dump and leave with Lily's stuff instead. But because of the sudden change in plans Lily had had to settle for the things she thought were most important.

She knew she could not take the front door. The gateman would see her the moment she stepped out because of the security lights that were usually kept on all night. She would have to take the back door through the kitchen.

The kitchen light was off but she could see her way because of the light from the hallway. There was a key in the keyhole of the back door but there was also a heavy metal gate, which was locked with two huge padlocks. She looked around wondering where the keys could have been kept. She checked in every single drawer and cupboard in the kitchen. She looked on every shelf and underneath. Then she remembered she had seen Ella take a bunch of keys from behind the pantry door once. She found two bunches of keys hanging on a rack that was almost coming off the door. She quickly unhooked them and went to the door. She dropped her bag on the floor and began to try the keys one after the other. She felt frustrated when none of the eleven keys on the two bunches opened the padlocks.

She tried to think of different places the right keys could be. Maybe Ella had them. If she did, then there was only one way to get them. She would have to steal them from her room.

She returned the keys to the back of the pantry door and walked towards Ella's room. It was beside the guest toilet, across the hallway from the sitting room. She stood before the door. What if Ella was still awake or what if she woke her up? Then she would have to come up with a good lie. She could pretend to be ill. She put her hand on the knob, took a deep breath and turned it. She pushed the door a little but it didn't budge. She felt an ache in her chest as she realized that the door could be locked from the inside. Out of desperation she pushed the door harder and with a scraping sound, it gave. She froze. When she was sure there was no movement from inside the room she gently pushed the door a little more and slipped inside.

The room was dark but not too dark for her see. She could see the bed in the corner, and on it Ella lay completely covered with a sheet. Her breathing was even. Lily looked around to see where she would start her search from. There weren't many places to look as the room was so sparsely furnished. Apart from the bed there was only a wardrobe and a chair. Ella's striped uniform was draped across the chair. She decided to look there because she now remembered that Ella always had a bunch of keys in one of her pockets that made it look like it was sewn on lower than the other pocket. She tiptoed to the chair and patted the uniform gently and almost immediately touched what could only be a bunch of keys. She felt elated. She put her hand in the pocket and brought it out slowly while stealing glances at the sleeping form. Then she quickly left the room and closed the door as quietly as she could.

Back in the kitchen she singled out the first key quickly and put it in the padlock. As she was about to turn it she heard a sound. It was the faint creaking of a door. Someone was opening a door! Her heart began to beat fast. In a moment a light would come on and she would be discovered. Her first thought was to run and hide fast. But did she still have enough time to pull out the key from the padlock before hiding? What if she did? Her hand trembled like a leaf as she pulled out the key. Then with legs that had turned to jelly she moved jerkily into the pantry and crouched behind the door.

In just a few seconds someone entered the kitchen. She swallowed hard. Her legs were shaking so badly. She waited for the light to come on but it didn't. Instead she heard the fridge door open and close and then the sound of the lid of a pot being removed. This was followed by some scraping sounds and then some slurping. It seemed like she was not the only one on a mission tonight. She hoped this person would hurry and get back to bed so she could get on with her escape. Besides her legs were beginning to ache and she couldn't change her position for fear of making a sound loud enough for the food thief to hear.

Finally the pot was covered and the fridge opened and closed again. Then Lily heard soft footfalls leave the kitchen and everywhere was silent. As she waited to hear the creaking door again she got up as quietly as possible to ease the ache in her legs. Just then she heard a sound in the kitchen. Had the person returned? Suddenly there was a bump, followed by a heavy thud which made Lily almost jump out of her skin. Then she heard some scrambling sounds. It seemed like the person tripped over something and fell. Her bag! She had left it in the way! Her heart sank. Why did this have to happen? If only she had put her bag somewhere else. But what if she still had a chance? Maybe she could stop whoever it was from raising an alarm and ruining everything. Slowly she slipped out from behind the pantry door and entered the kitchen. He was bent over the bag, fumbling with it. Though he had his back to her she recognized him immediately.

"Bernard," she whispered.

"Nnam o!" Bernard jumped up and spun round, his two hands on his chest.

Lily was startled by his reaction. "It's ok. It's me, Lily." She held out her two hands to keep him quiet.

"Aunty!" He stared at her wide-eyed. "Hey, Aunty. *I don fear.*" Then he looked at the bag and looked at her again. "*Wetin happen? Na you get di bag?*"

Lily hesitated. If she told him the truth would he help her or would he give her away? She had no way of knowing.

"Aunty…?" He searched her face for an explanation.

"Look, Bernard, I have to leave…I have to go out tonight. And I don't want anyone to know," Lily whispered.

He opened his mouth and shut it again. Then he shook his head slowly and turned away from her.

"Bernard, I'm begging you," Lily pleaded.

"*Na* big trouble *be dis o*." Bernard said, still not wanting to look at her. "Madam say…"

"All you have to do is pretend you don't know anything, just like I don't know anything about what you came to the kitchen to do." Lily was determined to try anything. "After all I could have left before you came out." Lily walked round and faced him. "Please, Bernard."

He kept looking away and for a while he stood there mumbling under his breath. He seemed to be asking himself questions and answering them. Then he shook his head determinedly.

"No. No, Aunty. *I no go fit. Madam dey ready to kill everybody."* Then he looked at her. "Why?"

"I'm her victim, Bernard. She took advantage of me because there was no one to save me from her," Lily explained. "I just need your help."

The young man shifted uncomfortably.

"*Ok, suppose I gree and I no talk, how you wan comot?"* He asked her. *"Wey key?"*

Lily showed him the bunch of keys and he gasped covering his mouth with both hands.

"I have the keys." She looked at him pleadingly.

"*How manage*?" His eyes were opened wide and he looked at her with admiration.

"It doesn't matter how I got them, Bernard. Just help me. Please."

"Ok," he finally said but still looked doubtful. "But Aunty..."

"I'll never mention your name," she said. "I promise." She walked past him to the gate and began to try the keys. One after the other the padlocks opened. Then she looked at Bernard who was still standing on the same spot.

"I'll just leave the keys on the table here and don't worry; I'll come back and lock the gate from outside after finding a way..." Then she realized she still didn't know how to get out of the yard.

"E get one place wey barb wire no dey," Bernard said after a while.

"I beg your pardon?"

"You want to climb fence?" He asked and Lily nodded. It seemed like the only option even though she had no idea how she would go about it. "No 'barb wire' by gardener's shed."

"Really?" Lily was excited. "Thank you. Thank you, Bernard."

"And ladder dey for ground for back of shed," he added.

She smiled at him, not knowing what else to say. Then she picked up her bag.

"Aunty. Wait." He walked up to her quickly as she was about to leave. She stopped. He stood in front of her but said nothing. When he started fidgeting with the buttons on his shirt Lily became worried.

"What...?"She began.

"Find me 'somtin'," he said with his head bowed.

Lily breathed a sigh of relief. "Of course." She brought out some money from her pocket, counted some notes and gave them to him.

"Thank you. Thank you, Aunty." He quickly stuffed them into one of his pockets. "And don't worry. I will lock gate."

Lily was relieved to be finally out of the house. Everything was just as Bernard said. There was a part of the fence, just about two feet wide, by the gardener's shed that the barbed wire had been removed. Also the ladder was exactly where he said it would be. What he didn't tell her was how heavy it was. It took her ages to drag it to the right spot and finally put it up against the wall. She was breathing heavily by the time she started climbing. Though her palms hurt and the weight of her bag bore heavily on her, she was glad to have come this far. However, when she got to the top she found out that the wall was really high and she didn't know how to get down the other side. Still there was no going back. She looked down and decided the only way was to jump. The wall was surrounded with shrubs and Lily wondered how safe they were. Well, there was no time to worry about that and only one way to find out. She put one leg over the fence and sat astride it. Carefully she moved her bag over and then she slowly carried the other leg over, being extremely careful not to touch the barbed wire or lose her balance. Then she jumped.

Nothing could have prepared her for the shock and searing pain from dropping off an eight-foot wall with only a thorny bush to break her fall. She scampered out clumsily, her heavy bag making it extremely difficult. Dazed as she still was she brought her phone out of her pocket and dialed.

"I've been beside myself." Lillian's voice sounded anxious on the other side. "What's happening?"

"Someone up there's watching over me," Lily replied breathlessly. "I'm out."

Chapter TWELVE

"OUT?" LILLIAN REPEATED TO herself. She couldn't wait to hear how she did it. She shook her head.

She had been standing by the kiosk for at least half an hour, but she was no longer agitated. Lily had been able to get out of the house and had called. She had spent the last hour worrying herself sick. She had been sure Lily was in danger and feared she would never make it. She couldn't imagine how Lily could have gotten out. She smiled now waiting to hear the story Lily must have to tell.

She spotted her immediately she emerged from the small lane. It was a good thing she lived off Allen Avenue. The place was always teeming with people both during the day and at night. Little wonder it was said that Allen Avenue never sleeps. If Lillian had been walking on the road at this time of the night with the kind of bag Lily was carrying near Anthony Village where she lived with Shade, she was likely to have been robbed moments after leaving the house.

Lillian walked up to her and gently slid off the strap of her bag from her shoulder. She looked like a weary traveler that had been on the road for days.

"Sorry," was all she could say at first as Lily let her have the bag. "But how did you do it?"

Lily shook her head and Lillian snickered.

"It's not funny, I promise you," Lily said unable to resist a smile.

"So did you drug your gateman?"

"That would have been a piece of cake compared to what I did, Lillie."

"Really? What did you do?" Then she noticed the small welts on her arms and neck. She lifted one of her arms gently and looked more closely. Anger was registered all over her face. "Who did this?"

"No one." Lily shook her head. "I jumped over the fence and landed badly. That's all."

"You?" Lillian blinked. "Jumped over a fence? Lily Parker?" She looked shocked. "I thought such bouts were reserved for tomboys like me." She looked at her other arm and her neck. "But what did you land on?"

"In, actually," she replied. "Some sort of bush, with lots of Melody's thorns."

Lillian's mouth hung open for a moment. "Wow. You've really had an adventure."

"And that's not all that happened."

"There's more?" The look on her face earned her a warning look from Lily and she struggled to look sober. "Sorry," she said.

"Let's get a taxi. I'll tell you the rest on the way."

In the taxi Lily began to tell Lillian all that happened.

"You went into her room and stole the key and she didn't wake up?"

"She didn't even stir. But someone else woke up."

"Who?"

"Bernard. He came to the kitchen to eat."

"What? To steal food?" Lillian was amused.

"Yes. So I hid behind the pantry door. Then he tripped over my bag and fell and I had to come out."

Lillian gasped. "I'll never know how you both didn't wake up the whole house," she said. "So how did you get past him?"

"I begged and begged him," Lily said. "Remember Melody's instructions."

"Can I forget?"

"Anyway it was a good thing he came out because he was the one that told me where there was no barbed wire on the fence and where the ladder was."

"He actually helped?"

"Then he asked for money," Lily said.

"My brother, Bernard!" Lillian slapped her thigh and shook her head. "Otherwise he wouldn't be my brother."

Lily laughed. "I really didn't mind. Truly. He deserved it."

"I'm not saying he didn't," Lillian said giggling. "Just that money must be involved. That's all. I'm just glad he didn't give you away."

"You know what I'm truly glad about?" Lily turned to Lillian. "God was watching over me."

"That." Lillian nodded in agreement. "And Melody doesn't keep savage dogs."

The taxi pulled up at the gate of the hospital and Lily quickly paid the driver.

"This is Alhaji's money," she said when Lillian wanted to protest. "Keep yours."

"So where exactly do we go now?" Lillian asked as soon as they were in the hospital premises. "Everywhere is so quiet.

It was really silly of me not to have asked the nurse I spoke to where to find Shade. I was just not myself."

"Don't worry. Let's look in the main building. I'm sure there'll be someone there to direct us."

They entered the building and saw a couple of patients but no nurse. As they were about to walk out again a man in green overalls walked into the building.

"Let's ask him," Lily said. "He looks like a hospital staff."

"Good evening."

"Good evening."

"We…came to see our friend," Lillian said to him. "Her name is Shade Oladimeji. She was brought here earlier on… and she is very sick."

"You say she's your friend?" The man asked.

"Yes," Lillian replied.

"She's a young girl like you?" The man pointed to both girls.

"Yes."

"They brought one girl like that around *that kind*…eleven or so," he said. "Is it not the girl with drug overdose?"

"What?" Both Lillian and Lily exclaimed at the same time and looked at each other.

"Oh, you didn't know?" The man asked. "Sorry. I thought you knew. Sorry."

"Where…where can we find her?" Lillian managed to ask.

"Emergency," he said pointing. "You see that building opposite this one, go there.

The second room on your left is the Female Emergency Ward. She's there."

"Thank you."

"Overdose?" Lillian asked herself as they hurried towards the place the man described.

"She didn't have to do this," Lily muttered.

Shade was deathly still on the bed with an intravenous tube attached to her arm when they found her. Lily was so overwhelmed she burst into tears. Lillian put her arm around her shoulders to console her, close to tears herself. Shade looked so ill.

They stood together by the bed until Lillian voiced out her thoughts.

"I wonder what really happened."

"That man turned her away and she couldn't take it and that's what happened," Lily said angrily, amidst tears. "They're the ones that mess you up and then they reject you for being messed up."

"Poor Shade," was all Lillian could say. She then got two chairs from the corridor just outside the room and put them beside Shade's bed.

"Let's sit and wait for her to wake up." She took Lily's bag from her shoulder and put it between the chairs.

Lily sat with her head bowed.

"What's going to become of her?" She was weeping again. "What are we going to do?"

"Shush, Lily." Lillian moved her chair closer to hers. "Shade will be fine. We'll do our best to make sure she comes out of this."

"And then what?" Lily asked helplessly. "What happens when she's all right and another man does this to her? Will we even be here?"

Lillian wanted to respond, to reassure Lily, but she had no answers. She didn't know what would happen if Shade went through this again. She had no idea what would become of her. Her heart-rending sobs after Fred broke up with her were still fresh in Lillian's memory. She felt frustrated, and angry.

Later a nurse came into the room. She nodded at the two girls and looked through the chart at the foot of the bed. She checked Shade's eyes and pulse and took her blood pressure. Then she examined the intravenous tube and turned to Lillian and Lily.

"Are you her friends?"

"Yes, we are," Lillian replied.

"Are you the one I spoke to on the phone?"

"Yes. Yes I am."

"Do you know anything about the circumstances that led to her being brought here?" the nurse enquired.

Lillian hesitated not knowing exactly what to tell the nurse. Then she decided she didn't know what really happened the previous evening.

"No," she replied. "She had left before I got back and I didn't know where she was until she called me from the hospital."

"Anyway," the nurse said after observing Lillian for a moment. "She took an excessive dose of a combination of drugs. Some good-natured people brought her here. They said they saw her sitting on a culvert by a fuel station looking very ill. They...thought she looked too decent to be there. They knew she had to be in some kind of trouble and decided not to leave her alone. They brought her here, paid some money and left, though not before she was made to call someone. Your friend is really lucky."

Both girls were speechless.

Finally Lily sighed. "So how is she?" She asked. "Will she be all right?"

"Oh, she'll be fine," the nurse replied. "Like I said she's really lucky to have been found and brought here on time. Thank God she didn't take any more than she already did and the rest of the drugs were found on her. It's also a good thing the consultant was here to see her and I assure you she was given the best care." She smiled. "We have run some tests and are waiting for the results. But I know she'll be fine."

"Thank you very much," Lily said comforted by what she had just learnt.

"She would get some counseling once she's well enough," the nurse continued. "You'll need to go and get some clothes and toiletries for her as soon as you can. Also come with me to collect her hand bag. I couldn't just leave it lying around because she has some valuables in it."

Lillian got up and went with the nurse. When she returned Lily was standing by the bed holding Shade's hand. She looked up as Lillian came in.

"I'm so relieved," she said.

"So am I." Lillian stood on the other side of the bed. "It appears those people saved her life. I wish I could thank them personally."

"Perfect strangers," Lily said. "I'm glad such people really exist. Sort of makes one feel better."

"Yes it does," Lillian agreed.

A few hours later Shade was still not awake and Lillian was ready to go and get her things.

"I won't be long," she said yawning and stretching. Spending the night dozing on a straight-backed metal chair wasn't her idea of a good night's sleep.

"Sure you want to go alone?"

"Yeah. It's better for one of us to be here when she wakes up." She picked up her purse. "Besides you should be in hiding."

"All right," Lily agreed. "But make sure you take a taxi straight there and back." She brought out some money from her pocket. "And I think Alhaji should pay for it. Take."

"I can't take it..."

"Listen." Lily stood up. "I never considered this as payment. To me it is still his money. And it is for Shade and not for you anyway."

"Ok." Lillian took the money hesitantly. "But…"

"Go. And don't be long."

"All right. Bye."

All Lillian intended to do was to get to the flat, take what Shade would need and rush back to the hospital. She really needed a shower but that could wait. Shade had to be taken care of and Lily needed to be kept safe. The plan was for Lily to leave Lagos for Port Harcourt immediately she was successfully out of Melody's house. That day Lily would see Lillian off to the gate as she usually did after a visit but this time a taxi would be waiting just out of sight. Both girls would carry nothing since Lillian would already have moved all of Lily's things and the gateman would suspect nothing. The driver was to pull up as soon as he spotted them. Since the gateman usually sat some distance from the gate they figured they would both already be in the taxi before he would be able to get to them. He would be in trouble with Melody of course but it just had to be done.

Lillian had been apprehensive even though they had both agreed it was a good plan. She was afraid a number of things could go wrong. But Lily was out now and she didn't have to worry about that anymore. The problem she faced now was how to keep her safe until she was able to leave for Port Harcourt. Shade's flat was out since it was probably the first place Melody would look. She wondered if they had discovered at Melody's house that Lily was gone. Of course they would have seen the ladder and known immediately. She felt sorry for Ella and the rest of the staff. Melody would go ballistic.

She got to the house and quickly gathered the things she thought they would need. She zipped up the hold all and slowly lifted the strap to her shoulder. It was heavy. She couldn't make up her mind what to leave behind. She felt it was better to take what they didn't need than to leave behind what they would.

She stepped out and locked the door. As she turned to walk to the stairs she saw some people walking towards her. Right in front of them all was a large woman dressed in a long lace robe and an elaborately tied head gear, with jewelry hanging from every possible place. Lillian heart lurched. She tried not to show any feelings as she walked boldly towards them, meaning to walk past. But Melody stopped a few feet from her.

"Are you the girl that lives with Shade?" she asked rather brusquely.

Lie. Lie to her and keep walking. "Yes," Lillian replied feebly, not understanding why her mouth didn't comply with her thoughts.

"And where is she?" Melody looked her up and down.

"I don't know," she lied. *Phew!*

"When was the last time you saw her?"

"Yesterday morning when I left for work."

"And she has not returned?"

"No."

"Ok," Melody pointed past Lillian to the door. "Open it."

"What?" Lillian looked back. "The door?"

"Yes," Melody cocked her head. "The door."

Lillian hesitated. *Who does this woman think she is?*

"I should open the door to a stranger…" One of the men stepped forward but stopped when Melody raised her hand.

"Let's make this easy, shall we?" Melody said. "As you can see it can be more complicated." She tossed her head in the direction of her over-eager henchman. "Besides I am not a stranger. I am Madam Melody, Shade's aunt."

"But what do you want me to open the door for?" The man took another menacing step towards Lillian and this time Melody didn't try to stop him. "All right," she said quickly. She walked back to the door and opened it and immediately two of the men brushed past her inside.

"What…?" She followed them in and watched them go from room to room and then she turned to Melody who had also entered the flat. "What are they looking for?" she asked. "Why are they going through our… what is it that you want?"

Melody kept her attention on the men and completely ignored her. They came out when they had finished their search.

"There's no one there, Madam," one of them said. "The place is clean."

"But I told you Shade isn't back," Lillian said.

"Keep quiet! I'm not looking for Shade," Melody snapped.

Lillian's eyes widened, but before she could say another word Melody turned to her fully.

"When you see Shade," Melody said narrowing her eyes. "Tell her that if she knows anything about Lily's whereabouts she had better let me know immediately otherwise this Lagos will not be big enough for both of us." She walked out and her men followed. Lillian walked out after them and stood by the doorway. It was then that Melody looked at the bag she was carrying. "Where are you going with that bag?"

Lillian's heart skipped a beat and she felt like a cornered animal.

"I'm…I'm traveling to the village…this morning… to see my sick father," she stammered. *Now where did that come from*?

Melody looked at her with narrowed eyes while her mouth worked rapidly in a way Lillian did not understand and then she nodded briefly before turning and walking off with her men. In a few seconds the last of the men disappeared round the corner and Lillian was left with only the strong scent of Melody's perfume lingering in the air. She dropped the heavy bag on the floor and fell against the wall, weak. The woman did have a presence. Little wonder she was able to keep all those girls under her control.

She locked the door and waited. She wanted to be sure that they had left before getting back to the hospital. When she got downstairs there was no sign of them and so she headed for the road.

The estate Lillian lived in with Shade was one of the four which were given out to contractors as part of the new housing scheme for the mainland. The houses were built according to plan and over the years the project had even been extended to cover more land. What no one seemed to have thought of was the expansion of the only access road that led in and out of the whole area or the construction of another one at the new extension. As soon as the houses sprang up people occupied them and the more the residents the greater the number of cars that used that one road. A gridlock was a regular occurrence at the junction before the Express Road.

It was difficult for Lillian to cross the road because of the traffic that was already building up and it wasn't even 7am yet. In less than fifteen minutes the cars would come to a complete stand still. She dashed across at the first chance she got and was about to step on the curb when she saw it. She wondered if it was what she thought it was or she was just being paranoid. Had her encounter with Melody got her so flustered that she was now imagining things? Still she wouldn't take any chances. She definitely hadn't been expecting it and would easily have missed it, but for that little detail. She made a few quick decisions and headed towards the bus stop. Lily and Shade would just have to wait a little longer.

At the bus stop she met a large crowd that seemed to increase with every passing minute in spite of the number of buses that kept stopping to whisk people off in dozens. Lillian decided to take a taxi. To struggle for, and get a bus with this heavy bag would be almost impossible. Finally she got a taxi at a rather high price and as it eased into the traffic she wondered exactly how far she would have to go if she was right. She also knew she could be in danger.

She was patient though tense throughout the ride and as the taxi made a U-turn at Jibowu she tried to look around without being too obvious. She panicked when she found out she was right all along. She was being followed.

Finally they arrived at the Eastern States bus parks. Before the driver could find a good spot to pull over she quickly scanned the different parks to see which one she could hide in. When she found the right one she told him where to stop, paid him and quickly got off. Her plan was to hide among the travelers for as long as she could, but as she made her way through the busy park she noticed a taxi at the back of the office building that had just dropped an old lady and her son. The driver had been allowed by the park security guards to drive all the way in because of the old woman. She made a quick dash for it and entered into the back.

"Listen," she said before the driver could utter a word. "I need to get to the General Hospital on the Island."

"I can't go that way at this time," he said, shaking his head vigorously. "There is too much traffic."

Lillian looked around quickly. There was no sign of her pursuers. She was safe for now but she didn't know for how long.

"Look, I will pay you," she said when the driver didn't look like he was ever going to comply. "How much?"

"It is not the money," he replied. "This Third Mainland Bridge..."

"How much?" Lillian repeated, interrupting him.

He hesitated and then sighed.

"If you can pay...Two thousand-five..." he began, rubbing his hands together. "I just hope..."

"Let's go," Lillian said just before ducking.

"We should go?" the driver wanted to confirm.

"Yes, go," Lillian replied. "And please don't act as if there's anyone in the taxi with you. Just keep your eyes on the road and don't stop for any reason."

The man laughed uneasily. "Are you in any kind of trouble?"

"No trouble," Lillian replied lying down on the back seat. "I'm just not ready to travel as far as my home town this morning. That's all.

Chapter THIRTEEN

IT WAS LIKE A miracle. The headaches had stopped completely. Why hadn't anyone told her about this before? And to think she actually believed there was something seriously wrong with her. But what was she expected to think when her head ached persistently for two days sometimes?

"The brain is mostly water," Esther had lectured her. "So when you're dehydrated what do you think suffers first? Drink up to eight glasses of water every day and you might never feel those headaches again."

And Esther was right. Amanda must have been dehydrated all her life. She stretched and smiled. It felt really good to wake up in the morning without a headache. That is except Sheyi, of course.

And he had been a real pain lately. He hadn't said a civil word to her in days. He complained about every little thing and seemed to look for opportunities for a fight. She tried her best to stay out of his way and totally ignored his criticisms.

"It takes two to fight, so don't give him a chance," was Esther's counsel. And Amanda took it very seriously. If he wanted a fight he wasn't getting it from her.

She got the children ready and took them to school. It was a good thing Sheyi had stopped taking them. At first she wasn't happy about it because he had the car, but now she was glad because she was able to go to certain places with them without raising any suspicions.

The car was outside when she returned. What could Sheyi be doing home at this time? Not knowing what to expect she opened the door and stepped in to see him sitting on a chair he had moved to face the front door. Immediately he saw her he started clapping his hands slowly. She shut the door behind her and stood still. What now?

"Congratulations," he said.

Congratulations? She frowned. Surely he couldn't have found out about… Could he? But she thought she had been careful.

"Tell me," he continued. "How did you do it?"

"Do what?" She would feign ignorance for as long as she could.

"Oh, please," he uttered in disgust. "Don't pretend." He leaned back, folding his arms. "No, no tell me. How did you pull it off all the way from Benin here?" Amanda stared at him. "I have to give it to you though. She made a clean escape. My aunt is at a loss."

Now Amanda was certain he was talking about something else and she was relieved.

"Who made a clean escape?"

"Stop it!" Sheyi looked away as if he couldn't bear to look at her. "Just stop it." He turned to her again. "But I assure you my aunt will find her."

Then it hit Amanda like a gust of wind.

"You mean Lily?" she asked, astounded.

"No, I mean rose periwinkle!" Sheyi glared at her his nostrils flared.

Amanda couldn't hold back the smile. *Good for you, Lily.* She couldn't wait to call her to make sure she was fine and to tell her to be careful.

"Yes. Look triumphant for as long as you can, you... lousy...good for nothing," Sheyi sneered. "It wouldn't be for long."

He got up and walked towards her. When he got close to her he stopped.

Amanda summed up courage and asked him the question she really needed an answer for.

"But why, Sheyi?" she asked. "What do you gain from keeping Lily with your aunt?"

He just grimaced, shook his head and walked out of the house. Amanda stood there with her eyebrows raised. She heard the car start and speed off. How exactly did Sheyi's head work?

She reached into her bag and brought out her phone. She had to speak to Lily now.

"Mummy!" She heard Lily's excited voice as she answered her phone. "I'm sorry. I should have called. Everything happened so fast and then I..."

"It's ok." It had never been more ok. "You're all right. I'm so relieved."

"I'm fine," Lily said. "Melody doesn't know where I am and... I ran away from her house last night. Or have you already heard?"

"Yes," Amanda replied. "Sheyi just brought me the news."

"She must have called him."

"And he thinks I'm the one that got you out."

"Oh? I hope he wouldn't do anything to you..."

"Don't worry about me. I'm fine. I just want you to be careful," Amanda said. "Melody is a heartless person. She might even have people out looking for you now. If you're sure you're safe where you are, stay there and I will come and get you. By the way where are you?"

"At the hospital. My..."

"What?" Amanda exclaimed. "What are you doing there? Are you hurt?"

"No," Lily replied. "I'm not hurt. It's my friend."

"Who? Lillie?"

"No, Shade."

"Ok. Which hospital?"

"General, on the Island," Lily replied. "But don't come. I...I can't leave Lagos yet."

"Whatever do you mean? Why can't you? You can't stay there."

"I'll leave as soon as I can. I can't leave Shade.

"But..."

"Lillie is with me. I'll be fine."

"I don't understand...but how long will she be in the hospital for?"

"I don't know. We just don't want to leave her here alone."

Amanda's sigh was long and deep. "What should I do?"

"I will call you as soon as she is discharged."

"Ok. But keep your phone on."

"Ok. I will."

Amanda sighed. "Be safe."

"You too."

"Bye."

Amanda hung up and headed straight for Esther's.

"You're just in time for a late breakfast...or an early lunch," Esther said as she opened the door and saw Amanda.

"Lily escaped from Melody's house."

"Come in." Esther grabbed her by the shoulder and pulled her in.

"How did you find out?" Esther asked as she sat beside her.

"Sheyi accused me just now of helping her get out," she said. "I came in from dropping the children at school and saw him. He had actually dragged a chair, a heavy chair, from where it was so that it would face the front door. And the first thing he did was to congratulate me. I wasn't sure I knew exactly what he was on about until he said it."

"But how did she do it?" Esther asked.

"I don't know."

"Have you spoken to her?"

"Yes. I called her immediately Sheyi left."

"What did she say?"

"That she's fine, thank God, and safe."

"Where is she?"

"She's still in Lagos."

"Shouldn't she be on her way here or to your cousin Agnes?"

"That's the problem. She says she can't leave yet. She said her friend is sick and she can't leave her."

Esther sat back and took a deep breath.

"I wanted to go and get her but she said not to." Amanda looked worried. "I just don't know how I'm going to cope knowing that she's still in Lagos with Melody and I am here in Benin."

"Calm down," Esther said. "You know what I see? I see the answers to our prayers coming in."

Amanda looked up at her.

"Of course you know we were expecting answers, or weren't you?" Esther asked.

"Yes, I was."

"God got her out, He will keep her."

Amanda nodded. They had both spent time praying for Lily since Amanda learnt to trust in God again. And she had decided to trust Him all the way, even for the impossible.

"Remember how Lily accepted you and forgave you even though you barely had any faith that it could happen?" Amanda nodded. "That's a miracle. Her getting out is another. I think there will still be lots more."

"Thank you, Esther."

"So…late breakfast? Early lunch?"

"I wonder though…" Amanda said as they ate. "I mean… Sheyi is…you know how he is. And I know he has this strange loyalty to Melody which I don't understand, but why is he so mad because I want to get Lily out of there? He knows why Melody wants to keep her there, but why should it be his business?"

"You mean why should he take it so personally?" Esther offered.

"Yes!" Amanda cried. "You should have seen his face today. And he couldn't even wait till he closed from work. He must have come home immediately Melody informed him. Imagine the traffic he has to face now on the way back to the office!"

"You said he is very close to his aunt," Esther said. "That he lived with her when he was in school and that she took care of him."

"Yes, and I even think she still gives him money," Amanda recalled. "I saw a cheque once with her name printed on it. It had dropped from his diary and when I picked it up for him he almost bit my head off." She smiled mischievously. "That's why I looked at it. Then some time later I saw another one in the car. This time I pretended I didn't."

"Why should he want to bite your head off just because you saw a cheque given to him by his aunt as if it were a big secret?" Esther wondered. Then she frowned. "Why should she be giving him money anyway?"

Amanda shrugged. "I don't know. It's not as if he still depends on her."

"When did you see the first cheque?" Esther asked.

"Oh it's a long time ago," Amanda answered.

"Hmmm."

"What? You have that look."

"I may be wrong," Esther began. "But if I am not it might explain a few things."

"What few things?"

"Could it be that Sheyi is being paid for bringing Lily?"

Amanda's jaw dropped and so did her fork, which clattered to the floor.

"Breathe," Esther held out her two hands to her when she saw how horrified she looked.

"No! I…I never…what…why…?" Amanda rambled.

"Take it easy," Esther soothed. "You need to calm down."

"Would he…? Is that why…? My God!" She cried and jumped up and began to pace back and forth. "The…the slimy…evil…shameless…monster."

"If it is true, yes, he's definitely all that and more," Esther said. "But you need to calm down. And hard as it may be, you still need to maintain the peace in your home."

"Peace!" Amanda cried. "There can never be peace in that house again. Ever! I'm going to descend on that scumbag…"

"And ruin all you've been working on, all your plans?"

Amanda stopped pacing. She sat down with her fists clenched, fuming. She closed her eyes tight and groaned. How come it had never occurred to her that Sheyi could be profiting from keeping Lily with Melody? No wonder he fought so hard to keep her from going to see her. He got a share of what Melody was paid, and he wasn't willing to lose it. She felt like she had just been slapped very hard across the face. She opened her eyes and looked at Esther.

"That's the lowest anyone can sink," she said. "The very lowest."

"If we are right," Esther said.

"How else can one explain it?" She drove a punch into her palm. "And I never, ever imagined it."

"Well, I did," Esther said.

Amanda looked a little surprised. "Then why didn't you tell me?"

"I imagined it, not that I knew for sure," Esther replied. "There was a man in my mother's village who got paid for delivering his two nieces to a brothel. He told all kinds of lies to their parents. Whenever they asked after those girls he would deceive them or get nasty or whatever. Soon someone got suspicious and did some investigation. That was how the truth came out."

"Some men are callous," Amanda said.

"And he is still there," Esther said. "My mother showed him to me."

"You mean he got away with it?" Amanda asked.

"He didn't," replied Esther. "The villagers seized all his property and gave him the beating of his life. Later he was arrested by the Police and locked up."

"Not enough," Amanda said, still angry but calmer.

"Would you have preferred if he had been hung upside down for days in the hot sun? Stark naked?"

Amanda shrugged. "Maybe."

"Or if his whole body had been rubbed with palm oil and he was made to crawl round the village market?"

Amanda tried to smile. "I just mean that..."

"I know what you mean," Esther said. "It's one of the worst things you can do to a child. I mean, you've taken away their childhood."

Amanda folded her arms tight around her stomach and grimaced as if she was in pain. "Sheyi is pathetic."

Esther studied her for a long while. "When are you going to speak to Lily again?" Esther asked.

"I'll call her later in the day." Amanda shifted in her seat. "I will be more comfortable if she is on her way out of Lagos. I feel so helpless being so far away from her and not being able to do anything."

"That's not true," Esther said. "You have been praying for her. You think you can protect her? Only God can keep her safe and you're the one that has been asking Him to. And He has been listening. I believe that He will work everything out perfectly, and you only need to trust in Him."

"I trust Him Esther. I really do. I just need to concentrate on that and not the circumstances."

"And He will help you. He's always there for you."

Amanda smiled. "No wonder I keep coming back here," she said. "You always know exactly what to say to encourage me."

"Oh," Esther said feigning hurt. "And I thought it was because of my pancakes."

"That too," Amanda said laughing. She looked at her watch and got up. "Your boyfriend and his sister will be closing from school soon and I still have one or two things to do before getting them."

"Wait." Esther got up quickly and went to the kitchen. She returned with a bunch of bananas. "This is for my two most favorite three-footers."

Amanda sighed.

"Will you take them? After all they are not for you."

"What can I say?"

"How about 'thank you'? And then I'll say 'you're welcome.'"

Amanda smiled and collected the bunch of bananas. "Thank you," she said.

Esther smiled and waved as Amanda walked back to her flat.

Chapter FOURTEEN

THE HOSPITAL GRADUALLY CAME to life as the morning wore on. Lily stood at the window of Shade's ward watching smartly dressed nurses walk purposefully around and attendants push overloaded trolleys from one place to the other. A few cars had been parked at the car park between the buildings. As she watched people generally mill about the grounds she couldn't help comparing the hum of activities to the stillness of the night before. It was almost like a different place. And she was in a different place. A few hours ago, she was held captive at Melody's house and now she was free. Melody would be looking for her, which was for sure. But she would never find her, even though she hadn't thought of where she would hide when Shade was discharged from the hospital. And Lillie was taking so long. She'd been gone for hours. She tried hard not to worry. She hoped she was fine.

"You ran away?" Shade's weak, croaky voice brought Lily back from her thoughts.

"Shade!" she screamed as she rushed to her bed side. "You're awake!" She put her arms around her and held on to her. "I have never been so worried in my life." She got up and looked into Shade's smiling face. "You're all right, thank God."

"I'm still here," Shade said. "And is it the cotton wool in my head or did I hear you say you ran away from Melody's house?"

"I did," she replied. "Last night. You must have heard me telling my mother on the phone."

"Good for you. How did you do it?" Shade asked.

"Plenty of time to give you the details but what happened is that when Lillian called me last night and told me you were at the hospital I wanted to come with her to see you," Lily said.

"Really?" Shade turned her head slowly as if it was twice its size. "Where is Lillie?"

"She went to your place to get some things for you, and she should be back any time soon." Lily didn't want Shade to know how anxious she was.

"No one has ever escaped from Melody's fortress before," Shade said. "She must be crazy by now."

"I can imagine," Lily said.

"Lily." Shade tried to sit up but she put a hand over her eyes and lay back again. "You really need to lie low. Listen, you can't even stay in Lagos. Melody is mean. She doesn't have a heart."

"Don't worry, Shade," Lily said. "I'm not planning to walk up and down the streets."

"You can't even ride in a car. She has eyes everywhere. If she wants to find a person she usually does. Except if you leave town."

"Well, she won't find me."

"Of course you know I'm not trying to scare you or anything. You can't even stay in this hospital for long. It's a public place and..."

"We'll go to a safe place as soon as you're discharged." Lily patted Shade's arm. "And you need to stop worrying. You look tired and you sound so weak."

A loud thud drew their attention to the door.

"Lillie!" Lily cried. "What happened to you?"

"Shade." Lillian climbed over the bag she had just dropped and ran in. "Thank God. You scared us last night."

Shade rubbed her eyes. "I was scared myself. It's all like a bad dream."

"How are you?" Lillian held Shade's hand with both of hers.

"I'm fine, I think." She sounded tired.

"And see Lily here," Lillian said. "She scaled Melody's wall last night."

"So I see," Shade said. "But like I told her she should be leaving Lagos immediately."

"Lillie," Lily said quickly. "Why did you take so long? I was beginning to worry."

"I just bumped into Melody, that's all."

"Where?" Lily asked puzzled.

"At the flat. She came looking for you, Lily," Lillian said. "I'd just locked up and was about to leave when she arrived with her thugs. They made me open the door so they could search the flat. Then she gave me a message for you, Shade."

"Me?"

"If you know where Lily is you'd better tell her or else."

"Or else what?" Shade grimaced.

"This Lagos will not be big enough for the two of you. Her words exactly."

"Shameless," Shade hissed.

"So when they left I got on my way," Lillian continued. "I actually thought they had left."

"They hadn't?" Lily asked.

Lillian shook her head and grunted. "And I would have led them right to you." Then she turned to Shade. "Shade, you know that barbing salon along Access Road with the broken down truck in front of it?"

"*Masculino*."

Lillian nodded. "That's where their car was parked, partly concealed by that old truck," she said. "And I would never have known but for the collar of the one in the passenger seat."

"What about his collar?"

"His shirt was black but the collar was white. In that brief moment I saw him on the road something tugged at my memory," she said. "One of Melody's men was wearing something like that and it had stuck in my memory. I don't know why. I don't even know what the guy looks like, if he is fair or dark in complexion. It was just that white collar on a black shirt. And I eventually told myself it had to be too much of a coincidence."

"So what did you do?"

She smiled and raised her eyebrows. "It was adventure time," she said. "You see, Melody had asked me where I was going with the bag. And I had told her that I was traveling to the village to see my sick father. So off I went to Jibowu to hang around East-bound luxurious buses."

"You don't mean it," Lily said. "But were you really followed?"

"Oh, yes!" Lillian nodded emphatically. "When we got to Jibowu Roundabout, I looked back and guess who I saw," she said looking from Shade to Lily. "It was Mr. 'white collar' himself in a car not too far behind."

"I would have been so scared," Lily said forming fists with her hands and holding them together.

"I was terrified," Lillian admitted. "I went straight into the bus park that was off the road and thankfully it was crowded. I found a taxi inside that had just dropped an old woman. I had to lie on the back seat. I didn't sit up until we were on Third Mainland Bridge and the driver had assured me that we were not being followed."

"I wonder what the driver was thinking," Lily said.

"He didn't need to think anything," Lillian said. "You gave me enough money to numb him. And I also hid in the gate house of the hospital for thirty minutes."

"Why?"

"To be completely sure no one followed me."

"I told you," Shade said. "Melody is a witch."

Lillian turned to Lily. "Have you called your mother at all?"

"She called," Lily replied.

Just then a doctor and two nurses appeared in the doorway. Lillian got up quickly to remove the bag she had dropped in the way.

"Morning, ladies," the doctor said.

"Good morning," they all responded.

"And how is our patient this morning?" he asked Shade as he walked to the bed. Then he turned to Lillian and Lily. "Could you please wait outside?"

They both nodded and walked out.

Outside Lily sat on a bench while Lillian leaned on the wall beside her.

"I've been wondering what would happen when Shade is discharged," Lillian said. "I don't want her to return to Melody's."

"She shouldn't, honestly," Lily said. "I hope she doesn't. We can take care of her."

"We?"

Lily looked up puzzled.

"I will take care of her," Lillian said. "You will be on your way to Port Harcourt first thing tomorrow morning."

Lily frowned. "What do you mean?" she asked. "You're joking, right?"

"You can't stay in Lagos, Lily." Lillian sat down beside her. "It's not wise. This morning's incident has shown me that we are dealing with a nut case. Besides, I feel responsible for what happened to Shade. It's my fault she's in this condition. I shouldn't have to involve you…"

"How is it your fault?" Lily looked at her quizzically.

"I'm the one who told her to tell the man about herself before he found out through other means. I was thinking… maybe I wasn't thinking. Maybe I should have left things the way they were. She was so happy…"

"Will you stop that? It was the right thing to do."

"I'm not so sure, Lily. She tried to kill herself because of what I told her to do. What if…?"

"Lillian, shut up." Lily looked at her sternly. "What if he found out later from someone else and we are not here to help her. What then? Please stop blaming yourself."

"I hope she doesn't blame me."

"Does she look like she does?"

"No, but…"

"I think you should forget about it. And I'm not leaving. At least not now."

"Why not?"

"I just can't leave like that." Then she turned to Lillian. "Could you?"

"No."

"Shade is my friend," Lily explained. "She was the only friend I had before you came. All the other girls hated me. I don't know how many times she defended me. She…she means a lot to me. And besides the two of us who does she have?"

Lillian was silent.

"Do you really want me to go?" Lily asked quietly.

"No! I don't," Lillian replied. "I don't want you to leave but I want you to be safe." She stood up. "Oh, I wish Melody would just disappear."

"In a puff of smoke," Lily said sadly.

Lillian was lost in thought for a while. "But where will you stay?" she asked finally.

"Somewhere safe."

"Yes. But where?"

"I've been thinking about a certain luxurious flat safely tucked away..."

"You don't mean...?"

"Victoria Island," Lily whispered.

"You really mean it, don't you?"

"We still have three weeks or so before Alhaji returns from his trip," Lily said.

"Three weeks." Lillian nodded. "Long enough."

"As soon as Shade is discharged we can all go there," Lily said. "I'm sure before the end of three weeks we would have left the place."

The doctor and nurses soon came out and Lily and Lillian returned to Shade's bedside. She was propped up against two pillows.

"The doctor said I can go home this evening," Shade announced as soon as she saw them. "He said someone will be coming to talk to me later in the day."

"You mean the counselor?" Lillian asked.

"Or something, yes," Shade replied. "I really don't think it is necessary though."

"Still listen to what he has to say," she said. "It's probably paid for anyway."

"I will, I will," Shade said. "Didn't say I won't."

"I'm hungry," Lily said.

"I am thirsty," Shade said.

"And neither of you has brushed her teeth this morning," Lillian said. "But Shade, are you allowed to eat with that tube still in your hand?"

"It won't obstruct the food from going down to my stomach," Shade replied.

"No. I mean…" Lillian began.

"I was just joking," Shade said. "Of course I'm allowed to eat."

"So what are we going to eat?" Lily asked.

"I brought the leftover from my birthday party last night," Lillian replied.

"Yesterday was your birthday?" Lily asked.

"Turned eighteen," Lillian replied gleefully.

"I'm sorry," Shade said remorsefully. "I'm sorry about everything. I was so…so…I didn't…" She burst into tears.

"It's ok," Lillian said trying to calm her down.

"We just want you to get better," Lily said.

"Besides we can celebrate my birthday when it is more convenient." Lillian put her hand on Shade's cheek. "Guess what?" She waited for her to look up. "We've been invited to a luxury flat in V.I. to recover from all we have been through."

"Very funny," Shade said in a tearful voice after blowing her nose into the tissue Lily handed her.

"But it's true," Lillian said. "Isn't it Lily?"

Lily just smiled.

"It's the flat Alhaji gave Lily," Lillian explained.

"Is that true?" Shade turned to Lily. "He gave you a flat?"

Lily nodded.

"That's very serious," Shade said. "Now you have another reason to be as far away from Lagos as possible. Girl, you're most wanted."

Lily and Lillian laughed.

"So tonight." Lillian tried to sound sinister. "Under the cover of darkness we escape to Lily's flat." Then she changed her tone. "But for now I have three toothbrushes and a large tube of toothpaste in the bag."

"And we can finally get down to the party leftovers," Lily said.

"How come no one is talking about a bath?" Shade asked.

"One step at a time," Lily said.

"Besides you're probably the only one allowed to take a bath here," Lillian said.

"And it isn't going to happen." Shade folded her arms across her chest. "Nothing is going to make me take a bath here."

"Then we shall all stink through the day," Lillian said.

"Stink?" Shade sniffed her blouse and smiled. "You're on your own. I can still meet the president."

"What about you, Lily?" Lillian turned to her. "Do you think you can pass through a group of people without turning heads? And I don't mean your fine face."

"Ha!" Lily laughed.

Lillian brought out a toilet bag from the hold all and they both helped Shade up. Then she put some toothpaste on a brush and handed it to her. "Hang on," she said and she brought out a bottle of water, a small towel and a bowl. Lily and Shade burst into laughter.

"What?" Lillian seemed at a loss.

"I'm surprised you didn't bring the bathroom sink," Shade said.

Lillian glared at her in mock anger. "Brush your teeth or I'll brush them for you."

After Shade was through Lillian helped her tidy up and then went with Lily to look for a place they could brush their teeth. Shade's phone was ringing when they returned.

"Melody," she announced. "I'd just switched on both phones when one began to ring. I let it ring until it stopped and now it's ringing again.

Lillian and Lily looked at each other and then at Shade.

"Are you going to answer it?" Lily asked.

"Wait, wait, everyone wait!" Lillian rushed forward. "I think you should know exactly what you're going to say before you answer so you wouldn't say anything that would make her suspicious."

"Lillie, she's already suspicious," Shade said.

"Well, then, so she wouldn't be sure of her suspicions."

The phone stopped ringing.

"Ok, she will call back." Lillian looked a bit nervous.

Almost immediately the phone rang again.

"Hello," Shade answered it. "The phones were off," she said after a moment. She listened to Melody for a while. "No I haven't been to the office…I'm not feeling too fine." Then she looked at Lillian. "She's right. I haven't been home since yesterday morning." A pause. "I *dey* with client." Another pause. "Lily? But she lives with you." Then she smiled and winked at Lily. "She what? But how did she get past the…? Are you sure she's not with her Alhaji? Have you checked with him?" Suddenly she held the phone away from her ear and grimaced. Moments later she returned it to her ear. "I swear," she said. "I don't know anything about it." Then her tone became harsh. "*How I wan take know now? We sail together? Wetin I wan carry her escape do sef? She dey dash me money?*"

Lily glanced at Lillian. She still found it a bit disturbing to hear Shade speak crudely like the other restaurant girls. She and Lillian waited as the conversation with Melody went on a little longer.

"I *don* hear you," Shade said finally and hung up. She tossed the phone on the bed and hissed. She looked like she had been drained of the little energy she had.

"Are you all right?" Lily asked her.

"I'm fine," she replied. "It's just that sometimes that woman annoys me so much I want to do something to her. And she wants to see me."

"Today?" Lillian asked.

"She said whenever I can," Shade answered. "And that means 'whenever I can'." She waved her hand. "Please forget Melody. She's the worst thing that can happen to anyone." She lay back on the pillows. "So where is that party food?"

The day wore on and the counselor came to speak with Shade. Lillian and Lily decided to walk around the premises. It gave them the opportunity to discuss how they could help her. They talked about what they could do to help her get over her ordeal. They also thought of trying to talk her out of going back to work at Melody's restaurant.

"Shade is very brilliant," Lily said. "Maybe we can convince her to take some of those professional exams she talks about."

"Studying would definitely keep her occupied," Lillian said. "You know, she has not been with anyone else since she met this Fred. It was like she had found a reason at last to stop prost…going out with men. She actually gave it up."

"Maybe she won't go back," Lily said. "Maybe…"

Lily's phone began to ring and she looked at it.

"My mum," she said.

It felt good to hear Lily's voice again.

"How have you been holding out?" Amanda asked.

"I'm ok, Mummy. And Shade is fine now. We are likely to leave the hospital tonight."

Amanda paused. "Where will you go?" she asked finally.

"There's…a safe place we can go."

"Where is that?"

"It's the flat the man I was…It's the flat Alhaji gave me." Lily was still ashamed to talk about Alhaji to her mother.

Amanda was silent again.

"Mummy?"

"How safe do you think it is?"

"Melody doesn't know about it and Alhaji is out of the country. I guess we'll be safe there for a while."

Amanda felt uneasy. In fact she still felt tense about Lily being in Lagos.

"How long do you intend to stay there for?"

"Just long enough for Shade to recover fully. Maybe two weeks or so."

Amanda was alarmed. "Two weeks? You can't be in Lagos for that long. What are you thinking? Melody has…"

"I will be safe."

"I'm coming to Lagos. Give me the address."

"Mummy…"

"The address, Lily."

Lily dictated the address and Amanda wrote it down.

"I can't leave right away. Shade…"

"May I come and see you at least?"

"Of course you can. I'm sorry. When are you coming? I really want to see you."

"Hearing that makes me so happy. I'll let you know. I'll call you, ok?"

"Ok."

"I'm praying for you Lily."

"Then why do you worry so much?"

"I…I…" Amanda was taken by surprise. Indeed why did she worry so much when she said she trusted the Lord? "You're right, Lily. I'll stop. And I'll always remember you asked me that any time I find myself worrying again. God will keep you. You mean the world to me."

Tears quickly filled Lily's eyes. "I love you."

"I love you too. Bye."

Chapter FIFTEEN

AMANDA LOOKED AT THE address Lily had dictated to her. It seemed like one of those newly developed areas in Lagos. Even though she had never been to that part of Lagos she was sure she could find it. And Lily was right. She would stop worrying. She had been praying to God to keep her daughter safe and yet she had remained fearful. God was dependable. She had asked Him to keep Lily and she would trust him to do it. She picked up the desk calendar to see when Sheyi would be traveling. He was in the Internal Audit Department of the company he worked for and was sometimes required to visit some of its branches especially those in and around Benin to supervise the auditing of their accounts. Usually he was away for only a couple of days but this time he had announced that he would be gone for a whole week. It was a blessing.

"Dear Lord," she prayed. "I know you can see the way out of all this, and so I'm going to trust you to lead me to it. You know my plans, the ones I'm sure of and the ones I'm still not clear about…" She looked at her two younger children as they sat on the rug watching one of their favorite cartoons on the television. "Don't let me do the wrong thing. You know that I want the best for them. So lead me and show me what to do every step of the way, in Jesus name, amen."

She had been given an appointment at the state secretariat for the next day. The sooner they gave her what she wanted the quicker she could move on to the next phase. Her colleague, Amina, who had also stayed back in Benin after their youth service had confirmed when she paid her a visit that she had obtained for her the document she required. Now it was only a matter of time.

She brought her thoughts back to Lily. In a few days she would see her again. She loved that girl so much her heart ached. Why had it taken her so long to realize how important she was to her? She just couldn't imagine how she could have allowed herself to miss out on her childhood. Lily was special and she could see it. She still felt some pain in her heart when she thought of what the girl had been through, what *she* had put her through. She couldn't change the past and she could not erase the pain she had caused, she knew, but she had made up her mind to do her best to ensure that Lily had a great future. She trusted God to help her.

Like so many nights before, Amanda was asleep before Sheyi got back. She hadn't been asleep for up to an hour when she was awakened by a sound. Suddenly she became aware of Sheyi's face looming over hers in the darkness, and then a strong offensive smell that filled her nostrils and almost choked her. Sudden fear made her try to get up but she couldn't. He was sitting with his thigh pushing against her and he had dug his fist into the bed on the other side. She was trapped.

"Sleeping beauty." He hiccoughed and belched directly into her face. She turned away, unable to bear the foul stench. He kissed her cheek and she struggled to get away.

She prayed silently but desperately that she would be able to get out of his hold. He was terribly drunk and was indescribable when he was like this. Why didn't she sleep with the children tonight as she had been doing for a while now?

"You think you can get away from me?" he asked menacingly. "I have you where I want you. You cannot escape." He grinned and Amanda panicked trying not to think of what he had in mind. It had been some time since he had been drunk like this but the memories were enough to make Amanda struggle the more. This only made him laugh and stroke her cheek.

"Look, Sheyi…" Amanda tried to see if she could get through to him while she continued to pray in her heart.

"Your mother can no longer save you," he muttered as if he hadn't heard her at all. "We have you where we want you and you cannot…" He hiccoughed again and seemed to find it difficult to continue.

Amanda was really scared now. What was he talking about and whom did he mean by 'we'? And what did her mother have to do with saving her from 'them'? It was difficult to think because she felt suffocated. She just needed to get away from him.

Sheyi found his voice again. "No woman, I say, no woman can ever rise above an Ibajeojo. I am an Ibajeojo," he said beating his chest with his hand for emphasis. "And no woman of mine can resist my command, so don't even try. See," he held up his fist, "your mind is here, I make sure of that every year and here shall it remain."

Amanda wasn't sure she was hearing right. Consumed with a desperate need to get away she raised both hands and pushed against him with all her might. She managed to get his fist off the bed and was able to roll quickly to the other side of the bed and get off.

"What do you mean by that?" She stood facing him, her heart beating wildly. "Whose mind?"

Sheyi threw his head back and laughed insanely. "Look at you," he said pointing to no one in particular. "You cannot fight it. Your mother…" he belched. "She is no longer in the way…"

Did he know what he was saying? Amanda didn't think so. He was really drunk. He got off the bed and stumbled forward trying to focus but found it difficult.

"You…you belong to…to me," he said waving his finger and then placing his palm on his chest. Then his head fell forward. He took a few sluggish steps towards her but Amanda had heard enough. She rushed past him and stood by the door.

He held out his arm to stop her but failed so he turned around looking for her. "Where are you? Where are you?" He raised his voice. "They have…they have…given you…given me you…given you to me," he slurred. He turned again and stumbled. This time he lost his footing and fell half across the bed. He tried to get up but couldn't. He raised his head. "Where…where is she?" He laid down his head again slowly and stirred a little. Then he stopped moving.

Amanda stared at his form on the bed and shook her head in disbelief. It was difficult to accept what she thought she had just heard. How could Sheyi have been telling the truth? How could he be so devious? How could anyone concoct such things in their mind? All those trips to Idipe, all those sacrifices, all those drinks, baths and seemingly harmless acts had all been against her. Her mother had been right all along. Angry tears filled her eyes as she remembered how she had refused to listen to her. Even though she had thought those things were rather crude and unnecessary she had allowed herself to be led into them. She had been unable to resist because of her desire to be a part of the family. Besides she'd wanted to impress them. She had even defended the practices.

She looked away from this man she had lived with for almost six years but hardly knew and quietly closed the door. She felt like a fool. How could she have ended up with a monster like him? He was capable of anything, anything at all.

At the earlier stage of their relationship she had objected to some of the things she was required to do. Sheyi had told her very little before they traveled to his village for the Christmas holidays the year after they met. All he said was that his family was a prestigious and respectable one and that what set it apart was its strict adherence to their unique family practices. It wasn't until the rituals began that he started telling her what was expected of her. She had walked out on him that morning in anger after telling him she could never be involved in such things. He'd run after her begging and of course lied that they were harmless practices that had been carried out for generations and were just for protection against his family's enemies. He'd said they were also for peace, stability, prosperity and fruitfulness. And since she was going to become a part of his family she was required to take part.

She had kept those things from her mother and everyone else. The truth was that she was ashamed that she took part in them at all. But somehow her mother had found out and warned her about them.

She went into the children's room and locked the door even though she knew Sheyi would not get up till morning. She lay quietly beside Ola, drained. She closed her eyes even though she knew sleep would not come easily. It was almost daybreak before she began to doze. She had spent the whole night praying to God to show her what to do concerning Sheyi.

"Mummy, I want to pee and I can't open the door."

Amanda stirred as Ola's voice woke her. "Oh Sweetie," she said, getting up. "Come on."

Sheyi had already left for work when she got out of the children's room. She wondered how she would relate to him now that she knew all that she did. The shocking discovery that he could be getting paid for getting Lily in Melody's clutches was difficult enough to deal with. Now coupled with the revelation of the night before, she didn't know if she could stay under the same roof with him.

Later as she sat at the dining table she tried to reconcile what she had heard with what her life had been like since she got involved with Sheyi. She had never been able to resist him in any way or stand her ground or question him about anything. She had always done whatever he told her, even when she didn't want to and she had always defended him whenever her mother raised any issue concerning him. She had thought she was protecting her relationship or that she was weak-willed, but never in her wildest imagination had it occurred to her that she was under any form of influence.

But she *had* been resisting him for a while now. And she was sure it was because she had renewed her relationship with God. He was the only one that could protect her; and yet she had ignored Him all those years.

Gradually it began to dawn on her what Sheyi meant when he said her mother was no longer in the way. Her mother never stopped praying for her and that had apparently been a hindrance one way or the other. She was scared to think what could have happened to her had her mother not been praying. This was too much. She had to see Esther.

"Who wants to go and say hello to Aunty Esther?"

"Me!"

"Me too!"

"That's settled then," she said. "Let's clean up and go."

It was Timothy that opened the door when she knocked half an hour later and she was surprised to see him at home at that time.

"No work today?" She asked him.

"No school today?" And they both laughed.

He bent and held Akin and Ola by the hand. "So are they on holidays or did you just give yourself one today?" He asked as he let them in.

"No holiday," Amanda replied. "We just didn't go."

Amanda took a seat while he went with the children to fetch Esther. They returned a few moments later with Ola struggling with a briefcase and Akin having a jacket draped over his outstretched arms.

"They insisted," he said quickly.

Amanda laughed. "And to think these two would never lift a finger at home."

"This is Uncle Timothy," he said. "There's that special something…" He let his voice trail off.

"You can keep them," Amanda sighed. "I could do with a break."

"You look weary."

"I am weary."

"Is everything all right?" Timothy looked at her closely. "All I can tell you, Amanda, is that God is at work on your behalf."

"I know," Amanda said. "I guess that's why I can…"

"What are you guys doing here at this time?" Esther asked the children as she walked into the sitting room. "Shouldn't you be at school?" She turned to Amanda. "Mummy?"

"No school today."

"Holiday?"

"No. Sheyi."

"Oh," Esther said blinking. "Oh, well then, how are you?"

"I'm all right.

"Of course you are. God is working out something great for you."

"Exactly what Timothy just reminded me," Amanda said. "And I was just trying to tell him that my strength comes from that knowledge."

"That's good to know." Timothy smiled and then turned to Akin and Ola. "Uncle Timothy has to go to work now."

"That's if Uncle Timothy still has a job," Esther said with a funny look on her face. "You're two hours late."

"What happened today?" Amanda asked.

"Esther let me oversleep. And that is what I am going to tell my boss."

"I let you oversleep? Weren't you ill when you got back from your 'over' overtime late last night and you needed a good night's sleep?"

"And you have also refused to give me my sandwiches."

"Your sandwiches were ready before you finished dressing up."

"Where are they?" He spun round. "I don't see them"

"Here." Esther got the package from the dining table and handed it to him.

"Why, thank you very much, my lady." He collected it and bowed with a flourish.

Timothy left and the two women settled on the sofa.

"I got the shock of my life last night." Amanda didn't waste any time.

"What happened? What is it this time?"

"It's a long story, Esther."

Esther whistled when Amanda was through. "Now I've heard everything. But why do they need to do so many fetish things?"

"Who knows?" Amanda shrugged. "Though with a name like theirs they probably need all the help they can get."

"What's with their name?" Esther couldn't help chuckling.

"I learnt it means that their creator should have made their own destiny like that of others that succeed."

"Meaning that they accept that they are failures? What kind of a name is that?"

Amanda shook her head. "I never told anyone about those things," she said. "I was ashamed to say that I took a bath with that stinky black soap every time we went to see his mother. And then I had to drink some…drink." She shuddered and stuck out her tongue as if she could still taste the repugnant liquid in her mouth. "They really had me, Esther. I even broke calabashes. Only God knows what I was really supposed to be breaking."

"Or what would have happened to you if your mother's prayers had not been covering you."

"Esther." Amanda put her two hands on Esther's shoulders. "He actually admitted that my mother was in the way. In the way of what?"

"Who knows?" Esther shrugged. "But you know what? You're the one in the way now."

"That's true." Amanda removed her hands from Esther's shoulders and interlaced her fingers. "Plus you and Timothy."

"And he feels threatened," Esther said. "He knows their manipulation is no longer working and he is afraid he has lost that control. And so long as God is on the throne he will never have control over you again."

"Amen."

"And did he involve the children in these practices?"

"Yes! Ola almost died when she was a baby."

"No way!"

"During that period we were staying with his mother she gave Ola a potion when I was out. By the time I returned it was like she wasn't the same baby I'd just left. Her tummy was running and she was throwing up almost every minute. She was reduced to skin and bones in less than a week. Esther, she was dying in my arms. How she survived is still beyond me."

"And you still didn't run for your life."

"And I still didn't run." Amanda sounded like she pitied herself. "Instead I lied to my mother that it was dirty water."

Esther shook her head. "God was on your case even when you were not aware."

"In fact I'm mesmerized sometimes. And I have the future to look forward to."

"Which reminds me. What time is your appointment today?" Esther asked.

"They said any time from 9am."

"Well, you can leave the children here."

"Thanks." Amanda held her friend's hand in appreciation. Even though Esther was always there for her she never took her acts of love for granted and she couldn't stop hoping that someday she would be able to really thank her.

"By the way would you be able to attend a meeting in church next week?" Esther asked. "It's actually running for three days but you could try to attend at least once."

"I could." Esther nodded.

"You'll be glad."

For the next few days Sheyi was his usual self. He seemed to be unaware of what had happened that night. Amanda decided to keep out of his way as usual and pretend that everything was just the same.

Finally the day came for him to travel, the day Amanda had been waiting for.

"I'll be back in a week," he said as he headed towards the door. "I want you to get the children ready. As soon as I get back we are going to Idipe to visit my mother."

The moment he shut the door behind him Amanda went for her phone.

"It's Amanda," she said as soon as Henry picked up.

"Hey Amanda. What's up?"

"Henry, I am ready."

Chapter SIXTEEN

"WHY DID GOD ASK them to go that way?" The minister asked. "What kind of God would do so much to get His people out of captivity only to put them face to face with an ocean and no ship?" He searched the faces of the people looking up at him. "I'd like to ask you a question. Did God know there was a Red Sea there before He asked them to take that route?" He nodded as he acknowledged the response of the people. "By the way who put the Red Sea there?" Again he nodded as the people echoed the universal answer. "But God has promised to take me to the other side," he continued. "Why am I facing this challenge? Why can't I have smooth sailing? Why can't this road just be a highway with no traffic and no speed limit?" He looked around and smiled. "My sister, has it occurred to you that you are no longer where you were when you first cried out to Him? Have you noticed that God has already miraculously put you on the journey to your desired destination?" He paused. "Then why don't you trust Him to take you all the way in spite of what you see?" He looked down at the Bible in his hand. "And when they cried to Him He told Moses to tell them to go forward." He looked up and frowned. "Go forward? March into the sea and drown?" Suddenly he lifted up his hand and raised his voice. "Oh no! No, My chosen people! I have just showed you what I can do! I have just visited your enemies with plagues! I have just rendered your captors powerless over you! I have just delivered you from four centuries of slavery just like I promised! I am the same God who just did all that and I can do more! Believe that, trust in me and go forward!" He lifted up his arms as the people stood up and cheered. "I will answer the question I asked you earlier," he continued amidst the cheers. "God told them to take that route because He knew that when they got to the Red sea *He would part it!"*

The noise was thunderous and it took a while for the people to settle down and be quiet. Amanda had never felt this jubilant in her life. The preacher went on to tell them that God always fulfilled His promises in spite of what was in the way and that what His people saw as setbacks were nothing to Him. He said that God wanted His people to see like he saw so that they would know that challenges were there to be conquered and not to conquer them because the all-powerful God was with them.

It was the first day of the convention, the only day Amanda could attend and it seemed as if all her questions had been answered already. In addition she had received the courage to face the difficult days ahead. Now she knew why God had made it possible for her to attend. If she didn't know better she would have believed that someone had told the minister about her because it had seemed like he was addressing her personally.

She had planned to leave for Lagos very early in the morning so that she could spend as much time as possible with Lily before returning late in the evening but she had let Esther convince her to spend the night there. She was excited because this trip was going to be different from the previous one. Then she had been afraid of what awaited her, but now she was just a mother going to her beloved daughter. And she had so much to tell her.

The morning Sheyi traveled, she had got on her knees and prayed that his planned trip to Idipe would be cancelled. Since nothing was going to take her to that place again no matter what and she was not ready for a fight, which could upset her plans, it was better if the issue of the trip never came up again. Only God could do that because from previous experiences Sheyi was ready to upset every other thing to favour his visit to his mother. But now after listening to this teaching she was ready to face any Red Sea. Even if it stood in front of her she would not be discouraged because she knew that the One that was with her was able to make a way right through it.

"Sheyi is not my problem anymore," she confessed in the taxi as they returned home from the meeting.

"What?"

"Sheyi is not my problem anymore," she repeated. "He's God's. And nothing is a problem to God."

"I'm glad to hear you say that," Esther said smiling.

"I'm glad to hear *me* say that," Amanda said.

"But that was a really powerful message by the minister," Esther said.

"It was also really encouraging. I don't think anyone that was present there tonight would disagree."

"It's always like that when Pastor Owen ministers. It's like God just tells him what people need to hear. You leave with the knowledge that things are never going to be the same."

"That's why I wish I could be there tomorrow."

"I'll get the DVDs for you, Esther said. "I have to get them for Timo too."

"Poor Timothy, having to work so late every day."

"That's what you get for being a honest and hardworking project manager at *NLDEngineering*," Esther said. "They use you."

"But they do compensate him for the extra hours."

"Hmmm…yes, but not the company."

"What do you mean?"

"His boss personally compensates him."

"You mean he pays him from his own pocket?"

"Yes. He knows how valuable Timo is to him, to the department, and he doesn't want to lose him. A few of Timo's colleagues have left because they felt the company was cheating them and he doesn't want the same thing to happen with Timo."

"But that company makes a lot of money."

"More than a lot."

Half an hour later Amanda lay on her bed thinking about what the minister had said. So if God has made you a promise even if it is something you read in the bible then you should just trust Him and know that he will fulfill it no matter what you face. She could believe that. In fact it was a relief. Let God worry about how to do the impossible. After all that is why He is God. Knowledge truly was power.

Esther showed up early the following morning to get the children and before 7am Amanda was already at the taxi park. There hadn't been enough time to do much else besides getting herself and the children ready and so she needed to get herself a snack at a nearby kiosk while they waited for more passengers to fill up the taxi. She didn't usually eat this early but she felt hungry.

"Amanda!" She heard someone call out as she walked towards the kiosk. "Amanda Parker!"

She turned to see a lady walking quickly towards her. Amanda wasn't sure she recognized her but the lady seemed to know her very well judging by the wide smile on her face.

"Amanda. Is it really you?"

Amanda smiled politely still having no any idea who the lady was.

"Hello," Amanda smiled back.

"It's Emmanuella," the lady exclaimed. "Federal Government Girls' College, Abuloma. I used to sit behind you in class."

Amanda cocked her head. She remembered Emmanuella from her science class and therefore for a few moments she tried to link the slim Emmanuella who won all the beauty contests in school to this plump lady standing in front of her.

"Emmanuella?"

"Of course, I have put on a little weight." She spread her arms. "But…it's me!"

"It *is* you." Amanda was certain now. The body may be nothing like it used to be but the face was definitely the same. And those dimples… Amanda didn't know why she hadn't recognized her immediately. "How are you? Quite an age."

They hugged.

"I'm fine," she replied boisterously. "How are *you*? You just disappeared from school and no one ever heard from you again. What happened?"

Amanda shrugged. "Issues."

"Just issues?"

Amanda shrugged again.

"Anyway that's such a long time ago," Emmanuella said, waving her hand. "So what have you been up to?"

"Well…" Amanda didn't know where to go from there.

"Married? Children? How many?"

"Three."

"No way! You look great," she said eyeing Amanda's slim, shapely figure in a fitted skirt suit. "Anyway you were always the 'belle'."

"I'm not the one who won all the beauty contests."

"That's because you never entered for them. And gosh, look at your hair." She reached out and touched Amanda's luscious long ponytail. "It's longer than ever."

Amanda smiled at her. She was used to people admiring her hair. But Emmanuella just amused her. "So do you live in Benin City or are you just visiting?"

"Work," Emmanuella replied. "One of our clients wants to open a major branch close to the university and my boss wants me to..." Suddenly she brightened up. "Speaking of my boss, you remember Robert, don't you?"

Amanda involuntarily sucked in breath. "Who?"

"Of course you remember him." She poked Amanda's shoulder. "Robert, Robert your boyfriend. He used to come to the school to visit you. You ought to remember him. Gosh Amanda. You really are the 'happening' girl. You mean you don't remember Robert?"

"Robert...yes...yes I remember him," Amanda said feeling really weird and hoping her effort to look composed was good enough.

"Well, he happens to be my boss," Emmanuella said. "He left his company to set up an advertising outfit, *Robsight*. Maybe you've heard of it..." When Amanda shook her head she continued. "Anyway he employed me when I was desperately in need of a job."

"I see." Amanda didn't know what else to say.

"So where are you traveling to?"

"Lagos."

"You live in Lagos?"

"No. I just have some things to do there." Amanda needed to get away.

"I hope you'll be staying for a while. It would be nice for you to drop in at the office." She reached into her bag and brought out a card. "Here's my card. I bet Robert will be glad to see you."

Amanda reached out and collected the card from her. "Thanks."

"So?"

"I beg your pardon?" Amanda was at a loss.

"Will you come by our office? It's very easy to locate."

"Oh…oh no…I'm sorry." Amanda replied. "I won't be in Lagos for that long."

"That's a pity. It would really be nice to catch up on old times."

Amanda wasn't so sure about that. "Yes. Well, thanks anyway. It seems like my taxi is full. It's really good to see you again."

"Good to see you too. Call me."

Amanda was no longer hungry as she returned to her taxi. An hour after the taxi left the park she was still taking deep breaths. Of course she had thought of the possibility of seeing Robert again. She just hadn't thought of how she would handle it. And she didn't think she could ever be prepared for it. Robert was Lily's father and he didn't even know she existed. Now she knew where to find him if she wanted. Could she keep this from Lily and let things remain the way they were? What if Lily wanted to meet him? What if Lily found out later that she had kept this from her?

They were in Lagos before Amanda realized it. She had been so occupied with her thoughts that the journey seemed to have taken half the time. Still she hadn't been able to sort out her thoughts or decide what to do. Things had taken a new turn so quickly she found herself becoming worried again. One moment she was Lily's parent and the only one responsible for making decisions regarding her future and the next another person was involved and everything might have to change. It didn't seem fair. This definitely seemed like more than she could handle. Though she desperately needed some encouragement she made up her mind not to be swayed. She would get back to these thoughts later. Right now she needed to concentrate on finding her way to where Lily was.

She took a bus to the Marina as she was instructed and waited for another one to Victoria Island. Her phone rang and she grimaced as she saw the name Fubara Jack, her mother's lawyer.

"Hello, Mr. Jack," she said.

"Hello Madam."

"I'm sorry I haven't called you. I've been so busy."

"It's ok. I was wondering if you…." The rest of the sentence was barely audible and Amanda couldn't make out what he was saying. There was so much noise around her.

"Hello…Mr. Jack?"

"Yes, Madam."

"Can I call you back? I'm in a very noisy place and I can barely hear myself."

"Ok Madam, I'll be expecting your call."

"All right then. Bye."

Amanda switched off her phone and tucked it deep inside her bag. She knew if she wasn't careful it could be stolen before she even left the bus stop. She had been putting off meeting with the lawyer concerning her mother's estate for some time now and she didn't know why. She wished Henry or Melissa were in the country. Sooner or later she would have to deal with it. Her bus arrived and she got on it. Since this was going to be a much shorter ride than the one from the mainland she quickly went over the directions again. Timothy had told her about three landmarks she needed to look out for. He had promised her that with his directions she couldn't get lost. She hoped he was right.

The marble building was where he had said it would be. She got off at the bus stop a few yards from it and waited for a taxi. He had said that a taxi from this point wouldn't cost too much, but if it did then she could still take another bus to the second roundabout. What the driver asked for wasn't too much for her so she took the taxi. It turned out that he knew the place and Amanda was relieved.

Amanda called Lily as soon as the taxi drove into the avenue.

"I'm very close to the house now," she said.

"I'll get the security man to open the gate," an excited Lily said.

As Amanda walked towards the gate it opened and a bare footed Lily ran out and threw her arms around her neck. And for that moment all the difficulties Amanda faced didn't matter.

Chapter SEVENTEEN

"THIS IS SHADE," LILY said as soon as Amanda walked in. Shade walked up to her and Amanda hugged her.

"Hello Shade. Heard you were ill. I hope you're better now."

"I am. Thank you."

"And this is Lillie."

Lillian also came forward and Amanda hugged her too.

"I've heard quite a bit about you, Lillie," Amanda said. "But don't worry. They are good things."

"I'm glad," Lillian said giving Lily a sideways glance.

"This is my mother," she addressed Shade and Lillie.

After the exchange of pleasantries Amanda sat and Lily got her a cold drink.

"Have you had anything to eat at all?" Lily asked sitting beside her.

"No, but this drink will do for now, thank you Lily."

Amanda turned to Shade. "I'm glad to see you're well now."

“I have no choice,” Shade said laughing. “These two mother hens have been doting on me for days. I’m fine now, thank you.”

“That’s good.” Amanda said. “So did you all meet at the restaurant?”

“Yes.” And Lily went on to explain how she got to know her friends.

“You look younger than I ever imagined,” Lillian said shyly. “No one would believe that you’re Lily’s mother.”

“I wouldn’t,” Shade agreed. “I would think Lily was your sister who’s just a shade darker than you.”

“Well, I was sixteen when I had her,” Amanda explained. “So how have you all been coping?”

“I love coping in this flat,” Lillian said making everyone laugh. “I could cope in here for a long time.”

“It is nice, I have to agree,” Amanda said.

“You’ve not even seen the rest of it,” Shade said. “It’s luxurious.”

“Pity we can only stay a few more days,” Lily said.

“What happens then?” Amanda wanted to know.

The room was silent. Finally Lily turned to her mother. “We haven’t really thought of it.”

“Don’t you think you should?” Amanda asked.

“Actually,” Lillian began and everyone turned to her. “I just imagined that since we can’t be here for long…I mean we have to leave this place soon, Shade and I would return to Anthony Village and Lily would go to Port Harcourt… as planned.” She put her hands together as if it was a settled matter.

“I think it’s a good plan,” Amanda said nodding her consent and smiling at Lillian. “Don’t you, Lily?” She turned to Lily.

"Yes…of course," Lily replied. "I wish Melody would leave me alone."

"It's my fault for bringing you here in the first place," Amanda ruefully said.

"You didn't know. And besides it wasn't your idea."

"No. It was Sheyi's." Amanda felt a little animosity as she remembered what she and Esther had talked about. "Although I let him convince me that his aunt's place was the best for you."

"That's because you had no idea…"

"Which Sheyi are you talking about? Melody's nephew?" Shade asked suddenly. Then she covered her mouth with her hand. "Sorry…I'm so sorry. I didn't mean to barge in."

"Ibajeojo," Amanda replied. "Do you know him?"

"Yes," she replied to the surprise of everyone else in the room.

"You know him?" Lily asked. "How?"

"He used to live with Melody."

"He did?" Lily was surprised. "I didn't know that."

"Yes, he lived with Melody here in Lagos." Amanda said.

"You said your mother's husband was related to Melody but you never said he was her nephew and you never mentioned his name."

"How well do you know him?" Amanda asked.

"He was living at Melody's house while I was there."

"What?" Lillian was shocked. "At that same house?"

"No, not at Allen. We moved to Allen Avenue after Sheyi left. We used to live at Palm Grove." Shade looked at Amanda and shook her head. "So you are the one that Sheyi married."

Amanda spread her hands. "I'm the one."

"You actually know him." Lily was still bemused.

"Very well," Shade said. "I'm not surprised it was his idea that you should come and stay with Melody."

"Why do you say that?" Amanda needed to know.

"Well…he's your husband and I don't…"

"He's all yours, trust me."

"Well then," Shade said. "I have an age-old grudge against men like him. He was a pimp for Melody."

Lillian and Lily gasped. Amanda wasn't surprised though her mouth suddenly tasted bitter.

"Go on," she told Shade.

"He was one of the men that brought girls for Melody and Melody paid him. They thought I was too young to understand then and so they weren't too careful around me. He did everything Melody wanted, everything. And he slept with the girls more than anyone." She saw Amanda wince. "Oh I'm sure you don't have to worry about catching anything. Sheyi is the most careful man I know. He sees his doctor more frequently than he goes to the toilet."

"Shade, I…think you've started talking in the present tense," Lillian said. "Is that on purpose?

"Just what I was about to point out," Lily said.

"Is it not Sheyi Ibajeojo we're talking about?" She looked from Lily to Lillian and then to Amanda who had gone silent. "You said I could…"

"Yes…yes, yes go ahead." She might as well hear the whole thing even though she felt a bit self-conscious now. She needed to know. "When was the last time you saw him?

"That would be…last month."

"No way!" Lillian exclaimed.

"He comes to Lagos every now and then, to pick up his cheque and to…" She paused and looked at Amanda.

"His cheque?" Lily asked. "Does that mean he still brings girls?"

"It's possible. I'm not really sure since he now lives far away," Shade replied, "but I'm guessing he still gets something for those he has brought already. You see, at the restaurant…"

"Ok," Amanda quickly interrupted her not wanting her to continue.

"Like Lily?" Lillian asked before Amanda could change the topic. "He gets paid for Lily?"

Lily looked shocked and Amanda quickly went to sit beside her.

"I'm sorry, Lily. I'm sorry for all these." Amanda soothed. "This didn't occur to me too until a few days ago. I didn't know the kind of person I was with."

"I resented him from the moment I set my eyes on him," Lily remarked bitterly.

"I don't know what to say." Amanda felt weak and very sad. She had wanted this time with Lily to be wonderful.

"Of course you must know he's in town now," Shade said getting everyone's attention.

"Sheyi in Lagos?" Amanda wanted to be sure she had heard right.

"You didn't know? Melody mentioned it the last time she called."

"Why does she call you?" Amanda asked.

"She wants me to come to the restaurant to see her. She knows I'm friendly with Lily. She wants to be sure I have nothing to do with her disappearance."

"And are you going to see her?" Amanda sounded a bit apprehensive.

"I have to, or she'll keep suspecting me," Shade replied. "It bothers her that she doesn't know where I am. I only have to prove to her that I have been with clients and she'll leave me alone."

"When are you going to see her?" Amanda asked.

"Tomorrow," Shade replied.

"And you'll let us know how it went?"

"Of course. Right away. And one has to be really careful. I think Lillie should tell you about her adventure with Melody's men." Shade turned to Lillian and bowed and waved her hand in a flourish as if welcoming her for a performance.

Within minutes Lillian had them all in stitches, even Lily who seemed to have forgotten her pain. She kept them all transfixed as she told her story again, making it even more intriguing than the first time. Amanda leaned back and observed her as the words flowed from her mouth with such ease. She could easily understand why Lily referred to her as her best friend. She seemed to have an amazing ability to ease pain. Amanda didn't know how else to explain it. She liked the girl.

By the time Lillian finished her tale, everyone had lightened up, and one interesting topic led to another. Through lunch they talked and laughed and Amanda felt especially happy that her visit would really be everything she wanted it to be. Lillian was something else.

As their conversations wore on Amanda found out a lot more about Shade and Lillian. Shade's story really touched her and she couldn't help imagining how complicated the journey out of her state of despair would be. But she was sure there was a way out. Now, she couldn't imagine anything God could not do. She felt sorry for Lillian who she thought was trying to be brave but really craved the security of her home and family. Amanda wasn't sure the girl even realized it. She also found out that none of the three girls really knew the Lord. This put such a burden in her heart that she began to pray silently for them. She prayed that she would have a positive influence on them even though the time was so short.

It wasn't until after dinner that she was able to have Lily to herself. Shade had gone to pack and Lillian was cleaning up in the kitchen. They went to the balcony and sat on the chaise longue Lillian had dragged there and sat on every night since they arrived, claiming that the view was worth millions. The flat was on the top floor of the building and they could see a considerable part of the Island all the way to the lagoon.

"This is a beautiful part of Lagos," Amanda remarked.

"It's for the rich and dubious," Lily said. "That's what Shade calls them."

Amanda looked at her and smiled. "They can't all be dubious. Surely some would be honest."

"Alhaji isn't one of them. No one spends honest money like that."

"So he actually gave you this flat."

"And a car and lots of other things. He thinks I would be impressed and agree to marry him and join his…"

"Marry?" Amanda was horrified. "He asked you?"

"Yes, he did. He thought I would be happy; you know… all the money and clothes and…things. He said I could live abroad if I wanted. He said any girl would be happy."

"You're not any girl."

Lily smiled. "That's exactly what I told him. He thinks I am just a poor girl with no one. He just couldn't understand how I can see how rich he is and still say no to him. He thought I would be swept off my feet."

"He doesn't know who raised you." Amanda took Lily's hand. "Mum did a better job than I or anyone could have done."

Lily looked up at her mother. "I loved her very much."

"I loved her too," Amanda said in a voice barely above a whisper. "I know you might find that hard to believe and I don't know how I could ever convince you, but it's true."

Lily's eyes were kind as she put her other hand over her mother's. "You don't have to convince me, I know," Lily said surprising her. "And Mama knew too."

At that moment Amanda tried to recall her relationship with her mother. She was selfish, stubborn and unyielding. She hardly listened to anything her mother said and she knew for sure she didn't show any love. She had felt guilty sometimes and had wondered what Lily thought of her. She didn't visit often and when she did she almost always made things unpleasant. At the very best her time with them had been passable. So how could Lily say she knew she loved her mother or that her mother knew? She struggled to form the questions into words and found it difficult. But Lily seemed to understand.

"Mama talked about you a lot. She said you had the biggest, kindest heart. She said it made people take advantage of you. I remember her saying that you were everyone's friend. You would do anything for them and they could always depend on you. She said you would go out of your way to make others comfortable even if it meant depriving yourself. She said you believed everyone was like you and that made her sad. She used to be afraid that someone would really hurt you one day. She said when you became pregnant with me you were more confused than any other thing at first. Then you found out the hard way what people were really like."

"And I flipped," Amanda said. It had been about sixteen years and she still winced as she remembered. The memory was too painful. She had thought that if she didn't think about it then it wouldn't hurt so badly and so she had managed over the years to push it to the recesses of her mind. She was surprised that her mother had said so much about her to Lily and that Lily had been able to understand even though she was so young.

Right from a young age Amanda had felt that it was her duty to make everyone happy. She had been a friend to anyone who needed her and had been too busy to realize that she didn't really have any of her own.

She took her hand from Lily's and wiped a tear from her cheek. "I was a friend that didn't have any. But I couldn't see it. I was there for them and they came to me when they needed my help. Mama warned me that people would take advantage of me but I couldn't understand. She knew me better than I knew myself. Even when I was hurt sometimes she reminded me of what she had said but I would only be back in no time doing the same thing all over again. There's nothing wrong with being kind to people but I overdid it. I was dumb. I bet people laughed behind my back."

"You were not dumb. You were kind and loving. There's nothing wrong with that. It's just that you got involved with the wrong people sometimes. I bet everyone wasn't bad."

"No," Amanda said after a moment. "Everyone wasn't bad. But I should have known when to draw the line. You don't know how far I went sometimes. Mum tried." Amanda sighed heavily as she remembered. "Mum really tried. But I wouldn't listen. It was like a drive. Then I got pregnant. When I found out he'd been lying to me, that he was married and I meant nothing to him but just someone to while away the time with, I was bewildered. I just couldn't comprehend it. When it hit me, it wasn't only what he did but what everyone who had ever taken advantage of me, did. And it hit hard. It was a rude awakening, Lily." She covered her face with one hand and took a deep breath. "Oh, Mum. She was the only one that could have lived with me then. Most days I was beside myself. I was angry, bitter, vengeful and also scared. And I was ashamed. Not just of being pregnant but also of being made a fool of by them all and so I refused to see anybody. I couldn't face them. Mum understood. She understood everything and just kept me away for as long as I wanted. She was priceless."

Lily let out a deep breath. "After you brought me to Lagos and you didn't come to see me like you promised, I tried to hate you. But Mama had helped me understand some things about you and that made it difficult. You see I have felt sorry for you all my life. Even when those things started happening to me I still struggled with my feelings. I wanted to hate you so badly I forced myself to believe you didn't want me in your life but still Mama got through to me with memories." She looked at her mother. "I understand why you left home in the first place."

Amanda put her arm round Lily's shoulder and drew her close. "Why I ran away, you mean."

"I don't blame you."

"I would."

"Why?" Lily asked. "You'd suffered a lot."

"Not enough to have abandoned you. It wasn't worth it. My pride, my ambitions…they just weren't worth it. Look at you, all grown up and I missed it all."

"Look, Mummy, I don't hold anything against you. You've been through a lot. Mama didn't blame you either. She always said that whenever you walked through our front door the first thing she always saw was how much you loved her."

Amanda looked up slowly. "What did you say?"

"It's true. She said that was the way it had been since you were very little. She said even though you were now angry and distant, that part of you had never changed. She said it was something you did every time you saw her for the first time after a long while."

"Wha…?" Amanda started laughing. Her laugh became uncontrollable and Lily couldn't help laughing too. "Oh Lily. Oh Lily she knew. She really knew."

"I told you."

Tears ran down Amanda's cheeks and she did nothing to stop them. "She used to call me 'baby' when I was young. Every time I walked in after school or any outing or whenever we hadn't seen each other for some time, she would go, "I love you, Baby," and I would give her a half smile and say, "I love you, Mummy." We did it for years. She used to tell me after I'd outgrown all that baby stuff that my smile still said it all. I guess I never stopped giving her the half smile. I didn't even realize it."

"She knew you loved her. She said it wasn't until you put it into words. She saw it in your eyes. She saw it in the way you mumbled whenever she asked you if you were hungry. She would put the food there and you would eat it all up. Sometimes she would wink at me behind your back."

"She did that?"

"Yes! She was never angry with you, even when you made her sad."

"I did that a lot."

"Yes, but she was always all right after she had prayed. She said there were forces. I didn't understand what she meant but she said they were…forces…that were holding you back but God was greater than them. She prayed a lot for you."

Amanda put her arm around Lily again and sighed. "I know." A soft breeze cooled the night air and Amanda felt at peace. It wasn't hard to see that tomorrow would be a better day. Things would work out well for her and her children. God would fulfill His promises.

But there was still something on her mind and she wasn't sure if she should tell Lily. But how could she keep it from her? Lily could hold it against her. Amanda was tired of making mistakes, especially where Lily was concerned.

"Lily," she said. "There's something I have to tell you."

Chapter EIGHTEEN

THE TRAFFIC OUTSIDE THE restaurant was unbelievable. Due to major repairs on Herbert Macaulay Way all cars going to the Island were diverted to Mainland Street because it was the only passable access to the old bridge. Some very impatient drivers, especially of public transit, took another route but it was at the risk of major damage to their vehicles due to the terrible conditions of the road. Cars were at a standstill because the road was too narrow and only one car could get on the bridge at a time. People were late for work, children were late for school and tempers were flaring. One could hear the blaring of horns and people screaming obscenities at each other.

Melody was oblivious to all these. She had been pacing back and forth for the past half hour or so with clenched fists. Why weren't things working out the way she wanted? She was used to having her way. If things didn't fall into place she always made them. She had the means. She enjoyed having power over people. She could make them do whatever she wanted. She could even make them disappear. Yet somehow she had let this one slip through her fingers. She wasn't usually this careless. She should have made the security tighter. The girl had taken her unawares. But it could still be rectified. After all, Melody always had the last laugh.

And that Shade. She always knew she had given that girl too much freedom. She should have been harder on her. Maybe she should have treated her like one of the other girls though that was something she had found difficult. The girl was too angry and strong-willed at the same time. Melody was impressed with her and had found it difficult to treat her like others. How foolish. Little wonder she had grown wings.

"Aunty, calm down."

"Don't tell me to calm down!" Melody snapped. "What do you know about anything?"

"I know that working yourself up like this wouldn't help matters."

"I say you don't know anything!" She walked to her office door, opened it and stuck her head out. "Has she come?" she bellowed.

"No, Madam," came the reply.

"Nonsense! Utter nonsense!" She slammed the door shut.

"She has said she is coming and it is only just past eight. Maybe she is caught up in the traffic."

"The traffic. The traffic." Melody went to the window and when she parted the curtains she became angrier than ever. "But this is madness. For goodness sake how long does it take to repair a road that they have to cause such a catastrophe? For how long are we expected to suffer like this?" She hissed and went to sit behind her desk.

"I hope it won't affect the customers."

"And what do you want to do if it does?"

"Sorry."

Melody hissed again. "Call Victor for me," she said into her intercom.

Shortly afterwards there was a knock on the door.

"Come in," Melody said.

A burly, dark-skinned man in a very tight t-shirt walked in, went straight to Melody's table and stood before her with his hands behind his back.

Melody totally ignored him and pressed the button on her intercom again to speak to her secretary. "Call Stanley and let him wait outside. Tell Mama Cook I want to see her before she closes today. Have you finished typing those letters?"

"No, Madam. I…" Her secretary began.

"You're not indispensable. Do you hear me? I will send you away and get me someone who would not use a whole morning to type three letters." She removed her finger from the button and rested her head on her hand. "Victor," she said.

"Madam."

She paused for a long moment and then sighed. "What do you have to tell me?"

"Shade has not shown up at her place and neither has the girl that lives with her."

"And?"

"She has not been seen by anyone."

"Anyone?" Melody was clearly irritated as she looked up.

"Car hire, hotel, police, hang outs, they've all turned up blank, Madam"

"So Shade is now invisible?" Melody raised her eyebrows. "So I would definitely be asking for too much if I ask about Lily."

"Madam, the boys are doing their best…"

"Don't give me that 'we're doing our best' line at all. It doesn't work for anyone!" Melody screamed. "Victor."

"Madam."

"You're playing with fire."

"Madam, we..."

He was interrupted by a knock on the door. They all waited as the door opened and Shade walked in.

Melody gave her a dark look and then turned to Victor. "You may go."

He left and Shade took a seat on the sofa in the corner.

"Good morning," she said to Melody. "Hello, Sheyi."

"Hello," Sheyi replied.

"*How una come miss like dat?*" Melody asked her.

"I no miss Auntie. I get client."

"What kind of client do you have that...?" Sheyi began.

"Hey!" Shade interrupted him at the same time Melody raised her hand for him to be quiet. "Paddle your own canoe."

"Am I the one you're talking to like that?"

"Are you not the one poking your nose where it does not belong?" Shade cocked her head.

"Look...look...look at this girl." He turned to Melody. "I should slap her..."

"You? Slap me?" Shade looked so angry. "I dare you!"

Sheyi looked around as if he was too shocked by what he was hearing. "Look at this girl of yesterday."

"Look again!"

"I think there's something wrong with you."

"I'm surprised you are just finding that out." Shade stood up and went to where he was. "I thought you always knew."

Sheyi stood up too.

"Ok, you two. That's enough." Melody couldn't understand what was happening with Shade. She had always been friendly with Sheyi. They had always got along well. As far as Melody could remember Shade had never been impolite to him. She had never seen her like this.

Shade looked at him disdainfully and went back to her seat in the corner. He sat down too frowning at her.

"What's the matter with you two?" Melody asked. "You want to fight in my office right in front of me?" She looked from one to the other. "Shade? Sheyi?"

Sheyi turned and faced Melody. "Aunty, forget," he said finally.

Shade refused to say anything. She seemed to have developed a sudden interest in her fingernails.

"Shade," Melody called her name again and she looked up. After a few moments Melody decided to let the matter rest. There were more important things to deal with. "Anyway," she said. "You already know why I asked to see you this morning."

Shade kept looking at her without saying a word.

That was the problem with Shade. You could never tell what was going on in the girl's mind and you could never predict her reaction. There were times she had really surprised Melody. Right now Melody couldn't tell if she knew anything about Lily's whereabouts. If she did she was sure she wouldn't give it away. It would be difficult to get anything from her, therefore Melody couldn't be straightforward. She would have to adopt a subtle technique that she hoped would work.

"I still don't know where Lily is and she has some money with me which she needs to come and collect. I also got her latest bank statement a few days ago." She pulled out a sheet of paper from a pile and spread it out on the table in front of her. "There's a lot of money in there. All hers."

"Wow," Sheyi said after stretching his neck to see the amount stated on the paper. "That's a lot to give up."

"She worked for this money," Melody continued. "I'd hate for her not to enjoy it."

"How do you know she has not withdrawn it?" Shade asked.

"I called Belinda this morning. She hasn't."

"Maybe she doesn't want it," Shade said.

"Ha!"

"What's wrong with him?" Shade asked reacting to the sound Sheyi had just made. "You think everyone follows the scent of money like you do?"

"Like you do not?" Sheyi turned to face her.

Shade seemed to have had enough of him. "Look, everyone is not like you. You have no shame. You would do *anything* for money."

Sheyi laughed derisively. "I don't collect money from everyone I sleep with, you do."

"Yeah? Well I don't remember collecting any from you!" Shade yelled. "Not at any time."

That seemed to take the winds right out of Sheyi's sails.

"It's like the two of you have problems this morning." Melody didn't think she would get anywhere with Sheyi in the office. "Sheyi, I think you should go and get some breakfast. You can come back later so we can discuss the other issue."

Sheyi got up and left the office.

"Shade," Melody said as soon as Sheyi shut the door behind him. "What is biting you this morning?"

"Nothing," Shade replied.

"Nothing," Melody echoed. "Have you seen a doctor?"

Shade looked up sharply. "A doctor? For what?"

"You said you were not feeling fine."

"I *dey* fine."

"Come," Melody said gently, beckoning with her hand. "Come closer. Come and sit here and let me show you this thing." Melody indicated the chair Sheyi had just vacated.

When Shade was seated Melody turned the bank statement round so she could see it.

"Look at the amount in her account. Even if she doesn't want to be with us anymore, I don't think she should leave without collecting her money. Apart from this she has two hundred thousand or so with me."

"That much? How come?" Shade eyed Melody suspiciously.

"I didn't have time to lodge it for her," Melody explained quickly. "I haven't been to the bank in a while." She tried to sound casual but she was studying Shade closely. "So have you heard from her at all?"

Shade sat back and sighed. "You've asked me before, Aunty, and I have told you I don't know where she is."

"I'm not saying that you do. I'm only asking if you have heard from her."

"I haven't," Shade replied. "Do you think she would tell me about her plan to run away or where she ran to, knowing you're my aunt?"

"You were friends."

"There are no friends here, Aunty," Shade said. "And I don't expect that she would still be in Lagos by now anyway."

Melody stiffened. The suffocating feeling she always had when it seemed like she was in tight corner was enveloping her again. She had tried her best to push the possibility of Lily being out of her reach from her mind, but it was becoming more difficult with every passing day. "She's still in Lagos," she said stubbornly.

"What would she still be doing in Lagos?" Shade asked. "She doesn't know anybody and you told me her Alhaji is out of the country."

To hear about Alhaji was like salt in the wound Shade had already opened. He didn't know that Lily was missing and Melody needed to find her before he returned. She found herself looking at the calendar on her table involuntarily. She didn't have long.

"She's still in Lagos," she repeated trying to fight the growing unease.

"Have you checked with her mother?" Shade asked her. "Are you sure she's not gone back to her? That girl is out of this city."

"She can't be with her mother."

"Why not? Have you contacted her mother?"

"No, but I'm sure she's not with her."

"Does her mother know she's no longer with you?"

"She knows...I don't know," Melody snapped.

"Anyway," Shade said after a moment. "The money is hers as you said. She can withdraw it any time she likes."

"And what about the one she has with me?"

"It's her loss if she doesn't come for it."

"I just want to give her the money and my conscience will be clear," Melody said. "You know I don't ever owe anybody."

Shade grunted. "It seems to me like there's more to this than the money," she said.

"What do you mean?" Melody was becoming impatient. Shade wasn't offering anything useful and now she was prying.

"There's another reason why you want this girl." Shade smiled at Melody.

"What are you implying?" Melody didn't smile back.

"I understand the fact that she's a hot one and she delivers," Shade said, tapping the bank statement with a long painted nail. "But still..."

Melody narrowed her eyes. "Now listen to me. My reason for doing anything is none of your business. Do you understand me? All I need from you is for you to let me know the moment she contacts you. Ok?"

"All right!" Shade lifted both hands in surrender.

"And what about the girl that lives with you? Who is she anyway?"

"Just someone's younger sister I decided to help," Shade said. "Besides I need someone in the house since I'm not there most of the time and she seemed trustworthy."

"And is she back from her village?"

"No," Shade said. "She would have called me."

"Ok." Melody let out her breath. "I'm counting on you."

Shade got up and smiled. "You can trust me." She left the office.

"That I can never do," Melody said to herself as she picked up her phone and dialed.

"Madam." It was Victor's voice.

"Make sure she's followed everywhere, and I mean everywhere."

"Yes Madam."

She hung up and dropped the phone in frustration. It was just as she had expected. Shade had given nothing away. It was possible that she truly didn't know where Lily was or she could be the brain behind it all. Melody had no way of knowing. That is except her boys could come up with something and she hoped they would. Time was running out fast. She pulled at the neckline of her fluffy chiffon blouse. She was beginning to feel suffocated again.

"Shade, you're becoming too scarce for me in this city o." It was Joe, Melody's driver.

"Oga Joe, Oga Joe." Shade took his hand. "It's a serious matter."

"It's like we need to pay a toll to see you these days."

Shade laughed.

"Aunty Shade, are you still in this country?"

Shade turned to see one of the cooks approaching.

"'Morning, Mama Junior." She hugged her. "You know I can't go anywhere without asking you first."

"How are you, my dear?"

"I'm fine, thank you. How is Junior?"

"He's fine. Good to see you, Aunty Shade."

"Will you be back tonight?" Selena asked Shade as she walked past the bar.

"I'm not sure, Selena." She had no intention of being back. "Bye."

Someone tapped her shoulder as she stepped out of the restaurant doors. She turned to see Sheyi standing there.

"You're not planning to leave without saying goodbye, are you?" He asked.

"I don't have to say anything to you." Shade continued walking.

Sheyi grabbed her wrist and tried to stop her.

"What the…?"

"Calm down, Shade," he said. "Come on. It's me, Sheyi. What's really going on?"

"Nothing is going on." She looked at her watch. "Look, I have to be at my office in a few minutes and you can see the traffic. I really don't have time for this."

"Shade." He looked at her pleadingly. "Ok, I'm sorry."

"You shouldn't be apologizing to *me*," she said with a meaning look.

"Then what's all this about?" Sheyi asked. "Wait a minute. Whom should I be apologizing to?"

"No one!" Shade twisted her hand free and walked quickly towards the gate. She looked back once and saw Sheyi still standing there with a suspicious look on his face.

Chapter NINETEEN

"SO WHAT IS SO urgent that cannot wait for me to finish addressing my staff?" Sheyi had just walked into her office without knocking and Melody was annoyed because of the interruption of her meeting with the storekeeper.

"She knows something," he said curtly.

Though still looking impatiently at Sheyi she gestured for Stanley the storekeeper to leave the office.

"Who knows something?" Melody asked in the same annoyed tone as soon as the man shut the door behind him.

"Shade. She knows something. I'm sure of it."

Really." Melody leaned forward and clasped her hands on the table. "And why do you think that?"

"You saw the way she was acting this morning, as if she was angry with me about something."

"Yes?" Melody sounded bored. "She was angry with you. I didn't know you've been sleeping with her and apparently more than once, without paying."

"It's…it's not that," Sheyi said, looking embarrassed.

"Then what is it?"

He took a seat and began. "I was surprised at the way she treated me this morning and I knew there had to be a reason for it. I sat at the restaurant trying to remember what I might have done wrong. I couldn't think of anything. Then I decided to wait for her outside so I could settle with her. I apologized and do you know what she said?" He leaned forward and pursed his lips. "She said something about not being the one I should be apologizing to."

"So? That could mean anything."

"No, Aunty." Sheyi shook his head vigorously. "There was something about the way she said it."

Melody thought for a moment. "Are you sure that's what she said?"

"Yes," Sheyi replied frowning, as if trying to remember. "She said…yes! That's what she said. That I shouldn't be apologizing to her."

"And who did she say you should be apologizing to?" Melody had picked up a pencil from her table and was turning it round with her fingers.

"She didn't say. When I asked her she said 'no one' and just bolted."

Melody dropped the pencil and folded her arms across her chest.

"Not to worry. If there's anything to it the boys will soon find out. She's being followed even as we speak. If she is connected to Lily in any way, my boys will find out. I intend to dig out that little nuisance as soon as possible from whatever hole she may have crawled into. She would not stand in the way of my contract." She slammed her fist on the table suddenly, startling Sheyi. "Oh why? Why didn't she wait for

Alhaji to return and sign this agreement before pulling her stunt? Nonsense!" She hit the table again.

Lily's phone was ringing.

"Lily!" Lillian shouted from the kitchen. "Your phone!"

I know!" Lily shouted back. "I'm looking for it. Do you know where it is?"

"It's in the…it's on the…now where did I see that phone?"

"Found it!" Lily screamed shortly after. She'd found it half hidden under a cushion on the sofa. She quickly reached for it. "Hello."

"Don't tell me you're all still sleeping?"

"Shade! Tell me, how did it go? Did you see Melody?"

"I did. Tried my best to throw her off your scent. Although…"

"What?"

"Nothing. How's everyone? How's your mum?"

"Everyone is fine. Did you see Sheyi?"

Lily thought Shade hesitated before answering.

"Yes, yes. He was there."

"Really. So…are you at work?"

"Yes. I've not been fired yet. I'll never know why."

"Shade," Lily said fondly.

"Just called to warn you that Melody is hot on your trail and I don't think she's ever going to give up," Shade said. "And she tried to work on me. Of course you know what I mean. She showed me your bank statement and also said you had some money with her. She wanted me to know how her heart would break if you left without getting your money."

"How sweet of her."

"She's desperate, Lily," Shade said seriously. "She doesn't keep a girl's money except if she really needs to lure her back. I think there's something very serious at stake."

"Yes. She doesn't want the money she gets from Alhaji to stop coming."

"No, it's more serious than that," Shade said. "I know Melody, Lily. She's tensed up. Something is really, really bothering her. She'll stop at nothing to find you."

"Well, she won't."

"Anyway there's nothing keeping you here in Lagos. I think you should leave with your mother today."

After a long pause Lily sighed. "I can't."

"Why not?"

"There's something I want to do first, something very important. I'll tell you about it later."

"Ok," Shade said after a moment. "Whatever it is, just make sure it doesn't take too long."

"I promise."

"I'll sleep better when I know you're out of town."

"And you call me mother hen."

"Be careful. I'll call after I've actually earned some pay in this company."

"Get to it then. Bye."

"Bye."

Lily turned around and saw Lillian setting the table for breakfast. "That was Shade."

"How did it go with Melody?" Lillian asked.

"She said she's bent on finding me, of course. And she thinks that there's another reason why she wants to find me, a very important reason."

Lillian stopped what she was doing. "And what's that?"

"Shade doesn't know but it is serious enough for Melody to be tensed up and desperate."

"What do you think it could be?" Lillian left the table and walked to where Lily was. She looked disturbed. "I think you should just go with your mother today. Shade is fine now and there's really no reason for you to remain in Lagos."

Lily sat down slowly. "Lillie, I can't go today. There is something my mother told me yesterday that..." She shook her head. "Look, Lillie, I just have to do some things."

"Do they involve going out into the streets beyond the corner shop?"

"Yes."

"Knowing you stand the risk of being spotted?" Lillian asked. "Come on. What are these mysterious things anyway?"

"Lillie, my mother has found...my father." She waited to see Lillian's reaction. "She hasn't actually seen him or contacted him but she met an old friend yesterday who said she worked for him here in Victoria Island. She gave my mother his office address."

"Your father? As in... your very father?" Lillian sank into the seat closest to her and gaped at Lily for a few moments. "And what exactly are you planning to do?"

"We...I want to see him."

"And your mother?"

"She would rather not but she said whether I wanted to or not was up to me," Lily said. "Lillie, I have dreamt about him all my life, hoping that one day he'll find out about me and want me. He's just a few minutes from here." She held a cushion to herself. "I don't even know how I feel."

"Is your mother going to call him first?"

"I guess. Lillie, she's finding this very hard."

"I can imagine. All these years."

"And she only found out about him yesterday herself. She hasn't even had time to sort out her own thoughts. She feels she will be making a mistake if she doesn't tell me and I find out after we have...Lillie, there's something else you should know."

"Something else..."

Just then Amanda walked into the sitting room. "Hello," she said.

Both girls looked up. "'Morning," they chorused.

"How are you girls this morning?" She curled up on the sofa.

"Fine, thank you," Lillie replied.

"Fine and you don't look like you want to be up yet." Lily said to her mother.

"I'm fine. I've just been so exhausted lately, that's all."

"But you slept well."

"I...you know, I'm not too comfortable staying in this house..."

"I am," Lillian said. "The only discomfort I've had in this place is the thought of leaving that bed soon."

"Maybe you should take it with you," Lily said eyeing her playfully.

"You know, I think I just might."

Amanda smiled at Lillian and swung her feet off the sofa. "We have a long day ahead of us today," she said. "I think I should take a shower now." She got up and stretched. "Lily, are you going to get ready too?"

"Yes, in a moment, Mummy," Lily replied.

"Breakfast will be on the table by the time you are ready," Lillian announced as Amanda was leaving.

"I'll be looking forward to it."

"We'll have to talk later," Lily said.

"I guess," Lillian said. "You'll have much more to talk about then anyway."

"Yes."

"Go on and get ready then."

"I'll be back in a minute."

"Your minute is equal to forty-five of mine. So go."

"Lie!" Lily cried as she hurried off.

In an hour or so Lily and Amanda were ready to leave.

"We won't take long," Amanda said at the door.

"Are you sure you don't want me to go and get you a taxi?" Lillian asked.

"No, don't worry, Lillie," Amanda replied. "We'll get one at that park up the road."

"Ok. See you later."

Orion House stood at the end of St. Gregory Close opposite the beach. It was a tall modern building adorned with huge mosaic designs. A company had to be doing very well to rent offices in this part of Lagos, let alone in a building as expensive looking as this one. Lily wondered what the inside was like.

As they walked through the glass doors she found herself in a massive reception area. A large stone counter stood facing them with at least ten people behind it busily attending to visitors. Two sets of elevators were on either side of the reception area. '*Robsight Exclusive Advertising Agency*' was among the names of the companies on a metal plaque on the wall to their right. It also indicated that it was on the third floor as the business card stated.

They got into the elevator and on the third floor the doors opened to a smaller but air-conditioned and tastefully furnished reception area. Dark brown leather upholstery against a backdrop of cream textured walls with a cream and brown rug gave the room an air of luxury. A large gold urn with multi-colored dry plants stood in a corner and a curved desk made of shiny wood completed the exquisite look. Two smartly dressed ladies sat behind it and they looked up as Amanda and Lily approached.

"Good morning," one of them said.

"Good morning," Amanda replied. "I'd like to see the Managing Director of *Robsight*."

"May I have your name please?"

"Amanda Parker."

"Please sit down."

The reception served the three companies indicated on the wall by the elevators, Lily observed. Two men and a woman were already seated when she and Amanda walked in. She hoped they were going to the other two companies. She'd hate to have to wait for them.

Amanda chose seats some distance from the others in the room.

"What do you think of this place?" She asked Lily.

"I've breathed in deeply about six times already," Lily replied. "I just love the effect."

"Can I tell you a secret?" Amanda asked.

Lily drew closer to her and smiled impishly.

"I wish I had dressed better," Amanda whispered.

"No!" Lily was surprised to hear it. "You look very elegant. You always look very nice. Your hair, your face, everything about you," Lily said. "And this navy dress, it was made for you."

Amanda now looked surprised. "Thank you, Lily."

"But it's true. You remind me of Mama, like a much younger, slimmer and more beautiful version of her even though you're really fair in complexion and she was dark." Then she grimaced. "And I'm a darker, shorter, bushier-eye browed, bushier-haired version of you."

"Are you through?" Amanda laughed. "I don't see any bushy eye brow or bushy hair."

"You should have seen my hair before Mama emptied two full tubs of hair relaxer cream into it. I had the most unruly afro. It seems you always saw it only after it was plaited. It was so long and thick and yet Mama refused to have it cut. She said she would rather tame it."

"And she did."

"Aunt Agnes didn't believe what she saw after the perm." Lily chuckled. "She actually jumped up and clapped her hands. She was glad she didn't have to face that hair again."

"Agnes made your hair?"

"Every week. And she complained from the moment she started till she was through."

"Excuse me." It was one of the ladies behind the counter addressing Amanda.

Amanda grabbed Lily's hand.

"You can go in now. It's the third door on the right around the corner." She indicated the passage way just before the desk.

"Thank you," Amanda said.

As soon as they were out of sight of the receptionists Amanda stopped suddenly and leaned against the wall.

"Ok. The truth." She took a deep breath. "I am so nervous I want to run out of the building."

Lily leaned against the wall too. "But you spoke to him on the phone earlier on."

"Yes, but that was different and...brief."

"Now it's face to face," Lily said. "I'm nervous too."

Amanda turned to Lily looking like she really wouldn't be able to go through with it. "He doesn't know why I'm here."

"You mean..." Lily didn't seem to understand at first.

"He still doesn't know about you, Lily. I didn't tell him."

"I see," Lily said quietly. "Well then I think you should go in first and talk to him and I can come in later."

Amanda placed her hands on Lily's shoulders and looked at her in disbelief. "I... Thank you. How have I lived without you?" She took a deep breath and stood before the door as if composing herself, and then she knocked and walked in leaving Lily just outside.

It had been more than fifteen minutes since Amanda went into the office and Lily was beginning to feel awkward standing there. Two of the visitors from the waiting room had passed and looked at her. Finally the door opened and Amanda stepped out, put an arm around her shoulder and guided her in.

"Lily, this is your father."

A tall and handsome man stood in the middle of the room. *This is my father*. The man she had dreamt of meeting for as long as she could remember. This was the man she had vowed she would look for as soon as she was able to. She had always known that he didn't know about her and she had decided long ago that one day she would change that. Now here he was standing just a few feet from her. It was overwhelming.

"Hello Lily," he said with a deep voice. He looked really composed unlike Lily whose stomach was so tied up in knots she couldn't speak. She was meeting him for the first time and had no idea what to expect. She could only nod slightly in reply.

"You look like your mother a lot," he said. "But…I'm certain that nose is mine. And that forehead." His voice was rich and Lily liked the sound of it. He extended a large hand with long fingers and when he smiled dimples appeared on both cheeks and his eyes shone. It wasn't difficult to see why her mother had been swept off her feet.

Lily was surprised at how easily he spoke to her. She took his hand.

"I am pleased to meet you," he said. "I never knew about you until now. Please forgive me if I don't know how to act."

Lily nodded again.

"Come and sit down." He led her to one of the chairs by the large desk in the room and turned another chair to face her before sitting on it. He looked over at Amanda who had taken a seat at the corner of the office, as if for support. Amanda nodded and smiled.

"What I did to your mother was terrible," he began as he turned back to face her. "I say so because I knew what I was doing but I did it anyway. She says she has forgiven me, hard as that must have been for her, and I have no choice but to accept that she has. But I must say at this point that something wonderful came out of it. And that is you." He sat back and seemed to be thinking of how to continue. He sighed heavily and nodded repeatedly. "I was foolish in those days. I lived carelessly as if I would never give account of the things I did. I thought everything within my reach was mine for the taking even if it belonged to someone else. And that meant I could steal, cheat on my wife and lie my way out of tight corners, anything. Would you believe I still thought I wasn't such a bad person? That I was just a regular guy who didn't do anything out of the ordinary?" He grunted. "I was dead wrong. Do you know what happened?"

Lily shifted in her seat waiting to hear more.

"Six years ago I was returning with two friends from a weekend trip to Ife when we had an accident. My friend somehow lost control of the vehicle and we came face to face with a trailer. That's all I remembered. The next thing I knew was that I was lying on a hospital bed with my head covered in bandages. They had removed pieces of glass from my head." He bent his head and showed Lily some scars that were barely noticeable. "I lay there feeling sorry for myself until my wife was able to find me. At first I was angry and thought it was unfair for me to be in that condition. It wasn't until I found out about my friends that I knew that God had been merciful to me. Wada died before we got to the hospital and Ben was paralyzed from the neck down. I had been spared. After that I wasn't the same.

"We were transferred to a hospital in Lagos and while I was discharged a few days later, Ben remained there. I visited him every day and would lie on his bed with him for hours. We would talk and laugh and throw insults at each other just as we always did." He smiled at the memory. "Everyone that saw us saw two men lying on a bed, talking. The difference was that at the close of visiting hours I had a choice to get up from that bed and leave. Ben didn't. That was when someone asked me a question that set me on the path of getting to know the Lord. It was a simple question. 'What do you do with your choices when you can make them?' He said there was going to come a time when you didn't have the power to make them anymore. And immediately I thought of Ben. Then this person spoke to me about God's love for me and asked me if I wanted to choose between heaven and hell. Lily I wanted to because I still could. I chose heaven, to spend eternity with God."

Lily looked at her mother. Amanda was smiling. Then she looked back at Robert.

"How did you choose heaven?"

"By making sure that is where I'm going."

"How do you make sure? How do you choose heaven? I don't think I've made that choice." Lily couldn't understand what was happening to her.

"By surrendering my life to Jesus. It was the first of the best and most important choices of my life. Would you like to make it?" Her father asked tenderly.

She looked at her mother again. Amanda had stood up and she had tears in her eyes.

"Yes," Lily said. "I would like to."

Robert picked his phone and said into it that he didn't want to be disturbed. And for the next few minutes he spoke to Lily about the love of God for her and everyone. He told her how God wanted to save people from their sins and hell and give them abundant life. And he told her that God was waiting for them to yield to Him and accept His sacrifice of Jesus. Then he led her in a simple prayer to accept Jesus into her heart.

"What has happened today is what only God can do," he said to Lily afterwards. "Every true Christian wants the opportunity to lead another person to Christ. Not only have I got that opportunity this morning, that person has also turned out to be my beautiful child whom I am meeting for the first time." He stood up and held his arms open to her. Lily got up too and quickly hugged him. Then he held out one arm to Amanda who crossed the room to join them.

"This is one of the happiest days of my life," he said as they all hugged.

Then Robert suggested that they go out to spend some time together before they left. When Amanda reluctantly agreed he made some calls and picked up his car keys.

"Let's go," he said.

"Where are we going?" Lily asked when they were on the road in Robert's car.

"First to the Plaza and then to the restaurant of your choice."

"The Plaza?" Lily asked.

"Yes. It is the biggest shopping mall in this area."

Lily had never felt this way before. She felt new, clean, as if she had never done anything wrong in her entire life. This must be what Mama always described as the 'new creation' experience. She'd said it accompanied what she called the new birth. If only Mama was still alive to see her now, to know that God had answered her prayers.

She listened to Robert and her mother laugh at something he said. This was just too good to be true. Not too long ago she was a lonely, confused girl without a family and now she was in a car with her own loving mother and father and she had just become born again.

Robert drove into the parking lot of the huge shopping mall and parked. "Where would you like to start, Lily?"

"I don't know," Lily replied shyly.

"Good," he said. "I love that answer. It's a great start to a wonderful day. Isn't it Amanda?"

Amanda shrugged looking like she didn't know what he meant.

"It means Lily is still a bit shy and I, Robert can lead while she follows. And I intend to. Come on."

They entered the brightly lit huge mall went from one shop to the other, while Robert kept them entertained with jokes. Lily had been thinking from the night before how awkward meeting her father would be for all of them. Now she knew that awkward was the last thing you felt with this man. When Lily's arms were full and she was exhausted, Robert seemed like he was just starting.

"Robert," Amanda said finally. "I can see that you could go on till the shops close if I don't stop you."

"Stop me? Why would you…?" He looked at Lily. "Are you tired, my dear?"

"A little," she said.

"Ah! Then we need to take a break." He signaled to a shop assistant and handed over some clothes he had just picked for Lily. "Please do this and let me know how much." Then he turned to Amanda. "You refuse to let me get you anything," he said quietly.

"You don't need to." Amanda shook her head vigorously.

"You haven't changed at all."

Robert paid and they left the shop to look for a restaurant. They found one they liked on a lower floor. As soon as they had ordered Robert took Lily's wrist.

"Now I want to know what has happened to you since the day you were born. Everything."

When Lily didn't speak but looked at Amanda instead he leaned back on his seat. "Are you still shy?"

"No," she replied after a few moments. "I just don't know..."

"Ok," he said. "I'll help. You were born in Port Harcourt, right?"

"Yes."

"Your mum said your grandmother raised you there until she died last year and you've spent the past year with a relative in Lagos but now you're going back."

"Yes."

"What class are you now?"

"I...I was in J.S. 3 last year."

"Oh, you've finished your Junior Secondary School," he said and then he frowned. "What about...?"

Amanda didn't let him finish. "Robert, Robert." She raised her two hands, quickly coming to Lily's rescue. "Lily has had a difficult year and she's just glad to be going back. She'll definitely be returning to school in a little while."

Lily was grateful her mother had quickly come in. She was happy she had found her father and though she could see he was a good man, she felt hesitant about letting him know how she had been living. If only the past year hadn't happened. She looked at her mother, silently thanking her.

"I'm sorry to hear that, Lily," Robert said. "I hope things will be better now that you're going back."

Their orders came and they ate silently.

"When exactly are you leaving Lagos?" Robert asked Amanda.

"Today, hopefully."

"But isn't it too late for Lily to go to Port today?"

"We...she..." Amanda looked at her watch. "I think we should let you get back to your work."

"My work can wait, Amanda. I want to spend as much time as I can with Lily. I don't know when I'm going to see you again." He brought out his phone and a note pad from his jacket. He scribbled on the pad and tore out a sheet for Amanda. "First, here are my numbers. I want to know what is happening with Lily at every moment in time. Now give me yours."

Amanda gave him her number and started to get up. "We still have to pack, Robert."

"Already?" He looked at his watch. "Can't you stay a few more days? What's the hurry?" Then he saw that the look on Amanda's face. "I can't convince you to stay?" Amanda smiled and shook her head.

"I wish I had known earlier," he said ruefully.

Later he picked three of the shopping bags in one hand and took Lily's hand in the other and helped her up. Amanda picked the rest of the bags and they headed for the exit. At the parking lot Robert turned to Lily.

"I want to be a part of your life, Lily. I want you to know that you have a father who cares about you. I know I have been missing all your life but I pray that God that brought you to me will help me make up for all the time I have lost." He dropped the bags and hugged her.

Lily hugged him back. In fact all she wanted to do was hold on to him and not let him go. She felt so secure in his arms. When she finally let go there were tears in her eyes. So this was what it was like to have a loving father. It was the best feeling in the world.

"Where am I taking you? Where are you staying?" Robert asked as he pulled out of the parking lot.

"At someone's place not too far from your building," Amanda quickly replied. "I think I can direct you."

Finally Robert parked in front of Alhaji's house.

"Thank you very much Robert," Amanda said as they got out of the car. "Thank you for everything."

"No. We should thank God for everything. I thank God for you and I thank God for Lily. Let me know how everything is going. Please call me if you need anything. And I would need an account number."

"I already told you Robert. I didn't come to you because..."

"I know Amanda. I know that isn't why you came. But I want to be a father to Lily in every way possible. Don't deprive me. I beg you. I've missed out enough already."

Amanda sighed. "I'll send it."

"Thank you."

Then Amanda looked at him intensely. "And Robert ... about Lily... your wife...your family... I didn't mean to ..."

"I've faced impossible situations Amanda," he tried to reassure her. "And with God on my side I have come out of them with positive results. This time won't be different." He gave her a reassuring smile.

After he had turned the car round he beckoned to Lily and she walked up to him.

"I'm only a phone call away." He smiled and drove off. As he got to the end of the road he honked and Lily waved. She had found her father.

The phone rang only once before it was snatched up.

"*Wetin?*"

"Chairman, it's me, Muftau.

"*Wetin?*"

"I just called to tell you that one of my taxi boys at Junction might have something."

Chapter TWENTY

"WHERE DO I START from?" Lily sat on to the sofa and kicked off her shoes.

"How about the beginning?" Lillian settled down beside her. "And don't leave anything out."

"Well..." Lily sat back. "We found the place easily enough, and we went in to see him. At the time we went he still didn't know anything about me so I let Mummy go in first and she was there for almost twenty minutes before she came out to get me." She looked at Amanda who was just returning from the room where she had gone to drop the bags.

"What happened when he saw you?"

"He just...I don't know." Lily shrugged. "He just accepted me, I think."

"Just like that." Lillian shook her head in wonder.

"He knew. He just knew. And Lillie, he's born again."

"Born again?" Lillian looked at Lily as if what she was saying was too much for her to comprehend.

"Like my grandmother. And Mary. And like my mum." She looked at her mother again. "He spoke to me about Jesus in a way I have never heard before. Not that I didn't know about those things but something happened to me while he was speaking. It was like the next step to take, the only step to take." She looked down at her hands. "I just gave my life to Christ and he prayed with me."

"Are you telling me that you are born again too?"

"Yes," Lily replied. "And I actually feel different. I feel forgiven."

"That's what happens when you decide to give your life to Jesus," Amanda said. "What Lily experienced today was a conviction and she knew she had to make a decision that could not wait."

"And the decision I had to make was very clear to me."

"To give your life to Jesus," Lillian concluded.

"Yes," Lily said.

"What's a…conviction like?" Lillian asked Amanda.

"The only way I can explain it is that it becomes all too clear to you that you are a sinner, and that you cannot stand before a holy God that way. So you realize your need for a savior and you accept His offer of salvation," Amanda explained.

"Is that all?"

"Acknowledging that you are a sinner is the beginning. You know that all your good works aren't good enough to save you. Jesus has already paid the prize for all your sins. All you need to do is accept Him and let the Blood He shed wash away your sins. Only then can you be acceptable to God. And when you accept Him, you have just fulfilled God's requirement for you to be called His child."

"So anything short of that…"

Amanda shook her head.

"My father said it is God's best way of showing His love and that is by sacrificing His best."

Lillian nodded. "What happens when I make that decision?"

"You become a child of God," Lily replied. "It means you have chosen heaven instead of hell."

"And if a person doesn't make that decision they would end up in hell."

"Yes."

"I don't want to go to hell that's for sure," Lillian said. "But…"

Just then there was a noise outside the door and Lillian jumped. The three of them looked at each other. Then it sounded like something heavy was dropped. Lily frowned, looking at the door with foreboding.

Who could it be? Who apart from Shade knew they were here?

"Shade?" Lily queried and began to walk towards the door. "But why didn't she call first?"

"Maybe she wanted to surprise us," Lillian said, though she sounded doubtful. "You know Shade. I just hope she was careful and wasn't followed."

A loud, quick rap startled Lily.

"I think you should ask who it is before you open the door," Amanda warned.

Before Lily could open her mouth to ask who it was there was the sound of a key in the lock and then the door swung wide open.

"Alhaji!" Lily exclaimed.

Alhaji Usman stood in front of her beaming from ear to ear.

"Alhaji, you're back!"

"And I'm so glad to see you." He held out his arms and moved towards her as if to embrace her but she moved aside so that he could see that they were not alone. "Oh," he said as he saw Lillian and Amanda, "we have company."

"Yes," Lily said quickly stepping out of his way. "Why don't you come in?"

He picked up his two suitcases and walked in while Lily locked the door. He set them on the floor just by the door and moved towards Amanda.

"Don't tell me," he said. "You're Lily's mother."

"Yes, I am," Amanda replied.

He held out his hand. "I'm Alhaji Usman," he said as Amanda took his hand. "Though you could easily be mistaken for her sister."

Amanda nodded and withdrew her hand from his.

"And you are?" He turned to Lillian.

"Lillian," Lillian said simply.

"She's my friend." Lily said.

"Well, I'm pleased to meet you both." He sat down on one of the chairs. "So Lily, how have you been?"

"Fine, thank you," Lily replied, sitting down next to her mother. She was dying to know why Alhaji had returned earlier than expected and whether he had had any contact with Melody.

"I know you weren't expecting me back so soon but I had some important business to take care of. I was just going to drop these things for you here," he pointed to the suitcases, "and surprise you this evening."

"I see," Lily said with an awkward smile. "Well, you surprised me now."

"Actually I am the one who is pleasantly surprised to see you here in this flat. And you are also very much at home." He looked at Amanda and Lily. "I was going to send Aliyu up to drop the suitcases when he told me you were here. So I decided to bring them up myself."

Lily still wondered what really brought him back to the country. She knew she had to think fast because Melody could be behind it.

"My mother has to travel back today. In fact she was just getting ready to leave when you came," Lily said. "And Lillie too has to return home."

"That's fine," he said. "That's very fine." He said to Amanda. "I hope you had a pleasant stay in Lagos. And I hope Lily has been saying good things about me."

"I had a good time, thank you," Amanda said politely.

"I'll go get some drinks," Lily announced. "Lillie, would you please come to the kitchen and help me fix some drinks for everyone before you leave?" Lily beckoned to Lillian stiffly as she got up and went towards the kitchen. Lillian got up quickly and followed her.

As soon as Lillian entered the kitchen Lily grabbed her arm. "Pack all our things into my bag and the rayon bag we got at the corner shop. And if there's anything that won't go in stuff them into my mother's bag and any carrier bag you find." Lillian nodded and turned to go. Lily held on to her. "Not now," she whispered fiercely. "We are fixing drinks remember?"

"Yes, yes," Lillian said walking in circles and touching her head intermittently. "But why did he have to come back today?"

"I don't know Lillie," Lily replied shaking her head. "I don't know."

"What exactly are we going to do?"

"Just look relaxed for a while after we've served the drinks..."

"And then I announce that I have to pack."

"And pack everything. I'm not ever coming back."

"All right." Lillian nodded.

"I'll pretend I'm seeing you off, just like we planned at Melody's house."

"And from there…" Lillian said excitedly. "Let's do it."

In a little while the drinks were served and Alhaji, Lillian and Lily had theirs in their hands. Amanda declined.

"Excuse me," Lillian said after a few minutes. "I need to finish packing."

"Oh, so do I." Amanda got up too. "Excuse me."

When they had left Alhaji smiled at Lily. "I have so much to tell you. First of all I'm glad you've finally accepted this flat. And I didn't know you had any contact with your mother."

"She…just showed up. And well…she couldn't have put up at Melody's house."

"This is your flat, Lily, to do as you will," Alhaji said. "So you told Melody you wanted to stay here with her?"

"This place is more comfortable." Lily carefully avoided the question. Maybe he hadn't had any contact with Melody yet. The sooner she got out of here the better. What was keeping Lillie and her mother?

Moments later they appeared.

Alhaji stood up. "Are you ready then?"

"Let me carry this one here." Lily quickly went and picked up a bag. "Let's go to the taxi park. I'm sure you'll get a taxi straight…"

"A taxi? What do you need a taxi for? My car is downstairs. I can easily drop you wherever you want."

Lily was about to protest when Amanda turned to him. "You don't need to bother. We'll get a taxi just as Lily said."

"Oh, Madam, it's no bother," he said as he walked towards the door. "In fact I won't have it any other way."

"I said we are fine," Amanda said rather firmly. And when none of them moved from where they were, Alhaji stepped out of the way.

"Ok," he said. "I was only trying to help."

"Thank you very much for everything," Amanda said. "Goodbye."

"Goodbye and have a safe journey," Alhaji replied. "And hurry back, Lily. I have so much to tell you."

The three of them walked out of the flat and Alhaji closed the door.

"I can't believe we're out of there," Lily said as they hurried down the road. "The very first taxi we see…"

They were able to get one just before they got to the park. Finally they were on their way.

"I'm switching off my phone." Lily looked back. "I can't believe he showed up today. I thought Melody sent him."

"Me too," Amanda said.

"And he almost ruined my get away plans," Lily said to Amanda. "He would have if it hadn't been for you."

"I said we are fine." Lillian mimicked Amanda. "I love the way you said that to him."

"I had to be firm."

"And I bet he wouldn't have relented if you hadn't been," Lily said. "I said we are fine." Lily clenched her teeth and they all laughed.

"I wonder why he came back earlier Lily," Lillian said.

"You can't believe how shocked I was to see him at the door."

"The good thing about it is that I don't have to leave you behind in Lagos." Amanda patted Lily's head.

"I'm going to miss you, Lillie," Lily said after a while. "I can't believe I'm actually saying good bye to you."

"Neither can I." Lillian turned from her front seat. "I can't imagine what it will be like with you gone."

They sat in silence for a while, each occupied with thoughts of the recent events and the future without each other.

"Lillie." Amanda reached out and touched Lillian's shoulder. "Have you ever considered getting in touch with Mary?"

"Mary? My sister?" Lillian asked. "Yes."

"I think you need to get in touch with her. You've been more than a friend to Lily. I'd like us to leave knowing that you will."

There were tears in Lillian's eyes. "I miss her today more than ever."

"That's why you need to find a way of getting through to her. You're going to miss her more when Lily's gone."

"She doesn't have a phone but I know someone I can call."

"Then promise me you will."

Lillian smiled. "I promise."

"Good."

Once again the taxi was silent. They would soon get to the taxi park for Benin-bound taxis where Lily and Amanda would get off and the driver would take Lillian back to Shade's place.

Lily looked forward to seeing her aunt Agnes again. She knew her experience in the past year would break her heart when she heard about it. But she would miss Lillian terribly. She wished they didn't have to part ways. She would make sure she spoke to her all the time. The voice of the taxi driver broke into her thoughts. It had a ring of anxiety.

"What's the matter?" Amanda asked him.

"Abi dis people be armed robbers?"

"Which people?" Lillian asked looking at the driver.

"What are you talking about?" Amanda asked him.

"One black car at the back." The driver looked really worried now. "*Dem don dey follow us since Victoria Island. If I change lane dem too go follow me change lane.*"

"What black car?" Lily asked looking back. "I don't see any…" She turned back suddenly gasping. "That's one of Melody's cars and it is full of her men!"

"What?" Amanda looked shocked. "How…?"

"Oh God, please." A sob escaped Lillian's throat. "What are we going to do?"

"*Wetin?*" The driver looked distraught. "*Wetin you talk? You know dem?*"

"Just when I thought we were out of this mess." Lillian was really scared.

"Mummy?" Lily was looking back again.

"Calm down everyone," Amanda said, raising her voice. "We are out of this mess."

"We are?" Lillian's voice sounded shaky.

"We are," Amanda affirmed. "Just calm down and believe…"

"Mummy?" Lily interrupted her. "There are two of them."

"Two?"

"Two cars. The other one is Melody's jeep."

"Don't worry," Amanda said in a voice that exuded confidence, smiling at her daughter and putting her hand on Lillian's shoulder again. "This is only a Red Sea."

Lily and Lillian looked at each other, confused.

"A Red Sea?" Lily asked while Lillian raised her eyebrows.

"Yes," Amanda replied. "Just like the Israelites faced in the wilderness when they first left Egypt. God knew they would come after us even before we took off. He knew they would try to stop us but that won't stop Him from finishing what He has started. He has already seen the end from the beginning." She turned to the driver. "Driver, keep driving there is no problem."

"Madam you say no problem?"

"No problem at all."

Suddenly Shade's phone in Lillian's purse started ringing, making her jump.

"It's Shade," she announced. "Hello, Shade."

"Lillie! Lillie! Where's Lily? Melody knows about the house. She's coming! Tell Lily to leave immediately! Do you hear me?"

"She's…we're out of the house…"

"Good, good. Tell her not to go back. She should just forget everything and just leave…"

"She's after us, Shade." Lillian cried. "We're on the road and she's been following us since with her men."

"She's been what?" Shade asked."

"Following us," Lillian replied. "Her men are on the road behind us."

"Ok, let me think." After a few seconds Lillian heard her voice again. "Where exactly are you now?"

Lillian tried to describe where they were.

"Ok. Give the phone to Lily's mum," Shade said.

"She said I should give the phone to you," Lillian said to Amanda as she handed the phone to her."

"Hello Shade."

"Hello Madam. This is what you're going to do."

Chapter TWENTY-ONE

THE TAXI DRIVER FOLLOWED Amanda's instructions and veered off to the right suddenly, taking the exit off the bridge. Only Melody's car was able to make the turn on time. Her jeep was too far left.

"Yippee!" Lillian couldn't help herself. "One down one to go and it's so far behind."

"That's good," Amanda said, looking back. She turned to the driver. "After that toothpaste billboard, take the next turn to the right."

The driver made the turn and increased his speed. It seemed like their pursuers were still far behind because Lily couldn't see them.

"I don't see them," she said. "Maybe they don't know where we turned off."

"It doesn't matter," Amanda said. "They wouldn't be following us for too long."

"Really?"

"Yes. We are going to the Army barracks."

"Army Barracks?

"Straight on to the gate," Amanda said to the driver.

"Barracks gate?" The driver asked.

"Yes," Amanda replied. The driver drove through the gates and came to a crossroad. "You will turn right here and drive on to the gate at the end of the road.

"That is the Senior Officers' Barracks. I *no* sure..." The driver looked troubled.

"Don't worry. Someone is expecting us."

Lily and Lillian looked at each other.

The driver stopped at the gate. Four armed soldiers were sitting on a bench while a couple more were standing and talking by the gatehouse. One of the soldiers on the bench got up and walked up to the taxi.

"Yes? What do you want?" He asked in a no-nonsense tone."

"Good Afternoon," Amanda replied. "We would like to see Major Ali."

The soldier looked at each of their faces. He then inspected the inside of the taxi for an even longer period.

"Driver, boot!" He ordered.

The driver got out and the soldier went with him to look inside the boot.

The soldier returned to Amanda's side of the car. "Is he expecting you?"

"Yes, he is," she replied.

"What are your names?"

"Amanda, Lily and Lillian."

After looking at Amanda for a few more seconds he took a step back. "Wait there." Then he walked back to the gatehouse.

"As if we can drive through your barricade," Lillian mumbled under her breath.

"And risk getting shot," Lily said barely moving her lips.

"By accidental discharge," Amanda whispered and they all fought hard to stifle their laughter. "Shush you two. I wouldn't want to have to explain to these soldiers what we find amusing."

The soldier returned shortly after. "Close 'B', bungalow 4," he said.

The heavy metal bar at the gate was raised and the driver was asked to drive in. They located the house easily enough and the driver parked the car in front of it.

"I'll be right back," Amanda said as she got off and headed towards the front door. The door opened almost immediately and she went in.

"You people said you are going to the motor park for Benin taxis," the taxi driver complained. "*Small time* armed robbers begin to pursue us. Now we're waiting inside the barracks. *Wetin* again eh? *Wetin* again?"

"It's ok." Lily tried to calm him. "We were not expecting those people to follow us. They are not armed robbers."

"If they are not armed robbers then what are they? What are they?" The driver queried. "People pursue us from V.I to Oworo. If I change my lane they change their own. And men fill the car. Now...now you're telling me they are not armed robbers."

"Are you not going to collect your money?" Lillian was beginning to get impatient with the man. "So even if they are armed robbers, have they caught up with you? Have they robbed you?"

"Me?" The driver cried, turning to face her. "Rob me? Why will they want to rob me? Am I carrying anything? Are you not the ones carrying something? Or did you see armed robbers pursuing me before I carried you people?"

"Who is carrying something?"

"It's ok." Lily intervened. "Nobody is carrying anything. And like we said they are not armed robbers. By the time my mother comes out now all this would be solved. I know this is not what we agreed but we will pay you and you will be on your way."

"Better," he said, eyeing Lillian who chose to ignore him. "This is the kind of thing we taxi drivers pray about every day, that we will not pick 'problem passengers'."

Lillian turned her back to him and began to look outside the window. Lily decided to concentrate on the door her mother went in through.

"It won't be long," she said.

"I hope she won't take too long in that place because I have a family to feed," the driver continued. "I am just a simple man going about my daily bread. I don't look for anybody's trouble. Let nobody bring their trouble to me."

Lillian sighed, took one look at him and turned back to the window.

"Look at the time," Lily said looking at her watch. "I hope the roads will be free. Oh, here comes my mum."

Amanda had just emerged from the house with two men and they were walking towards the car. When they got to the car, Amanda opened the door where Lily was sitting.

"Come down, girls," she said.

"What's happening?" Lily asked as she got down.

"We're changing cars," she replied. "Driver, please open the boot for us."

The driver got down and opened the boot. "You people are entering another car," he said to Amanda.

"Yes." She opened her handbag and brought out some money as Lily and Lillian got the bags out. "So how much is our extra fare?"

"You know that we have wasted time," the driver said. "It's because those people were pursuing us, otherwise..."

"How much do we owe you?"

"Just add two thousand five hundred. It's because...I don't even know whether..."

"Take," she handed the money to him, cutting short his rambling. "Thank you. And instead of turning right at the beginning of the close, turn left so you can go out through the other gate."

"Thank you." He got into the taxi and drove off.

"This way Madam," one of the men said to Amanda. He led them into an open garage beside the house and loaded their bags into the jeep that was packed in it. "The windows are tinted so no one can see inside." He opened the car door for them and they all got into the back, while he got into the driver seat and the other man got into the passenger seat.

As they drove out of the gate Lily looked out for Melody's car but didn't see it. They must have missed them when they turned into the road that led to the barracks.

"I hope you can still make it there on time," Amanda said.

"I have to, Madam. It's the only one for the day."

"The only what?" Lily whispered to her mother.

"Flight," Amanda replied. "We have to get to the airport on time for the only flight to Benin."

"Airport?" Lily asked.

"Airport?" Lillian looked surprised.

"Yes," Amanda replied. "The major thought it was better for us to go by air. He was able to call the airline and make three bookings."

"Who's the third booking for?" Lillian asked.

"You," Amanda replied. "They have probably seen you with us. There's no way I'm leaving you behind."

"You're taking me with you?" Lillian's face lit up. "Lily… I'm going with you?"

"Are you serious? Lillie is coming with us?" She threw her arms around Lillian. "This is just the best thing."

"That way I can keep my eye on both of you."

The roads were quite busy and it was an hour before they were at the local airport. Their flight was at a quarter past four and they had only minutes to get their tickets and get on the plane. The driver stopped at the entrance while the other man grabbed the two heaviest bags and made a quick dash for the counter. Amanda and the girls followed quickly.

"This will be my first time on a plane," Lily said to Lillian as they stood behind Amanda waiting for their tickets.

"This is my first time in an airport," Lillian said.

"My second. Not like I remember the first time. Mama took me with her once when I was really small."

Later the man turned around and handed the tickets to Amanda. "Your tickets Madam. You need to hurry."

"Thank you very much. And please thank the major for me. It was really generous of him to pay for the tickets."

"I will. Have a safe trip." He waved to Lilly and Lillian and they waved back.

"Thank you." Amanda picked up her bag. "Come on girls.

They had to rush through the security checks and run all the way to the tarmac. They were panting by the time they got into the plane. It seemed they were the last ones to board.

"You'll have to take any vacant seat you see," a flight attendant told them. "We are already set to take off."

"Oh no," murmured Lillian.

They settled in their different seats and the plane took off. There was no way Lily could see where Lillian was sitting because Lillian was the last to be given a seat and was taken towards the back of the plane. Lily wished they were sitting together. She still couldn't believe Lillian was traveling with her. It meant they were not supposed to part ways just yet. A wave of sadness swept over her as she remembered Shade. She knew she still hadn't recovered from her recent ordeal and she felt deeply for her. She had watched sadly as Shade fought hard to pull herself together after they left the hospital. She had tried to be brave. It was what she had done all her life. She always said that she had to be strong to survive because no one fought for her. But Lily had seen her weak and defenseless after her suicide attempt. Lillian had been full of words of encouragement and counsel and she, Lily, had tried her best to make her as comfortable as possible. And when Melody came after them, it was Shade that came to their rescue. It mattered to her a great deal what the future held for her friend and she hoped desperately that things would turn out well for her.

The plane landed in Benin just after five and the passengers began to disembark but Lily stayed in her seat until she saw Lillian beside her. Then she got up and they both moved towards the front with the other passengers.

"How was it?" Lillian asked Lily when they were on the tarmac.

"It would take some getting used to," she replied. "Were you scared?"

"Was I scared?" She raised her eyebrows.

They both laughed.

"What's that?" Amanda asked.

"It's Lillian's first time on a plane and her heart was in her mouth throughout the flight."

"Really? And where was yours?" Amanda asked laughing.

"I wasn't really scared," Lily said.

"Liar!" Lillian cried.

"Truly! I just didn't like the lurching and the noise and the…ok, just a bit." She giggled.

"Ha!"

After picking the only bag that was checked in they went in search of a taxi to take them home. The roads were very busy as usual. The airport was quite some distance from where Amanda lived and it was already getting dark by the time the taxi pulled up at the gate.

"Thank God," Amanda said as she opened the taxi door. "Thank God for everything."

"I can't wait to see them again," Lily said as they headed for Esther's flat.

"You mean Ola and Akin," Amanda said.

"Yes."

"Pity, the time you have with them is so short."

"I'm going to make the most of it."

Amanda knocked on the door and Esther opened it smiling with Ola jumping up and down beside her. Akin whom she was carrying immediately reached out for Amanda.

"Hello everyone," she said. "Good to see you all." Amanda had called her earlier to inform her that she was coming with both Lily and Lillian.

"Good to see you too and you don't know how much." Amanda hugged her with Akin still in her arms then she took him and held Ola close. "How are you all?"

"We're fine," Esther said hugging each girl in turns. "Please come in."

As soon as they were in, Lily picked Ola up.

"Well, Esther," Amanda said. "You know Lily, my daughter, and this is Lillie her very, very good friend."

"I'm pleased to meet you both."

"And girls, this is Esther," Amanda said. "My very own Lillie."

This made everyone smile.

"I hope you're all hungry because the children and I have cooked dinner," Esther said.

"Really? Akin, is it true?" Amanda tickled her son who started giggling immediately. "Did you help Aunty Esther cook dinner? Ola?"

"Ola is still a bit shy," Lily said. "I don't think she's going to say anything."

"And she's been nattering all day. Both of them have," Esther said.

"Timothy still at work?" Amanda asked.

"Yes he is. He called about an hour ago. He said he would try to get away early so he can see you all tonight. So what really happened?"

"Esther, everything happened." Amanda put Akin on a chair and walked with her to the kitchen. "But let's feed these people first."

"Your brother and sister are lovely," Lillian said as she went to sit beside Akin. "He's the cutest boy I've ever seen. Just look at his curly hair."

"He looks a lot like my uncle Henry. That's my mother's elder brother."

"And Ola is beautiful."

"Very."

"It's a pity we have to leave tomorrow morning," Lillian said. "I would have loved to spend some more time with them. I could stare at them all day."

Lily laughed. "Now you'll have only me to stare at all day."

"Help!"

Later Amanda and Esther walked in with the food and asked them to come to the table. Before long they were all enjoying Esther's Fried Rice and chicken and reliving the events of the day.

"That is a real "Red Sea" experience," Esther agreed with what Amanda had said. "So how exactly did you cross? After all, here you are."

"Shade called just then."

"That's Melody's niece that was with them when you got there."

"Yes. She wanted to warn us that Melody was on her way to us. When she found out that we were already being followed she told us to leave the bridge at Oworo and drive as fast as possible to the barracks," Amanda said. "And that was a move our pursuers did not expect because one of the cars was too far from the exit to come after us."

"So how did you get rid of the other car?"

"We don't really know." Amanda shrugged and looked at Lily and Lillian.

"Maybe they didn't know what turn we took when we turned to the barracks," Lillian said.

"Or maybe they got into the barracks and lost us because we drove into a restricted area," Lily said.

"Yes," Amanda continued. "Shade had called someone, a major, through whom we had access into the senior officers' section. He provided a vehicle with tinted windows and gave us a bodyguard to take us through another gate to the airport. We were just on time to make the flight."

"Sounds like a movie." Esther stared wide-eyed at each of them. "You mean that woman really came after you? What was she planning to do? Take Lily by force?"

"I tell you, only God knows." Amanda replied. "I'm just glad it's over."

"So first thing tomorrow morning they're off to Port Harcourt."

"Before the cock crows," Amanda said. "I wouldn't be surprised if Melody puts her nephew on the night bus. I want them to be long gone before he gets here."

"There's nothing he can do though," Esther said.

"I know but I just don't want them to have to deal with him at all."

"It is better they don't, definitely. I still can't believe he was actually in Lagos."

"Tell me about the Robert part." Lily and Lillian had gone to the kitchen to do the dishes and Amanda and Esther were left alone at the dining table. "Just when I think it can't get any more interesting something new pops up."

"'Pop' is the right word." Amanda nodded. "Opening his office door and walking in took all the courage I had, Esther, as I didn't know what to expect. And of course I completely forgot everything I had rehearsed as soon as I saw him." She smiled as Esther laughed. "I was so nervous that what I meant to say last was what I said first."

"Which was?"

"That we had a child together. That was supposed to be revealed at the tail end of my speech. So I quickly let him know that I had made a lot of terrible mistakes where Lily was concerned and I was sure that I would be making another one if I didn't tell her about him now that I knew where he was. I told him that I had no other reason than for my daughter not to hate me again. And Esther, the man *don* born again *o*."

"Slow down," Esther drew her chair closer to Amanda. "Real or fake?"

"As real as can be," she replied. "He led his daughter to the Lord."

"He led Lily to the Lord."

"And he is ready to take care of her."

"Amazing," Esther said. "And he just accepted her."

"He just knew. Another Red Sea split right apart."

Esther sat back. "To think that all this time God was taking care of that aspect of Lily's life."

"Without anyone's knowledge."

"And then He set up a timely arrangement for you two to see each other again."

Amanda took a deep breath and closed her eyes for a moment before looking at Esther again. "I used to think that Robert would always be a dark side of my life. When I found out about him from my old school mate I thought I was going to face something really heavy. What would he say? How would he receive me or my news? For me it was a destabilizing development. What if he didn't believe me? I kept wondering what I was doing to his family bringing my fifteen year old daughter into his life so suddenly. But the whole thing was nothing like I expected. God gave me a miracle. The only thing is that he now has to face the challenge of telling his family."

"You know," Esther said reflectively. "These things we do have consequences. It's so much better not to dabble into them at all. But I believe God will help him." Then she smiled. *"Ama, your story don pass a movie part one, part two and part three o."*

"You think?" Amanda giggled.

"By the way, how far with the forms?"

"You mean…? Well now that Lily is here latest by Monday I'll send them."

"No matter how long or dark the night is…" Esther began.

"Morning must surely come."

"And the sun will come out." Esther added. "No one can stop that."

There was a knock on the door and Esther got up to answer it.

"Where are the Lagos people?" The room resounded with Timothy's deep voice as he walked in.

"Uncle Timothy! Uncle Timothy!" Ola and Akin got up from the floor where they had been playing and ran to him."

"Hello my mini friends," he said excitedly as he picked them up, one on each arm. "How have you been?"

"Hello Timothy."

"Hey. How was your trip?"

"Eventful."

"Esther said you were returning with your daughter," Timothy said.

"Yes," Amanda said. "And her friend too."

"Where are they?" Timothy asked.

"In the kitchen."

Lily and Lillian came from the kitchen just then. Timothy put the children down.

"Hello Lily and…" He shook Lily's hand.

"Lillian." Lillian took his extended hand.

"Nice to meet you both. I'm Timothy, Esther's husband."

Timothy took a seat and turned to Amanda. "So what's the plan?"

"They both leave for Port Harcourt tomorrow morning and stay there till further notice," she said.

"And when is Sheyi coming back?" He asked.

"Most likely tomorrow," she replied. "I think we should let you eat and rest. Besides we have to set out early ourselves. And…I'm still bringing the children here in the morning."

"What time would you like me to wake you up?" Esther asked.

Amanda stood up and eyed her playfully. "I promise you that I'll be the one to wake you up tomorrow morning."

"If you say so," Esther said stifling a smile.

Amanda thanked Timothy as he dropped the bags inside her sitting room a few minutes later.

"You're welcome. Good night."

"Good night all," Esther said.

Amanda shut the door. "We need to go to bed early. Everyone come this way." She led them to the children's room. "You can sleep on the children's beds. They'll sleep with me tonight. We're all getting up by four." She turned to leave.

"Four?" Lily exclaimed. "Is it because we have to set out early or because you want to win your bet?"

"Bet? What bet?" Amanda feigned ignorance. Then she smiled. "Take a quick shower if you want, both of you, and Lily please come when you're through. There's something I need you to do tonight before you sleep. Go on all of you," she said as she hurried out.

Amanda lay awake long after everyone had slept and let her mind go over all that had happened. However was it possible for anyone to survive in this world without the help of God? No. Survival was not enough. People survived, though defeated, beaten down, cheated, discouraged, frustrated, and even suicidal. No, survival was certainly not enough. To be victorious. That was it. So how could one be victorious without God's help? It just wasn't possible. There were too many forces working against you. Sometimes it seemed like life was one big calculated effort to knock you out and if you didn't take a stand it would defeat you. But to take a stand was not all. One needed to take the right stand, the one that would ensure that victory; the one that would put you above all those opposing forces and give you strength to withstand them. The one that would give you the courage to carry on no matter what you faced. And that was where God came in. Amanda was glad she had taken that stand. She couldn't say that all her problems were solved but she knew she was on God's side and He had all the answers. And she knew it didn't mean she wouldn't get into difficult situations but she knew for sure that He would always guarantee her victory, even if it seemed sometimes like it was by the skin of her teeth.

By the time she finally fell asleep it was with joy that God had made it possible for Lily to escape Melody's clutches and in a short while she would be safe in Port Harcourt.

By the time Amanda opened the door for Esther in the morning they were almost ready.

"Told you," she said as Esther walked in.

"What time did you people get up?" Esther asked glancing round. "Sure you slept at all?"

"Good morning," Lily said smiling. "Mummy got everyone up by four."

"And we're ready to go," Amanda said smugly.

"Good for you," Esther commended her. "Where are my little angels?"

"Still sleeping," Amanda replied. "We'll get them."

Esther helped Lillian with the bags.

After they had dropped the children at Esther's place they were on their way. It was still dark but Amanda was determined to get them out of town as early as possible.

They got to the taxi park in no time because they were usually very few cars on the roads at that time of the morning. Their taxi was full in no time.

"It seems you're not the only early birds this morning," Amanda commented as she observed the number of people milling around the park and how quickly the taxis were filled up.

As they waited for the driver to settle some things with the park officials Amanda hugged both girls again.

"Take care of each other," she said. "I know Agnes is there and of course she was over the moon when I called her last night to tell her you were coming. But Lillie," she turned to Lillian, "while you're still in Port Harcourt, please keep an eye on Lily for me. And I trust you because I have seen how genuine you are. I only pray that you would make the right decision to give your heart to Jesus. And I pray that God will touch your father's heart." She turned and put her two hands on Lily's shoulder. "You have a real friend in Lillie. But she needs you too. Help her to make the right decisions. And when she decides to go back home," she wagged her finger in Lily's face, "help her pack her things!"

"I promise!" Lily said laughing.

"And I promise to do what you said," Lillian said. "Thank you for everything."

Amanda reached into her bag and gave them an envelope. "Give this to Agnes and don't listen to any protest from her."

The driver returned and Amanda stepped back. "Have a safe trip."

Amanda got home expecting to see Sheyi but there was no sign of him. She had taken the children from Esther's and had settled down to some housework when the phone rang. The wiped her hands on a towel and picked it up.

"Hello." She didn't know whose number it was that showed on the phone.

"Good morning. It's Shade."

"Hello Shade," Amanda said. "How are you?"

"I'm fine thank you," she replied. "And how are Lillian and Lily? I guess by now they should have left for Port Harcourt."

"They have," Amanda confirmed. "And I am so relieved. Shade, I don't know how to thank you for your help."

"You've thanked me too much already. I am just glad that you got out of Lagos safely and Lily is out of Melody's reach. And speaking of Melody, she was so angry when she got back last night she broke a window."

"You don't say," Amanda said, laughing.

"I wasn't there of course. I'd decided to make myself scarce. I only went there today looking all sweet and innocent. Joe the driver gave me the full gist. Apparently she threw something at someone and missed."

"Sheyi, maybe?"

"Maybe." Shade snickered. "But Joe didn't know whom. He was still in the corridor when it happened. He said she was shaking all over. He had never seen her so angry. And Melody can get angry. You see it is the highest level of offense in Melody's world for a girl to run away. She's usually hunted down. And anything could happen to her. That's why I was so concerned for Lily."

"So girls have been hurt before for running away?"

Shade sighed. "Let's just say I've seen things." She paused. "But it turns out that there is even more to Lily's case than her just running away."

"What do you mean?" Amanda asked.

"Melody was supposed to get a contract through Alhaji Usman that involves a rather large amount of money."

"And?"

"She couldn't afford to lose Lily before clinching the deal," Shade replied. "I called Lily yesterday morning and told her about my suspicions."

"She didn't tell me anything."

"Maybe she didn't want you to worry," Shade said. "Now I don't think Alhaji would be so eager to sign anything. Besides I learnt he had also told her about his intention to marry Lily and that she was to take care of her until he returned from his trip abroad."

"And Lily escaped. I see. No wonder she broke a window. How did you find out about this?"

"News travels fast in the restaurant," Shade said. "And even when I saw her this morning she still looked like she wanted to commit murder. I just avoided her and stayed at the bar until I left."

"Can't anyone stop her from doing all these things?" Amanda wondered aloud.

"In this city? I don't know."

"And what about you Shade? What are you going to do?"

"You know, I've been thinking seriously about that lately," Shade replied. "It seemed all right to keep on enduring my life here before Lily and Lillian came to Lagos. But after having friends like them, things have changed."

"How do you mean?"

"They have left and I can't imagine staying on without them. There's nothing here for me anymore. Lillian asked me once why I didn't leave earlier. I went for youth service in the East and still returned to the restaurant and she couldn't understand why. I tried to explain to her that the restaurant was all the family I had. Now I know the restaurant is what I need to get away from."

"I bet she'll be glad to hear that. What are you going to do?"

"I'm leaving," Shade said triumphantly. "I have some friends in Abuja who are willing to help."

"What would you do there?"

"Nothing like I have been doing, I assure you," Shade answered. "I'm not just leaving Lagos, I'm leaving that way of life completely. I'm just glad I'm still alive."

"I'm happy about this Shade." Then a thought occurred to her. "But what about Melody? How are you going to get away?"

"My next call will probably be from Abuja, you know." Shade laughed. "No, Melody doesn't have to know anything. And even if she does I don't think she'll be able to stop me."

"I don't doubt you for a second," Amanda said. But as soon as she said it she became unsure. An uneasy feeling had come over her suddenly. Should she tell Shade about it? What exactly would she say?

"I'll call Lillian and Lily later," Shade said. "It's been nice talking to you."

"Nice talking to you too." But Amanda felt compelled to warn her. There was nothing wrong with that. "Shade I feel the need to tell you to be very careful. I just…want you not to… you know…not to…take anything for granted…"

"I'll be careful," Shade reassured her. "Don't worry."

Amanda hung up feeling she should have done more, said more to let Shade know how strongly she felt about this. She checked how long Shade had been on the phone with her and tried to justify hanging up. Twelve minutes was a lot of airtime. She still couldn't deny this sense of foreboding even as the day wore on.

"O God," she prayed aloud. "Let Shade be safe. Please take care of her."

Hours later Shade was still on her mind. She decided to call Esther. She couldn't continue like this.

Esther came in shortly afterwards with some of the cakes she had baked earlier on in the day.

"What's on your mind?" She asked as she sat on the sofa.

"Shade," Amanda replied. "Their friend in Lagos."

"What about her?"

"She wants to leave Lagos too and I can't seem to shake this…feeling I have about it."

"You don't want her to leave?" Esther enquired.

"No, not that." Amanda shook her head. "Of course I want her to leave. It's just that I feel she's not safe, as if something bad is going to happen," Amanda explained. "It's this strange feeling I have."

"She can't be safe if she wants to leave. Wouldn't Melody try to stop her, just like she tried to stop Lily?"

"She said she wouldn't let her know and I know she can get away. After all she helped us. But I can't shake this thing." Amanda shook her head.

"Have you tried to commit her to God?" Esther said.

"That's why I called you. I've prayed but I thought if we prayed together…"

"Let's pray."

After about fifteen minutes of earnest prayers for Shade they both thanked God and Amanda looked up and smiled.

"You don't look worried anymore," Esther observed.

"I'm not," Amanda confirmed. "In fact I am relieved. I feel confident that God will keep her."

"Amen to that," Esther said jubilantly. "Let's celebrate with some cakes."

Amanda fetched two plates and sat down with Esther who put cakes in them.

"It is confirmed that Sheyi is a pimp," Amanda announced. She looked directly at Esther who stopped chewing for a moment. "Shade was also living with Melody when he was there. She didn't know all this time that the mother of her new friend was connected to the same Sheyi. It was when we were talking about him in Lagos that she found out."

"And she confirmed it."

Amanda nodded. "In addition to the fact that he is still very much in the business and that he is in Lagos every now and then."

"When does he go?" Esther asked in wonder.

Amanda shrugged. "He also still sleeps with the prostitutes…"

"Please don't say it!" Esther looked away as if she couldn't bear to listen.

Suddenly Amanda laughed. "You know what she said? She said I shouldn't be bothered about catching anything because Sheyi sees the doctor more frequently than he goes to the toilet or something like that."

"What kind of man is he?"

"That's a mystery to me."

"He'll now come and ask you about your trip to Lagos," Esther said.

"Yes, but he'll have to admit that he too was there and then we start opening one page after the next."

"Till all is revealed."

"Till all is revealed."

"It's a good thing I wasn't there with you in the taxi when you were trying to get away," Esther said after a few moments.

"Why do you say that?" Amanda asked.

"My first thought would have been that it was Shade that told Melody where you were."

"No…" Amanda began.

"No, really! After all she was the only other person who knew and she had gone to see Melody that morning."

"Yes…but you don't know her. She would never…"

"I know that now but then I would have been sure she either gave you away willingly or was coerced. And I would have tried to discourage you from accepting her help."

Amanda cocked her head for a moment, thinking. "Well, thank God you were not there," she finally mumbled before biting into her cake.

"Exactly what I said," Esther said smiling.

"Suspicious," Amanda said with her mouth full. "It's not good to be suspicious."

"I agree that it's not good," Esther said. "It's *better.*"

"You're impossible!"

Later Esther got up to leave. "Were you able to get to the courier company on your way back from seeing Lily and Lilian off?"

"Oh sorry. I forgot all about that." Amanda scratched her head. "Yes I was. I was their first customer. Had to wait for them to open their doors. I got there rather early."

"Good." Esther stopped at the door. "I wonder what's holding Sheyi in Lagos."

"I hope whatever it is keeps him there."

Esther laughed and Amanda couldn't hold herself.

Chapter TWENTY-TWO

LILY'S BACK WAS STIFF as a board by the time she got out of the taxi at the park on Aba Road in Port Harcourt. She stretched, not caring who was looking. She never stretched in a public place. Her grandmother had told her it wasn't proper.

"Sorry Mama," she said as she swung her arms down elaborately.

"Who is Mama?" Lillian asked as she got out of the taxi to get their bags.

"My grandmother," Lily replied. "I was just apologizing to her for stretching in public."

Lillian paused for a moment and looked at her. She was about to say something but thought the better of it and shook her head instead. Lily laughed and went to help her with the bags. They didn't stand by the road for long before a taxi stopped for them.

"I can't get through to anyone on the phone," Lily complained after trying her mother's number again. "I want my mum to know we got here safely."

"Didn't your mum give you your aunt's number?"

"Yes but I can't get through to her either."

"At least she knows we're coming so she'll be expecting us," Lillian said.

"Yes," Lily said. "I am so excited. You'll love her, Lillie."

Lillian smiled. After a while she sighed heavily, looking out of the taxi window.

"What?"

"For seventeen years I didn't leave Anambra State. And in just four months I have been in Lagos, Edo state and Rivers state."

"You're the real adventurer," Lily said.

"And I thought Lagos had it all for me." She sounded wistful.

"Things aren't always as we want them," Lily said regretfully.

"You can say that again," Lillian agreed. "Do you know what I was thinking about all through the journey?"

"What?" Lily looked at her.

"How much I miss my family and how much I would like to go back home but can't," Lillian replied. "If my father is still planning to marry me off then no matter how much I miss home I can't go back."

"Lillie," Lily said, "if there's anything I have learnt in the past few days it is that God can make anything happen. Think about what we've all been through. Could you ever have imagined that we would be where we are now? I think that if He can save me from Alhaji, get us out of Lagos in one piece, save Shade's life…He can make this marriage issue disappear completely and you can go back home."

Lillian sat there without saying anything. Then she looked up. "I hope so," she said finally. "And you forgot to mention meeting your father for the first time."

"Yes, that too. The truth is I can believe anything now. I am so sure of God's love that I don't think anything is impossible. I am certain that things are working out for all of us. You need to speak to Mary soon just like you promised my mum. I remember you said there's someone you can call."

"Yes, there is."

"Who knows? She might just tell you that you're free to come home now."

Lillian sighed. If only she had Lily's faith.

The taxi turned into Albert Street just after the Woji roundabout. Lily wiped a tear from the corner of her eye discreetly. Everything on the street she had grown up on seemed exactly the same; the houses, shops, even the road was as bad as ever. As the taxi driver drove in, out of and around the potholes Lily felt she was the only one that had changed. And she would never be the same again. She would never be that young girl that left just over a year ago oblivious of what world out there had for her.

"What number?" Lillian asked, bringing her back to the present.

"What? Oh. Sixteen. The blue and white house just up there."

"It's cute," Lillian said.

"Everything about Mama is cute. You'll soon find out."

As soon as the taxi stopped in front of the house someone came running out of the gate.

"Lily!"

"Aunt Agnes! Aunt Agnes!" Lily quickly paid the driver and bounded out of the taxi. She ran all the way into the open arms of her aunt who lifted her completely off the ground and swung her round. It was on this exact spot she had clung to her sorrowfully a year ago.

"My baby! My baby is back!" Tears welled up in Agnes's eyes.

"Oh Aunt Agnes." Lily too had tears in her eyes. "I've missed you so much."

"Lily." Agnes held her at arms' length. "Let me look at you."

Lillian walked up just as the taxi left. Lily looked up at her.

"Aunty, meet Lillie, my friend."

"Lillie." Agnes held out her arms again and held Lillian close. "You're now my friend too. You're welcome." She collected the bags from her. "Let's go inside."

"The house looks just the same," Lily said as they walked in. "Except Mama is not in it."

Agnes dropped the bags and put her arm around Lily's shoulder. "Yes, the house looks the same, but it can never be." She smiled. "I miss her too."

Lily smiled sadly. Her grandmother used to fill the whole house with her warmth and her love. Now it seemed like just a nice house.

"But we still have our wonderful memories of her. And we have all that we learnt from her. Even the answers to the prayers she prayed for us are still coming in."

Agnes tried to cheer her up.

"That's very true, Aunty."

Agnes turned to Lillian. "Sorry Lillie for ignoring you like this," she apologized. "Mama was just like that."

"It's ok. I understand. Lily has told me so much about her."

"Thank you." Agnes picked up their bags again. "Come inside and freshen up while I try to call Amanda to let her know you have arrived. I have made pounded yam and native soup. The soup is full of periwinkles and stock fish, Lily, just as you like it."

Lily winked at Lillian. "Welcome to my world."

After they had both taken a shower Agnes asked them to sit at the dining table.

"I got through to your mother. She has been trying to call too. She said she'd call back in a few minutes."

"A table cloth," Lillian said in childlike wonder as soon as Agnes disappeared into the kitchen. "What if I told you I have never sat at a table with a table cloth?"

"No."

"Yes."

"Not even at home?"

"At home?" She laughed. "We don't even have a dining table. All we have is this dilapidated wooden structure a local carpenter's apprentice constructed for my mother ages ago for something or the other, and it is covered from one end to the other with our books, especially the old ones, and all kinds of junk. It was even pushed to the corner of the sitting room so it is out of the way. For you to eat on it you have to be really determined. You would have to clear up a part of the mess and endure looking at the rest it." She laughed again.

"And your mother didn't mind?"

"My mother?" Lillian shook her head. "Mama doesn't care for such things. She usually scoffed at anything modern and told me I had a silly head."

"Of course you know you don't."

"What does it matter if she still thinks I do? She never listened to me."

"Well, you don't," Lily persisted. "I think you're the person with the most 'unsilly' head I have ever known."

"Thank you very much."

Agnes came in with a tray just as a telephone began to ring.

"Lily, please fetch the phone from the kitchen," she said. "I'm sure it's your mother."

Lily was speaking on the phone when she returned. "Tiring but we're fine. We tried to call you too." She smiled at Lillian as she listened to her mother. "Yes, she's fine. Hold on for her." She gave the phone to her.

"Hello." Lillian said. "I'm fine." And then she laughed. "I stayed awake throughout." After a little while she thanked Amanda and handed the phone back to Lily.

"Hello," she said. And then, "ok Mum, I won't forget. Bye." She gave the phone to Agnes. "She wants to speak to you."

Lily sat at the table next to Lillian.

"Your mother wanted to be sure we didn't both sleep off in the taxi and end up beyond Port Harcourt," Lillian said.

"Thank God Port Harcourt is the last stop." She opened the dishes. "Let's eat."

It didn't take that long before neither girl could eat anymore.

"I can't even move," Lillian said when Agnes told them they were supposed to empty the dishes. "I guess it was so good I didn't know when to stop."

"I always have this problem when Aunt Agnes cooks," Lily said. "My waist line increases by an inch."

"It was so frustrating not to know where you were and not to be able to speak to you at all," Agnes said when they were seated in the cosy living room. "At first I was really angry with Amanda because she refused to tell me. Then I committed it to the Lord and waited. I just couldn't understand why she blocked me off like that. It wasn't until I said I was going to Benin that she told me you were in Lagos. Tell me how was life in Lagos?"

"Aunt Agnes, don't blame my mother," Lily said. "She's had a lot to deal with…"

"I know she's passed through a lot. Even though we didn't really talk much in the past year we still talked more than many previous years put together. I knew after a while that she had been restored to the Lord completely and that was my greatest joy. Mama would have loved to see that."

"Yes." Lily dreaded having to tell Agnes about the past year but she knew the time would come when she wouldn't be able to avoid it.

"So what did you do in Lagos?"

Lily felt uneasy and hesitated.

"Lily is now born again," Lillian quickly came to her rescue. "She met her father. And he was the one who…who… prayed her in."

Agnes looked at Lily as if in a new light. "Lily? Tell me what Lillie is talking about."

Lily smiled shyly. "Mummy met one of her old classmates who worked for my father and she gave her his office address. She decided to tell me because she didn't want to do anything wrong anymore." She paused when Agnes sighed. "She said it was up to me to decide whether I wanted to see him or not. And I did, so we went together to see him."

"That's in Lagos."

"Yes, in Victoria Island. And he was nice and told us how he became born again. He told me about the love of God and how God wanted to bridge the gap between Himself and me. He told me about Jesus and I believed."

"Amanda didn't tell me," Agnes said. "This is great news. So you spent a lot of time with your father. Was he the one you stayed with in Lagos?"

"No. Actually I only met him yesterday."

"Yesterday?" Agnes looked confused.

Lily sighed. "Aunt Agnes, I really don't know how to tell you about Lagos but I can't keep it from you. I don't know if you could ever be prepared for what you are about to hear. I don't know if I'll be able to say everything. Maybe Lillie will help me when I can't…" Lillian moved closer to her to assure her that she would.

For about half an hour Lily spoke about her ordeal, from the moment she first left Port Harcourt to the moment she returned. For about half an hour Lillian helped her when she needed to. And for about half an hour Agnes listened and wept.

"I promised Mama that I would take care of you," she finally said as she sobbed. "And I failed."

"No." Lily quickly went to her and put her arms around her. "You didn't fail, Aunty. I'm here now and I'm alive and well and even born again. And do you know why? Because you prayed for me and God heard."

"God knows," Agnes said amidst sobs, "that a single day did not pass without me lifting you up into His everlasting arms."

"You see?" Lily tried to pacify her. "You were always there for me."

"I'm so sorry about everything that happened to you," she said, holding both sides of Lily's face. Lily hugged her again. "I don't know why it had to be that way. Only God knows why we pass through rough patches. But we need to be grateful that He helps us through them and brings us out victorious. But let that woman come here…"

"It's ok, Aunty," Lillian soothed. "She would never dream of coming here."

Agnes calmed down after a while. "And Lillie, did that woman hurt you too?"

"No," Lillian replied. "Actually I ran away to Lagos a few months ago because my father wanted to force me to marry one of his friends."

"In this day and age?" Agnes was shocked.

"I couldn't do it. Besides I'd always wanted to get away but I was going to wait until I was admitted into a university far away from home. I jumped over the fence just before the man came to propose and ran to Lagos. That's where I met Lily. My friend that helped me get away was actually at the restaurant as well. She's the one that Lily was talking about.

"I always thought Lagos was where I was meant to be but I hated it. The strong people took advantage of the weaker people and everyone just seemed to have it in for everyone else. Friendship and love is so minimal compared to the hatred." She shook her head ruefully. "I'm out and I don't miss the place."

"My dear Lillie," Agnes said. "You've described not just Lagos but the whole world. The devil is the god of this world and until Jesus comes again to take us His children, we are going to continue to see the hatred and the evil that pervades the worldly system. But we have our consolation in our personal relationship with the Lord Jesus. Even though we are in this world we are not of it and He knows His own and He preserves them."

Lillian listened intently as Agnes spoke. The look on her face bothered Agnes.

"What's the matter, Lillie?" she asked.

She wrung her hands and looked down. "It's just that...I'm not yet a part of His own. I have never made up my mind. Mary, my sister who has been born again for quite a while, had been speaking to me about it for a long time but I always put it off. I always felt I wasn't ready. I never made up my mind."

Agnes hesitated for a moment. "And now?" She asked tenderly.

"I think I have," Lillian said quietly. "I have decided I want to be born again. I want to be a Christian."

Lily's face broke into a wide smile. She left Agnes's side and came and sat beside Lillian, holding her hand. Lillian smiled shyly as she looked at her.

"You've already decided," Agnes said to Lillian. "But you need to tell the Lord what you have decided. Would you like to tell Him yourself or would you like me to lead you in prayer?"

"Please lead me," she replied. "I don't think I know what to say."

"Ok." Lillian bowed down and Agnes led her in the prayer. When they were through Lily reached out and hugged her friend warmly.

"Now we're sisters in Christ, aren't we, Aunt Agnes?"

"Indeed we are." Agnes hugged Lillian too.

"I'm born again," Lillian said shyly. "Just like Mary."

"Mary will be pleased," Lily said. "I bet she's been praying for you. And now you will have this good news for her when you call. I can imagine how hard she must have tried to get you to understand."

"But I just couldn't see," Lillian said. "Not the necessity or the importance. I had nothing against it but I always thought it was something to be put off until a later date. I was sure there would be a convenient time. I'm glad I didn't die before now."

"All God's children are glad they didn't die before they knew the Lord." Agnes stood up. "Of course giving your heart to the Lord is only the beginning of what is called 'the Christian race'. You need to grow just like a baby grows. But you grow by God's word. I will get you both a few books you can read that will help you understand better. And if you have any questions you can ask me." She left the room to get the books.

"Your mum will be glad," Lillian told Lily

"Yes! I'm going to call her later and tell her."

"And I've not even been here for a full day."

Agnes returned and handed them the books. "They're very easy to understand. I expect you'll find them so. But if you still have any issue you want me to clarify, don't hesitate to ask me. I'm very happy about what happened today." She sat down again.

"And I am also happy to be back home. I thought it would never happen," Lily said. "It feels like a dream. And to think I brought back the good in Lagos with me." She smiled at Lillian.

"Shade is still there and I just can't stop thinking about her," Lillian said. "She's a very good person."

"I pray she'll be all right."

"For her to be all right she would have to leave Lagos and be as far from Melody as possible." Then Lillian turned to Agnes. "You know we went to the hospital to see Shade the night Lily ran away from Melody's house."

"Yes."

"Shade wasn't just sick. She had tried to kill herself."

"Kill herself?" Agnes stared wide-eyed.

"Yes. That's why we had to stay with her and try to help her. She's a good person, but she just fell into the wrong crowd."

"So how did she get to work for Melody?"

Lily chuckled. "Can you really say that Shade works for Melody?"

"Exactly," Lillian agreed, chuckling too. "But it was Melody that got her into prostitution. She lost her parents when she was very young and Melody was the only relative that would take her. And by the time she was fifteen Melody started giving her to men."

"How wicked." The anger was evident on Agnes's face. "Where I work I deal with lots of similar cases but I have never been able to come to terms with how callous some people can be. We have even had cases where it was the mother that introduced her own daughter into it." She looked from one face to the other. "Two months ago a seventeen year old girl was brought to us by some Nigerian Youth Service Corps members.

She had just had a terrible experience and had traveled a long distance. A lot of her journey had been done on foot and she was looking half dead."

"What happened to her?" Lily wanted to know.

"The most unbelievable thing you've ever heard." Agnes looked at her watch. "But I'll have to tell you later. Will you both be all right if I get back to work? I took the day off today because you were coming. But I promised that I would show up if I could. We have two new cases today."

"Cases?" Lillian asked. "Are you a lawyer?"

"Yes, but I work for an NGO full time now, doing mostly other things," Agnes replied. "And when I said cases I didn't mean legal, I meant the new arrivals at our office."

"You work for an NGO? That's a non-governmental organization, right?" Lillian asked

"Yes, it is," Agnes confirmed. "It's called The State Charity Foundation but we like to call it *Rest for the weary*."

"What exactly do you do?" Lillian looked really interested.

"Basically we welcome people, mostly women and children who are victims of abuse and have no one else to turn to, give them a place of rest and help them start again. Most importantly we introduce them to Jesus and watch them 'come back to life'."

"Sounds interesting." She moved to the edge of her seat.

"And rewarding. You wouldn't believe how much. With a little love and attention a person can be lifted from despair to a point where they can maximize their potentials. When I return I will tell you about it. Lillie, you look like you could sit me down here all day."

Lillian's face was glowing. "I can't wait."

"What…is the matter with you?" Lily asked Lillian as soon as she had closed the gate after Agnes.

"What do you mean?" Lillian asked as if she didn't know what she was talking about but the smile on her face showed otherwise.

"There was this look on your face when Aunt Agnes was talking about her work," she said. "And I can still see it."

"What look?" Lillian still feigned ignorance.

Lily eyed her and walked into the house. When they were inside Lillian went and stood by a window, looking outside. She seemed to be lost in thought. Lily watched her for a long moment wondering what was going through her mind. She had noticed a change in her countenance while her aunt was talking. She had also noticed how she drank in every word. Something was definitely on her mind. Lily decided not to press her. Maybe she would talk when she was ready.

Finally Lillian turned around and sat on the window seat. "You're right," she said. "So much has happened to me today I can hardly contain myself. Today I finally understood the need to be born again, the importance of accepting the sacrifice Jesus made for me and I have accepted Him. I pray that I will belong to Him for the rest of my life and nothing will ever take me away from Him." She stood up and walked towards Lily. "Now I want to explain that 'look' you were talking about." She sat on the sofa beside her. "Your aunt…I'm sure she's dedicated to what she does."

"Aunt Agnes? It's all she's ever done as far as I can remember," Lily said. "She worked at night sometimes. She used to talk to Mama a lot about it. Mama always said she was the only person she knew that had a heart big enough to take in so many strangers, people she has never met before."

Lillian nodded. "A heart big enough," she said thoughtfully. "She definitely has that. The way she spoke about her work… she got through to me."

"She's passionate about her work."

"Yes, but she defined for me what I have been trying to understand for some time now."

"What's that?"

"What I want to do with my life," she said decisively.

Lily looked at her enquiringly. "What you want to do with your life?"

"Of course I still want to go to the university and study Law…"

"Law? Like Aunty Agnes? You know she read Law."

"She said so." Lillian nodded. "But what she does now, helping people who have been victims of others and are so badly hurt that they need help seems to me the most important thing anyone can do with their life."

"You…I can't explain the look on your face," Lily said.

"I have discovered my life's purpose." Lillian pointed at her face. "This is the look."

"Really." Lily smiled. "You know, if I didn't know you as well as I do I would think you didn't know what you were talking about. I would say you were just carried away by the way my aunt spoke, and probably by the things you saw in Lagos. But I know you really mean this. You have been my friend and I've never met anyone like you. If anyone can help those that are broken, it's you."

Lillian couldn't help the tears that welled up in her eyes. She tried to smile but her lips only twitched. "Thank you," she managed to say.

"My mum noticed it immediately," Lily said.

"Your mum? Lillian looked surprised. "What did she say?"

"She said you had a gift of giving comfort to others," Lily said.

"That's amazing. Thank you for making me surer than ever." She nodded. "I'm going to hear more about it from Aunt Agnes and then discuss my intentions with her."

"Intentions?" Lily asked.

"Yes," Lillian replied. "I want to do what Aunt Agnes is doing."

"Are you planning to start right now?" Lily was wondering when Lillian would decide to see her family again.

"Maybe, maybe not." She shrugged. "I still want to get a degree and I still miss my family…"

Lily heaved a sigh of relief. "I'm sure there's no hurry," she said putting a hand on Lillian's shoulder. "The NGO will always be there. If there are some important things you need to do first then do them. There's nothing wrong with that."

"You're right," Lillian agreed. "Though I really feel like starting right away."

And that was exactly what she said to Agnes when she returned late in the evening. Agnes was thrilled when she heard, especially after Lily described the kind of friend she had been.

"Zeal, perseverance and a willingness to help others are just about all you need to qualify. And from what I have heard I think the organization will welcome you with open arms." Agnes smiled at Lillian's gleeful countenance. "It's only sad that quite a number of the people that work with us are only there because they need something to do until they can get a better paying job," Agnes sounded mournful. "So what exactly are your plans? But you're so young. What about school? You have my full support of course but don't you think you should consider studying first and getting a degree, you know, a good background?" She spread her hands. "It's really up to you."

"I was just telling Lily that I want to study law."

"Good. You do that first."

"I can't write my matriculation exams this year anymore. So while I wait I'd like to make myself available."

"That's wonderful. But I want to warn you. The money is not that much."

"I will be paid?"

Agnes chuckled. "Of course you'll be paid."

"That's settled then." She rubbed her hands together. "I have a job."

Chapter TWENTY-THREE

IT WAS ALREADY PAST eight when Shade got home. She shut the door behind her and felt unusually happy. It would be at least ten hours before she saw anyone again. She had been home early every night since she returned from Lily's flat and she intended to spend every night at home until she left Lagos. If by some uncommon miracle there was still anything left of her dignity she was determined to preserve it. As a result she had refused to answer any calls from her numerous acquaintances, most of who were men she had been spending time with.

She would have been dead now, she imagined, but for the timely intervention of strangers. She shuddered at the thought. She would have killed herself because of a broken relationship and then what? Life would have gone on without her. People like Melody would have continued in their vices and their victims would have continued to suffer the consequences. The world would have just been one prostitute short. And who cared about that?

She was grateful for her friends. They had helped her more than they could ever know. During the time she had spent with them all her suicidal thoughts had vanished and her despair had gradually been replaced by a determination to prove that she would not remain anyone's victim. Where this new strength came from she didn't know but it was unlike anything she had ever experienced. She felt for the first time that her life could become something worthwhile, and since she was at the reins, the direction it would take from now depended on her. Nothing from her past would determine for her how she lived anymore. She would make her decisions now. And prostitution would certainly no longer be a part of them.

She took a shower, prepared a light meal and settled in front of the TV. This had been her routine for a while now. She would listen to the Network News while she ate and maybe watch a movie before going to bed. But tonight she was not in the mood for a movie. She wanted to think.

Things had not been the same at the restaurant since Lily slipped through Melody's fingers. She had learnt that Melody was determined to make everyone pay for it. She had fired more of her staff than she had ever done in such a short period of time. She was even reported to have resorted to a physical abuse of one of the bar girls. Shade sighed as she remembered how the girl's face was described after the incident. Melody didn't take kindly to a girl getting away, especially one as important as Lily. There was no knowing how long the effect would last.

Joe, Melody's driver, had appeared at Shade place of work that afternoon to inform her that he had been fired. He said Melody blamed him for Lily's escape. She said it was his incompetence at the wheel that made them lose the chase. He was looking so forlorn that Shade was tempted to help him. Not too long ago she would have contacted one or two of her 'friends' and got him another job. And of course a 'return favour' would have been required of her. But she was resolute in her decision to desist from anything to do with prostitution. Even though Joe was one of the few people she liked at the restaurant, she refused to let his lamentations weaken her resolve. She wouldn't succumb now, or ever. She let him go with a promise to see what she could do, a promise she knew she would not keep.

She had begun processing a transfer from the head office of the insurance company to a branch office in Abuja. Her boss was really helpful and agreed to be discreet about it even when he didn't know why she wanted the transfer. In a week or so she would have her transfer letter and then she would leave.

She had already dozed off when there was a knock on the door. She raised her head and looked around, not sure exactly what had awakened her. The sound came again, louder, and this time she knew someone was at the door but she didn't get up. If she didn't answer maybe the person would go away. She couldn't imagine anyone in Lagos presently that she wanted to see. The rapping became more urgent and she thought she could hear someone calling her name. It was a female voice. She looked at the time. It was past midnight. She dragged herself from the bed and went to the sitting room.

"Who is it?" She asked through the closed door.

"Shade, it's me Jacinta," the person replied. Even though she didn't shout the urgency of her tone could still not be played down. "Jacinta! Jacinta!"

Shade had heard the name before at the restaurant. She was sure it was one of the newer girls but she was having a difficult time putting a face to the name. Even if she knew who it was she still wasn't ready to open the door.

"What do you want?"

"Please open the door for me."

"Why should I when I don't even know you?" Shade maintained an unfriendly tone.

"Ah! Shade, you know me," the girl pleaded. "You know me. Please."

"From where?" She asked rudely.

"From the restaurant." She sounded like she was at the brink of tears now. "I've been working there for about a month now. I know you very well. Please."

"How do you know where I live? What are you doing here at my place at this time? Who opened the gate for you?" Shade felt more reluctant to open the door.

"I have nowhere to go." The girl replied and began to weep. "I have nowhere to go tonight."

Shade hesitated for a long moment wondering what to do and then she opened the door. A short disheveled young girl stood outside.

"Come in." Shade stepped out of the way for her and she quickly entered looking over her shoulder once.

Shade locked the door and turned to face the girl who had crossed the room to stand at the kitchen doorway holding one side of the frame with both hands.

"Who or what are you running away from?" Shade asked peering at her. She found the way the girl cowered at the kitchen door almost amusing. "And who gave you my address?"

"I collected it from Brother Joe."

"Joe gave you my address?"

"Yes."

Shade felt angry but she just shrugged. She was more interested in why the girl had come to her place at this time of the night.

"Where are you coming from?" She asked her. "Why did you come here?"

She began to wring her hands. "I've told my 'man' before that I cannot stay a whole weekend at a client's place," she explained. "At first he agreed. Then when he asked me again and I refused he went to report to Madam. I told him before that I didn't have any excuse to give my mother. Where will I say I went?"

Shade was familiar with the different kinds of problems that arose between the girls and their pimps. There were usually disagreements over how far the pimps wanted the girls to go and how much the girls were willing to succumb to. To the pimps it was all about the money and being in Melody's good books. They didn't care about what the clients required of the girls.

"Why don't you sit down?" Shade indicated the seat closest to the girl. She looked closely at the girl as she went and sat down. She couldn't be more than seventeen. "So what happened after he reported you?"

"That man, Victor, just came to where I was sitting in the restaurant. He just 'jacked' me and dragged me to Madam's office. When I got there, Madam asked my 'man' again what happened and he said I refused to go to where we had agreed before. I tried to explain but they didn't let me talk. They were just insulting me. Then Madam warned me that if I didn't obey my 'man' I would regret it. She told Victor right there in front of me that he was to deal with me. And honestly my 'man' was lying."

"Who's your 'man'?" Shade wanted to know.

"Sheyi."

"Who?" Shade cursed under her breath. She didn't even know he was still in Lagos.

"And he was pretending to be my friend. I can't believe he could ever do such a thing." Jacinta shook her head, looking down.

"So what happened that you ended up at my place tonight?"

"When the client came for me at the restaurant I went with him because they were watching me. We first went to *The Interior*. After having some drinks he said he wanted us to attend a party before we went to his house. He then told me he wanted to see some people before we left. It was when he went to meet those people that I just made up my mind and got up and walked out," she said. "I got on the first bike I saw and just as the bike man 'entered' the road I saw that Sheyi and Maxwell were driving behind us. I begged the bike man to make sure that they didn't catch us." She lifted her hands, clearly exasperated. "I want to quit. I am afraid. I don't want to do again."

"I still don't know why you came to me."

"Brother Joe was standing outside after he left Madam's office earlier," she said. "Madam had just sacked him. I told him what happened and that I was afraid. He said it was better if I just did what they said. While we were talking I found out he was going to see you. He said you're the only one he knows that can help him." She looked down again. "So I begged him for your address."

"So what do you expect me to do?"

"I don't know, maybe advise me?"

"Advise you?" Shade looked frustrated. "What kind of advice do you expect me to give you? How did you get into this in the first place?"

Jacinta frowned and muttered something under her breath.

"You wanted money, didn't you? You wanted to enjoy the good things of life."

"That's why we're all in it," Jacinta said rather pertly.

Shade shook her head. "You don't know anything. You chose to do this. You had a choice. Some of us didn't."

"How?"

"I became an orphan at twelve and Melody was the only relative I had that was willing to have me. At fifteen she sent me out to 'sail'. Sheyi was my 'man' until I dropped him."

"Dropped him? How?"

"Never mind," she said with a wave of her hand. "If I had a mother like you do, I wouldn't care how poor we were. I would never become a prostitute." Shade let out her breath loudly. "Tell me, are you proud of what you do?"

"No," Jacinta replied after a long pause. "But a lot of girls are doing it."

"It doesn't mean you have to."

"My friends said it wasn't that bad. Just some nights of fun and our purses will be loaded."

"But you have seen that there's more to it than that now, haven't you?" Shade asked. "You have seen how dangerous it can be. Anything can happen to you. No one would admit anything and most people would never know what really happened."

"But if it is so dangerous, why are you still doing it?"

"Not for long," Shade said and suddenly realized she was about to reveal her intentions to a stranger.

"You're quitting?" Jacinta was alarmed.

Shade tried to find a way out without sounding too obvious. "Everyone will quit one day."

"But you're quitting soon." It was a statement rather than a question.

"Look whether I am quitting soon or not is not the issue here. What you should be concerned about is what we are going to do about your case. Where does your mother think you are?"

"I told her I was going to a friend's birthday party and if we didn't finish on time I would sleep there and return home in the morning."

"I hope they don't know where you live."

"I don't think so."

"You don't think so." Shade looked her up and down.

"I didn't tell anyone," she said quickly. "Do you think they could find out?"

"It's possible."

"O God, I'm dead." She placed both hands on her head and looked like she would start weeping again as the corners of her mouth began to turn downwards.

"Not yet, Jacinta. Calm down," Shade said. "They cannot come to drag you from your house. They can only catch you on the streets."

"Catch me on the streets?" She stared wide-eyed like a little child listening to a scary story.

"Yes. If you didn't live in Lagos then I would say you had nothing to worry about, but the streets of Lagos belong to Melody."

"But I live in Lagos," she said. "So if I live in Lagos they would get me?"

"Just be careful from now on. That's all I can say. Don't go to deserted places, don't go out late at night again and don't be alone anywhere." Shade leaned back on the chair. "The truth is Melody doesn't like to lose her girls."

"It's true," she acknowledged nodding firmly. "See how she searched for that half-caste girl that ran away. It was almost as if she would run mad." She eyed Shade. "Do you think it is possible for me not to be in serious danger if I stop going to the restaurant?"

"Your case is very different from Lily's, don't worry."

"Different? How?"

"There was more to Lily's case than just a girl running away."

"What is special about her case?"

Shade shook her head again. "Let's just say your quitting will not raise as much dust."

"Truly?"

"Trust me."

Jacinta paused for a moment and then she looked up at Shade. "But do you know how she got away? People are saying maybe…"

"How will I know?" The look on Shade's face made Jacinta drop the matter immediately.

"You said I am not really in danger?" She asked after a few moments.

"I hope not. But just be careful as I have told you and make sure you never 'sail' again."

"Never again, I promise."

Shade let Jacinta spend the rest of the night with her and gave her some money to take a taxi straight home and still have some to hold on to. She had tried to reassure the girl but she knew her safety could not be guaranteed. She felt sorry for her.

A week later Shade had packed her bags. She had made up her mind that even if the transfer could not be arranged yet she would still move to Abuja but recently she found out from her boss's personal assistant that her letter was ready. All she needed to do was get to the office to pick up her copy and book her flight to Abuja on her way back home. She was taking the first flight in the morning. She had no reason to wait a moment longer.

Lily and Lillian were excited about her plans. They said they would be praying for her. They were the first people she had ever known to offer to pray for her since her parents died and it meant a lot to her. In fact she felt like she really wanted them to. They said they were both born again now. She didn't know what that really meant but she knew it had to be a good thing. Maybe she would ask them about it later.

She picked up her letter as planned and made her booking on her way home. She had no qualms about deserting Melody. True, she was the only one that was willing to give her a home when she had nowhere to go but she felt she had paid her dues. Maybe she had paid more than her dues. She should have left much earlier.

She had just walked into her gate when she saw a familiar car parked in front of the building. She slowed down her pace immediately and wondered whether to double back or keep walking. A voice behind her helped her make a decision.

"Hello Shade. You've been so scarce." The voice was suave.

"What do you want here?" she asked without looking back.

"*Haba*! Is that how to welcome a friend?"

"You're not a friend and you're definitely not welcome here."

"Well, I'm here, welcome or not," he said. "Let's go upstairs."

"Upstairs where?" She stopped suddenly.

"Don't fool around with me." In a second he had her upper arm in a tight grip. All the smoothness had gone from his voice. "Let's go upstairs."

Shade knew better than to resist. It wasn't as if she couldn't try to free herself or reason her way out of a tight corner. This was different. Victor wasn't human.

At the door she struggled to free her arm. "Let go of my arm!" He released her so she could open the door.

They both entered and Victor whistled.

"Going somewhere?"

Shade's suitcases were right in the middle of the sitting room. At that moment she wished more than anything that they were anywhere but there.

"You know, Madam asked me to bring you in tomorrow but I said today." He tapped his temple. "Instinct." He smiled. "Tomorrow would have been too late, wouldn't it? You're all packed and ready to go. Tell me, where to?"

"As if I would tell you," Shade said between clenched teeth hating the humour in his voice.

"Oh you will. In due time," he said with a wide grin that showed his silver tooth.

Shade hated him. She always had. He was responsible for all of Melody's dirty work. Their paths had crossed a few times but Melody had always taken her side. She knew he hated her too and must have been looking for a way to get back at her. How he must be enjoying this. But Shade wasn't going make it easy.

"What makes you think I'm bothered about going to see Melody?"

"You should be," he said raising his eyebrows and folding his arms across his massive chest. "She wasn't particularly thrilled to find out the part her little Shade had to play in Lily's disappearance."

The look on Shade's face seemed to satisfy him.

Shade felt like lunging at him and scratching out his eyes just to wipe off the smug look on his face. "You…"

"Don't even think about it," he said with a warning look, as if he could read her mind. "I'm still taking you to Madam tonight no matter how many pieces you've made me break you into." He bowed and pointed towards the door. "Shall we? We don't want to keep Madam waiting."

Shade needed to think. If she went with him now she didn't know what would happen. Melody would try to stop her from leaving Lagos or worse…

She was seated between Victor and another thug in the back seat of the car as they set out for Melody's restaurant. There was nothing she could do at the moment except to think. How could Melody have found out about how she helped Lily escape? Maybe this crazy Victor was just bluffing. And she had fallen for it. Well, if that was the case then it was his word against hers. She would deny knowing anything about Lily's escape and rail against Victor. Then Melody would side with her as usual. She hoped. But the fact still remained. Her bags were packed and Victor had seen them. And what if Melody had truly found out about her involvement? She would have to hear from Melody first before trying to figure a way out. She felt so helpless.

"Out," Victor said to her at the restaurant after he had got out of the car. He took her arm as she got out and she yanked it out of his grip.

"Don't…touch me!" She sniffed and walked straight to Melody's office without breaking her stride. She entered without knocking. The last thing she was going to do was act guilty.

Melody looked up suddenly to see who was barging into her office. Her stern look slowly changed into an almost friendly one. "Well, well, well, who do we have here? Folashade. Where have you been all my life?"

"Yes, Aunty?" Shade stood staring at her. She didn't know whether to challenge her or wait for her to ask a direct question. She decided to wait.

"I see you have honoured my invitation," Melody said appearing unperturbed in the least by Shade's bravado. The two seats in front of her table were occupied, one by Sheyi who looked at Shade once when she came in and turned his back to her, and the other by a man Shade had never seen before. "Please sit down and make yourself comfortable." She pointed to the sofa in the corner. "It's going to be a very long night."

"Ok." Shade maintained an angry countenance but went to take the seat. "But I'd like to know why I had to be roughened up by Victor to get me here. You could have just called me."

"Shade, Shade, you were becoming increasingly difficult to reach." Melody sounded casual and friendly but Shade could see through the false façade. The woman was fiendish. She knew she had to get out of this place and fast.

"So what do you want with me?"

"All in good time, my dear. All in good time."

If Melody was trying to unnerve her she was doing a pretty good job. But Shade would rather die than let it show.

Melody leaned forward and began to speak to the man beside Sheyi in hushed tones. Shade didn't like this at all. There was no knowing how long she would be kept here. She looked at her watch and saw that it was getting really late. This was bad. Sheyi turned to look at her and she met his gaze with a cold stare. What was that she saw in his eyes? Pity?

Twenty minutes lapsed and Shade couldn't bear it any longer. She had been totally ignored while the three of them continued to whisper. She was about to protest when there was a knock on the door.

"Come in," Melody said immediately.

Victor walked in with two other men. Shade's heart skipped a beat as soon as she saw him.

"Why did you take so long?" Melody asked him.

"We had to look for her, Madam," Victor replied.

"And did you settle with Gogo?"

"Yes, Madam. He has disposed of the goods."

"Very good." Then she turned to Shade. "Do you know what I can do to you?"

"Do to me?" Shade felt her heart lurch. Melody's face had suddenly taken on an expression so evil it gave her goose bumps just to look at it. The party had begun in earnest.

Melody's devilish laughter suddenly filled the room and for a moment it seemed like there were more people there than Shade could see.

"It rankles me to think of how ungrateful you are, how easily you forget all I have done for you," she said with so much malice quick chills ran down Shade's spine.

"I…I don't understand." Shade's heart was racing.

"Oh, you don't. You don't understand how you stabbed me in the back."

"Stabbed you in the back? What are you talking about?" If she couldn't get out at least she could prolong this. Maybe she could still find a way out.

"You betrayed me, Shade!" Melody cried. "The very first chance you got you didn't hesitate to betray me."

"Betray you…how?" Shade feigned total ignorance.

"You think you can hinder my progress and get away with it?" Shade was about to ask her what she was talking about when Melody raised a hand to stop her from speaking. "Do you know what you cost me by helping Lily escape? I will kill you and nothing will happen or have you forgotten you have no one? You've made a terrible mistake."

Shade steeled herself. She wasn't going to let the words affect her. Or at least she wasn't going to let it show. "Who told you I had anything to do with Lily's escape?"

"Shut up!" Melody screamed making Sheyi jump. "Do I look like a fool? You've been with me all these years and you still take me for a fool? Eh? Shade?" Not letting her reply she continued. "You knew where she was throughout the period

I was looking for her." She pointed to Sheyi. "Sheyi here can confirm that." Shade looked at Sheyi enquiringly but he kept his back to her. "I know there is no way that girl could have gotten away without the help of someone like you."

Was it possible that Melody still didn't know for sure? That she could still play along?

"Ok. So what if I knew where she was? Does that mean I helped…?"

"Just…stop," Melody said, cutting her shut.

"She was at her Alhaji's place at Victoria Island." Shade raised her voice so Melody would not be able to stop her easily. Maybe she could try her best to confuse Melody. "Doesn't that tell you anything?" She was satisfied to see Melody's face darken in a moment of confusion. Shade had been on the streets for so long and had gotten herself out of dire situations numerous times. Maybe all those years of practice would pay off tonight. They had to. "Maybe you should sit him down and ask him some questions. Maybe he has a good reason for hiding her."

Melody pursed her lips and her eyes roamed the room but settled on no one in particular. She seemed to be considering what Shade had said.

"Don't…don't listen to her Madam." Victor rushed forward and said quickly. "I'm sorry Madam, but she isn't telling the truth."

"Who…is this?" Shade asked condescendingly, turning towards Victor and pointing at him with an upturned hand. "Who asked you anything? You that could not find a girl that was under your very nose."

Victor looked desperate. He eyed Shade and continued. "She knows about the escape and I have someone outside the office to prove it." He walked quickly to the door and opened it.

"Someone outside to prove…" Shade laughed in disgust and prepared to continue ridiculing him. "You want to save face with a false accuser. How much did you pay him? Who's going to fall for…?" Her voice trailed off as Jacinta appeared through the door. "Jacinta?" She walked up to Jacinta who appeared unwilling to meet her eyes. "You sent Jacinta to spy on me?" Shade was apparently shocked.

"Not really." Victor looked triumphant. "But she was willing to trade anything for her safety."

"And…what did she say about me?" Shade didn't recognize her own voice.

"That you were going to help her just like you helped Lily." Victor turned to Melody. "And Madam, her bags were all packed when I got to her place this evening."

"But I never told her anything like that. Jacinta! Why did you…?" Jacinta only looked away.

Melody had heard enough. "You ungrateful girl! You think you can do what you like." She got up. "I'll show you that you have messed with me for the last time." She turned to Victor. "Victor!" He was instantly by Shade's side. "Take her."

Agnes had just returned home. She had had a particularly busy day attending interviews at the Local Government Council and meeting with the management of a multi-national company. All she wanted to do was take a shower, have a quick meal with the girls and head straight for bed. But as Lillian set the plate before her she found that she couldn't bring herself to put as much as a spoonful in her mouth. It wasn't because there was anything wrong with the meal, Lillian had proved her culinary skills again and again, but because she had a burden, an uneasy feeling that something bad was going to happen if she didn't pray as soon as possible. She looked at the girls who were busy chattering about one thing or the other.

"I can't eat," she announced to them. "I can't eat now."

"Are you ok?" Lily asked.

"Yes, I'm fine. I'm fine," she replied. She got up from the table. "But someone somewhere isn't."

"What do you mean?"

"I feel a strong urge to pray."

"For whom?"

"I don't know but it's urgent."

"Mary used to have that," Lillian said seeming to understand. "And it was always urgent too."

"So if you will both excuse me." Agnes left the room.

Fifteen minutes later Agnes was still praying. Both Lillian and Lily had decided not to eat as well but wait until she was through.

"Maybe we should join her," Lillian suggested.

"Ok," Lily agreed.

They both stole into Agnes's room and found her kneeling by her bed praying. Lillian sat on the couch by the door while Lily went and sat at the desk across the room. They had agreed that they would both pray that God would answer Agnes's prayer and do whatever it was she felt the need to pray about.

The page became blurred again and Amanda shook her head so she could see the words. Finally she closed the book she had been trying to read for over an hour. True, she had been enjoying the peace and quiet, but she couldn't help wondering why Sheyi had not returned to Benin. She had made up her mind not to call him. She could call Shade to find out if he was still in Lagos. She had been meaning to call Shade anyway.

Ever since she had first been concerned about her safety she had called her several times just to be sure she was fine. Once again a deep concern for Shade's safety enveloped her like a thick fog. She knew she had prayed for her before but right now she was certain she needed to pray more than ever. It was just something she had to do. She slipped off the bed to her knees. She was going to pray hard tonight, hard enough to deal with this concern and for Shade to be safe.

Chapter TWENTY-FOUR

FOR THE SECOND TIME that evening Shade found herself wedged between two men in the back seat of Melody's car. The heavy set one on her left was already in the car when she entered while the man that had been sitting beside Sheyi in Melody's office had got in after her. This time Victor was in the front seat. They had another business to take care of first, one that involved the man called Gogo and some mysterious 'goods'. She knew because she had overheard part of the conversation. Melody had spent a long time briefing Victor and the man on her right on how to 'tidy things up' and she had looked very intense when she was speaking to them. Shade wondered what it was really about. One thing was sure though, they were up to no good.

They had been waiting in the car for all of thirty minutes for no apparent reason. The longer Shade sat there the more nervous she became. She had no idea where they were taking her or what they were going to do with her and she was scared.

She knew what Melody could do, what she had done in the past. If anything happened to her, no one would ask any questions. She had no family to miss her, no relatives to make enquiries. She felt hopeless and abandoned. Suddenly her mind was drawn to the promise Lily and Lillian made to her that they would pray for her. It seemed like the only ray of hope she had. That their prayers would work seemed remote but she desperately needed to hold on to something. If she didn't, the wave of despair washing over her would probably destroy her before Melody did.

The driver started the car finally and the sound of the engine seemed to reverberate through Shade's body. He was about to drive out when a car suddenly pulled up at the gate blocking the exit. Immediately another car drove up and men began trooping out of both cars and shouting at the top of their voices. Shade couldn't make out what anyone of them was saying as they were all barking out orders at the same time but she could see they were policemen. In a flash a few of them had surrounded the car she was in while others ran into the restaurant.

"What the...?" Victor looked around, wide-eyed, totally confused.

"Get out!" She heard one of them bellow. She saw the man on her right open his door and get out immediately, standing away from the car.

"What the...? Victor exclaimed again when he looked back and saw that the man had complied.

"It will be in your best interest to come out of the vehicle immediately Mr. Man, or else we will have to use force!" An armed man was addressing Victor.

Shade was in shock but she managed to get herself out of the car as quickly as she could, her heart beating wildly in her chest.

"Raise your hands!" One of the men barked at her. She raised them quickly. She was shaking like a leaf.

Then she saw Victor being dragged out of the car and searched. The other thug and the driver were also searched.

In a short while Melody was led out yelling and threatening. A group of people, including Sheyi, followed closely behind her with their hands raised. Two policemen followed the procession. The car blocking the exit was removed and a Police van was parked in its place. Then they were all ordered to march into it as well as Victor and the other two men.

"You! In!" One of the detectives shouted, walking towards Shade. She was about to comply when the man that had been in Melody's office earlier and in the car with her held her back. Shade looked at him in confusion. Then it suddenly occurred to her that he hadn't been rough-handled, asked to get out of the car or marched into the van.

"She's not involved," he quickly said in her defense. "In fact she's a victim. They were about to do away with her. Thank God we were delayed. I was beginning to wonder how I would save her if you and your men didn't arrive on time."

"Ok, sir." The other man withdrew immediately making Shade even more confused. "But she will still need to come along to make a statement."

"Yes, of course," the man replied. "She will ride in the car with me."

He took Shade by the arm and led her to one of the cars parked outside the gate. He opened the door for her and she got in and sat with her palms together between her knees. She was shaking so badly she couldn't think. A few moments later the man returned and sat with her in the back while two other men squeezed into the front seat and a third man got behind the wheel. Before long they were in a convoy of Police vehicles heading for the Police Headquarters.

Less than half an hour later Shade was in a small office waiting to write her statement. She could hear the pandemonium going on somewhere outside as Melody and the others were being booked. Once in a while she could still make out Melody's voice above the racket.

If there was anything she thought could be a fate worse than what was originally planned for her tonight by Melody, it was to be arrested by the Police. To be picked up in a raid like tonight was the one thing she had dreaded the most since she had begun working at the restaurant. One could be left in the cell for a long time without even being tried according to what she had heard. Besides she had been told a lot of gruesome stories about the things that happened in the prisons.

So why had she exposed herself to such risks and danger by staying on at the restaurant? It all seemed so stupid now. And a Police raid was only one of the risks. So many other things could have happened, things that could have ended her life. Of course one or two very nearly did. She smiled as she remembered Lillian describing her as the girl with nine lives. She knew she didn't have nine lives, just the one. And somehow it had been spared.

The man whom she now knew to be Police Detective Al Hassan entered the room and sat behind the desk.

"Your name is Shade isn't it?" He asked as he pushed a sheet of paper and a pen towards her.

"Yes sir," Shade replied.

"We just need you to write a statement because you happened to be at the scene when the arrests were made. It's procedure." He sounded almost apologetic.

She couldn't understand why she was being treated so kindly. It wasn't what she had been told about the Police, but she was grateful.

"Just write from when you got there this evening, why you were there, and all you did until the policemen arrived. Can you manage that?"

"Yes." She began to write as best as she could and when she finished she handed the paper back to him. He scanned it for a few seconds and then laid it on the table and looked directly at her.

"Tell me, how did you get mixed up with a character like Madam Melody?"

"She…adopted me." Shade knew more questions would follow and she had to quickly decide how much she was willing to expose to the detective. He looked at her enquiringly as if he needed her to explain further. "I…my parents died when I was…very young and she was the only relative I had that would take me in."

"You mean you're related to that woman and she was going to…" He shook his head and shrugged his shoulders. "Only God knows what she was going to have them do to you tonight. Some people are callous. Did you really help that girl escape?"

Shade hesitated.

"You don't have anything to be afraid of. I just want to know."

Finally Shade nodded and the man smiled.

"Ok, Shade. You're free to go." He stood up. "But I'll advise you to steer clear of Melody from now on." He wagged his finger. "I've been hanging around her, working undercover for some time now and I can safely say we have something on her. Finally. But we don't really know how much. Our men have gone to pick up her colleague, Gogo, thanks to her. He has been connected with human trafficking amongst other nefarious acts in the past. But she's very crafty, and slippery.

She doesn't do the dirty work herself. So I can't tell for how long she will be held."

"Thank you, sir." Shade stood up. All she wanted to do was get out of there and as far from Melody as possible.

"Here." He handed her some money. "I hope this will get you home."

Shade nodded and got down on both knees as she took the money from him. "Thank you very much."

She walked out of the office and out of the building into the streets. She was free to go, the man said. It could have been a different story.

She stood by the road and waited but no taxi came. Finally she decided to walk to the nearest bus stop. It was late but being out alone at this time of the night was nothing new to her.

"Thank God the man gave me some money," she said to herself as she walked. She had left her purse on the chair in her living room when Victor came for her. "No phone, no money. How would I have got home?" She tried not to think about what she would have done in the past if she had truly been stranded.

She got off the bus at a busy bus stop and was able to get a taxi home. She asked the driver to wait at the gate while she got her luggage. Nothing was going to make her spend the night in that flat even if she was assured that Melody and her goons had been locked up and the key thrown into the ocean from the Bar beach. She would sleep in a hotel as close to the airport as possible. She had settled with the landlord earlier and all she needed to do was hand over the keys. It had been difficult to dispose of her cooker, TV and some of her furniture but she'd finally found someone to take them for less than they were worth. She was in a hurry to leave and didn't really mind. She'd left the rest of the furniture for the landlord to do as he wished.

By 8am the next morning the Abuja bound passengers began to board the aircraft and Shade was one of them. She had allowed herself only two hours sleep for fear of oversleeping and missing her flight. As she walked into the airplane she felt tired and sleepy but elated. A new world awaited her, with new opportunities, new goals and new ways of achieving them.

She took her seat and quickly brought out her phone. She needed to make a few calls before she had to switch it off. First she called her friend in Abuja to let her know what time to pick her up at the airport then she called Lillian.

"I'm calling from the plane going to Abuja," she announced as soon as she heard Lillian's voice.

"That's wonderful!" Lillian said excitedly.

"Not as wonderful as knowing that Melody was in trouble with the Police the last time I saw her and would most likely still be in jail as we speak."

"Lily!" Lillian screamed. "Shade has some good news for you!" She put the phone on speaker. "How did it happen? And it's about time."

"Melody planned to get rid of me last night," Shade said and she heard Lillian gasp. "Yes, but some policemen came and raided the restaurant. They arrived just in time because they were about to take me away when they came. Apparently they were already on to her and there was actually an undercover detective in her 'employ'. And if it hadn't been for the fact that he knew what Melody was about to do to me, I would have been in jail too."

Lillian and Lily listened attentively as Shade recounted what took place the night before. They could hardly say anything.

Suddenly Lillian cried out. "Then you really are the one we were all praying for last night!"

"I beg your pardon?"

"Last night when Lily's aunt got home she couldn't eat. She said there was someone that needed to be prayed for. Then when her mum called we told her we had spent some time praying but didn't know whom we were praying for and she told us she had been praying too but that it was for you. So we thought it might be for you."

"I don't know what to say," Shade said, baffled. "I was really in trouble. They would have killed me or I would have been thrown in jail. I escaped the two. But I didn't know such things happened, that a person would feel the need to pray and wouldn't know what they were praying for. Or that people would be praying for the same person at the same time without communicating with each other."

"Intercession is what it's called," Lily said. "And it is so amazing."

"Melody was going to kill me. And you all prayed for me. And the Police were there just in time." Shade seemed to be thinking aloud.

"Thank God you are out of Melody's grip too."

"Yes, indeed I'm out." She looked up. "Oops. Have to hang up now. We're about to take off. I will call you from Abuja."

The flight to Abuja was only an hour or so and Shade had planned to spend it sleeping but she couldn't. Her conversation with Lillian and Lily kept her awake. How could it be that Lillian, Lily and her aunt were praying for her in Port Harcourt at the very same time Lily's mum was praying for her in Benin without previously planning it? And why was it at one of those times she was most scared in her life? The only other time she had been this scared was when her mother had died suddenly and she was alone. She was beginning to believe it was because of their prayers that she was in an aircraft on the way to Abuja and not in a police cell or an unmarked grave.

For long minutes she turned these thoughts over in her mind. Did it mean she was an individual in God's eyes? She had never paid Him any attention for as long as she could remember. She had always felt that if He existed at all then He couldn't possibly notice her if He noticed anyone at all. But there was no way she could deny His existence now or the fact that He knew about her. Not after what had just happened. But if He had truly been seeing her why hadn't He done something earlier? So many unpleasant things had happened to her that He could have saved her from. She pondered on this until it suddenly hit her. Of course she hadn't been associating with the kind of people that were likely to be called upon by Him to pray for her. That was for sure. Then God Himself must have brought her friends to her. She hated to think that she had been indifferent about Him. She hadn't cared whether He existed or not. She had thought her life was whatever the world had to offer and that she didn't need God. But now she could see that He had had a lot to do with her life. She had lived so dangerously for years and somehow she hadn't been swept away by the tide. God had protected her. And she was grateful. She didn't know what she would do about this discovery but she made a mental note to ask her friends some questions as soon as she had the chance. If God cared for her and had cared for her all this time then she would start caring about Him too.

Kuukua with her short-cropped hair looked exactly the same as when they were students at the university. She was standing just outside the arrival gate in a faded t-shirt and an oversized jean skirt with a sweater tied around her waist. Huge beads hung around her neck to complete her typical dressing.

She waved as soon as she saw Shade and Shade felt like she had never been happier to see her. They hugged each other and Kuukua helped her push the trolley out of the building to the parking lot.

"I can see you're still a 'clothes' person," she commented as she observed the number of suitcases.

"And I can see you're still not." They both laughed.

"Tell me," Kuukua said as she seemed to be pushing with all her strength. "What are clothes made of these days? Lead?"

"You need to put some meat on your bones, girl. Then you wouldn't be complaining about my 'light' suitcases."

"Light? Light?"

"Complain, complain."

"You haven't changed."

"Neither have you."

Chapter TWENTY-FIVE

"SHEYI IN PRISON?"

"That's what they said." Amanda stood on the verandah in front of Esther's flat shifting her weight from one foot to the other. "I was on my way back from the children's school when they called."

"Did they tell you what happened?"

Amanda sighed deeply. "They said the policemen raided the restaurant last night and arrested everyone there."

"Who told them?"

"Shade. It was Shade that called them this morning and told them everything that happened."

"Don't tell me she was there."

"She was." Amanda sighed even more deeply than before. "Melody had given instructions for her men to do away with her when the Police came."

"Do away *ke*? But is she now…? Was she too…?"

"No, thank God. In fact she should be landing in Abuja any time now."

"How did she manage?"

"God was with her. He answered our prayers. Remember how I felt she was in danger and we prayed," Amanda said. "Last night the need came differently but stronger than ever. So I prayed. The amazing thing was that when I called Lily last night she told me that Agnes had returned from work yesterday with a burden to pray."

"For Shade."

"Yes, but at the time she didn't know for whom. Lily and Lillian joined her to pray. When they told me I was sure it was for Shade."

"And first thing this morning she calls them," Esther said.

"To say she had a narrow escape last night." Then Amanda let her head drop. "But what do I do about Sheyi now?" This was the question she had been asking herself from the moment she heard the news. She couldn't just sit here in Benin and do nothing when she knew he was behind bars. But what could she do? "Should I go to Lagos or what?"

"Don't be hasty about...."

"But I can't just leave him there."

"Of course you can't. I'm not saying that. All I'm saying is that you should not rush into any action. You need to be sure of what you are to do even if you are going. We could speak to Timothy."

"Timothy? Yes. Of course."

After speaking to Timothy Amanda found out that the only way was probably to go to Lagos or get someone in Lagos to make enquiries about Sheyi's conditions and explore the possibility of bailing him out. But Timothy didn't want Amanda to go herself. There was only one person Esther thought she could ask for help. Reluctantly she picked up her phone and dialed again.

"Amanda! What a pleasant surprise. How are you?"

"I'm well thank you. And how are you?"

"Great. How's Lily?"

"She's fine."

"Are you sure? Are you all right?"

"Yes. Yes we're all fine." Amanda paused and Robert waited for her to speak. "Something came up Robert and I…" All of a sudden she was overcome with doubt. What was she thinking? "I shouldn't have bothered you. I don't know what I was thinking. I shouldn't…"

"Will you stop rambling and tell me what it is?" Robert interrupted her. "It's too late anyway. I'm already bothered and you were right by calling me. Please. Please let me help."

Amanda sighed. "It's Sheyi, my...my…"

"What about him?"

"He…he was in a place that was raided by the Police last night. And he was locked up with the other people there."

Robert was silent for a few seconds. "Do you know where they took him?"

"The Police headquarters in Lagos."

"Oh, in Lagos here?"

"Yes. Yes, he's been in Lagos for a while."

"Let me call you back."

"Ok."

"He said he'll call me back," Amanda explained to Esther.

"Sounds like he's willing to help."

Amanda nodded and her phone rang.

"Hello."

"Yes Amanda, I want you to tell me everything you know. Everything."

After listening to her he told her he would make a few calls and get back to her and she was not to worry.

"Oh, Esther," Amanda lamented after hanging up. "Why didn't I end up with a regular guy?"

"Shut up Amanda," Esther chided her. "You haven't ended up yet."

She looked at Esther and smiled. "You think so?"

"I'm sure of it. Thank God Robert's willing to help. So what did he say?"

"He's going to make a few calls. And that means that if Sheyi can be bailed out he would take care of it."

"All this for Sheyi."

Amanda shrugged.

She waited patiently for Robert to call and it wasn't until after she had picked the children from school that he did.

"I have made some enquiries," he said. "And it turns out that he's not an innocent bystander, if you catch my drift. But he can be bailed out."

"Thank God."

"He won't be entirely free because some serious allegations have been leveled against him, so they'll want him close by for further questioning. But they'll still release him this evening if everything goes according to plan."

"Thank you Robert." Amanda felt truly grateful.

"You're welcome. But let's just hope what they think they have on him is baseless. Because if it isn't he could be back there in a flash."

What had Sheyi got himself into? He may not be the best thing that ever happened to her but she still didn't want him in prison. She really hoped the investigations wouldn't yield anything concrete. Everyone deserved a second chance, even Sheyi. She hoped he would have learnt his lesson from his night of incarceration and done some serious thinking about mending his ways.

"You're a good friend, Robert."

"I'm glad you see me that way."

That night Henry called and Amanda told him Sheyi had spent the night in prison.

"Do you think his hands are really dirty? I mean really, really dirty?" Henry asked.

"Honestly Henry, I don't know. I don't even want to think about that."

"Are you saying there's a possibility?"

"He's…he's…Look, he lied to me about where he was going and that could mean anything." Amanda had never told Henry about Sheyi's involvement with Lily and she wasn't planning to.

"Well, I hope for his sake that his hands are clean," Henry said. "I for one am glad you've realized you and your kids are better off without him."

"He's still their father."

"Second thoughts?"

"It just…doesn't feel right, you know?"

"I don't know."

"Henry."

"You're a sensible girl Amanda."

"Girl?"

"Ok, woman.

Amanda laughed. "My love to Bianca and Shirley."

"They're sending their love too."

"Bye."

"Bye."

The next morning Amanda woke up to the sound of the front door opening and closing. She was sure it was the front door. She looked at the time. It was just past 4am. She sat up straight on the bed and began to pray silently. There was nothing else she could do since it would only take a few seconds for the intruder to get to where she was. The bedroom door opened and Sheyi stood there.

Amanda heaved a huge sigh of relief. "Sheyi."

He walked towards her and stood by the bed. "Who is he?" He asked accusatorily.

Amanda ran her fingers through her hair and blinked, not knowing what he was asking her.

"Don't pretend with me," he said coolly. "Who is the guy that bailed me out?"

"Robert?"

"Yes. Robert," he said with a hint of mockery in his voice. "Tell me." He came and sat on the bed. "What's between the two of you?"

Amanda looked at him with disgust and began to get off the bed. She planned to go straight to the children's room and lock the door but he held her arm and stopped her from getting off.

"Why? You don't want to tell me?"

"What's wrong with you? Let go of me." Amanda tried to free her arm.

"Not until you tell me what I want to know," he said bringing his face close to hers. "Not until you tell me who Mr. Nice Guy is and what's going on between you two." He tightened his hold on her arm and clenched his teeth. "He seems to think the world of you. Of course you're a beautiful woman and I'm not surprised. So, how long as this been going on?"

"You're talking rubbish." Amanda looked away unable to tolerate his blood-shot eyes and bad breath any longer.

"Don't lie to me," he said glaring at her. "You don't know what you're playing with. Imagine you sending your clean-cut boyfriend to come and look down on me."

"Will you stop this? He's not my boyfriend or anything like that and you're hurting me." Her arm was really beginning to hurt.

"Oh. You expect me to believe that you just got a 'nobody' to bail me out of detention?"

"Robert is not a 'nobody'," Amanda said shaking her head.

"Then tell me now what's between you two," he snarled.

"Lily! Ok? Robert is Lily's father."

He let go of her arm as if it had burnt him and Amanda could see the shock on his face. She got off the bed and rubbed her arm.

He got up too and began to pace. Then he stopped and looked at her. "Lily's father," he said, as if to be sure of what he had heard. "You've been involved with Lily's father. For how long?"

"No, I have not!" Amanda said firmly. "I only met him again recently after fifteen years!"

"And you hit it off!"

Amanda sighed and lifted her arms as if admitting defeat. "I can't talk to you." She walked towards the door.

"Where do you think you're going?" He quickly got between her and the door. "You've been sneaking around behind my back…"

"I could never do that Sheyi, even if I wanted to," Amanda cut him short. "I could never stoop that low."

"You expect me to believe that," he sneered.

"Believe what you like," she said coldly and made to walk past him and out of the room.

"I'll have you know that I won't tolerate any hanky-panky from you…" He moved menacingly towards her.

"No?" Amanda asked and something in her demeanor stopped him short. "God knows I have tolerated enough *hanky-panky* from you." It was her turn to advance towards him and to her surprise he began to step backwards. "I know about those secret trips to Lagos and wherever else, to pick up girls for Melody, and sleep with them as you wish." To see his face suddenly twist and his mouth hang open was a delight to her. "Oh, I know more than you think. And I only need to let Robert know what you did to his daughter..."

"Stop it!"

"And that you were paid. And with your new criminal record and the allegations..." Amanda continued as if she hadn't heard him.

"Ok, what do you want?"

"I don't want anything from you except that you should just...leave me alone." She brushed past him and went to the children's room.

By the time she came out two hours later he was sitting on the sofa with his head in his hands. She pretended not to see him as she went to the kitchen to put the kettle on. On her way back he looked up.

"We need to talk," he said.

"I'm sorry I can't. I need to get the children ready for school."

"What about when you return from school?"

Amanda hesitated before replying. "All right."

The children were excited to see him. She watched him for a few moments as he played with them while she packed the lunch boxes. He was like any loving father. But Amanda knew better. He was no role model, not for her children. Yet...

Sheyi was waiting for her when she returned. She sat opposite him and waited.

"I have to return to Lagos this morning," he announced. "I wasn't supposed to have left in the first place. I…I don't know if I…I don't know what their investigations will turn out. Aunty is trying to implicate me and I am innocent. She's the one telling them stories about me and they are all lies. That woman is capable of anything." He stood up. "I just can't believe she could do this to me." He walked round the chair. "She's still locked up, you know, and I don't know why. But she hates me for it. And I know she's going to try to make things even more difficult for me." He stopped and turned to Amanda. "But you know I'm innocent, don't you?"

Amanda didn't meet his eyes. How could she know? She didn't even know what he was being accused of. When she didn't reply he asked her again.

"Don't you?" Still Amanda didn't reply. "Well, I am." He nodded. "I may have done some things, and I regret them, but abduction and child trafficking?" He shook his head vigorously.

A gasp escaped Amanda's lips. "Is…is that what you're being accused of?" Amanda tried to keep her voice as calm as possible. Suddenly it was a little bit difficult to breathe.

"Yes! Can you imagine? Unbelievable isn't it?"

"Is Melody smuggling children out of the country?" Amanda was almost afraid to ask.

"She must be. They have reasons to believe that she is."

Amanda was horrified. How could there be so much evil around one person? "And you had no idea anything like that was going on."

"No! I can't even believe she could ever be involved in such a thing."

To think that Lily had been in more danger than she thought…

"If you're not involved," she said. "then you don't have anything to worry about."

"You don't know my aunty. If she's bent on implicating me she'll do anything to make sure I'm put in jail. In fact, I'm afraid of her now."

"But what can she do?"

Sheyi laughed bitterly. "Anything."

"So what are you going to do?"

"I'm going back to Lagos to defend myself as much as I can. I can only hope…I need your help."

"My help?"

"Rather, Robert's." He refused to meet her eyes. "I…I still need his help."

Amanda took a deep breath. "What would you like me to tell him?"

"That I'm innocent of the allegations. That I'm a good father to my children…" He seemed at a loss for words. "That I'm a responsible, hardworking man."

"What about your company?" Amanda asked. "Have you contacted them and told them what is going on?"

"My company? No. I still want to have a job when this is all over. I sent in the report of my audit by courier and took some leave. Health grounds. I expect that this will end quickly with your…with Robert's help."

"I'll call him," Amanda said finally. "I'll tell him what you said."

"Thank you." He walked towards her with a smile on his face and Amanda got up quickly and headed for the kitchen before he got any closer.

"Ok. All right." She heard him say. "I'll just get my things."

She pretended to be busy in the kitchen until she heard him return to the sitting room.

"I'll be off now," he called out.

"Safe journey," Amanda said from the kitchen doorway.

"I'm depending on you," he said as he walked out the door.

Amanda tried to smile.

Long after he had left Amanda couldn't move from where she was. *Sheyi, please don't be involved in this horrible thing,* she thought. Because if he was she didn't think there was anything Robert or anyone could do to help him. There had been a lot of campaigns against such vices in recent times and the government had begun to pay more attention particularly to crimes against children. More young people were being smuggled out of the country never to be seen again by their families. A new agency had been set up and a harder sentence had been introduced for offenders. He could be imprisoned for a long time if found guilty. She felt sorry for him.

She waited till she was sure that Sheyi was in Lagos before calling Robert who promised to do all he could.

"That was Sheyi I saw this morning, wasn't it?" Esther asked Amanda a few hours later. She was traveling to see her mother and Amanda had gone to see her off.

"Yes, but he's gone back. He wasn't even supposed to have left Lagos at all."

"Did he come in peace?"

"No. At first he wanted to fight. He wanted to know who my boyfriend was that bailed him out."

"Don't…don't even tell me you're serious. He's not even grateful he was bailed out."

"He was so angry and he kept bullying me until…" Amanda pouted.

"Until…?" Esther prompted when Amanda paused.

"I don't know." Amanda shrugged and continued pouting. "Something snapped."

"And what did you do?" Esther asked looking at Amanda as if she was a pre-schooler who had been naughty.

"I told him what I knew, about what he did for Melody... about Lily, told him we could take it up, and with his recent experience..."

"Tell me he cowered in a corner."

"He changed his tone. Asked for help."

"And?"

"I called Robert again. Apparently Melody has been linked with abduction and smuggling of children out of the country and she doesn't want to go down alone. If he's innocent Robert will try his best to clear his name."

"What?" Esther looked at her aghast. "Of all the wrongest things to be involved in. But what if he's not innocent?"

"I pray he is. He's still my children's father.

Chapter TWENTY-SIX

IT HAD BEEN OVER an hour since Amanda sat on her doorstep. It wasn't hot inside but she still felt stifled. Besides, her thoughts had been going back to one thing and she needed some distraction. An incident on the street had provided some a while ago. A motorcyclist had dropped his passenger close to her gate and both men had begun screaming and waving their fists at each other. Passers-by had intervened and this had resulted in the gathering of a small crowd and a lot of noise. Even after the problem was solved and the two men had left, a few people still stayed back to discuss what had happened. Amanda was sure from their occasional outbursts and from how much longer they stayed that their discussions had gone on to other issues. Moments ago the last group dispersed and now there was a lull in the activities on the street. She wished she had someone to talk to. Esther wasn't due back till the end of the week.

For Amanda most things were working out as she wanted, Lily was safe in Port Harcourt and what she had been working on in the past few months had been successful, but an ache in her chest reminded her that there was still something she needed to deal with. This was a hurdle she didn't know how to scale. She had committed it into God's hands and tried to trust Him but every time she got off her knees she seemed to take it back with her. She was sure it wasn't going to be easy. That she had made her decision was certain, and that it was the right decision was undisputable as far as she was concerned, the problem was whether Sheyi would allow it. She couldn't blame him, of course, if he tried to stop her. After all he was their father and in his own strange way he loved them. But things couldn't continue this way, not for her or for her children. So if she had to she would fight with everything she had

She would have to tell him very soon. She could already imagine what his reaction would be but there had to be a way around him, or through him. God would make a way, she was sure. He had to. Things had come too far for anything to go wrong now. She got up and dusted her skirt. She still had some work to do before going to bed. She needed to sort through the children's things to see what they would need. After locking the door she went to the children's room and began her task. As she opened the wardrobe and brought down clothes from the shelves she pushed all thoughts of Sheyi out of her mind. Let God take care of him.

One of the pictures showed three men and a woman lined up against a wall handcuffed. Another picture showed a large truck with children being lifted out from the back by policemen. A third one was of the Inspector General speaking

to reporters, and at the bottom of the page was that of a tearful mother being reconciled with her ten-year old daughter. *Judgment Day for Child Traffickers*, the caption at the top of the page read. The story went that seventeen children between the ages of six and fifteen had been rescued from people believed to be part of a large human trafficking ring as they were about to be driven across the border. The children had been locked in the back of the truck for almost two days without food, water or any convenience. The driver and his companion were arrested immediately. A man and a woman who were found close to the border and suspected to be part of the ring were also arrested after the driver was interrogated. Other members were still at large but the Police had commented on their commitment to finding them and putting an end to this crime. Their Inspector General also told the Press that further arrests would be made as soon as they found further evidence as a result of more intensive investigations.

Robert put the newspaper down and sighed. This was the third time in less than two months that this kind of news would make the headlines. Why would anyone still be involved in human trafficking with all the attention it was getting? Why should anyone even be involved at all? There shouldn't be any pity for such a person. They needed to go to prison. Yet for Amanda's sake he prayed for Sheyi.

He exchanged looks with the man sitting across the table from him when he heard the knock on the door.

"Come in."

Sheyi opened the door and walked in. "Good morning. I hope I'm not late. The traffic was something…"

"It's ok, Mr. Ibajeojo. You're still on time. Please sit down."

A smallish man in a very smart navy blue suit sat in the chair directly opposite Robert. The lady sitting next to him looked like a model from a designer office wear catalogue while

Robert himself was impeccably dressed in a perfect grey pin striped suit. Sheyi took his seat on the other side of the man and immediately began to regret his decision to dress casually in an opened neck shirt and khaki trousers, which was borne out of his resentment for Robert. He had told himself that he only had to put up with the man for as long as he needed to. As soon as the case was over and he was free he would get as far away from him and his condescending attitude and snootiness as possible. How dare he feel so superior just because he was in a position to help? People helped one another every day. And how dare Amanda think she could flaunt her boyfriend at him? He would deal with her later. Who did they think they were?

"This is Barrister Allen," Robert addressed Sheyi, "and this is Miss Ojo. They are from the law firm I told you about."

The man shook hands with Sheyi while the lady merely nodded.

"They would be representing you in court which…"

"Court?" Sheyi sat forward in his seat. "But I thought you said we wouldn't have to except…you gave me the impression that since I am innocent and am only being implicated by that mad woman, all we need is to wait for the Police to finish their investigations…Paper work! That's all you said is left, paper work!"

The room was silent after Sheyi's outburst. It was the lawyer that finally spoke.

"Listen Mr.…" He leaned forward to look into the file on the table. "Ibajeojo…" he said, pronouncing the name wrong.

"Ibajeojo," Sheyi corrected firmly.

He glanced at Sheyi before continuing. "Yes, it would have been just paper work after the Police investigations and you would have been free of all allegations," he said. "The reason

Mr. Robert here is saying we might have to go to court which is very likely, I might add, is that…"

But Sheyi didn't let him finish. "You can't just come up with…court now," he burst out again. "No, we can't let this get to court. Don't you know what that means?" He stood up and looked round the room. "It means months and months of hearings and whatever you call it. And if something goes wrong I could be sentenced to a long prison term." He shook his head vigorously. "No! No way! There's no way this case is going to court. It is completely out of the question!" He turned to Robert. "You told me…"

"I think you should sit down and let the barrister finish," Robert said.

"It seems like no one is listening to me. How can I sit…?"

"Sit down!" Robert yelled suddenly and a startled Sheyi sat down meekly. "Please continue Barrister Allen."

Barrister Allen cleared his throat. "As I was saying, the reason we are very likely to go to court is that what the Police investigations turned out is not what was expected."

"What…what do you mean?" Sheyi asked stealing a quick look at Robert.

"They claim that they have evidence to prove that you were involved in the abduction of a Miss Celestina Otto who is still missing. A relative of hers is willing to testify that she spoke about leaving the country to work abroad shortly before she disappeared. She has been linked with Madam Melody and Madam Melody, of course has involved you. And now the Police suspect you are involved. So you see," he looked in the file again, "Mr. Ibajeojo, we are looking at a possible trial here."

"But this is…this is ludicrous! This is…utterly… unreasonable! I had nothing to do with anyone's abduction. Celestina Otto," he spat. "I've never even heard the name before."

"That may be true but what we need from you now is..."

"Celestina Otto," Sheyi continued as if he hadn't heard the lawyer. "Who is Celestina Otto? How can this devilish woman do this to me after all I have done for her?" He looked at the lawyer. "It's not true. I promise you." He turned to Robert. "To God who made me, I have nothing to do with anyone's abduction." He swore violently and hit the table hard with his fists. "Look, I may have done certain things I'm not proud of but I have never abducted anyone. I could never do that, not even for Melody. She tried to get me to do certain things but I refused. I told her to let me do...the other things..." He wrung his hands. "And let the others take care of those... Honestly, I never got involved. If...if the Police say they have anything it is just a case of me being in the wrong place at the wrong time. You know? What you people call being guilty by association. I'm telling the truth."

Barrister Allen took a deep breath. "We don't disbelieve you but we will need you to convince us in order for us to provide enough evidence to put up a formidable defense in court."

"Oh God," Sheyi lamented. "What kind of predicament is this?"

"Just tell us what we need to know about what went on in that syndicate, I mean everything you know."

"I've told you. I don't know anything about any abduction or...or...trafficking or anything like that." He looked like he was close to tears.

"What about the 'things' you know about? I mean what you said earlier that you are not proud of?"

"Yes, Mr. Ibajeojo, what exactly did you do for the woman?" Robert asked.

After a trying hour of prompting, cajoling and a little intimidation, Robert and the lawyers were able to get some tangible information from Sheyi.

"This information you have given us would be very useful for the Police in their investigations and hopefully the rooting out of Madam Melody's 'associates' and partners in crime," Barrister Allen said, handing the file to Miss Ojo. "I'm therefore willing to indulge myself in the belief that we have something to bargain with."

"Does this mean…?" Sheyi began.

"I…don't know what it means yet," he replied quickly. "But we are going to try to get the best deal we can. The problem now is whether it is enough."

"Enough?" Sheyi asked.

"To keep the case out of court," Barrister Allen replied. "The extent of our bargaining power depends on how much useful information we can give them. The prosecutor's office will be represented at the next meeting. What we place on the table at that meeting will determine the course your case will take. Already, one thing we can see is that the only tie you have to the abduction of that girl is Madam Melody's accusation."

Robert leaned forward intertwining his fingers on the table. "What the barrister is telling you is that if the information you disclose now is not good enough for them you could be tried and sentenced, but if you have been able to produce enough to satisfy them you may never step into the courtroom."

Sheyi shifted in his seat and sighed heavily. "But I've told you what I know."

"What about names?" It was Miss Ojo who spoke. "Do you know the names of anyone else who is involved and is still at large?"

Sheyi was silent for a moment. He could give names. He could definitely give names. He had been around Melody long enough to know a few of her criminal friends. But these people were murderers. What if they found out that he was the one that gave them away? He would be history. There had to be another way. He couldn't do it. And as if the lawyer knew exactly what he was thinking he broke into his thoughts.

"If you don't give their names you stand the risk of going to prison for a long time but if you do and they are caught they will be locked up for so long they would probably die there."

"But you don't know these people. You will just..." He snapped his fingers. "Disappear."

"No one needs to know where the information came from."

When Sheyi still hesitated Robert became impatient. "Mr. Ibajeojo," he said. "It seems you're forgetting something." He paused for a brief moment looking directly at Sheyi. "You could be tried and sentenced as a murderer and human trafficker due to lack of evidence. Would you rather go down for a crime you did not commit, or would you tell the lawyers what they need to know in order to get you out without a trial?"

They all waited patiently as Sheyi stared into space. Finally he looked down and drummed on the table with his fingers.

"Ok," he said. "But you have to promise that my name will not be mentioned at all."

"Your name will not be mentioned. You would not even appear at any of the meetings involving the Police or anyone else apart from your lawyers, and the lawyer from the prosecutor's office," Barrister Allen assured him.

"Oh, thank you," Sheyi said, heaving a sigh of relief. "I'm so glad to hear that. I promise to tell you everything I know."

"That would be a very good thing for you to do." The lawyer sounded as if a heavy weight had been lifted off his shoulders.

Twenty minutes later, Barrister Allen stood up and so did Robert and Miss Ojo. He shook hands with Robert and turned to shake hands with Sheyi who had stood up too.

Sheyi pumped his hand with both of his. "Thank you, sir," he said grinning broadly.

"I hope everything works out as planned."

Barrister Allen and Miss Ojo left and Sheyi was left alone in the office with Robert.

"Thank you," Sheyi said when they were both seated. "And I'm sorry about my behaviour earlier on. The thought of being sentenced...I almost lost my mind. What would happen to my aged mother? I'm the only one of her children she depends on. And there's my family to consider. I have two very young children. How would they live with the shame of knowing their father is a prisoner? How would they live with that stigma?" He shook his head. "That cannot just happen." He shuddered as if he actually had a chill.

"First of all, Mr. Ibajeojo, you're welcome. And it is my hope that this case doesn't get to court at all. Like the barrister said, we are in a good position to hope. I'll also say that I'm glad you mentioned your family and I can see you care about your children and want the best for them."

"Yes, yes. Yes of course." Sheyi nodded vigorously.

"And I'm sure you already know the relationship between Amanda and I, that I am Lily's father. I want you to know that the only reason I am helping is because Amanda asked me. Even though there's nothing between us, I still care about her welfare and Lily's as well. I know the idea of going to prison is unthinkable to you and so I need to let you know that there's still one condition you need to fulfill."

Chapter TWENTY-SEVEN

"THE WHOLE HOUSE SMELLS of food," Agnes commented as she walked into the sitting room. She went into the kitchen and saw pots and pans arranged on the counter top. She began to open them one after the other. "Three different kinds of soup? Fried rice? *Moyin-moyin*? How much could your mother possibly eat?"

"Actually, we're trying to present a wide variety for her to choose from," Lillian replied. "And we are not even through yet."

Agnes looked at her from the top of her glasses. "I think I'll leave you to it."

"And you know she's not coming alone," Lily added.

"She's coming with one adult and two toddlers," Agnes reminded them. "But we have enough food here to feed the entire neighbourhood."

Lily giggled. "At least we won't run out."

Amanda arrived several hours later with Esther and the children. They had left Benin later than they had planned and it was getting dark.

"I'm so glad to see you Agnes," Amanda said hugging her warmly. "This is my friend Esther. Esther," she let go of Agnes and turned to Esther. "This is my cousin Agnes."

"I'm pleased to meet you," Esther said. "I've heard so much about you."

"And how is your husband?" Agnes asked.

"Oh, he's well, thank you. He sends his love."

"And a few other things to the girls," Amanda added looking at Lily and Lillian who were just running into the sitting room.

When they were all settled, Agnes picked up Akin and drew Ola to her side.

"These children have really grown," Agnes remarked. "Akin is just like Henry."

"And not only in the way he looks," Amanda said.

"You mean he acts like him too?"

"In addition to being hyperactive…" Amanda shook her head. "He never gets tired. He's always ready to go."

"Good boy." Agnes hugged him fondly.

"I should leave him here with you."

"If only he would stay."

Esther laughed. "I doubt. He's so attached to his mummy it seems there's an invisible rope holding them together."

"Just like Henry and Mama so many years ago," Agnes reminisced.

"We'll just take your bags inside now and then we would lay the table," Lillian announced. "We hope you're hungry."

This made Agnes start to giggle, setting Lily and Lillian off too. "Sorry," she managed to say while trying to restrain herself. "They really, really hope you're hungry."

"Why?" Amanda didn't understand.

"You need to see how much food these girls have prepared," Agnes replied.

"I see," Amanda said smiling at Esther. "No problem. We'll just see how far we can go."

"Good," Lily said as she and Lillian picked up the bags and headed for the room.

"So how's your work at the NGO?" Amanda asked Agnes after the girls had left.

"Great. There's a lot of work but we're doing fine. The girls have been helping."

"Really helping or just hanging around?"

"Really helping, and they've been very useful. They have both been invaluable but Lillian has a particular interest in helping people with problems. I'm beginning to wonder if she doesn't have a sort of calling in that area. She even intends to continue when she's out of school."

"You know, I noticed something special about her almost immediately I met her. She had this 'healing touch' kind of thing." Amanda sat forward.

"You noticed!" Agnes exclaimed. "I've been trying to put words to it but I think you just did it for me."

"She has a way of bringing comfort by the things she says, the way she acts. She can soothe a troubled person. She's a friend indeed."

"That she is," Agnes agreed. "I'm sure she'll be a treasure to any charity organization."

"I was so glad when I found out the kind of person she is. She's a good friend to Lily."

"And now they're going to be separated," Agnes said wistfully.

"How are they taking it?"

"Lily is sad sometimes and she expresses it, but it's Lillian I'm really concerned about."

"Why?"

"She's not facing it."

"How do you mean?"

"She doesn't talk about it or show any feelings at all," Agnes replied with her brow creased. "It's like she's...denying it. I feel she's pretending it's not going to happen."

"Maybe she just doesn't want to deal with it," Esther suggested. "Maybe she's afraid that if she faced it, it might be too hard for her to bear."

Amanda slumped in her chair. "That's terrible."

"After she left her family Lily and Shade were the ones to fill the vacuum," Esther said. "She must be terrified of being separated from Lily and the loss she feels might follow."

"I've got to find a way to help her," Agnes mused.

"We'll all pray," Amanda said. "Maybe she'll decide to go back home."

"Then we'll have to pray first that the situation there has changed," Esther said, nodding thoughtfully.

Their conversation had to come to an end when Lily and Lillian walked in with their arms laden.

"Do you need any help?" Amanda asked them.

"No," Lily replied. "You're guests."

"No, we're fine," Lillian said. "Just get ready to be well fed."

"I am," Amanda said.

"So am I." Esther smiled at them.

"I've been ready all day," Agnes said as she put Akin on the seat beside his sister. "But I'm not a guest." She got up and went to the kitchen with them.

After the table had been set Lily and Lillian put some food in little plates for the children.

"I think the best place is the coffee table," Lillian suggested. "We can put cushions there for them to sit on."

"Are you sure you want to clean up any mess?" Amanda asked. "I can manage with Akin here and Ola can sit…"

"I'm sure I want to clean up any mess," Lillian replied smiling.

"You're supposed to relax and enjoy your meal without any distractions. We'll take care of the children," Lily said.

"Well then, this is a meal to remember."

"I don't even know where to start," Esther said as she took her seat at the table.

"I knew we were going to have that problem," Agnes said, taking off the lid from the last dish. "This spread is overwhelming."

"I don't have any problem," Amanda surprised everyone by saying. "I'm going to start with the pepper soup, and then continue with some pounded yam and native soup… and then I'm going to have a little of that wonderful looking *Egusi* soup… and then I'll take a little fried…"She looked up to see everyone looking at her. "What?"

"Amanda." Esther had a surprised look on her face. "When did you start liking food?"

"I like food!" Amanda looked from Esther to Agnes.

"Since when?" Agnes asked. "Mama used to say that if it was declared that there was no more food in the country Amanda would be the last person to be bothered. It was a task to get her to eat when she was younger."

"And Ola is taking after her," Esther said. "Akin is always ready to eat her food."

"Well, I like what is before me and I'll show you."

"Seems like she means business," Agnes said nudging Esther.

"I'd like to see it happen." Esther wasn't convinced.

Amanda smiled and began to put some soup in her bowl. Others followed suit and in a little while everyone was eating. After a few minutes Amanda paused and looked at Agnes.

"I'm really grateful for all you've done, Agnes," she said. "And I'm really going to miss you."

"I'm going to miss you, all of you." She looked at Lily. "I wonder when I'm going to see you again."

"I hope I'll be able to come for your wedding," Lily said. "Now that is something I really want."

"Wedding?" Amanda looked from Lily to Agnes who looked somewhat embarrassed. "Is there something I should know?" She frowned even harder when Lillian cleared her throat noisily and rubbed the back of her neck. "Come on Lillie, out with it!"

"Who? Me?" She asked feigning ignorance.

"Agnes?" Amanda had a warning look on her face.

"Ok, I'll tell you," Lily began. "Aunt Agnes has…"

"No, you won't!" Agnes quickly interrupted her. "There's really nothing…" Lillian cleared her throat again and Agnes glared at her in mock anger. "What's wrong with you girls?"

"Are you going to talk or do you want them to tell me?" Amanda dropped her fork and folded her arms.

Lily bounced up and down on her chair as if she was ready while Lillian quickly raised her hand and nodded.

"There's a…close friend of mine…" Agnes began self-consciously. "If you clear your throat one more time Lillie…!" Lillian looked surprised not knowing how Agnes knew she was about to. Esther couldn't resist laughing. "He's a Christian and he's very nice and…"

"He's drop dead handsome and he's crazy about her."

"Lily!"

"He has a fantastic job with one of these UN organizations and he's ready to marry."

"Lillie!"

Esther couldn't take anymore. She dropped her fork and had to cover her mouth with her hand. It made everyone laugh.

"Just keep me posted," Amanda said picking up her fork again and waving it at Agnes. "Do you hear me?"

"I hear you. I'll let you know when… if there's anything to know."

"There is," Lily mumbled under her breath and Lillian cleared her throat.

"All right you two," Agnes warned, trying to look serious. "You're going to join the children at the coffee table if you don't behave."

"We'll behave," Lily said, giggling.

"Our lips are sealed." Lillian went through the motion of zipping up her lips and tossing the imaginary key over her shoulder.

"How do you cope with these two?" Esther asked.

"You don't," Agnes replied simply.

They finished their meal and everyone pitched in to clear up and put the leftovers in the freezer.

"We should all go to bed early tonight," Agnes announced after helping to put the children in bed. "I asked the taxi driver to be here before six. We must leave by six."

"You're right," Amanda agreed.

Lily and Lillian left for bed after a while and a little later Esther yawned and stood up.

"The journey and the heavy meal have taken their toll," she said. "I'm closing for the day."

Then Agnes and Amanda were left alone.

"I wish I hadn't stayed away, Agnes," Amanda said ruefully. "We could have spent more time together."

"I guess."

"I feel like I cheated myself."

"Don't."

"I don't know how to thank you, Agnes."

"For what?"

"Everything."

Agnes just looked at her and smiled.

"You never gave up on me for one thing. If I were you I would have a long time ago."

"No, you wouldn't," Agnes said after a pause.

"Yes, I would. I was so mean to you. I shut you off completely."

"No, you wouldn't," Agnes persisted calmly. "Not if God told you not to."

Amanda raised her eyebrows enquiringly.

"Oh yes. And He gave me the grace. I had no business giving up on you. I asked for wisdom and He gave me every step of the way."

"And I was busy being so disagreeable and selfish. I even kept Lily out of your reach."

"You were going through a tough time."

"Still not an excuse. You've always been good to me."

"Do you know that I still wonder if I would have coped as well as you did if I had been in your shoes?"

Amanda grunted. "You call that coping?"

"Well, here you are, still in one piece."

"Still in one piece. But I have God to thank for that. I have God to thank for everything. And I wouldn't wish Sheyi on my worst enemy."

Agnes moved to the seat next to Amanda's. "You remember you said you would call to tell me what happened after you told him. You never did."

Amanda shook her head and sighed as if there were no words to describe what she was about to say.

"How did he take it when you told him?"

"He didn't."

"But...he still let you go. I don't understand."

"Neither do I. He disagreed completely and told me nothing positive could ever come out of such a move. But it was as if something held him back. I don't know what it was but I could sense it. We talked for a long time and he told me clearly that he didn't support it at all. He even begged me to reconsider. But he didn't try to stop me. I don't understand it and I'm not trying to."

"So long as he doesn't stand in the way."

"Yes."

"I'm sure the Lord is at work."

"So am I. I had worried about it for ages, wondering what he would do when I told him I was leaving the country with the children. I knew this was something he would never let me do ordinarily. He knows now that it's over between us but he still let me go. And he knows he may not see them for a long time. But somehow...here I am."

"God answers prayers. He brought you this far and I believe He will take you through."

Early in the morning Agnes went out to see if the taxi had arrived.

"The taxi's here and counting," she hollered as she entered the house. "Lily and Lillian bring out all the bags please. We need to be out of here in a few minutes."

The bags were arranged by the front door and everyone gathered in the sitting room.

After a few moments Agnes cleared her throat and smiled at everyone. "Inasmuch as we know that we are about to be separated," she looked at Lillian who fixed her gaze on the ground, "we must be thankful to God for today. This is because what is happening now is an answer to fervent prayers. God has granted His children's hearts' desire and we are happy for that. Oh, we will miss you, of course, more than you can ever know but in the midst of this sadness and seeming loss and probably even fear of what the future holds," she looked at Lillian again, "we must know that all things work together for good because we are God's children. Also we must know that this is a new beginning for each one of us. One door closes behind us today, leading us into a new place, with new experiences and new opportunities to prove God's love for us." She nodded and cleared her throat.

"I'd like to say something," Amanda said when Agnes was quiet. She looked round the room and her gaze settled on Lillian. "Lillian, I couldn't leave without telling you what's in my heart. I've never met anyone like you. You are a special gift from God. I'm glad He sent you to Lily. I don't know how she would have pulled through those dark and horrible days without your friendship. I want to thank you specially for being there for her. I pray...that God will keep you close to Himself. I also pray that He will help you make the right decisions. And I pray that He will fill your heart with joy always."

Lillian nodded but refused to look up.

"Let's all hold our hands," Agnes said.

They held hands and formed a circle while Agnes led them in a short prayer for a safe journey and the fulfillment of God's purpose in everyone's lives. A few minutes later they were on their way.

At the airport, after Amanda, Lily and the children had checked in Lily took Lillian's hand and drew her away from the others.

"Do you know how many miles will be between us by lunch time?" Lillian asked.

"I wish we were going together."

"As much as I do?" She raised her eyebrows and shook her head.

"More than you do. Thank God we can speak on the phone everyday if we want," Lily squeezed Lillian's fingers. "That means I don't have to worry about who will keep me laughing with the craziest jokes."

"You tell crazier jokes than I do," Lillian said looking down.

"Me?" Lily laughed heartily. "You invented crazy jokes."

They both laughed.

"Will you contact Mary?" Lily asked suddenly looking intense.

After a brief moment Lillian replied. "I will. You know I have been planning to. I just haven't gotten round to it yet."

"Well, get round to it."

Lillian smiled cheekily. "I promise."

"I'll keep calling to find out." Lily made it sound like a warning.

"You won't have…" Lillian was interrupted by a sudden noise coming from the other side of the lobby. She turned to see that everyone's attention was on a man who was shouting as he bustled through the crowd. He seemed to be heading towards them.

"Sheyi!" Lily exclaimed as soon as she recognized him. "What is he doing?"

"Amanda! I can't let this happen! I cannot sit back with folded arms and watch you take my children away!" Sheyi was shouting as he marched straight to where Amanda was standing with Esther, Agnes and the children. "Not today!"

"Sheyi, what are you doing? I thought…" Amanda stared at him in disbelief.

"I am stopping you! That's what I'm doing." He reached for Ola's hand and tried to take Akin from her but she refused to let go. "You think I will just let you take them away?" He sounded breathless.

"You didn't try to stop me in Benin. Why are you doing this now?" Amanda looked round and noticed that everyone around them had stopped what they were doing to watch. "And you're making a scene."

"My mother wants to see them."

"What?" Amanda's eyes were like saucers. "It's too late for that."

"Look, my mother will see them first and then we can discuss this traveling thing…"

"That is not going to happen!" Amanda said firmly.

"Look, they are my children. I can walk out of here with them and no one can stop me."

Amanda looked frustrated. "Look, Sheyi…"

"They are not going anywhere," he insisted. He tried again to take Akin from Amanda's arms and when she wouldn't let go he started towards the exit still holding on to Akin, therefore dragging Amanda along too while he held on to Ola firmly with his other hand.

"Lukman!" He called out looking round angrily as weaved through the on lookers who tried to get out of their way. "Now where is this useless taxi driver? Lukman!" A man quickly walked up to him. "Get the taxi round. We're leaving now!"

Agnes and Esther had stood in shock and were speechless until Sheyi began to draw Amanda and the children away. They quickly followed each one at a loss as to what to do. It was Lily who ran and held on to Ola's hand slowing Sheyi down and taking him by surprise.

"What do you think you're doing?" He looked at her as if she was an abominable sight. But Lily refused to leave Ola's hand. Sheyi stamped his foot in disgust and groaned loudly.

"Like mother, like daughter." He hissed. "Lukman! Come and hold this girl for me while I collect this boy…"

Just then the flight announcement was made and Amanda and the children needed to proceed to the departure lounge.

"Sheyi, stop this." Amanda spoke quietly but she looked furious. She held on to Akin more tightly and looked determinedly at Sheyi. "You are too late…"

"Stop deceiving yourself, woman. These children are not going anywhere…"

"Mr. Ibajeojo."

Sheyi suddenly froze at the sound of the voice that came from somewhere behind him. Without turning around he seemed to know whose it was.

"Yes?" He answered shakily.

"Is there a problem here?" Everyone's attention had been on the ruckus and no one had noticed Robert approach.

For a few moments Sheyi couldn't say another word. "No… no, no," he said finally as he let the children go and turned rather stiffly. "There's no problem at all. I…I…only came to wish my family a safe journey."

"I see," Robert said coolly. "I came to do the same."

Amanda looked at Robert confused and so did Agnes, Esther, Lily and Lillian. Lily took Ola away from Sheyi as soon as he released her hand and went to Lillian. "Lillian, that's my father!" She whispered.

"Really?" Lillian was pleasantly surprised.

"He came."

"But what just happened here?" Lillian whispered to Lily. "I mean between Sheyi and your father."

"Search me. But I'd really like to know." Lily grabbed Lillian with her other hand and began to walk towards her father.

Amanda looked at Robert enquiringly but he only winked at her and smiled reassuringly.

Lillian stopped and drew Lily back. "Tell him a smile and a wink won't work for you," she whispered again. "You want all the gory details."

Lily shook her head. "I'm really going to miss you, Lillian Obimali." She smiled and continued to walk towards her father.

"Hello, my dear," Robert said as he turned towards Lily when he saw them approaching. "I've been looking forward to seeing you again."

"Hello," Lily said. "This is my friend Lillie. Lillian. Lillie, my father."

Robert nodded and smiled at Lillian. "How are you?"

"Fine, thank you sir," Lillian replied.

"And who is this little miss?" He crouched down in front of Ola and smiled at her.

"My sister, Ola."

"I'm so glad everything has worked out well," he said to Lily as he stood up. "But you won't be rid of me."

Lily smiled shyly. "I don't want to be rid of you."

Lillian took Ola away and left Lily to speak to her father alone. Agnes, Esther and Amanda stood together talking while Sheyi went to sit on a bench not too far away.

"Blackmail," Lily said mischievously as soon as she was alone with Lillian again. "He actually admitted it."

"I don't understand," Lillian said.

"He said he suspected Sheyi could try to stop my mother from traveling with the children. So he told him that if he was to keep helping him with his case..."

"He should back off," Lillian said looking directly at Sheyi even though she knew he couldn't see or hear her. "That's ingenious."

"I'm just glad it worked. I can't believe he actually came here to stop her." Lily shook her head. "What if my father had not thought ahead? What if he had not shown up on time?"

"Sheyi would still have had to face us all," Lillian said. "Though I can't really say we formed a formidable resistance. At least you still tried. I can't say the same for the rest of us. I for one was shell-shocked." She made a funny face. "I'm glad your father came."

"I'm so happy he came." Lily nodded in agreement.

"You should be," Lillian said raising her eyebrows. "He was about to set hairy Lukman on you."

Lily tried to speak but went into a fit of laughter instead.

"You're all better off if you travel, really," Lillian said thoughtfully. Your mother deserves a fresh start and so do you. And the little ones don't have to be brought up in an unhappy home." She looked over at Sheyi. "And Sheyi, well, he can… live his life. What did he expect to achieve today? He doesn't even know if he will still end up in jail. After all, nothing is guaranteed."

"And it's not as if they are no longer his children."

Lillian hesitated before asking the questions that had suddenly popped into her mind. "But…is your mother still his wife? Would there be a…divorce?"

"A divorce? That would mean that there was ever a marriage."

"They were not…?" Lily shook her head. "My mother told me they were never properly married."

Amanda called out to Lily just then and they both knew they had to say goodbye. Lily looked at Lillian.

"I guess this is it." She put her hand on Lillian's arm and tried to look brave.

Lillian took a deep breath. "Let's join them," she said quickly.

They all hugged each other amidst tears and said their final goodbyes. But Lillian stood back watching them.

Agnes noticed and went to her. She placed her hand on one of Lillian's folded arms. "Are you part of this company?" She asked with tears still in her eyes.

Lillian just smiled but said nothing.

"Or are you traveling with them?"

She shrugged.

"This is going to be the last hug in a very long time, the one that would be freshest in your memory," Agnes nudged her. "Go on."

After waiting a few more moments she walked to Amanda and Amanda quickly drew her into her arms affectionately.

"You have been a great blessing, a treasure, and I want you to know I will never forget you." Amanda said.

Then Lillian knelt down in front of Akin and Ola and held them tightly. She got up and walked towards Lily and it seemed like everyone was watching. Lily's eyes glistened with tears as Lillian approached her and stood in front of her. Lily opened her arms and waited. Finally Lillian smiled and hugged her friend. "Don't catch a cold," she whispered into her ears.

This door was closing all right and they couldn't stop it. But it meant that they had entered into another phase and were hopeful that this was the beginning of a future that would be kinder to them because of the One they now both knew as their Father.

Chapter TWENTY-EIGHT

"THIS IS BLESSING. THE girl I told you about," Agnes said as she pulled out a file from the pile in front of her. She opened it to show Lillian the photograph of a teenage girl. "She was found and brought in by those NYSC members. She had been wandering for days."

"Why was she wandering?" Lillian got up from the chair she'd been sitting on and perched on the edge of Agnes' overcrowded table to get a closer look.

"Lillian, I've been looking after young people with different kinds of experiences for a long time but I have never quite come across anything like this."

"What happened to her?"

"This is what she told me." Agnes rested her elbows on table and held her hands together. "She grew up with other kids in the home of a man she referred to as 'Uncle'. She said there were seven of them. One day some people came to see him, that is the 'Uncle' and when they left he told her that she was to go with them when they returned. She said she didn't want to go but I guess the kind of relationship she had with him was such that she couldn't disobey him and so when they returned she went with them."

"Where did they take her?"

"No one knows. She had never left the village so she didn't know any other place. She said she rode in the back of a van for a long time. She didn't know how long.

She said the van had no windows at the back."

"She might as well have been blind-folded."

"Yes. They didn't want her to be able to retrace the place. She said she was asleep when they got there and it was dark. She was taken into a very big house and locked in a room. That room was to be her home for a year."

"Why did they take there? What did they do to her?" A frown was already forming on Lillian's face.

"Are you ready for this?" Agnes asked and paused for a moment. "To have a baby."

Lillian's frown deepened. "To have…I don't understand."

"I'll tell you what I understand from what she told me." Agnes and the other workers at the NGO sometimes had to try to fill in the missing pieces from the disjointed stories told by some of the distressed people that came to them for help. "A childless couple used her to have a baby." She watched Lillian shake her head slowly as she bit her forefinger. "She never met them, at least not in that sense. A woman counseled her when she first got to the house and told her that a man would visit her and she was not to resist him. They took her blood and urine for tests, of course, to make sure she was suitable. They fed her with the kind of food she never even knew existed, and they also gave her drugs. She said the man came three times."

"At least she would be able to recognize him if she saw him again."

"Oh no", Agnes said quickly.

"Why not?" Lillian asked.

"She said he only came late at night and the light was always switched off when he did. She never saw his face but she said she would always remember his 'scent'."

"That means his perfume." Lillian laughed sadly. "That's a lot to go on."

"Anyway she became ill, or so she thought since she had never been pregnant before and a mid-wife came to the room to attend to her until she had the baby."

"Are you saying she was never allowed to leave the room? At all?"

"She said she was allowed sometimes to walk around the yard in the morning and evening, but the woman was always with her. She spent most of the time in the room actually."

"What happened when the baby was born?"

"He was taken away immediately but not before she saw that it was a boy. And that was the last time she saw the mid-wife as well. A few days after, the woman that had been assigned to her told her to come outside with her bag. She went with her and a man told her to enter a van."

"Just like that?"

"You understand."

"They were through with her." Lillian shook her head. "Where did they take her?"

"Back to 'Uncle' who took one look at her and said she couldn't live with him anymore."

"Why not?"

"He said she was no longer a child."

"What? Was he not the one that…? Didn't he know…?" Lillian was angry.

"Calm down, Lillian." Agnes tried to pacify her. "If you get fired up every time you hear about what brought these people here you'll be worn out in no time. Sometimes you have to harden up just so your heart won't break."

"It's just so...unfair." Lillian's voice was squeaky and filled with emotion.

"Yes, it is. She had a lot of money tucked in her bag when she got here. I asked her where she got it from and she said the man in the van gave it to her. She said she had forgotten about it."

"Good thing. Who knows whether her uncle would have taken it if he had known?"

"I think they must have settled him very well before they took her. They're obviously very wealthy," Agnes said.

"So anytime you discover your wife can't have a baby you just grab a helpless, healthy girl and have a child with her. Then you tuck some money in her bag and send her on her merry way. While the wife puts a cushion under her clothes until one day..." she raised her hands up and shook them, "*ta-da*, it's a baby!"

"Lillie, let it go. I would rather have you divert that energy to caring for the victims. Ok?"

"Actually I have enough energy..." She smiled when Agnes raised a finger. "All right!"

Agnes closed the file and returned it to the pile. Then she took three other files and handed them to Lillian. She leaned back on her seat and looked closely at her.

"So what are your plans?"

"I'm going to work on these," she said indicating the files Agnes had just handed to her. "And then I'm going to see that the records in the store have been brought up to date. And then I'm going to spend some time with the babies..."

"You know what I'm talking about."

"Aunt Agnes..."

"Lillian."

"Can we talk later?" And she quickly left the office.

It had been four weeks since Lily left and Lillian had spent most of the time working as if her life depended on it. It seemed to Agnes as if she couldn't cope with Lily's absence any other way. Though they spoke on the phone often she still looked like she had lost her best friend. Agnes missed Lily too but Lillian was finding it hard to deal with. She had tried to get her to talk about it but had failed. Agnes could feel her sadness as she moped around the house. Maybe it was time for her to go back home. They had talked about that when Lily was around and Lillian had actually expressed her desire to see her family again. Yet she had also felt the need to be sure it was safe. If her father was still bent on marrying her off then she couldn't go back. But Agnes had been praying. She had an assurance that God was doing something but she needed Lillian to contact home. Maybe she could try talking her into making that decision tonight. She wouldn't force her. That was the last thing she wanted to do. And she really liked having her around. She was a wonderful individual and she was very useful at work. If the other members of staff were as dedicated as she was and had half her zeal, there would be far better results. She prayed silently that everything would work out right.

They both fell asleep that night before they could talk because they were exhausted by the time they got home. Agnes woke up in the morning wondering if they would ever have the chance. The days almost always followed the same trend until one Saturday afternoon Lillian returned from the market with a huge smile on her face.

"I was able to do something today," she announced gleefully as she unpacked the shopping bags.

Agnes hadn't seen this happy in a long time making her really curious. "What were you able to do today?" She asked as she folded the laundry.

"I…spoke to Mary."

Agnes looked up sharply. "You called Mary?" She couldn't have heard anything more pleasing.

"I didn't tell you because…because…Oh, I don't know why I didn't," Lillian said lifting up her arms. "I had called her church earlier and the office clerk promised to help. She spoke to Mary and when I called again she told me when Mary would be there. And today I spoke to her."

"Lillie, you don't know how happy I am that you did," Agnes said. "What did she say?"

"Could she say anything? She was just weeping. Well, so was I."

"I can imagine, all this time."

Lillian went and sat beside Agnes. "Aunt Agnes, she said everything has changed. She said when I left my father became subdued and that he admitted his regret about the whole marriage issue. She said my mother now goes with her to church sometimes." She paused. "She wanted to know when I was coming back."

"And what did you tell her?"

"Something that would make you and Lily happy," she said shyly.

Agnes opened her eyes wide. "We are going shopping." She cupped Lillian's chin. "We are going to buy the whole town."

Lillian looked deep into Agnes' eyes. "I'm not going to stay away from you for long Aunt Agnes. I'm going to come here every time I can."

"I wouldn't have it any other way, Lillie."

Lillian worked harder than ever during her last few days at the organization. It was a sad period for the workers and the beneficiaries and some actually wept when they learnt that she would be leaving them. Lillian would miss them too, especially the babies. She had grown so fond of them.

A party was organized for her on her last day at work and everyone attended, including the workers that were not on duty. It was an emotional time for them all because several people came out to talk about how she had touched their lives. She fought hard to control her tears but couldn't. When they finally left for home she had two carrier bags full of gifts. Almost everybody had brought her something.

"I told you you're special," Agnes said when they got home. "Those people really appreciate you."

"I appreciate them too, Aunt Agnes. I wish I didn't have to leave."

"I will miss you."

"Oh, I will miss you too." She ran to Agnes and hugged her.

At the taxi park the next morning they both discovered that saying goodbye was harder than they had thought it would be. "Dear Aunt Agnes," Lillian said wiping her eyes. "You're one of the best people I have ever met."

"That's a very sweet thing to say. And remember, one door closes…"

"And we find ourselves in a new room with more opportunities to prove God's love for us."

"I couldn't have said it better."

The driver started the car and as it pulled off Agnes realized that though she was sad that Lillian was leaving she was also very happy that the girl could return home to the family she had missed so much. God's purpose was at work and it was best for everyone. Besides she had her own new door she had walked into. She smiled as she turned and walked away. All she could see were opportunities to prove God's presence with her.

"Nna anyi! Nna anyi o!"

"What is it woman?" Victor Obimali came out of the house looking around to see where his wife was. "Have I suddenly gone deaf that you have to scream the whole place down before I can hear you?" He saw her by the gate with a basket lying on the ground beside her, the vegetables in it spilled.

"What is it Mama?" Mary had run out from the kitchen when she heard her mother screaming.

IK and the younger ones too came out of the house to see their mother bent over and dancing.

"My sun has come out," she chanted as she lifted one leg after the other, her waist shaking like a tambourine in the hands of an avid player. "My darkness is gone. My enemies are put to shame."

Mama?" Mary looked at her quizzically as she stopped running and walked towards her.

"*Nna anyi!* It is Adaeze."

"Adaeze?"

"She is coming." She started marching down the path.

"Lillie!" Mary screamed even though she hadn't seen Lillian yet. She raced after her mother. "Lillie!" She screamed again.

Coming down the road was Lillian with a big smile on her face as she drew closer to Mary and her mother. She dropped her bags and ran the rest of the way into her mother's waiting arms.

"Mama," she cried as she buried her face in her mother's shoulders.

"Ada."

Lillian looked up at the sound of father's voice.

"Papa," she said and went and knelt before him, all animosity and anger gone. He lifted her up gently and held her to himself.

"Welcome home Ada."

THE END